Lynette Eason is a bestselling, award-winning author who makes her home in South Carolina with her husband and two teenage children. She enjoys traveling, spending time with her family and teaching at various writing conferences around the country. She is a member of RWA (Romance Writers of America) and ACFW (American Christian Fiction Writers). Lynette can often be found online interacting with her readers. You can find her at facebook.com/lynette.eason and on Twitter, @lynetteeason.

Books by Lynette Eason

Love Inspired Suspense

Visit the Author Profile page
at Harlequin.com for more titles.

CONTENTS

Recycling programs
for this product may
not exist in your area.

ISBN-13: 978-0-373-60117-2

A Silent Terror and A Silent Fury

Copyright © 2015 by Harlequin Books S.A.

The publisher acknowledges the copyright holder
of the individual works as follows:

A Silent Terror
Copyright © 2009 by Lynette Eason

A Silent Fury
Copyright © 2009 by Lynette Eason

⊕ HARLEQUIN®
www.Harlequin.com

Printed in U.S.A.

Lynette Eason

A SILENT TERROR
and
A SILENT FURY

❖ HARLEQUIN® LOVE INSPIRED®CLASSICS

A SILENT TERROR

Keep me as the apple of your eye; hide me in the shadow of your wings, from the wicked who assail me, from my mortal enemies who surround me.
—*Psalms* 17:8–9

As always, to Jesus Christ. Let me be a good steward of what You've given me.

Thanks go out to:

The wonderful crime scene writers group on Yahoo. It's such a relief to know if I have a question, I can ask it and get an accurate answer in, sometimes, under a minute! You guys rock.

Emily Rodmell, editor extraordinaire. I'm honored to work with you. Thank you so much for taking a chance on a newbie and for making all my books shine.

Thank you to my deaf friends who are always eager to share their ideas, culture and language.

Thank you, dear hubby, for all the time and effort you put into getting my books out there and for being proud of me.

Thank you, Lauryn and Will, I love you so much.

ONE

Something was wrong. Goose bumps pimpled on Marianna Santino's suddenly chilled flesh as she walked up her driveway. The door to her small home stood open. That in and of itself didn't bother her. The open door combined with the facts that it was January and slightly below freezing didn't bode well. And where was Twister, her large German shepherd, who normally bounded out to greet her?

Her internal fear alarm screeched. Adrenaline rushed.

Run. Get away.

She turned to run—and paused. But what about Suzanne?

Investigate or flee? What if Suzanne, her roommate, needed her? What if she was hurt?

What if whoever broke in was still in there?

Jamming her right hand into her coat pocket, she pulled out her Blackberry and punched in 911. When the screen lit, indicating the call was connected, she put the device to her ear to hear someone speaking. Unable to make out the words, she spoke softly into the phone. "Someone broke into my house." She gave the address and clicked off to wait. No doubt the dispatcher was probably yelling at her about hanging up, but it wouldn't do any good to stay on a phone with a person she couldn't hear.

Marianna scanned the house again. Her hearing aids picked up nothing out of the ordinary, just the wind whipping all around her, causing a whooshing sound to rumble in her ears. Other than that, all was quiet. Silent. Like a tomb.

Was the person still in there? Did Suzanne need help? Again the questions swirled in her brain, worry agitating her. Please God, don't let anything be wrong. Maybe the wind blew the door open.

But that didn't explain Twister's absence. And Suzanne, who always arrived home before Marianna, would have shut the door immediately.

Her eyes darted to the street. No police yet. Fear for her friend finally overrode her concern for her own safety. Slowly, she walked forward until she reached the front porch steps that led up to the door. The stain on the step stopped her.

Blood.

In the form of a shoe print. Leading out of the house.

She was beyond fear. Now she was terrified.

"Suzanne? Twister?"

Desperately, she strained for any sound that would penetrate the shroud of silence she lived with on a daily basis. With a shaking finger, she bumped up the volume on her hearing aid. Slowly, she stepped toward the door once more. The footprint led away from the house. That was good, right? Whoever had been there was now gone.

Or watching.

Glancing over her shoulder, she scanned the quiet street. After school normally meant children on bicycles and neighbors walking dogs. But the frigid weather had everyone inside. The street was deserted. Suddenly, the windows seemed ominous, staring back at her like empty eyes.

Where were the police?

Shivering, she stepped closer, avoided the bloody print and slipped inside the door. Looked down. Another print. A blast of warm air from the vent above her blew a lock of raven-colored hair across her eyes. Pushing it aside, she swallowed hard and made a concerted effort to control her fear-induced ragged breathing.

She continued on.

The kitchen to her right. Peered in. Nothing but an empty mug on the counter.

The den to her left. Again, nothing seemed out of place.

That left the three bedrooms down the hall. And the trail of bloody footprints leading to the room at the end.

With nerves taut, the hairs on her neck standing straight up, she took another deep breath and stepped into the hall, doing her best to avoid smudging the prints, which grew darker with each step.

Was she destroying evidence the police might need?

Hesitating, she chewed her lip. Her instincts screamed at her to get out. To leave.

But Suzanne might be hurt. What if she needed immediate medical help?

Those thoughts kept her going, ignoring the raging fear flowing with every heartbeat.

"Suzanne?"

A noise, caught by her hearing aid, pulled her to the left as did the prints. Suzanne's bedroom. The door was shut.

Reaching out, she almost touched the knob. Stopped. Every crime show she'd ever watched seemed to replay through her mind in a five-second span. She caught the edge of her shirt, gripped it with her thumb and pointer finger, and twisted the knob to open the door. No sense in marring any fingerprints that might be there.

No, you're just possibly wiping them off.

But Suzanne was her priority.

Another muffled sound. What was that? Run! Please, God!

The knot in her throat grew tighter as the door swung inward. A bloody smudge marred the hardwood floor. And another one just behind it. The room lay trashed, items broken and strewn about.

Oh, please, Jesus, let the police get here soon.

"Suzanne? Twister?"

Another sound. From the closet. Slowly, she walked toward it. Using her shirt again, she grasped the knob and turned it.

The door exploded open, pushing her backward to land on her rear. She let out a little scream, then groaned.

Twister. Licking her face, he expressed gratitude for his freedom.

"Get off. Down," she ordered.

Immediately, he dropped to his haunches, ears perked, brown eyes gleaming. Cocking his head, he whined, seemed restless, his attention on something beyond her bed.

She whirled, rounded the bed and stopped.

"No!" she screamed and dropped to her knees.

Suzanne lay faceup, eyes fixated, unseeing, on the ceiling above her. Beneath her dark hair, a pool of blood soaked into the light brown carpet.

As Ethan O'Hara approached the house, the scream reverberated from within. The wide-open door and the brown bloody footprint on the front porch told him that the 911 hang up call signified real trouble. Definitely not a prank. Catelyn, his partner, pulled her gun and gave him the nod; he entered the house, his own weapon held ready in his right hand. They'd been passing by the neighborhood when the scanner went off. When Catelyn heard the address, she gasped, "That's Marianna's house, I think."

"You know her?"

"I'm better friends with her sister, Alissa, but I've met Marianna a couple of times."

Instead of waiting for a unit from the county, he and Catelyn had simply made a right turn into the subdivision, calling in that they would handle it.

She followed behind him, covering his back. Silently, senses on high alert, he tracked the prints.

Again he heard, "No!" coming from the back bedroom on his left.

Not wanting to call out and possibly alert the perpetrator who could still be around, he controlled his breathing, felt the familiar rush of adrenaline he always had going into a potentially dangerous situation and stepped into the bedroom.

The bed sat centered on the opposite wall. Sobs came from the right of it. He took in the debris-littered room. Someone had put up a violent fight. Catelyn came up behind him indicating the rest of the house was clean.

Lowering his gun to his side, he met her eyes, then turned back to see a woman lying on the floor beside the bed, her head resting in a stain of red. The crying came from the other woman who knelt at the figure's side, long dark hair hiding her face.

"Ma'am?"

No response.

"Ma'am?" He touched her shoulder.

She jerked, screamed and scrambled sideways. Movement to his right brought him around and face-to-face with a German shepherd, whose sharp teeth, bared in a snarl, looked capable of tearing Ethan's throat out.

"Easy, boy," he soothed, backing up a step, flashing his badge to the scared woman trembling just out of reach.

"Twister, no. Sit," the woman commanded, her voice clogged with tears.

The snarling stopped. The dog sat, popped a yawn, then, with his tongue lolling out of the side of his mouth, grinned up at Ethan.

Breathing a little easier, Ethan was able to turn his attention back to the body on the floor…and the woman whose liquid ebony eyes flicked between him and Catelyn. Catelyn moved over to see the action this side of the bed. In a gentle tone, she said, "Marianna, it's me, Catelyn, Alissa's friend. This is my partner, Ethan O'Hara. What happened?"

Marianna blinked, swiped a few stray tears and gave a shuddering sigh. "Oh, Catelyn. I…I don't know. I just… came home from work and found…this…her. The front door was open and…I called 911, but couldn't wait for help. I had to make sure she was all right, but…she's not."

Another muffled sob, more silent tears.

No, the woman definitely wasn't all right. The coroner would need to make a trip out here. Ethan asked, "Who is she, your sister?" They looked enough alike.

A negative shake caused her hair to shimmer, a few strands stuck to the salty tracks on her cheeks. She brushed them aside. "My roommate. Suzanne Miller."

Twister crawled over to rest his head on his mistress's knee. Her slender fingers buried themselves in the animal's silky fur.

"Who are you?" he asked.

He knew Catelyn could fill him in, but he wanted to know now. He told himself his wanting to know was strictly professional and had nothing to do with the fact that she was probably the most gorgeous woman he'd ever laid eyes on. He blinked, forcing himself to focus on her words, not her looks. Or the sound of her voice, which had an accent he couldn't quite place.

Marianna glanced at Catelyn, then looked back at him. She said, "I'm Marianna Santino. I teach at the Palmetto State School for the Deaf across the street."

The deaf school. He'd refused to acknowledge it as they'd passed it on their way to this subdivision. His sister had gone to school there for many years. It held a mixture of bittersweet and painful memories for him.

Looking straight at her, he said, "I hate to tell you this, Ms. Santino, but it looks like your roommate either surprised the perp…or he was after her and caught her." He looked around, then motioned to Catelyn. "We need to get out of here. This scene's been contaminated enough. Call it in and secure the area, will you?"

Catelyn went to do as he requested. Ethan held his hand out to the woman.

"But everyone loves Suzanne," Marianna protested even as she accepted his helping hand. Twister stayed right beside his mistress. "She teaches kindergarten at Pine Wood Elementary School."

"Well, it looks like she made someone really mad about something."

Marianna missed that last part; he'd turned his head and she'd not been able to read his lips. Something about someone being mad. But who?

She followed him from the room, down the hall and out the door. What had Suzanne stumbled upon? Had she been up there all day, or had she come home early from work?

A hand on her arm brought her attention back to the man before her. His concerned blue-gray gaze narrowed, zoomed in on her. For some reason she noticed the touch of gray at his temples. "Oh, I'm sorry. You said something. I was thinking, picturing poor Suzanne…" She bit her lip. He didn't need her to break down again. He needed her help.

"Are you with me here?"

"Yes, yes, I'm sorry." She really needed to stop apologizing. None of this was her fault. "I'm almost deaf and need you to face me when you talk to me so I can read your lips, all right?"

Understanding flashed across his rugged features. The flicker of pain she glimpsed on his face confused her, but then it was gone and he was all business. "I need to ask you some questions, all right?"

Marianna nodded. Probably the same questions she had running through her mind. They walked to the curb, Twister trotting beside her.

Ethan asked, "Does Suzanne have any enemies?"

"No, like I said, she teaches…taught…kindergarten."

"A fight with a boyfriend?"

"She doesn't have a boyfriend right now. She recently broke up with a guy named Bryson James, but it was amicable."

He jotted something in the small notebook he had pulled out. When he looked up, his electric gray-blue gaze connected with hers again and she felt a pull, sensed comfort, strength…a hidden pain?

She jolted, not wanting to feel anything right now or notice the good-looking cop sitting on her couch. Suzanne was dead, and the police needed her full attention to help solve her murder.

"Family?"

Marianna rubbed her hand across her forehead, swallowing another wave of grief. She whispered, "Her parents live here in town. They'll be devastated." He shifted next to her. She stared helplessly at him. "What can I do? How do I help?"

His big calloused hand reached over to take hers, his gaze intense as he said, "You're helping in just answering the questions. Don't leave anything out, tell me everything you know about her. The smallest detail could wind up being the biggest clue, okay? Then we're going to have to find you a place to stay for a couple of days until we can release the scene—" he cleared his throat "—um, your house, back to you."

Marianna nodded and sucked in a fortifying breath, and for the next hour and a half, while officers, a CSI unit, the medical examiner and the coroner paraded through her home and Suzanne's privacy, she did her best to give Ethan O'Hara something to work with to enable him to find Suzanne's killer.

Ethan waited while Marianna sent a text message to her parents that she would be coming to stay for a couple of nights. He was glad texting was such an in thing these days, since it made communication so much easier for the deaf. His sister would have loved the technology. Instead of dwelling on the past, however, he focused on what the crime scene investigator was saying.

"The medical examiner ruled out suicide. Ms. Miller was killed when she cracked her head on the corner of the bedside table. Blunt force trauma, if you want the official term. The M.E. said she'd do an autopsy to be sure, but she doubted she'd find anything else."

"I'll talk to her later. Thanks for the help and let me know if you find anything else, will you?"

"You bet, Ethan."

Marianna walked toward him, her beauty not one bit diminished by her puffy eyes, red nose and blotchy cheeks. The grief stamped on her face pierced him. Why was it always the good ones? The ones who didn't deserve to have their lives shattered this way? Not that anyone *deserved* to come face-to-face with murder, but...

Melancholy thoughts would haunt his after-hours work tonight. He smirked at that thought. What after-hours? As a homicide detective, he lived his job twenty-four/seven. Maybe if he had a family, someone to go home to at night, he'd make more of an effort to work less and spend time at home.

He smiled at her and noted the well-trained Twister at her side. Ethan commented, "He reminds me of the dogs on the K-9 squad."

Tilting her head, she grinned. His heart slammed against his chest, and his breath whooshed from suddenly constricted lungs. Wow. Twin dimples flashed at him as her eyes crinkled at the corners. "Twister is a special dog, specially trained to be my ears. I don't know what I'd do without him."

Then the dimples disappeared, the brief moment of levity gone. It shocked him to realize how much he wanted her to smile again. "Do you need a ride to your parents' house?"

"No, but thank you. My brother, Joseph, is on the way to pick me up. He's home, visiting. My mother let him know I needed a ride, but she didn't tell him why." Her hands clasped in front of her, she kept her eyes on his face. She looked lost, shell-shocked.

The urge to gather her in his arms singed him. Instead, he cleared his throat. "Why didn't she tell him?"

Well-shaped shoulders lifted in a shrug. "A lot of reasons. The main one being the safety of the other drivers on the road between her house and mine."

"Right. Okay, well, there's nothing else we can do here."

He placed a hand on her shoulder, felt a tremble run through her.

Don't do something dumb, O'Hara, like hug her.

He pulled her to him for a brief moment, patted her back, then stepped back. The surprise on her face matched the disbelief he felt. He'd hugged her. Now why did he go and do that? What was it about her that had him tossing his professional detachment to the wind? She offered him a small smile filled with gratitude.

Swallowing his rampant thoughts and emotions, he realized he'd only just met the woman and was getting in deep, reacting with his heart, instead of his head. Clearing his throat, he said, "Hey, it'll be all right. Everything will work out, okay?"

Unblinking identical vats of chocolate stared up at him.

Her eyes made him think of Hershey's—and kisses... and not necessarily the candy kind. She asked, "Will I see you again?"

"Oh, yeah, I think that's definitely going to happen." He didn't realize he'd spoken the words aloud until he watched the flush rise from her neck to her cheeks.

Oops.

Catelyn stomped the mud off her shoes, diverting his attention from the woman in front of him. When he looked to the door, Marianna did likewise.

His partner said, "I've questioned all the neighbors I could find." Her lips twisted in disgust. "Nobody saw anything. Her next-door neighbor was home from work with the flu. Said he heard a crashing sound sometime this morning but felt too bad to get up to see what it was."

Ethan's eyes sharpened, "Probably that trash can that was overturned. Check that out to make sure he didn't dump anything."

A car turned into the drive. He turned back to Marianna. "I think your ride has arrived."

Marianna winced. "You mean trouble has arrived."

TWO

How was she supposed to go back to a normal life? Marianna had taken off yesterday and the day before, calling in sick and staying at her parents' house, she and Twister fortunate enough to be wrapped up in her mother's love and concern. Now it was Friday morning and she was on her way to the school. According to Suzanne's mother, the autopsy had been finished and her funeral was tomorrow.

But, first, Marianna had to make it through today. She'd chosen to go to work instead of sitting around thinking about the brutal loss of her friend, so she was expected to teach without falling apart. But how? My strength is in You, Lord. Please get me through this day.

The day of the murder, Joseph, her eldest brother, had picked up her and Twister up from her small house and taken them to her childhood home, drilling her like a dentist for the entire ten-minute drive. When she'd said trouble had arrived, she should have said the Spanish Inquisition had been *revived*.

She chalked it up to his being an FBI agent and the boredom of vacationing having set in. And the fact that someone had just killed his baby sister's roommate. Concern came naturally for him, overprotectiveness his first instinct. One of the reasons her mother hadn't told him about the murder when she'd ask him to pick her up. Joseph could handle just about any situation with a coolheaded professionalism except when it came to his baby sister.

It drove her nuts.

Throughout her entire childhood and most of her adult years she had fought to prove she could take care of herself and to get her family to stop hovering simply because she was deaf. She was just glad Joseph had agreed to go get her car yesterday afternoon. Being stuck without transportation made her feel trapped, like a bird with clipped wings.

She'd snuck out this morning, avoiding her mother's delicious-smelling breakfast. When she'd considered eating, her stomach had lurched in protest. The only thing she'd been able to force down yesterday had been soup and some fruit.

As the school building came into view, she glanced across the street at the entrance to her neighborhood. Would it hurt to drive by? Just to see? A quick glance at the clock told her she'd be late if she did. Resisting the urge to spin the wheel to the right, she entered the campus. Waving to the guard at the entrance, she made her way down the road, cut a right into the first parking lot she came to and whipped into an empty spot.

The building where she taught sat up on a hill. A big hill. Unfortunately, some brilliant architect had designed the nice building but neglected to add a parking area anywhere near it. Hence the lower-level parking and the breath-stealing hike to her classroom.

At least she got her exercise every day. Grabbing her ever-present backpack from the passenger seat of her car, she slammed the door and began the ascent. Other staff members were in the process of arriving and several waved.

"Marianna!"

She turned at the sound of her name. Julie had obviously been calling it a few times as the woman rushed up to her, panting, bending over to catch her breath. "I keep forgetting you can't hear people yelling at you."

Marianna laughed for the first time since Suzanne's death. Julie Thomas, friend and fellow teacher, could always be counted on to produce a smile. "Nope. You just have to hit the right pitch. How long have you been calling me?"

Julie shot her a dark look. "Long enough." A frown knitted her blond eyebrows together. Sucking in a deep breath, she said, "Okay, I can finally breathe again."

She waved toward the hill they still had to climb. Fortunately, some bright soul had taken pity on the Green Hall staff and had built steps into the side of the hill. Marianna headed for them, watching Julie's lips and listening intently as her friend asked, "Are you all right? I mean, I can't believe someone broke into your house and killed Suzanne. It's just…"

"Insane?" Marianna asked quietly.

"Yes. That's the only word for it." Thankfully, while Julie had her funny side, she could be serious when the time called for it. Marianna felt Julie's hand on her arm. She stopped walking and looked around into her friend's green eyes, which held a sheen of compassion-induced tears. "Truly, are you all right?"

Sighing, Marianna leaned over to give the concerned woman a hug. "No, I'm not all right yet, but with God's help and by finding Suzanne's killer, I will be," she whispered. "I have to be."

They finished the walk to the two-story building in silence. Julie went to the bottom floor, which contained the middle school. Marianna went upstairs to the multi-handicapped school. The middle school students were on an academic track that would prepare them for college.

The students in the multi-handicapped school were on the occupational track. They would find themselves with a job suited to their needs and live either with family or in a group home.

And while their IQs might not be the highest, they still had a great love for socialization. In fact, most of her students were just like any other teenagers, discussing the current television programs and the newest dance, and using the latest technology to communicate with each other. The school was a great place and Marianna loved it.

She greeted the secretary with a smile. "Hi, Jean."

"Oh, you poor girl." All five feet two inches of Jean Witherspoon ejected from behind her desk, and she rushed over to give Marianna a maternal hug. "What on earth happened? Has there been any word on who…well, any more developments?"

No one wanted to say the word *killed* or *murdered*. Marianna certainly didn't want to either read the words on peoples' lips or hear them with the help of her hearing aids. No, she'd rather avoid both words.

She shook her head. "No, nothing. I'm hoping to hear something soon."

"Are you going to be okay? Do you think you can concentrate today?"

Leave it to Jean to cut to the heart of the matter. "No, probably not, but I'm going to give it my best shot."

A pat on her arm pulled her attention to the boy standing next to her. Actually, the word *boy* wasn't exactly accurate for this student, Josh Luck, who was six feet four inches tall and would normally be called a man if it weren't for the fact that he had the mental capacity of about a five-year-old. At twenty-one years old, he would "age out" and graduate in five months. His handicapping label also read "autistic," but he had a mild form of it, because he enjoyed hugs and physical touch.

And he loved to bring her gifts. Specific gifts.

Just about every day Josh would bring her some new computer piece from his seemingly endless supply. She'd talked to his father about it and the man just laughed it off, told her to throw them out or whatever. Josh had so many computers and parts at home that there was no way to keep up with it all. If the boy wanted to give her something, he obviously didn't think he'd need it. But each week she would send the parts home…just in case.

Josh was also known as a savant. He knew how to take apart a computer down to the last screw and put it back together almost with his eyes closed.

He was going to have a great career in computer repair… with a little help from the school-to-work transition team.

Marianna said, "See you later, Jean. I need to see what Josh's brought me today."

She led Josh down the hall to the third classroom on the right. He followed her and tapped her shoulder again. Marianna shook off her coat and hung it in the closet. Josh waited patiently.

Then she turned and held out her hand, palm up.

Josh placed a computer piece in the center of it, then clomped off to sit in his specially designed desk. His lumbering, bulky frame had decimated several regular student desks before the maintenance department workers finally took it upon themselves to build him an indestructible one. So far, so good.

Several more students made their way into the classroom, stopping for their morning hug and encouraging word.

The single wooden door to her classroom suddenly seemed to morph into a revolving one. One by one, other teachers and staff stopped by to express concern and condolences. Marianna kept a smile on her face and the tears at bay by sheer willpower.

It wasn't until she placed her purse in the bottom drawer of her desk that she realized something seemed...off. She turned to her assistant, Dawn Price, and said, "Did you move things around on my desk?"

Forty-five years old and a veteran assistant, Dawn looked up from where she'd been asking a student about his morning. "No, why?"

Marianna looked at the small potted plant that normally sat on the back corner of her desk. It had been moved up closer to the edge above the drawer. Her stapler was on the left side instead of the right. Several papers she'd stacked neatly looked as if they'd been rifled through.

She shook her head. "Things just aren't where I left them." She shrugged. "Maybe the cleaning crew had to move my desk and things got shifted."

Soon, a student had her attention and she focused on getting through the morning.

Praying the day would end soon, she did her best to concentrate on the students, pouring as much as she could into their eager minds.

Ethan threw the pen down on the report and rested his head in his hands.

"What's wrong, partner?" Catelyn asked as she found a perch on the side of his desk.

"This case," he mumbled into his palm.

"Yeah." Confusion colored her voice. "I don't understand the complete lack of evidence."

He snorted and looked up. "We've got evidence, such as the shoe print, it just isn't leading us anywhere. The fact that there were no viable fingerprints leaves us cold. Not even a stray hair. I don't get it. Suzanne put up a struggle—didn't she? The room was torn apart."

"There's no indication she fought back." Catelyn dropped a sheaf of papers on his desk. "The M.E.'s report. Nothing under her fingernails, nothing on her clothing."

"Then she surprised him. The room's not trashed, because she fought him, he trashed it before she got there." Tapping his chin, he looked at the papers but didn't pick them up. "He wasn't expecting anyone to be there."

"Okay, so he broke in, started gathering his loot in the bedroom, was there maybe a couple of minutes when Suzanne walked in on him."

Nodding, Ethan said, "She startled him and he grabbed her, she probably would have pulled back, maybe stumbled and fell, hitting her head? Or maybe he pushed her trying to get out of the room. I don't know, just speculation, but…" he said, shrugging.

"But where was her car? The one in the driveway was registered to Marianna. And it was clean. No sign of a search or tampering."

His gaze snapped up to hers. "You're right. There was only Marianna's car. The garage was empty."

"Suzanne may not have owned one."

"One way to find out." A few taps onto the computer keyboard brought up a number of Suzanne Millers in the Spartanburg area. He scrolled down to the right one listing her address and clicked. Suzanne's pretty features as shown on her driver's license filled the top right corner of the screen. Finding the area of the screen he wanted, he clicked again.

She owned a black Honda Accord. Glancing up at Catelyn, he pointed to the monitor. "Look."

Catelyn looked at him. "So, what are you waiting for?" She glanced at the clock on the wall opposite his desk. "It's twelve forty. I've got another appointment, but it's plenty of time for you to be waiting on Marianna when she walks out of class. Actually, she's probably at lunch. It's Friday, so the buses start picking up the kids at one." The residential school dismissed the students early on Friday because some of the kids had a four- to five-hour trip home. The drivers and attendants who staffed the buses stayed the weekend in whichever city was at the end of their route, then brought the students back on Sunday night.

"Yeah, I know the schedule." Without another word, Ethan grabbed his coat and headed out the door.

Fifteen minutes later, he'd flashed his badge to the guard at the entrance and refused the offer of directions to the building called Governor's Hall, the cafeteria where the students gathered each day to eat, then stand outside to wait for the buses. He knew the way.

Ethan now sat outside the building watching the end-of-day activity. Two high school boys tossed a football with one hand and signed back and forth with the other, talking in a language Ethan had done his best to forget, yet remembered with no trouble. Another young man stole a kiss from the girl he held hands with as they strolled up the hill toward the area where they would wait for the bus to pick them up. A group of elementary students crossed the street at the crosswalk, and a little girl about seven years old stooped to entice a cat to come to play until she was hurried on by the worker bringing up the rear.

Nothing changes, he thought. When his sister had been a student here a little over three years ago, the same two boys played football, the same couple held hands—everything was the same. Then he shook himself. Of course everything wasn't the *same,* but it sure did bring back memories.

Memories that brought the pain of his sister's death to the surface one more time, along with the resentment of his parents' just moving on as if nothing had happened, as if his world hadn't been ripped apart. A week after her funeral, his parents had left to tour Europe. Sure, they'd asked him to go with them, but he'd been shocked at their plans, had thought they were crazy, insensitive, unfeeling.

Forcing his thoughts from the past, he concentrated on watching for the one person he hadn't been able to push from his mind.

Marianna Santino.

And then there she was. Coming out of the cafeteria, her heavy wool skirt swaying against her endless stretch of legs. The baby-blue, cable-knit sweater only enhanced her dark beauty. She had her raven-colored hair flowing around her shoulders and down her back, just as she had two days ago.

His palms suddenly itched, curious to feel what it would be like to let that hair flow through his fingers. Curling his traitorous hands into fists, he told himself to focus. He was here on a case, not a date.

And soon she would be gone from his sight. Where was she going? Climbing from his car, he followed her. She was on her BlackBerry, texting someone, her fingers flying over the keys. Totally focused on her task, she kept her head down, never looking left or right—not exactly the best defensive walk. But then she wasn't the one who needed to be on the defensive; Suzanne was the one who'd been killed.

He wondered how Suzanne had walked. Probably like Marianna, completely unaware of her surroundings. The thought chilled him.

"Marianna!"

She didn't turn. Instead, she flipped her phone shut, pulled open the glass door and slipped inside the building. Closing in fast, Ethan saw her enter the third classroom on the right.

Reaching the door, he entered after her. Her desk faced the door and she stood behind it, pulling a box from a drawer. "Marianna?" He moved farther into the room.

Looking up, she gasped. "Oh, Detective O'Hara."

"Sorry, I didn't mean to startle you. And it's Ethan."

"Ethan, then. And it's all right." She held up a shoebox. "I'd forgotten to give this to Josh to take home last Friday, and with all the craziness *this* week, I forgot to give it to him today. He loves to bring me computer parts each week. I believe in recycling, so I was just going to rush down to the bus pick-up area and give it to him."

"Come on, I'll drive you. I've got a few questions to ask if you don't mind."

She blew out a sigh, grief crossing her flawless features for a brief moment. She shut the drawer and walked around the side of the desk. "I don't mind. I can't think of anything I haven't already told you, but maybe your questions will jar something."

Together, they walked back to his car, with Marianna greeting various staff and students along the way. When they reached his vehicle, he drove her around to the where the buses picked up the students and she hopped out. Ethan stayed put and watched her approach an on-duty staff member. She asked in sign language while voicing, "Cleo, has Josh already gone?"

Cleo signed back, "Yes, his bus left about five minutes ago."

Marianna sighed, hands gracefully forming the words, "Oh well, it wasn't anything major, just his box. I guess I'll save it for next week."

"You want me to keep it until Monday? I have to go back to my classroom anyway, so I don't mind."

"Sure, thanks." Marianna handed over the box of treasures with a dimpled smile, then walked back to climb in Ethan's car. "Do you want go up the street to the coffee shop to talk?"

"Sounds good to me."

The sooner he got this investigation out of the way, the sooner he could start thinking about asking Marianna Santino out on a date. Maybe. If he thought his heart could handle it.

Ice Cream and Coffee Beans, home to tasty milk shakes and fresh-brewed coffee. Sandwiches could be ordered, too. Marianna chose a peanut butter shake with whipped cream. Ethan decided on a chocolate one, sans the white topping, and a club sandwich.

A plain, no-frills kind of guy, she thought. Nice. He kept his beard trimmed close and his mustache neat. A well-shaped mouth with firm lips smiled at her through the facial hair. Sometimes it was hard to read the lips of people who hid them behind beards and mustaches, but not Ethan. He was an easy read. His lips anyway; his eyes were another story.

He said, "I can't believe you went to work today."

Taking a sip of her milk shake, she relished the sweet richness on her tongue for a minute before swallowing. "I had to." She leaned back against the booth. "I love my parents, and my mom would like nothing better than for me to come home on a permanent basis, but one day was enough." She gave a wry smile. "And Joseph was driving me nuts."

"Your brother?"

She nodded, admiring the breadth of his shoulders, the strength that he exuded. "He's an FBI agent who works in New York. He works a lot of missing person cases. It's the first time he's been home in almost a year, and he gets confronted with this. I told him to stay out of it, but don't be surprised if you get regular calls for updates from him."

"Not a problem."

Sucking in a deep breath, she asked, "So, what kind of questions did you have?"

"Catelyn and I were hashing over the case and we realized there was only one car in the driveway—yours. Where's Suzanne's?"

Marianna furrowed her brow. "Oh, I'd forgotten all about that. It's in the shop getting new brake pads. She was supposed to pick it up yesterday. Since we live so close to my school, I let her use my car to drive to work and I just walked." She rubbed a hand across a forehead that was beginning to ache. "I'll have to call her parents and let them know to go get it."

"I'll take care of that. I also called Suzanne's school. They said she arrived on time Tuesday morning and signed in but left early because she was sick. We do know that she signed out at four minutes after ten. Assuming she didn't stop anywhere because she felt bad and wanted to get home and go to bed, I think it's safe to say she probably arrived home around ten-fifteen. The murder happened shortly after that."

Grief cut into Marianna. She didn't want to think about it anymore but was determined to do whatever it took to catch Suzanne's killer.

Running a hand over her hair, she smoothed it down around her ears, a habit she'd picked up two years ago. Curt Wentworth, her ex-boyfriend, hadn't wanted to see her hearing aids. They made him self-conscious and uncomfortable. Which was really strange, since he'd chosen audiology as a profession. She hadn't realized until too late that his constant stroking of her hair hadn't been out of affection; he'd been covering up her hearing aids. Marianna sighed. No use thinking about him.

Forcing her thoughts away from Curt's unpleasant memory, she focused on an awful thought. "So, Suzanne came home sick and walked in on a burglary. He killed her and ran."

"That's what it looks like."

Tears choked her, blurring her vision. She blinked, refusing to let the endless tears fall. "She should have stayed at work," she whispered.

His hand covered hers, and she shivered at the contact. It had been a long time since she'd been attracted to a man; she had been a little gun-shy since she and Curt had broken up six months ago. Her surprising feelings scared her and yet...

She watched his mouth and focused on his words. "Yes, if she had she would probably be alive. But, she didn't and..." he sighed, then looked up at her. "Was Suzanne a Christian?"

That question startled her. "Yes, she was."

"Then there's comfort in that, right?"

Marianna relaxed a fraction but nodded and offered a feeble smile. "Yes, of course, but I, and everyone else who loved her, will miss her." Tears gathered again. She sniffed, grabbing up the napkin with her free hand to dab her eyes.

"I know." His fingers squeezed. Marianna started at the tingle that raced up her arm. Trying to be discreet, she pulled her hand from his and picked up her milk shake. The sparkle in his eye said she hadn't fooled him.

But now wasn't the time to pursue the mutual attraction. Marianna had a funeral to attend, and Ethan had a murder to solve.

* * *

Feet thudded against the stairs, phones rang, voices raised in argument filled the air. The person seated at the desk ignored the chaos coming from the room to the right. "Where have you been?" Tense fingers gripped the phone as the frantic voice shook, wobbled, fought for control and said, "I had things to take care of. The girl's dead. She surprised me. I didn't mean to kill her. She fought back and I pushed her…."

"Do you know what you've put me through having to explain your absence? Look…never mind. So, you didn't find it."

"No." Harsh, frantic breathing.

"Calm down. We have to have it. If the wrong people get their hands on that…everything we've worked so hard for is down the toilet." A string of curses rent the air.

"I know, I know. But she probably doesn't even realize what she has."

"Doesn't matter. If she looks at it…"

"I can't do this. If anyone finds out, if I get caught, our careers are finished. I can't believe this. I never meant for…" A frustrated sigh sounded, then, "Let someone else do it. I can't."

"Are you crazy? The last thing we need is someone else involved. Right now, the only people who know about this are you and me. We need to keep it that way. This is your fault. If I have to come up there and take care of this…"

"I know, I know. Maybe I should just go to the police… explain that it was an accident."

A harsh laugh echoed. "What fantasy world are you living in? Now, quit being a wimp and fix it."

"No way. I'm out. *You* fix it. Tonight."

THREE

Thunder rumbled, shaking the air surrounding the mourners who'd come to the afternoon funeral to say goodbye to Suzanne Miller. Thankfully, heavy rain continued to hold off, but Marianna knew it wouldn't hold much longer. The fine mist they'd started the service with had progressed to a steady drizzle; soon it would be a downpour. She clutched the curved handle of her umbrella and scanned the crowd.

She spotted Ethan and Catelyn a few yards away, looking alert and watching those gathered. Their diligent surveillance sent a shiver crawling up her spine to settle at the base of her neck.

The minister spoke but she couldn't see his face clearly through the sea of shifting heads and the service wasn't interpreted, so Marianna couldn't actually understand much of anything being said. Which gave her time to focus on the people.

She knew a lot of them, their sad faces grabbing her heart. But it was Suzanne's parents who speared her emotions and clogged her throat with tears yet again. Unmitigated grief, stunned disbelief and rampant rage alternated across their faces. Marianna could relate. She hoped they'd gotten everything they'd wanted from the house this morning. Suzanne hadn't had a lot of things and as soon as the police had cleared the scene, her family had wanted to gather the last of their loved one's items.

Marianna shivered again. When she took her focus off Suzanne's family, became aware of her surroundings, she felt...watched. After finally admitting the unsettling sensation wasn't just in her imagination, her stomach quivered.

And then she realized...he probably was here.

Suzanne's killer might be somewhere in this crowd.

She'd heard of killers showing up at their victims' funerals but couldn't fathom that she might actually be standing somewhere near a murderer. Shuddering, she wrapped an arm around her middle in a one-arm hug.

Fear churned; she swallowed it down.

Ever since the viewing and short service at the church, and then upon arrival at the burial site, she'd felt someone staring holes in her back. Yet each time she turned, she saw nothing strange and no one out of place. At first, she chalked it up to being the dead woman's roommate. Of course people would stare at her.

But maybe it was more than that.

As though in slow motion, she turned a full circle, examining every face, trying to see around hats, scarves and umbrellas.

Movement caught from the corner of her eye brought her head around. Ethan headed her way. Nerves cluttered up her stomach. If he leaned over and whispered in her ear, would she be able to catch the words? Pulling the collar of her coat snug around her neck, she stepped to the left to get a better view of the minister. She'd been invited to sit with the family, but the number of relatives in attendance had clearly been underestimated, so Marianna had surrendered her chair to an elderly aunt.

Ethan stepped next to her. She looked up at him. He smiled and mouthed, "Are you all right?"

She shrugged, ignored the threat of tears for the hundredth time that day, then dared to ask, "He's here, isn't he?"

Ethan didn't bother to pretend he didn't understand who she meant. She could see it in his eyes. "Probably." Keeping his voice low, he looked over her shoulder and asked, "Do you see anyone who *shouldn't* be here?"

Once again, Marianna let her eyes trail over the people. The minister had finished and the mourners started their exit. "There're too many people, too many hats and umbrellas. I can't see all of their faces."

"I'm having that problem, too." His eyes scanned the group, but his body remained relaxed, hands tucked loosely in his pockets. "Who did you come with?"

"Just myself. My parents didn't know Suzanne very well, and my dad wasn't feeling well anyway, so Mom wouldn't let him come out in the cold." She paused, bit her lip and looked away from him. "I spent the night at my parents' house again last night. I just couldn't...I guess tonight I'll stay at my house." Tears pooled and this time she couldn't fight them. Several dribbled down her cold cheeks.

A warm cloth swept them away. Ethan had pulled out a handkerchief. Grateful, she took it from his hand and finished mopping up. "Thanks. I'm sorry. I suppose the tears will stop one day."

"Let yourself grieve. It's okay to hurt. And it's okay to stay with your parents awhile. No one would blame you." All gentleness and compassion, his eyes said he hurt for her.

She pocketed the handkerchief. "I'll wash it and get it back to you."

"No hurry. Come here." He took her hand in his and urged her along behind him.

She followed, stopping when he placed a hand on her

arm. Wondering what he was doing, she watched his face, waiting for him to speak. "Okay, now, you can see the people getting in their cars. Tell me if you see anyone who sticks out."

Marianna turned. She and Ethan stood at the top of a gently sloping hill, making it easy to watch the crowd scatter to their various vehicles below. The rain had slacked off. People closed their umbrellas, affording Marianna a pretty good view of faces she hadn't been able to see earlier.

She gasped, "There's Bryson."

"The ex-boyfriend, right?"

"Yes. I mean, I don't know why I'm surprised he's here. It was a mutual breakup without any hard feelings. Of course he would be here. I'm sure Suzanne's death came as a shock."

"I still want to talk to him and maybe catch him off guard so I'll see a true reaction. Excuse me, okay?"

Marianna watched the good-looking young attorney head for his black BMW. Ethan set off after the man, leaving her trailing slowly behind and watching the two of them. Then the feeling of being watched caused her to glance over her shoulder once more. Nothing and no one around her stood out as suspicious.

Her BlackBerry vibrated. Shoving her hand in her pocket, she kept her eyes on Ethan as he approached Bryson. When the device hummed again, she glanced at it. And groaned.

Curt Wentworth. Why wouldn't he leave her alone?

She flipped the cover and read his text.

"We need to talk. Stop being so stubborn and meet me this evening for dinner."

Not in this lifetime, buster. What would it take for him to get the message she wanted nothing more to do with him? He'd put his hands on her in anger and left bruises on her. He'd also been verbally abusive. He was the last person she wanted to have dinner with. For at least two minutes, she stared at it, debating what to say. Unable to come up with anything she wouldn't regret, she closed the unanswered message and the machine, clenching her fist around the device.

A gentle hand covered hers. Startled, she realized Ethan had come back. She shivered. And realized something else. The feel of his hand on hers felt right.

"Problem?" His brows climbed to reach into the shaggy blond hair that lay across on his forehead.

"What?" She'd missed what he'd said. Trying to speech read through a red fog of anger didn't come in her little bag of tricks.

"Is there a problem?" he repeated.

"Oh. Yes. But nothing I can't handle." And she would handle it. Just as soon as she figured out how.

"I don't mind helping out."

"I said I could handle it." She appreciated the offer but didn't need another person in her life trying to take care of her. Winning her independence had been a tough battle, but she'd done it.

Hands held up in a gesture of surrender, he backed up a little. "Gotcha."

Feeling a tad guilty at her snappiness when he'd been nothing short of wonderful, she bit her lip and sighed. "I'm sorry. I'm just a little…"

"…stressed," he finished for her. "Understandable."

"So, what did Bryson have to say?"

"I get the impression he was truly upset." Ethan recalled the man's red-rimmed eyes and genuine air of grief. "He said something about the fact that they'd been talking about getting back together."

"Really? I didn't know that."

"I asked him if he'd be willing to give us a DNA sample so the crime scene investigators could compare it with anything they found…if they find something. He said he'd go down first thing Monday morning."

"I always liked Bryson. I'm not exactly sure why they broke up, but I think he was pressuring Suzanne to get married and she wanted some space. She never really talked about it, though, even with me." She shrugged. "I didn't push, figuring she'd tell me if she wanted to."

Ethan watched her features, marveling once again at her physical beauty. And yet she was so much more than just a pretty package. In just the short time he'd known her and under the worst circumstances, she'd shown herself to be the epitome of…what? He searched his brain for the right adjective.

Class. The woman was pure class.

Shadowed dark brown eyes stared at him, and he realized he hadn't responded to something she'd said. "Sorry, my mind went wandering." No sense in telling her where.

Marianna flashed a dimpled smile, brief but sincere. "It's fine. I was just saying that I needed to get…home." She grimaced, and he knew she wasn't excited about the idea. After a minuscule hesitation, she took his hand between hers and gave it a quick squeeze, her closeness and light, fruity perfume scrambling his senses. Biting her lip, she gave him a shaky smile. "Thank you for everything. I hope you'll keep me updated on the case."

"Absolutely."

Marianna left the cemetery and began the short drive home. She dreaded going into her house alone, yet had turned down several offers of accompaniment. Not exactly sure why, she just knew she didn't want to be around a bunch of people, including family. She knew she faced a lot of cleaning up and most likely more uncontrollable tears. Better to do that without an audience. Ethan had started to insist that he follow her but had gotten a call and had to leave. That had been fine with her.

She'd texted Joseph, asking him to bring Twister home so the dog would be there to greet her. He'd agreed against his better judgment, arguing she didn't need to be by herself.

She pulled into the driveway and turned the car off. The house loomed, small and empty. It shouldn't seem particularly scary, yet a tremor shook her at the thought of walking up the path to her porch. Memories almost overwhelmed her, tempting her to once again run home to her mom and dad.

At least the door was closed today. Please, God, take this fear away. I know it's only natural after what's happened, but I don't want to be afraid. Help me trust You.

The curtain in the window to the right of the door moved; a black nose pressed against the glass. The familiar sight caused her to release a relieved breath.

Twister's welcome home. He was waiting for her.

Marianna scrambled from the car, grabbing the overnight bag Joseph had packed for her the day of the murder, and headed for the door.

Climbing the steps, she paused, noticing the footprint had disappeared. Someone had scrubbed it away. Shuddering, unease still very much present, she unlocked the door and pushed it open.

And gaped.

Her house sparkled, from top to bottom. Someone had scrubbed, mopped, vacuumed and more.

How…what…who?

Ethan.

She frowned. Now why did she automatically assume it was him? It could have been Joseph or some other member of her family.

Someone had hired a professional to clean up the mess left by the criminal and the crime scene investigators. Her heart warmed at the thoughtfulness as grateful tears blurred her vision. A piece of paper lay on the table just inside the foyer. Picking it up, she read, "I didn't want you to come home to a mess. Hope everything is better than when you left it. Ethan."

"Thank you, Ethan," she whispered.

Twister nudged her hand and whined. Absentmindedly, she scratched his head as she went from room to room, examining everything.

A lump clogged her throat as she moved, sensing Suzanne's presence even though she was now with the Lord.

When she reached Suzanne's room, the door stood open, inviting. Hitching her breath, she stepped in and looked around. It, too, had been scrupulously cleaned.

And stripped bare. Suzanne's family had come and gone, leaving not even a trace of their presence. Or Suzanne's. Unable to stop herself, she looked to the spot where her roommate had died.

Even the stain was gone. It was as if Suzanne had never been there. Marianna walked over and knelt, running her hand over the area, feeling the carpet spring back beneath her palm. Anger, fear and a troubled helplessness burned within her.

Help the police find her killer. And help me deal with this, Lord. Please give me peace.

Tired beyond belief, Marianna called to Twister and stepped from the room, pulling the door shut behind her.

Entering her bedroom next door, she stared at the familiar sight of her haven that was supposed to offer comfort and knew she couldn't sleep here tonight. Her stomach rumbled, but she had no energy to fix anything to eat. Doing a one-eighty, she trod the short distance to the small living area and crashed on the couch. She pulled out her hearing aids and laid them on the end table beside her.

All sound ceased to exist for her, and all she wanted to do was snuggle into the silence.

Twister settled on the floor beside her and she let her hand dangle over the edge to rest on his back as she stared at the ceiling, thinking, praying, drifting....

With a start, Marianna's eyes popped open, confusion holding her captive until her brain caught up. She'd fallen asleep on the couch. But something had awakened her. A vibration: Twister?

Darkness blanketed the room broken only by the glow of the night-light coming from the hall. The clock on the DVD player read 3:18 a.m.

What had awakened her? Rubbing her face, then running a hand through her tangled hair, she swung her feet to the floor, eyes probing the blackness. That was odd. Where was Twister?

Uneasiness swept over her. The hardwood floor beneath her trembled. No doubt the vibrations had awakened her. Fingers groped the table beside her, grabbed up her hearing aids and shoved them in her ears.

Still, mostly silence surrounded her.

Again the floor shook. As though cushioning a footstep? Uneasiness climbed into fear. She strained to hear something, anything. Her breathing quickened as spider feet scrabbled up her spine. Her stomach cramped with a sudden thought, what if the killer had come back?

Would he do that? But why?

Adrenaline pumping, she fumbled to remember where she'd left her purse, which held her BlackBerry.

The recliner. In the corner by the fireplace. Guided by eyes adjusting to the darkness and the dim hall light, she crept across the floor to the chair and shoved her hand into her purse, located the device and snatched it out.

She realized she still had her shoes on: low-heeled black pumps she'd worn to the funeral. Sliding them off, she set them aside and tried to think of a possible hiding place. The kitchen pantry? Or should she try to slip out the front door?

Lord, what do I do?

A sense of urgency caused her hands to shake. She felt more vibrations and a hard thud sent her adrenaline into overdrive. Was that a muttered curse she picked up? She inched the volume up on her hearing aid but had to be careful not to bump it up too far or it would start whistling.

Then she tuned in to Twister's furious barking, causing her to flinch. He'd probably been barking for a while if he'd already reached the pitch she needed to hear him.

With her heart thudding and her blood pounding, her brain switched to survival mode. Her fingers found the numbers on her BlackBerry and punched Send.

She needed help fast.

Someone was in her house.

FOUR

Ethan leaned back in the squeaky chair, tapping the pencil against his chin, staring at the ceiling as weariness washed over him. He should be in bed. But the nightmare had returned full force, and his escape to his desk had been the only thing that had allowed him to push the memories to the back of his mind.

Thankfully, it hadn't been the dream about the death of his sister. Unfortunately, it had been the one about his other failure. A hostage situation. The one where he'd been in charge and the woman had died. He'd just finished his crisis negotiation training, fresh from his sister's funeral… and drunk. Oh, not stumbling, falling-down drunk, but he'd definitely had one too many. And he'd made a very bad decision that cost a young woman her life. At least he felt as if it was his fault. He was supposed to have had backup, someone with more experience, but the man hadn't shown up in time. So, it had fallen to Ethan…and he'd failed.

His fault…all his fault.

The words echoed in his mind. *I'm sorry, God. Are You listening? I'm sorry.*

The pencil snapped with a crack. Startled, Ethan dropped the pieces to his desk, then rubbed his bleary eyes, wishing he could make it all go away. But he couldn't.

So, here he sat at approximately three o'clock in the morning, trying to make sense of Suzanne's murder. The place wasn't exactly a ghost town, since other officers, suffering a similar affliction to Ethan's, chose to work the graveyard shift. He grimaced when realizing he felt more comfortable at his desk than he did in his home.

His personal cell vibrated on his hip, and he sat up with a start. Who in the world...? A quick glance at the caller ID showed Marianna's cell number. He'd memorized it with ease the first time he'd seen it in her file.

Dread hit his chest. She must be in trouble. Why else would she be calling at this time of night...morning. With his left hand, he grabbed his keys; with his right, he pulled the phone from the clip.

"Hello?"

No answer.

"Hello?" He raced for the door and down to his car. She couldn't hear him, but surely she could see that he'd answered. Why didn't she say something?

Unless she couldn't. He had the bad feeling his first re-action—that she was in trouble—was right. Indecision, fear of making the wrong move, made him pause for a fraction of a second; then he found himself praying. A simple litany. *Let me get there in time. Let me save her.*

Bolting from the office, he raced for his car.

Marianna prayed silently as she felt another tremor be-neath her stockinged feet. The vibration felt stronger. Once again she had called 911 and had no way of knowing if the police were on the way. She'd placed a call to Ethan as backup, praying he would wake up to hear his phone ringing.

More vibrations. Was that a door slamming? It felt closer. Was he searching for her? Whatever he was doing, he was heading her way. Panting her fear, she clung desperately to control, forcing her mind to think, to reason, to figure a way out. Visions of Suzanne lying on her bedroom floor, blood pooling beneath her head, caused a wave of nausea followed by dizziness to rush through her.

Her world turned choppy, the survival instinct strong. Her eyes darted around the room.

The fireplace. The poker. A weapon.

Then a thump. Vibrations. Marianna quickly moved toward the front door, her hand now on the knob. It was locked, of course.

More of Twister's furious barking, then nothing. Worry for her pet churned within her. Oh, God, protect Twister. Did she have time to get out, or should she hide? Would whoever was in her house come looking for her? How much time had the dog bought her?

Shaking hands fumbled with the dead bolt. Precious seconds ticked by as the key fell to the floor. The thumping stopped, vibrations ceased. She froze, her breath strangling her as she tried not to gasp, desperately wishing she could hear how much noise she was making.

Her BlackBerry buzzed in her pocket; she ignored it. Trembling, she bent down, snatched the key, jammed it in the lock and finally got the door open. She slipped out the opening, onto the porch, and felt hard hands grasp her upper arms.

Marianna's screech nearly ruptured Ethan's eardrums. He hadn't meant to scare her, but she'd come stumbling out the door so fast that if he hadn't caught her, she'd have taken them both to the floor of the cement porch.

Twisting, struggling against him, she had her eyes closed. "Marianna, it's me." *She can't understand with her eyes closed, remember?*

Not knowing whether to let go or give her a shake, he figured releasing her might surprise her into opening her eyes. He let go and stepped back. She stumbled, gasped and opened terror-filled, tar-black eyes to stare at him. Finally, recognition dawned, and relief swept away the fear…for a moment. Then she whispered, "He's in my house. I dialed 911, so the police should be on the way."

Ethan set her behind him and stepped in. His right hand pulled his ever-present gun from his shoulder holster. Pointing the weapon to the ceiling, he turned and mouthed to Marianna, "Stay here, okay?"

She nodded, then whispered in a small, worried voice, "Something's happened to Twister, too. He was barking his head off, then stopped abruptly. So be careful."

Lips tight, Ethan gave a nod, pulled his cell phone from the clip on his belt and dialed a number requesting backup. After he hung up, he stepped back farther into the house. He started to shut the door—only to stop when Marianna stepped in behind him. He frowned at her. "I told you to stay out here."

"Please, I'll stand right here." Fear oozed from her, and his heart clenched in anger at the person doing this to her.

A small crash from the back of the house snapped his attention in that direction. If the noise was coming from back there, she was probably fine standing next to the door—probably. He gave her another pointed look, then started making his way toward the sound, nerves tense, senses alert.

A whispered curse followed by the sound of glass breaking.

Then silence once again.

With quick, measured steps, he headed toward the back room, gun ready. Adrenaline flowed, but he kept his breathing steady. The memory of the first time he'd entered the house haunted him. He felt as if he was in a time warp, déjà-vu kind of thing. Ignoring the sensation, he moved into the first bedroom on his left.

Marianna's room. Empty. Except for shards of broken glass littering the area under her window and—his gut clenched—Twister, lying motionless at the foot of the bed.

Marianna cowered by the front door, torn with the desire to run and the determination to back up Ethan should he need it. Squaring her shoulders, she watched Ethan disappear down the hall, then crept over to the fireplace to grab the poker she'd considered earlier.

Hefting the weight of it in her right hand, she felt slightly more prepared to face the danger that lay just down the hall. *Oh Lord, protect Ethan. And I know Twister's just a dog, but please take care of him.*

The hardwood floor vibrated once more, and she tightened her grip on the makeshift weapon, ready to swing if an unfamiliar face appeared in front of her.

But it was only Ethan, looking grim and tight-lipped. He held up a finger as he walked past her to the front door and yanked it open. Flashing red-and-blue lights fought for space in the small opening. The cops were here, she realized belatedly.

Her gaze followed Ethan's retreating back as he flashed his badge to the two startled officers, who'd started grabbing at their guns the minute the door opened. At the sight of the badge and the man behind it, they relaxed. He said something and their posture tensed once again. One took off around the side of the house; Ethan went the other way, and the third man walked toward Marianna.

She looked at him. "What's going on?"

"I'm Officer Tom Bell. Ethan thinks the guy slipped out of your bedroom window and headed off through those woods in the back. Ethan didn't want to follow him out the window in case the guy left behind some evidence." He kept his face turned toward her and enunciated his words clearly. Ethan must have told him she couldn't hear. She didn't know whether to be annoyed or appreciative. She settled for appreciation…this time.

Within minutes the two men were back. The disgust on Ethan's features said whoever had been in her house had escaped.

Dread crept around in her stomach, finally settling in a hard knot at the pit. She looked at Ethan. "Now what?"

"We need to get the crime scene team back over here and see if he left any evidence behind." Concern slid across his face as he laid a hand on her shoulder. "Twister's hurt. Who's your vet?"

"Oh, no." She whirled to rush back into the house. His hand grasped her upper arm, halting her progress. She spun around. "What?"

"Let me get him. I don't want you destroying any evidence."

"Is it bad?" Anguish squeezed her heart.

"I don't think so. The guy hit him with the lamp from your end—" Ethan blinked, his attention caught by something behind her. She followed his gaze—Twister slowly made his way down the hall, his eyes cloudy with pain but fixed on his mistress. A trickle of blood made its way from the middle of his head down over his brown-and-black snout.

"Oh, Twister," she whispered, dropping to her knees. He came slowly, weaving slightly. When he arrived at Marianna, he dropped to the floor with a cross between a whimper and a grunt to lay his head on her knee.

"Will you make the call for me?" She wondered if he

could hear the tears she felt clogging her throat as she asked him the favor.

"Sure." He squeezed her hand in silent sympathy and pulled his phone from the clip. She looked up the number on her BlackBerry and Ethan complied.

As once again her house flooded with authorities and crime scene investigators, Marianna gave her statement, then sat in the back of Ethan's car, hugging her beloved pet to her as Ethan drove them to the vet's office.

After leaving Marianna's dog at the emergency veterinarian's office, Ethan replayed his part in the scene of the break-in. What had he done wrong? How had he let the guy get away?

Fatigue gripped him. It had been a long while since he'd had a good night's sleep. And now the sun crept toward the horizon. Soon it would be dawn...and he'd yet to go to bed. Oh well, he'd survive.

Marianna, however..."Hey," he said as he touched her arm. She swung her head around to look at him. He kept his face angled toward her so she could see his lips but he was still able to keep his eyes safely on the road. "Where do you want to go, your parents'?"

She gave a listless shrug. "I guess so."

"Twister is going to be all right. You heard the doctor."

Marianna blew out a sigh. "I know and I'm grateful, but I'm also terribly frustrated. What is going on, Ethan?" Tears surfaced once again. He watched as she held them at bay with sheer determination.

He shook his head. "I don't know, Marianna. I think you're the only one who can really answer that. Unfortunately, you might not even know what you know."

"Well, that's clear."

A rueful chuckle slipped out. "I'm sorry. I wish had something more to tell you."

"I've racked my brain trying to come up with something. Why someone would kill Suzanne? Why did, possibly, the same someone come back to the house and was willing to break in with me there?" She turned thoughtful. "Although, he may not have known anyone was there, because I parked my car in the garage when I got home." Her eyes narrowed. "Do you think he's looking for something?"

Ethan pulled into her parents' driveway and glanced at the dashboard clock. It read 6:42. "It's certainly a possibility. At first, when I got to your house the day of the murder, I thought there'd been a huge fight in Suzanne's room. But there was no evidence she'd struggled. So, it could be the guy was definitely looking for something. Could Suzanne have been involved in something shady? Something you wouldn't have known about?"

"Absolutely not." She spoke without hesitation. "Suze was a great girl and a devoted Christian. There's no way she would be associated with something illegal."

"Then the incidents may not be related. It's possible our burglar read the story about Suzanne's murder in the paper, did a simple online search to find out where Suzanne lived and decided to help himself to anything he could find."

"Only I was there." She frowned, her dark, finely arched brows coming together above the bridge of her delicate nose. "It mentioned me in the article, so he had to know she had a roommate."

"Maybe. Then again, he may have figured no roommate would want to stay in a house all by herself after her friend had been killed in said house, and therefore he would have free rein."

She rolled her eyes, her gorgeous, chocolate eyes. He blinked. She was saying, "There are so many possible explanations it makes my head hurt. Thank you for having my house cleaned up, by the way. That was a very thoughtful thing to do."

Ethan could feel the heat rising to his face. He didn't really know why he was embarrassed; it was just that her smile did crazy things to his emotions. He reached out to brush a finger under her hair, to push it away from her face, then moved his hand, cupping her cheek. "You're quite welcome." She looked…kissable. He leaned closer and let his hand slide to the back of her neck.

The porch light came on; a face appeared in the window. Ethan felt another flush start to creep up his neck as he slowly pulled back, turning from the watchful eyes peering at them from behind the glass and connecting his gaze with Marianna's once more. He felt as if he was back in high school on a date and his girl's dad had just sent him a warning.

Marianna's short, lilting laugh told him she'd read his thoughts. He smiled at her. "Aw, stop," he drawled. She grinned, her dimples flashed and his heart sputtered. Crazy.

A light tap on his window jerked his attention from the woman beside him. He pressed the button and the glass slid down in a smooth ride. A tall, dark-haired, dark-eyed male replica of Marianna stared down at him. In his early thirties, the man had the air of one who knew what he wanted and had what it took to get it.

Ethan had the uneasy feeling this man wanted him, or at least Marianna, out of the car.

Marianna leaned forward and asked, "Joseph, what are you doing up?"

"When I hear a car pull up in the driveway and then silence, I'm going to investigate a bit." Sarcasm dripped, but Ethan could tell the man wasn't angry. Joseph, FBI agent and big brother. He could handle the FBI agent part; it was the big brother part that had him leery. But there was no way he was letting that little secret become public knowledge. Ethan gave Joseph a cool nod and held eye contact as he shoved open his door.

Joseph stepped back and Marianna took the cue to climb out her side. She walked around and slid her arms around Joseph's waist. Ethan felt a twinge of jealousy that took him by surprise as her brother gave her a comforting hug. He wished she trusted him that way. Then he gave a mental roll of his eyes and told himself to get it together.

He said, "Marianna had another little incident early this morning."

Joseph's gaze sharpened. "What kind of incident?"

"Someone broke in my house. Twister scared him off. I called 911 but must have hung up too soon. I couldn't tell if someone answered or not. Then I called Ethan and he came to the rescue. Now, I want to go to bed."

Joseph's expression said he wouldn't be satisfied with that piddling explanation, but wasn't going to push it for now because he could see the exhaustion on her face. Ethan's respect for the man went up a notch…and it was already high to begin with.

The light flickered off, then on, then off, then back on—a way of getting a deaf person's attention. Marianna pulled away from Joseph, turned and saw her mother standing on the porch, her fingers on the light switch. The glow from the ceiling fan light illuminated the area. She signed. "Hey, Mom, it's just me. I'm moving back in for a little while, if that's okay."

Questions formed in her mother's eyes, but she didn't say anything, just motioned for Marianna to come in. Then she gave a pointed look at Ethan. Marianna signed, "Mom, meet Ethan O'Hara. He's the detective working on Suzanne's case." Then she said, "Ethan, meet my mother, Maddelena Santino."

Ethan walked toward the women, his smile sincere and charming at the same time. He signed, "Nice to meet you." Surprise lit Maddelena's eyes and Marianna gasped.

He directed a sad smile toward her as he signed and spoke at the same time. "Yes, I sign. I had a deaf sister. She was…she died…three years ago, but I've never forgotten her language."

Marianna thought her jaw might hit the ground. Then her mother said with graceful hands, "It's freezing out here. Everyone come in and let me feed you breakfast."

Her mother's answer to every disaster: Food. Right now, Marianna wouldn't complain. With her life so crazy, she'd welcome the familiar routine. Plus, she was cold and wanted to get inside.

Once Maddelena had everyone settled, she fired up the gas stove and cooked a breakfast fit for a five-star restaurant. The rest of her family made their way into the kitchen, and the introductions began.

Her terror fading in the chaos of family, Marianna felt herself relaxing and enjoying Ethan's shell-shocked look. She said, "You don't come from a large family, do you?"

He shook his head. "Nope. It was just me for a long time. My sister was almost ten years younger. Then, she died…." He trailed off, his gaze fixed on two of her siblings arguing over who got the next piece of toast. Alonso, her sixteen-year-old deaf brother and youngest member of the clan, had lightning-fast reflexes and beat out Gina, her twenty-six-year-old hearing sister who was a real estate attorney in North Carolina. Gina had come home last week to visit and announce her recent engagement.

Gina punched Alonso in the arm hard enough to make

him wince. She signed, "You need to learn to respect your elders, boy."

Alonso signed back, "When I see an elder that deserves it, I'll give it."

Gina very maturely stuck out her tongue, then turned her back on him to plop another piece of bread in the toaster.

Marianna smiled at the craziness. She told Ethan, "If you think this is bad, you should see us all at Christmas!"

"I can't even imagine." He took a bite of his eggs and chewed, but she noticed he never took his eyes from the antics of her family.

She also noticed Alonso refused to look in Ethan's direction. Lasering the evil eye on her brother, she subtly signed, "He's not the cop who arrested you. Be nice." Unfortunately, about six months ago, Alonso had been arrested for being in the wrong place at the wrong time when a friend of his decided to shoplift. Protesting his innocence to this day, he still had an aversion to cops. Including his own brother, Joseph.

Alonso rolled his eyes and ignored her order.

Then she noticed Ethan's frown. He placed his fork on his plate and reached for his phone, lifting it to his ear. He listened for a minute and a half, then hung up. His fierce expression was back, his tenseness from the break-in returning twofold.

She raised a brow in question.

He signed, "That was Catelyn. The lab found some evidence, and I need to get over there to find out what's going on."

"On a Saturday?"

He gave a small smile. "No rest for the weary." When he stood, everyone looked up at him. He signed, "It was a pleasure to meet you all, but duty calls."

Marianna's mother frowned and signed back, "They don't let you eat?"

Joseph shot him a sympathetic glance and saved him from having to answer by saying, "Mama, you know how it is in law enforcement. You've got to do what you can when you can."

Maddelena rolled her dark eyes and signed, "Bah, you go do your job, then, but only if you promise to come back when you can eat a decent meal. And come to church with us tomorrow. We go to the church with the interpreter on the other side of town."

Ethan said his thanks for the breakfast, made no comment about church and headed out the door.

Marianna stabbed a bite of pancake as she watched him leave, wondering why the fact that he was so comfortable with her family made her nervous.

Ethan climbed into his car, never so glad to get out of someone's home. Not that he hadn't enjoyed the crazy clan, but they made him think about the past. About what might have been.

Guilt pierced him as it did every time he thought about his sister, Ashley. And the more he was around Marianna, the more he thought about Ashley. A vicious cycle if there ever was one.

Poor Ashley. She'd been ten years his junior and stuck with him as the one person she could count on…and he'd let her down. True, it hadn't been intentional, but in the end it hadn't mattered. She'd died.

And his life had spiraled downward into a hole he'd almost been unable to claw his way out of. If it hadn't been for his ex-partner, Mac McCullough, Ethan might still be drowning his sorrows in a six-pack each night. Mac had eventually quit the force and gone on to be a missionary overseas, but Ethan thanked God for the man every day.

His phone rang, yanking him from his memories. Thank goodness. "Hello."

"Hey, it's Catelyn. Where are you?"

"Almost to the lab. Why?"

"We got a shoe print from under her window."

"Does it match the bloody one from the porch?"

"Nope. Unfortunately, not."

"Are they the same size?"

"Negative on that, too."

"All that means is that the guy wore a different pair of shoes."

"Or this break-in is totally unrelated to the murder." Ethan could hear her frustration. She wanted to catch this guy as bad as he did.

He said, "Yeah, I've already thought of that."

"So, what's Marianna going to do? Is she staying with her folks right now? I'm really nervous about her going back to that house by herself. Something's just weird about the whole situation. The murder, then the break-in…weird."

"I agree. But I'm stumped as to a connection. And yes, right now, she's staying with her folks." He sighed, ran a hand through his already mussed hair. "Listen, I haven't been to bed yet. If you don't actually need me there, I'm going to run home, take a shower and crash for a couple of hours."

"Sure, I've got it covered. Go get some rest and call me when you get up. I appreciate you not calling me in on it last night."

"Nothing much you could have done. I didn't figure you'd hate me for letting you sleep."

"Never. That's why I'm willing to put in a few hours on the weekend. I'll get it back after we catch this guy."

"Thanks, Cate."

He hung up, did a U-turn, then took a left to head home. Just a few hours sleep, then he'd be back on it, he silently promised himself...and Marianna.

FIVE

As Marianna dressed for church in the morning, she studied the childhood room she'd shared with two of her sisters, Catherina and Alissa. She smiled when she thought of her twin, Alissa.

As children and even teens, they hadn't wanted to be separated and had shared a room up until graduation from high school. They'd gone to different colleges, Marianna to Gallaudet University in Washington, D.C. and Alissa to the University of South Carolina in Columbia, just a couple of hours away.

Being the parents of six children, her mother and father had had to get creative when it came to sleeping arrangements. The house had four bedrooms and a basement that had been converted into a small apartment for Marianna's grandmother, who'd lived with them until she died last year.

Marianna appreciated the fact that her mother still kept the double bed and bunk beds in here so that the sisters could have their "reunion" during holidays. Often all four sisters usually wound up in the one room, staying up all night catching up, then crashing wherever they found a spot.

She said a small prayer of thanks for her childhood,

knowing she'd been blessed. Oh, not always with material things but with the things that mattered. And one more thing to be thankful for was the fact that the vet had sent a text message saying Twister would be able to come home Monday. Marianna missed her four-legged friend.

Attached to the pocket of her black dress pants, her BlackBerry buzzed, pulling her from her thoughts. She slipped it from the clip and checked the caller ID.

Curt Wentworth. Why he continued to bother her, she had yet to figure out. This was the man who'd wooed her, had her tumbling head over heels in love, then had turned around and emotionally stabbed her in the back. When he finally let her know she wasn't good enough for him. Add his physical aggression into the mix and she just wanted him to leave her alone. She read, "Why aren't you answering my messages? I want to see you, Marianna. It really makes me mad when you just ignore me. Rather rude, don't you think? At least have the courtesy to answer me."

She punched the reply button on the machine and typed, "Leave me alone, please, Curt. ALREADY TOLD YOU I'M NOT INTERESTED IN SEEING YOU ANYMORE. If you would stop texting me, I wouldn't have to ignore you. You are the one being rude."

He responded, "But I've apologized, what else can I do?"

"Honor my request to LEAVE ME ALONE."

"I made a mistake, Marianna. As a Christian, aren't you supposed to forgive me?"

This called for caps again. "I HAVE FORGIVEN YOU, JUST DON'T WANT TO BE WITH YOU. I wouldn't mind trying to build a friendship with you, but it would go no further than that, and you and I both know that you're unwilling to accept that right now. Late for church. Bye."

She replaced the device back into the clip and grabbed

her purse. When it vibrated once more, she pressed the 'Ignore' button, resolving not to respond to him anymore. Maybe that was the problem. She kept answering him intermittently instead of being consistent in just deleting his messages, and that encouraged him or gave him hope. Quite possibly if she just didn't acknowledge his texts anymore, he would give up and go find someone more suitable.

Such as a hearing girl, one he wouldn't be ashamed of. Absentmindedly, she smoothed her hair down over her ears, then stared at herself in the mirror above the dresser. In a fit of pique, she grabbed a hair tie and pulled the silky mass into a casual ponytail, exposing her hearing aids for the world to see. There. Eat your heart out, Curt Wentworth.

Marianna clamped the lid on the memories and the feelings they still invoked. Not feelings for him, just the feelings of not measuring up or being good enough.

He'd certainly fooled her for a long time. But she'd learned her lesson well. And while she'd been honest when she'd said she'd forgiven him, she sure hadn't forgotten his behavior. Or his constant pushing for her to get a cochlear implant, a surgically implanted device that worked as a "mechanical ear." It was great for some people, she just chose not to go that route right now. She shook her head at her stupidity. He could have asked her for almost anything that wasn't illegal or immoral, and she would have done her best to oblige.

Anything but to get a cochlear implant. And he'd refused to listen to her or her reasons why she didn't want one. She didn't want to risk destroying the hearing she had left. She was also comfortable with her deafness and didn't need to be "fixed." It was a concept Curt couldn't compute and refused to accept that she knew her own mind on this topic. Marianna grimaced. *Okay, Lord, give me something more pleasant to think about this morning, please?*

Immediately, Ethan's face appeared in her mind's eye. She grabbed her jacket as she allowed herself to think about the good-looking cop. She'd been surprised he'd fit in so well with her family—and to find out he'd had a deaf sister…well…

The lamp on her bedside table flashed. All of the bedrooms were wired with a flashing light to alert the occupant that someone was "knocking" on the door. There was actually a small button to push, similar to an indoor doorbell that activated the light.

She opened her door to find Gina standing on the other side. Her sister signed, "You ready?"

"Yes, I guess. Curt's bugging me again this morning."

Her sister sighed and shook her head. "I hope you told him to leave you alone."

They started the walk down the hall to the stairs. Gina turned and walked backward down the steps, gripping the rail with her left hand as she signed with her right. Marianna smiled at the leftover childhood behavior and answered, "I did, but it doesn't seem to faze him much."

Gina, dark hair, dark eyes and slightly overweight, still had all the features of the Santinos. Full lips and slightly slanted eyes gave her an exotic look, showing off her Italian heritage, but somewhere down the line the family had some Japanese blood, too. Her sister wore it well.

"Want me to get rid of him for you? I know a guy or two."

"No, I wouldn't want to get Mario in trouble before you guys even get married." Her sister's fiancé was an army ranger. "I'll handle Curt. Now, let's get to church."

The rest of the family, including her father, who was

finally looking a little better after his bout with whatever had laid him low the last couple of weeks, dispersed to their respective cars. Marianna rode with Gina, who planned to have lunch with friends after church. As they drove, Marianna couldn't help thinking about the break-in from Friday night. As much as she didn't want to, she remembered the terror she'd felt, the pure fear that had almost held her paralyzed.

Did the guy find what he was after? Did that incident have anything to do with Suzanne's murder?

She shivered in spite of the heat blowing from the vents.

Would he be back? Would she feel safe staying there by herself now, unable to hear if danger came prowling again?

A nagging sense of unease kept her nerves on edge. She couldn't seem to focus on anything much but the continued flashes of remembered terror.

Think of something else!

Her parents and Alonso led the way ahead of them. Marianna looked in the side mirror to watch the traffic behind them, mulling over her options: Stay in a house where she'd constantly be scared. Go stay with her parents. Move in with a friend from school.

None of the options really appealed to her. As she'd told her mother, it looked as if she would be moving back home temporarily.

A silver sedan with tinted windows cruised sedately behind her and Gina. At the traffic light, the man in the green SUV that pulled up next to her seemed to be watching her. She smiled, then kept her eyes straight ahead. The SUV turned right and she wilted. Paranoia is only a good thing when someone's after you, she reminded herself. Otherwise they lock you up in the loony bin, okay? Relax.

By the time they reached the church, Marianna's nerves

were shot. And it didn't help that the silver sedan that had been following them most of the way turned into the parking lot behind her.

Feeling refreshed from a good night's sleep, yet antsy at the lack of progress in the case, Ethan determined to work on finding the man—or men—who'd broken into Marianna's home. He needed to see her, to dig deeper into her past and Suzanne's.

You've already done that, O'Hara. You're just looking for an excuse to see her.

The thought taunted him. He blew out a sigh. Oh, all right, he admitted it. He wanted to see her. But he really did need to hash the case out with her, too. Sometimes the victim is so busy being the victim that he or she subconsciously refuses to bring memories to the surface until later, after the passage of time when once again the individual is feeling secure, safe.

Acting completely out of character, Ethan impulsively decided to meet her when she came out of church and see if she would have lunch with him. He'd almost gotten up to go, but had wimped out at the last minute. It had been a while since he'd been to the large church downtown that his parents had frequented. Since Ashley's death, it just hurt to go back and be reminded of how much she'd loved being a part of the youth ministry, how much she'd loved giving to and serving others. But maybe he'd been wrong. Maybe if he'd have let people reach out to him…

Questioning his motives during the ten-minute drive to the church she'd mentioned attending, the one with a small deaf ministry, he pulled up outside of the sanctuary to sit and stare at the door. After a few minutes, his gaze wandered and the political poster in the window of the building across the street caught his attention.

It was election year and the campaigning was fast and furious, narrowing the candidates down one by one. Clayton Robertson seemed to be the favored one of the more conservative party, while Terrance Sloane ran a strong opposition.

Should be an interesting political year all the way up to the day in November when people would stand in line and vote in the next governor of South Carolina.

Ethan shook his head. He was all for democracy, but the money that went into these campaigns galled him. When he thought of the good those funds could do and how he always wondered if it was spent as it was supposed to be, he shook his head and sighed. Well, he voted; not much else he could do about politicians and their issues.

A movement from the doorway of the church pulled him back to the reason he was here.

Marianna Santino.

A whole herd of people stampeded toward their vehicles after shaking hands with the pastor standing at the sanctuary exit. Finally, Marianna came out signing animatedly with a young girl. Ethan didn't mean to eavesdrop, but he caught that Marianna was reminding the girl about basketball practice tomorrow afternoon. The girl agreed, then said something about being ready for the big game on Thursday.

Ethan opened his door and stepped out, intending to approach Marianna and ask her to lunch, but he stopped when a clean-cut man in his early thirties walked up to her and took her hand. Regret cut through him. Who was this? A boyfriend?

Relief followed the regret when he saw her expression change to one of annoyance as she yanked her hand away from the guy.

Unfortunately, Ethan was too far away to hear what she

was saying. But when the man grabbed her upper arm and Marianna winced, that was enough for him.

Marianna thought about giving Curt a good kick in the shin but didn't want to make a scene in the church parking lot. If he didn't let go of her arm in the next two seconds, however, she'd toss aside her inhibitions and give her foot permission to do its worst.

Then she was free, her arm throbbing from the grip Curt had had on it. What? How?

"Ethan? What are you doing here?" The question came out before she could stop it. Surprise and relief held her captive.

Fury emanated from his blue eyes and if he lasered Curt any harder with them, the poor man would be incinerated on the spot. Through gritted teeth, Ethan said, "Touch her again and I'll arrest you for assault."

Curt's Adam's apple bobbed. Then he bravely stuck out his chest. Funny how it seemed thin and pitiful next to Ethan's broad shoulders and muscular physique. Not that she had any business noticing that.

"Who are you?" Curt demanded.

Marianna stepped in. "This is Ethan, one of the detectives investigating Suzanne's death."

"Yeah," Ethan growled, "so where were you a week and a half ago on Tuesday, around ten in the morning?"

Curt's eyes shot wide and he stammered, "Um…uh…I…was at a conference…in…in New York."

Marianna elbowed her protector. "All right, Ethan, that's enough. Curt didn't kill Suzanne."

"What about breaking into your house?"

Curt looked ready for the ground beneath his feet to swallow him. "Look, I didn't kill anyone, and I certainly didn't break into Marianna's house. I don't have any reason to."

Marianna took Ethan's arm. "Come on. Walk with me to my mother's car. She's probably waiting on me."

Ethan gave a final, hard look at Curt and said, "My pleasure."

"Goodbye, Curt."

Marianna and Ethan headed in the direction she led. He asked, "Why'd you tell him bye?"

She blew out an exasperated breath. "I don't know. Because it was the polite thing to do?"

"When a man lays a hand on you like he did, the last thing he deserves is politeness. How's your arm?"

It hurt. "It's fine. Forget him and tell me why you're here."

Ethan spotted her parents and brother standing beside a white Suburban. "Why don't you have lunch with me and tell your folks I'll bring you home later?"

Nerves suddenly swirled in her stomach. What kind of lunch was he talking about? A date lunch? Or a business, let's-talk-about-the-case lunch? She bit her lip and he gave her a knowing smile.

"Please?"

She couldn't resist. "Okay." Catching her father's attention, she signed that she was going with Ethan and would be home later. He frowned but nodded.

Ethan took her hand and led her to his car.

That's when she noticed the silver car parked four spots down. Earlier, when it had turned in behind her and her sister, she'd tried to get a look at the driver, but it had gone on past them and around the side of the building. She'd given up trying to figure out if someone was following her and if the occupants of the car had been members of the church arriving at the same time as she.

Seeing the car still parked there, and her sister long gone, along with her parents, she decided she was definitely being paranoid—not that she didn't have good reason to be, but obviously the silver car belonged to a member of the congregation. Relief replaced her momentary anxiety.

Ethan tapped her shoulder to get her attention. "So, what are you in the mood for?" His touch lingered, causing her stomach to do a series of flip-flops.

Pushing her attraction aside for now, she thought. "Something...relaxing."

"Huh?"

"You know, relaxing food. Fruit, ice cream, soup."

"I never knew food could be relaxing."

Marianna reached up and took his hand in hers, feeling the calluses of a man used to hard work, yet one who used his hands for gentle comfort, too. Somehow, Marianna knew Ethan would never raise a fist against her—ever.

"Well, you're about to learn something new. How about we go to Panera?"

"The one on East Main?"

She laughed. "Yes, since it's the only one in Spartanburg."

"Right." He pulled his hand from her grasp and cranked the car to head across town. Once there, Ethan ordered while she got a table. From her seat, she watched him smile at the young girl who flirted outrageously with him while punching in the order.

Marianna was impressed that while Ethan smiled in a friendly way, there was nothing encouraging or flirtatious about him. Curt would have...nope, not going there.

Soon, Ethan brought their food to the table, and Marianna enjoyed her salad while he sampled the soup.

After a few minutes, Marianna placed her fork on the table and looked at her companion. "So, let's get to the point. You have something else you want to discuss with me, don't you?"

Startled bemusement flickered briefly, then, turning serious, he said, "I don't think you're safe staying at your house."

"I've already thought about that."

"And?"

Marianna sat back, munching the last bite of salad. She swallowed, took a sip of water, then said, "I hate to admit it, but you're probably right. I don't want to, but I guess I'll be staying at my parents' longer than I thought."

"What's your hesitation?"

"I've fought so hard to be…" Did she really want to share this with him? A man she'd known for only a little over a week and met under extreme circumstances? Yet, there was something about him that pulled her, drew her to him.

He finished the sentence for her. "…independent?"

She nodded, guilt hitting her hard. Her family was so wonderful, yet they had a way of being a little smothering sometimes.

"They just want to make sure nothing happens to you."

Marianna straightened, agitation making her words sharp. "I can take care of myself. I don't need someone watching to make sure nothing happens to me."

Something flashed in his eyes. Hurt, anger, grief? She couldn't place the emotion she saw but wondered at the cause.

Abruptly, he said, "Okay, so this guy that broke in. His shoe print is different than the one we found from the murder."

Marianna blinked but allowed the topic shift. "Does that mean it was two different people?"

"No, not necessarily. He could have just worn a different pair of shoes this time. We did rule out Suzanne's ex-boyfriend, Bryson James. He had an alibi, plus his shoe size is about a size and a half too small for the print we found. That's too much of a difference to suspect him."

"What about the two prints from the different incidents. Are they the same size?" Marianna wondered.

"No, but there's only about a half size difference. Which, again, doesn't mean much. Some people buy their shoes according to fit and feel, not size. But the difference is small enough that we can't rule out it's the same person."

"So, basically, we know nothing."

"That's it in a nutshell."

"And there wasn't any DNA or anything found either time?"

"Still waiting on that. And you can't think of anything you might have that this guy could be after?"

Marianna threw her hands up. "No. I can't think of a thing."

"Well, my guess is that he didn't get whatever he was looking for Friday night."

She looked up at him, fear flowing freely. "So, I guess that means he'll be back, huh?"

SIX

Monday morning Marianna hurried to school, anxious for the day to be over so she could see Twister. She'd missed his comforting presence. Joseph had volunteered to pick up the dog for her and have him waiting at her parents' house since she had basketball practice this evening. Twister would greet her when she walked in the door later tonight.

After she and Ethan had finished eating the day before, he'd driven her home to retrieve some of her things and taken her to her parents' house. Her mom welcomed Marianna like a long-lost child even though she had just spent Saturday night there, while her father's furrowed gray brows told her he worried silently.

In the classroom she flipped on the television so the kids could watch the morning news. It was filled with mostly political happenings owing to the upcoming election, and her students found it fascinating to be informed of the latest in the process. Oh, they didn't understand it in detail, but they knew it was a big deal and therefore wanted to be involved. Marianna was happy to oblige. She and the other teachers had even arranged to have a mock election day for the entire school, with several voting booths loaned to the school by the local voter's registration office. The workers had agreed to volunteer and run the day like a normal voting day, even having the students register to vote just like any other citizen. The only difference was no one had to meet the age requirement. Everyone was really excited about it, even the staff members.

Josh entered the room and handed over another computer part. Marianna went to her desk, pulled open the drawer and realized she'd left his box in the other teacher's classroom. Making a mental note to get it later, she dropped the part into the drawer and said, "Thanks, Josh."

"Welcome," he signed. Then looked at the television. His eyes went wide and he signed, "Daddy!"

"What?" Marianna glanced up at the screen and noticed a well-dressed man in his mid-forties speaking to the reporter to his right.

Josh jumped up and down, causing the room to shake, his large frame causing the effects of a small earthquake. Books tumbled from the shelves, and the desks danced across the floor. Marianna went to him and laid a hand on his arm. "Josh, calm down." Josh stopped but didn't take his eyes from the television.

"Daddy," he signed again.

Sure enough, that was his father. Marianna had met the man only once at the beginning of the year. The campaign manager for one of the gubernatorial candidates, he would be campaigning from Charleston this week, only about three hours away. Marianna wondered if the man would try to make it down to visit Josh before heading off to the next city on the list. Hmm, probably not or she would have been notified by now. Closed captions played at the bottom, displaying the conversation taking place between the reporter and Josh's father.

No wonder Josh lived with his grandparents. His father was a busy man, and his mother had died a few years ago.

"...overhead transparencies?"

The question came from the door, catching Marianna's attention with the noise. Misty Williams, late twenties, tall, red hair, green eyes. And a teacher with an attitude. Why the woman had taken a dislike for Marianna was beyond her.

"I'm sorry?"

Misty rolled her eyes, then stomped into the room to pull open a file cabinet.

Marianna felt her jaw drop but swallowed her desire to snap the woman's head off. As if she didn't have enough stress in her life right now without adding Misty's nastiness to it.

"Excuse me." Marianna stepped forward and placed a hand on the drawer. The woman's gall was unbelievable.

Misty stopped her search. "Transparencies. Jean said you have some."

Marianna sighed. Perhaps if she kept her cool, one day Misty would reveal why she disliked Marianna so much. "Sure, Misty, how many do you need?"

"Four or five should be fine."

Handing them over, she tried to see beyond the anger—and saw nothing but the raw emotion directed solely at her. She shivered. Why did the woman display such malice toward her?

Misty snatched them and left without a word of thanks.

Shaking her head, Marianna welcomed the rest of her class as they filed in. Her assistant hurried through the door and tossed her lunch bag on her desk. "Sorry I'm late—my car wouldn't start this morning, so I had to catch the bus."

"No problem, I'm just glad you made it." She placed a hand on the woman's arm, glanced around to see that the students' attention was on the news and asked, "Dawn, do you know why Misty is so hateful to me?"

Dawn's eyes went wide, then her lips thinned. "No, but I've noticed her attitude toward you."

"She seemed friendly enough initially, after she first started working here a couple of months ago, but something definitely happened to put her off of me, that's for sure."

"I don't know, but I'll keep my eyes and ears open for you."

"Maybe I should just ask her."

Dawn shrugged. "I guess you could. Or maybe it's just a phase and she's having a couple of bad weeks. Who knows?"

"Maybe."

And then there was no more time to worry about the situation. Soon, Marianna found herself caught up in the business of teaching and the endless stack of paperwork that went with it.

Before she knew it, the day had passed and the final bell had rung. Basketball practice wasn't until after supper, so Marianna stayed late working on papers. Around five o'clock, she pulled a frozen dinner from her dorm-sized refrigerator and walked toward the teacher's lounge to zap it in the microwave.

As she stepped from her well-lit classroom into the dark hall, she noticed how empty the building was.

Empty and spooky.

She didn't need her imagination to fill in what could happen to a lone female in a deserted building. She paused, trying to decide whether to keep going or turn around, grab her purse and get out. Which was silly, because she'd done this routine of staying late ever since basketball season started. Only now, with Suzanne's death and the break-in...

Adrenaline kicked in as she relived the terror of seeing Suzanne lying lifeless on the floor, of being alone in her house, grief stricken and weary, then terrorized once again when the intruder climbed through her bedroom window.

Returning to the scene of the crime.

Fear seized her, cramped her stomach as a terrifying idea flashed through her mind.

What if Suzanne was not only in the wrong place at the wrong time, but also was the wrong person?

What if the killer originally thought Suzanne was Marianna, learned of his mistake, and Friday night was his idea of trying to finish the job?

Ethan sat at his desk, flipping through the case files, his mind about as alert as mush. He couldn't keep his thoughts focused as he worried about Marianna. For some reason he couldn't convince himself that this last break-in was unrelated to Suzanne's murder.

He glanced at the clock. Almost five thirty. Catelyn had left forty-five minutes ago to meet up with Marianna's sister Alissa.

Marianna had basketball practice with her team at six, but no doubt she would head over to the gym early to make sure everything was ready. Tapping his pen against his chin, he thought. Should he go over just to check on her? What if something happened to her while he sat here worrying about her?

She's a big girl, O'Hara—she doesn't need you checking up on her.

But his mind kept playing the "what if" game. What if there was something behind her and she didn't hear it? What if someone tried to warn her of the danger coming and…

Stop it!

Although…what would it hurt? Just run by, say hey, and then head home. To his empty apartment. Where he would grill chicken for one. Fix one glass of iced tea. Set one place at the table. Growing up, he and Ashley had shared thousands of meals together, just the two of them, while their parents traveled the world, jet-setting with their country club friends.

Ah, Ashley, sweet sister, even after almost three years, I still miss you terribly at times.

He let his gaze slide to the picture on his desk, the last one he'd taken of Ashley. She had her long dark hair pulled up into a messy ponytail, had on sweats and a ball cap. Her grin pierced him as he remembered the last time he'd seen her, tried to warn her about the car speeding toward her.

She hadn't heard him. Instead she'd hurried toward him, stepping into the path of the vehicle. And he'd been unable to do anything about it. To stop it. His fault...

Ethan slapped the picture facedown, stood and gathered his leather jacket. He'd just go by the school and see Marianna, make sure she was all right. But he sure wouldn't tell her that was his reason for stopping by. She was certainly little Miss Independent.

And she was probably fine, but what could it hurt? Just to see. To reassure himself.

Marianna hurried up the walkway to the dark gym. Puzzlement made her frown. Where were the lights? Her assistant coaches and student helpers?

Granted, the players wouldn't show up for another fifteen, twenty minutes, but everyone else should be here by now. Reaching the heavy glass doors, she saw a sign:

Basketball practice has been canceled.

"What?" She hadn't canceled practice! Well, that explained why no one was here. Had someone decided to play a practical joke on her? It was too early in the year for an April Fool's Day prank. They'd gotten her good last year: every one of her starting players had texted her claiming to be sick and unable to attend the big play-off game. She still hadn't come up with an appropriate retaliation.

She pulled on the door. Locked. Digging in her pocket for her key, she opened it and stepped inside.

Great, another dark hallway.

She slapped at the light switch on the wall. Nothing.

Weird.

Now she started to get that feeling in the pit of her stomach that told her something wasn't right. The same feeling she'd had when she'd first seen her door standing wide open the day of Suzanne's murder.

Invisible fingers tickled the nape of her neck.

She whirled.

"Who's there?" Because someone was there. She couldn't hear anyone, but she could *feel* the presence of someone. A dark, sinister feeling that shot adrenaline double-time through her body.

Not again, God!

Her breath came in short, whispered pants as she slipped behind a display board for the moment. She had to make a decision, but her brain felt as if someone had used the remote to put it on pause.

What to do?

Think, Marianna, think!

Her BlackBerry. She slapped her side...and felt nothing. She'd left it charging in her classroom.

Although the darkness pressed in, she wondered if she could use it to her advantage. She knew the layout of the building. Hopefully, whoever was in here with her didn't.

With what she prayed were silent steps, she slowly moved her sneaker-clad feet toward the inner door of the gym. If she could get inside the storage room, she could lock herself in.

Tears threatened as her fear mounted. But she kept her cool and took another step. And another. The door to the court lay just beyond her. One more step and her fingers brushed the cool metal. She knew it would clang loudly as soon as she pushed it inward. She'd have to move fast once inside the door.

With another prayer and a deep breath, she gave it a shove and rushed in, spinning to the left. Pure darkness pushed against her eyes. Silence thundered in her ears, even as her hearing aids picked up heavy footsteps behind her.

Trailing her fingers along the wall, she moved as quickly as she dared.

Almost there.

If memory served her right, she needed to go only a few more feet after she passed the bleachers. Praying the room would be unlocked when she got there, she kept moving. The wall ran out, her shin hit the lowest bleacher and she flinched but ignored it.

Then she felt him, her, it.

Breathing on her neck. Smelling of stale cigarette smoke. She turned to flee.

Pain ripped through her scalp and down her neck as a rough hand gripped her ponytail in a vise.

She screamed, tears leaking down her cheeks.

"I'm deaf! I can't hear you if you're talking!"

The hand shoved against the back of her head, and she went down, cracking her cheek against the edge of the wooden seat.

Marianna screamed again.

SEVEN

Hand on the gym door, Ethan paused. Darkness greeted him. He frowned, his gut shouting at him that something was wrong.

Had she canceled practice? The sign on the door said she had. He grabbed the handle and pulled. Locked.

Unclipping his phone from his belt, he sent a text to Marianna's BlackBerry. "Are you having practice tonight? I'm at the gym and no one's here. You okay?"

Anxiety caused sweat to bead on his brow. Should he call for backup?

But backup for what, canceled basketball practice?

The comfortable weight of his gun rested snugly under his left arm. He reached up and loosened the strap but didn't pull the weapon out…yet.

Retracing his steps, he climbed back into his car and drove around to the girls' dormitory, located within sight of the gym.

Several stood outside talking, signing fast, using a word every now and then that Ethan didn't understand. Must be slang he wasn't up to date on.

When they spotted him, the conversation ceased. Ethan looked around for a dorm parent and spotted her talking to one of the girls near the door to the building.

The girl she was talking to pointed to him and the woman turned, frowning. "May I help you?" she signed.

"I'm sorry to bother you, but I was looking for Marianna Santino. I thought she had basketball practice right now, but there's no one in the gym. Do you know where I can find her?"

One of the teens signed, "Basketball practice was canceled."

Ethan signed back, "Did Ms. Santino say why?"

"No, just that it was canceled."

That still didn't sit right with Ethan. "You talked to her?"

The girl nodded. "On the TTY." The telephone device used by the deaf to type messages back and forth. Just like texting, but the TTY used a landline, and the person could read the message as it was being typed out.

"And you're sure it was Marianna?" he asked.

A shrug. "That's what the person typed."

Ethan touched the tips of his fingers to his mouth and brought his hand down, palm up. "Thank you."

"Welcome."

Walking back to his car, he checked his phone. No response to his text to Marianna. His gut tightened. Not necessarily alarming, but unusual. And in light of recent events...

Should he check her classroom or go back to the gym once more? Should he call campus security and see if they'd had any report of a disturbance?

He glanced at the gymnasium and thought he saw something move. Lights dotted the campus at night, lighting the walkways and streets, but there were still spots that remained dark, places someone could hide.

The movement caught his eye again, and he moved toward it, hand on the butt of his gun.

* * *

Marianna lay against the floor, not daring to move. Her fingers gripped the object her attacker had shoved into her hand before releasing her.

Slowly her senses returned, and she felt warm wetness flowing from the throbbing gash on her cheek, absent-mindedly wondering if she'd need stitches.

Every muscle tense, she concentrated on the floor. About a minute earlier, she'd felt the person move away from her, fleeing feet pounding across the surface, the vibrations under her prone body growing fainter with each step.

Dare she pray it was over? How long should she stay there? Should she try to leave and get help?

A light flickered in front of her. The terror returned full force, and she scrunched down into a little ball, not wanting to move and take the chance on making noise that would draw attention to her.

The light passed over her. More running feet, headed in her direction. She scrambled to her feet, adrenaline flowing, anger surging. This time she'd fight back and with fists still knotted, tightly clenched. Ignoring the throbbing pain in her cheek, she tried to remember every self-defense move Joseph had taught her.

Then she was staring into Ethan O'Hara's worried face as he turned the light on himself to show her who was there.

Her muscles wilted, pulling her back to the floor she'd just risen from, and she burst into tears.

Ethan had never felt such murderous rage as he did at that very moment. Not even toward the two teens who had drag raced in the high school parking lot, their irresponsible actions leading to his sister's tragic death. Ashley's death had been an unintentional act.

This, though, this attack on Marianna had premeditation written all over it. He sat on the floor beside the sobbing woman and gathered her into his arms. More beams of light entered through the door held open by the officers Ethan had called when he realized the lights in the gym didn't work.

Campus security arrived and everyone began talking at once.

The young man in his mid-thirties who held the title of head of campus security, Kevin Manning, sat on his haunches, pushed his cap back on his head and asked, "She all right?"

Through gritted teeth, Ethan muttered, "Does she look all right?"

Kevin's expression didn't change although his eyes sharpened. He ignored Ethan's question. "I'll need her to tell us what happened just as soon as she gets it together."

Ethan thought about putting his fist together with the man's nose, but reined in the impulse. The guy was just doing his job. He had the safety of all the residential students and staff on his shoulders. Of course he would need information as soon as possible.

Marianna pulled away from him, and his arms immediately missed her slight form. Using the heel of her palms to swipe the tears from her face, she squared her jaw and looked at him. He flinched when he saw the gash on her cheek, the blood on her face, smeared and still seeping. He made sure his face stayed illuminated by one of the flashlights. She said, "I want this person caught."

"Do you remember anything about him? Did you see him?"

"No, it was pitch-black. But I *felt* him." She shuddered

and the tremble went straight to his heart. Then he felt guilty. Once again, someone he cared about had been hurt. If only he'd come to check on her earlier; if only…

His fault…his fault…

Shrugging those memories aside, he told himself to focus. "Did you notice anything about him? Did he have on a mask? Come on, Marianna, give me something to work with."

Overhead lights came on, slowly brightening in intensity as they warmed up. Flashlights flicked off, and Ethan finally got a full look at her face, noticing the gash on her cheek looked worse in the glaring brightness.

"We need to get you to a doctor to check that out." He reached out a hand as though to touch it, and she flinched away from him. His hand dropped.

"He…pushed me into the bleacher and…"

Ethan pulled out a clean handkerchief and pressed it to the wound. "I think it's slowing down, but you may need a stitch." He backed up a bit and turned to see paramedics coming through.

Ethan glanced at Kevin, who shrugged. "Didn't figure it would hurt anything to call them."

Respect for the man went up a notch. "Good move. Thanks."

Marianna fought the idea of going to the hospital. "Just put a butterfly bandage on it and it'll be fine."

One of the paramedics said, "If you insist, but you still might want to have a doctor look at it. It may need a stitch or two. If you don't get it taken care of, you might end up with a scar."

She nodded and Ethan vowed to see she took care of it.

Finally, after all the commotion calmed down, the statements had been taken and the gym closed off so crime scene staff could do their job, Ethan said to Marianna, "I'll give you a ride to your parents' house."

"That's all right. I have my car."

"Then I'm following you home."

At first he thought she would protest; then she gave a weary nod and headed for the exit.

Before she could place her hand on the door, it burst open and a young teenage boy exploded through. Spotting Marianna, he broke into a flurry of signs. Her face paled and she looked at Ethan. "Did you understand what he said? Someone vandalized my car!"

Grim, jaw tight, he nodded. "Let me call the police back."

"Why would someone do this? What did I do? Who hates me so much? What is going on?"

Stunned, Marianna could only stare in disbelief. Every window in the little red Honda gaped as if it, too, were shocked at the violence perpetrated on it. Glass lay shattered on the ground around the perimeter of the vehicle. Sickness swirled in her stomach. The glass was on the outside. Someone had kicked the windows out…from the inside.

"Seems to me trouble keeps following you, little lady."

Marianna read the policeman's words, her brain on autopilot as it took in the shapes formed by his lips. Her hearing aids picked up some of the sounds and she processed his sentence.

"No kidding," she muttered.

Grateful for Ethan's supporting arm around her shoulders, she leaned into his embrace. It appeared that was going to be his job tonight, holding her upright.

The officer spoke again. "We'll let the investigative

team haul the car down to the lab, since you're concerned this may be in connection with that other woman's murder."

Weariness like nothing she'd ever felt before made her light-headed. She must have sagged slightly, because Ethan's arm tightened. He turned her to face him and said, "We need to get you home. There's nothing more you can do here."

With a grateful heart, she allowed him to lead her toward his car, then stopped abruptly when she remembered the paper.

"Oh, no!"

Ethan looked alarmed. "What? Are you okay?"

"No! He shoved something in my hand. What did I do with it?" She opened both hands, palms up, and there it was, still in her right hand, crunched and crushed into a flat mess. Her fists had been clenched the entire time, she realized, even when she'd used the heel of her palms to wipe her tears and the blood from her face. Dried, dark streaks still stained her skin.

He sucked in a deep breath. "Hold on. Just…don't do anything with it yet." Turning, he hollered over his shoulder. "Hey, Henry, you got a pair of gloves and a plastic bag on you?"

Henry hurried over, a frown on his slightly pudgy face, which hadn't seen a razor in a while. "Of course I do, I'm working a crime scene," he said, holding the items out. "Why?"

Ethan took the gloves and pulled them on. To Henry he said, "Hold that open, okay?"

Still frowning, the man complied. With one gloved hand, Ethan reached for the paper in Marianna's shaking hand. Gripping it with the edge of thumb and forefinger, he held it and, with his other hand, unfolded it.

Marianna looked over his shoulder and tried to see what

it said, but it was too dark. Ethan moved about ten yards to his right and held it up to the light. She watched his lips as he read aloud, "Keep your mouth shut, or else."

EIGHT

Exhausted, worried, frustrated by the lack of progress on the case, Ethan had fallen into bed after making sure Marianna was safely ensconced in her family's care. Her mother had seen Marianna's cheek and immediately ushered her off to examine the wound. Now, he lay sleepless once again, staring at the ceiling. Slowly, his body relaxed and he drifted.

The bright sun pounded the asphalt, sending heat waves radiating over anyone brave enough to expose himself to it. May wasn't supposed to be this hot, he remembered thinking.

Then he was in the huge, almost deserted parking lot, waiting for Ashley. Somewhere in his sleep-fogged brain, he knew he was dreaming, yet hope remained that this time the ending would be different.

As he watched his Camaro pull under the lone tree providing the only shade in the entire parking lot, he told himself to park in a different spot. Suddenly, he was behind the wheel, watching, still waiting, clueless. He told himself to crank the car and drive off, move, park anywhere but there.

Instead, he just sat there.

The familiar blue hatchback pulled in and parked about

forty yards away. The occupants couldn't see him positioned as he was behind the tree.

Drive over there! he tried to order himself.

His dream self didn't hear.

Now, the events started clicking, one after the other, only now he was a spectator watching a movie. One he'd seen before and didn't like, didn't want to watch again, not if he couldn't rewrite the ending.

Ashley stepped from the car and looked around. Two other girls clambered from the backseat. One headed for the building; the other walked backward, signing, talking to Ashley. Ashley finally spotted him under the tree.

She waved to him and he waved back. She turned to say goodbye to her friend.

Engines revved.

The sound caught his attention because it seemed close.

But he kept his eyes on his sister, still walking backward, talking, signing, laughing. Grabbing a few last words.

Tires screeched as the black, low-slung Mustang hurled into the parking lot through the open gate. Its white twin followed seconds behind.

The dream seemed to slow, the camera panning back and forth between him and Ashley and the racing cars. Back to Ashley. Laughing, waving, long hair swinging around her face as she turned to run toward Ethan.

Fresh horror, remembered agony of what was to come screamed at him.

Ashley! Stop!

Still laughing, running toward her rock, the one person she could count on. Her stability in a silent world.

No! Look out! The words echoed in his mind even as he saw himself screaming at her, his shout falling on her deaf ears, sliding away.

Desperately, he tried to wake up.
Screeching tires, burning rubber.
The thud.
Ashley!
He ran to her, grabbed her, looked into her face. But it wasn't Ashley this time. Marianna's features mocked him, her eyes fixed on his but empty of the vibrant life that so defined her.

Terror and grief had him screaming out his denial. Once again, he'd failed. It was his fault...his fault....

Gasping, he sat up in bed, panting, his chest aching, the tears falling, great heaving sobs escaping. And he let them. Even after three years, the dream made the loss fresh, brought back the crushing pain of Ashley's death... and the guilt that plagued him.

If only...

Only this time, he'd failed Marianna, too.

He rolled off the bed, knelt on the floor, ignored the sweat dripping from his brow and leaned his head against the mattress. *Father, please, help me keep my focus on You. I know You don't blame me for what happened to Ashley, but no matter what I do, I can't forgive myself. I also know I've been a little slack in coming to You with my problems lately. For that I'm sorry. Forgive me, God. Help me deal with what's going on in my crazy head and mixed-up job. And Marianna...God, that's a tough call. I'm not even sure what to pray here, except to ask that You watch over her. And please don't ask that I be the tool You use to do it. I failed Ashley, God. I failed that poor woman who died on my watch.... I can't go through that again.... Please don't ask me to.*

He didn't bother adding an Amen to the end of his prayer. He had a feeling the conversation was far from over. The clock read five fifteen. Should he call Mac, the man who'd gotten him through the worst time of his life and kept him from destroying himself and his career? Mac was overseas, working as a missionary now.

Ethan wondered what time zone Mac was in, then sighed. No, no sense in both of them being awake. No need to bother Mac when he couldn't do anything but worry about Ethan. It would drive the man nuts knowing that Ethan might need his help and be unable to provide it. No, he'd have to deal with this one on his own.

Unfortunately, there'd be no more sleep tonight; might as well work on the case…cases. Suzanne's murder, Marianna's attack, the car vandalism, everything. Somehow, when he connected all the dots, he was going to come up with the big picture of how all these separate incidents were related.

Before Ethan had gone to bed last night, he'd called and filled Catelyn in on the night's events. Her comment had been, "How is it I'm never with you when all this stuff keeps happening?"

"Because it keeps happening after we're off the clock."

"So, why do you keep clocking back in?" Her voice had been low, knowing. She'd always been good at reading people.

"Lay off, Cate, she needs help."

"Hey, I'm not fussing."

His mind's eye pictured her pointing a finger at his nose as she said, "But you'd better call if you find yourself in trouble. I don't care what time it is, on the clock, off the clock, whatever. You hear me?"

Saluting the phone, he'd said, "Yes, ma'am."

"Good, glad we got that straight."

"I'm supposed to meet her after she gets out of school. Once again, I want to find out if she remembers anything else from any of the incidents, especially the one last night."

"Let me know what she says. Listen, I've got class—gotta run. But call me if you need me, seriously."

He knew she meant it. And she knew he'd call if he needed her. That's what good friends and partners were for. And that's all it was between them. Once upon a time, they'd tried for something more, but both had quickly realized they were only meant to be friends—period.

Ethan had been disappointed at first, then grateful. Now as he thought about Marianna, he wondered what God was doing in his heart and if, after all the craziness was done, God had something in mind for Ethan and Marianna. The thought made him a little...antsy.

Right now, he didn't have time to explore that weird feeling. His phone buzzed as he pulled open the door to his car.

He glanced at the number and his heart chilled once again.

Six ten in the morning and Marianna was texting him. Uh-oh, that couldn't be good.

Marianna kept her eyes glued to the television, absorbing the news, the shock sending shivers through her body.

Josh's father had been killed in a car wreck. The station went to a commercial. Her fingers flew over her Black-Berry keypad as she texted the message to Ethan that she wouldn't be able to meet him today. Already she was making plans to be the one to drive Josh home to his grandparents. She knew they'd want him there, especially for the funeral. And she planned to be there for him, too.

When the station came back from the commercial, she read the captions unable to tear her eyes from the breaking news story. The reporter announced, "Roland Luck, campaign manager for Clayton Robertson, was killed in a car wreck early this morning. Roland apparently lost control of his car soon after leaving a private meeting at a secluded resort atop Breakaway Mountain, just twenty-five miles north of Asheville, North Carolina. His car swerved over the side and crashed into the wooded area below. His body has been recovered. For now, Steven Marshbanks, Roland's assistant, will take over the campaign management until a replacement is named. Mr. Marshbanks is currently unavailable for a statement. We'll have more details as they become known."

With hands shaking, Marianna closed her eyes. *Lord, what is going on? My world is spinning out of control, and the only thing I know to do is hold on to You and pray You make everything work out how it's supposed to. And poor Josh, I don't even know if he'll understand what's happened. Just...help me, Lord. Wrap us all in Your strength.*

She felt a hand on her shoulder and turned. Her mother stood there, concern in her gentle brown eyes, her apron already tied around her ample waist. Maddelena signed, "What's wrong, honey?"

Marianna hadn't realized she been crying until her mother's soft fingers reached up to wipe a few tears from Marianna's cheeks. She flinched when the woman brushed the cut she'd incurred on the bleacher the night before. It throbbed a steady beat, encouraging her to find some aspirin soon. And hide it from Joseph. He'd been asleep when she'd gotten home, leaving her mother and Twister to greet her at the door, to smother her with care and questions Marianna had only partially answered.

"Oh," she sniffed, "thanks. One of my students' father was killed in a car accident this morning."

Her mother's eyes went wide. "I'm so sorry." She gathered Marianna close for a tight squeeze, pulled back and signed, "I think we need extra prayer these days. I'm going to e-mail my ladies' Bible study group if that's all right with you."

Marianna nodded and brought her hands up to say, "More than all right. Thank you."

"Now, come eat."

A watery chuckle escaped her lips. Of course, tragedy had struck and her mother's solution was food. Right now, it worked for her. She'd need her strength in the coming few days. It was only Tuesday and already she felt as if she'd done enough, had enough happen, to fill the entire week.

Twister sat at her feet while she ate. Absentmindedly, she rubbed one of his ears and thought back to the incident of the night before. She'd purposely avoided thinking about it—one of the reasons she'd turned on the news—but now she needed to make sure it was all right for her to leave with the ongoing investigation. Most likely it would be fine as long as she left a contact number where she could be reached.

Swallowing the last of her eggs, she reached once again for her BlackBerry and typed a message to her principal, asking permission to be the one to drive Josh home and attend the funeral. Within minutes, she had a reply giving her permission. Relief flowed over her. Her principal promised to have a state car ready and waiting for her.

After explaining her plans to her mother, who promised to take care of Twister, Marianna headed to school. When she arrived at her classroom, her five homeroom students, Josh, Peter, Christopher, Lily and Sarah, were already there, seated at their desks. The two girls had their Sidekicks out, texting. A firm look from Marianna had them tossing her sheepish smiles and tucking the devices away.

Her assistant, Dawn, stepped into the classroom, mug of coffee in hand.

"Good morning, Dawn."

"Heard you had quite an adventure last night."

Marianna winced, reaching up to touch her cheek. "I suppose it's all around the school."

"Yep. Your activities are a hotbed of gossip."

"So, is it accurate?"

Dawn shrugged. "I don't know." She gave a small grin. "Whatcha think I've been waiting to find out?"

Before she could answer, she got her usual greeting from Josh, since he couldn't stand it anymore and leaped up out of his seat. He signed her name sign, fingers shaped in the letter *M* and pulled it down from scalp to shoulder, symbolizing her long hair.

"Hi, Josh." She forced herself to smile through her sadness for him. He didn't have a clue. But then his life probably wouldn't change that much in the coming days, although he would probably wonder where his father was eventually. Possibly. Who knew what he would think, how this would affect him?

Marianna started to answer Dawn when Peter, one of her higher level, if extremely shy and sensitive students, with a rapt expression on his face, caught her attention and waved her toward the door.

She turned to find Ethan standing there, one shoulder leaning negligently against the doorjamb. Her heart caught her by surprise and did a little flip-flop before resuming its normal rhythm.

She stared. What brought him here? Biting her lip, she prayed it wasn't more trouble.

Accurately reading her expression, he gave that little one-sided quirk of his lips that did funny things to her stomach. Then he said, "After you sent me that text this morning telling me about Josh's father and that you were going to take him home, my boss thought you might need a little extra protection with everything that's been going on. He asked me if I'd be willing to take on the job."

The inscrutable expression in his blue eyes caught her attention, and she wondered at the meaning behind it. Instead of asking, she looked around the classroom with alarm churning through her. "Does he think I'm endangering the kids by being here?"

Ethan shook his head. "No, not really. We did discuss it, but his theory is that you have something this guy wants and he's only going to come after you."

She chewed her bottom lip. "I don't know whether to be relieved or scared." A half laugh escaped.

"Well, the one sure way to stop all this madness is to find out what it is you have that he wants."

Marianna sighed, then turned to her assistant. "Dawn, would you mind handling the class for me? I need to make sure everything is ready for Josh."

"No problem." Dawn shooed her out the door, taking over the class with skill.

Marianna and Ethan walked outside, where the sun shone bright, casting a deceptive-looking warmth over the grounds. She shivered, pulling her sweater tighter around her shoulders. "So you got my text about Josh's father."

"Yep." He sat on the bench just outside the door of the building.

"I'll be leaving in just a short while to take him home."

"He doesn't have anyone that could come get him?"

"Sure, but why make someone drive all the way down here when I'm going that way?"

Ethan nodded. "Makes sense. And yet…" He eyed her petite frame, and she flushed at his scrutiny. "Are you sure that's safe? He's a pretty big boy."

"He's big but wouldn't hurt a fly. At least not on purpose. And maybe if I leave for a while, things will calm down around here." A thought struck her, causing her blood to hum a little faster through her veins. "You don't...you don't think whoever's the cause of all this mess will follow me, do you?"

Ethan noted the renewed stress on her pretty face. The thought had occurred to him. What better timing than a lone woman out on the road with no way to defend herself? He definitely didn't like it.

"None of the other teachers are going?" It was really pointless to ask and go through these motions. He knew what he had to do, had been ordered to do.

She shook her head. "No, there's so much going on around here, and my principal really can't spare that much manpower. Subs are few and far between."

"So, guess that means I'm your copilot."

Her jaw dropped. "Did you say copilot?"

"Indeed." He gave a mock bow and said, "At your service."

"But...but..." she sputtered. "Why? No. I don't need you to look after me."

He smiled, hoping she couldn't see the battle raging inside him. "Sorry. You've got your own personal bodyguard for the next few days. At least until we get a break on Suzanne's case and the person targeting you. And, to be honest, my boss doesn't want to take a chance on something happening to the kid who'll be riding with you. Potential negative publicity, backlash about the department being slack and all that." She still looked as if she was in shock. He signed, "So do you want to drive, or should I?"

Two hours later, ensconced in a state van—the transportation people had taken pity on Josh's very long legs and provided the larger vehicle rather than the usual tiny Taurus—Ethan found himself with special permission to drive, Josh in the back and Marianna in the passenger seat.

He didn't have to have special training in reading body language to understand what hers shouted. Arms crossed, toe tapping the floor board, chin jutted, jaw tight, lips pursed. Yep, she was mad. In her eyes, he was tramping all over her independence; no doubt making her feel like he thought she needed a keeper. He refused to tell her he was just as thrilled with this assignment as she.

God, I remember specifically praying that You NOT use me to watch out for her. Yet here I am. Exactly what do You have in mind?

Not really expecting an answer but hoping for one regardless, Ethan drove along silently, waiting—and watching his back. Not a lot of traffic was a good thing, since it allowed him to see each and every car that came near.

"I can take care of myself, you know."

The words came out machine-gun fast, startling him into looking at her for a brief moment. Eyes back on the road, he could feel her staring at him. Quirking a brow, he tilted his head so she could see his lips. "Really? Like you did last night?"

She wilted. "Well, no. Last night was…horrible. Terrifying. I just meant I'm perfectly capable of driving myself and a student to Beaufort, South Carolina."

"Marianna, I never questioned your abilities. But who knows what this guy is capable of?" On impulse, he reached over and took her hand to give it a squeeze. "I…we…just want to make sure that nothing happens to you."

Narrowed eyes nailed him. "Then why didn't you want to come?"

Her question sucker punched him. She'd read him, his reluctance. "No offense, but I don't want to talk about that."

The fact that she let it go amazed him. "Then tell me about your sister."

Another direct hit, that one to the gut. He swallowed—hard. "Ashley was…amazing. She went to the deaf school."

"Ashley O'Hara." Realization dawned. "I knew her. The girl who was killed in the parking lot of the local high school by the…"

"…drag-racing teens," he finished. "Yeah, she'd been to a ball game with some of her hearing friends from church. They were a little late getting back, and with the parking lot almost empty, she wasn't paying attention when she headed toward…" The lump in his throat surprised him. After almost three years you would think he'd be at the point where he could at least talk about the accident without getting so emotional. If only the regret, the feeling of being responsible for…

"Oh, Ethan, I'm so sorry."

Fresh guilt sideswiped him. He dodged it. "She would be twenty years old this year."

"And the boys who were responsible? I don't think I ever heard what happened."

"It was ruled a negligent vehicular homicide. Both boys had stiff fines and the one who actually hit her served some jail time. They're still doing community service stuff."

Time to change the subject. He asked, "Did you call the school dormitory and cancel basketball practice yesterday?"

Blinking at the sudden turn, she answered, "No, of course not."

"Yeah, that's what I thought. Someone called the dormitory on the TTY and pretended to be you, canceling practice."

Anger flashed over her features, mixed with fear and frustration. "So, this person not only knows my schedule, but also knows who to call, how to call and what to say to impersonate me."

"I've got Catelyn working on tracing the phone call. Unfortunately, I wouldn't hold my breath on finding anything out there."

"I know. That call could have been placed from anywhere that has a public TTY." She leaned her head against the window, staring at the passing scenery. Josh held a Nintendo DS game that kept him enthralled.

Unable to stop himself, Ethan reached over to grasp her hand once more. Her eyes shot to his. He squeezed, a gentle pressure meant to offer reassurance. He felt the fragile bones, the slender, graceful fingers, and he appreciated her courage as she gave him a wobbly smile and squeezed back.

Ethan returned his attention to the road. Checked the side mirror, the rearview mirror.

Made a mental note about the car coming up behind them.

And noticed it was coming fast.

NINE

Marianna registered the sudden tensing in Ethan's shoulders, his body's abrupt shift to alert mode. Wondering at the lightning-fast change, she watched his eyes, not wanting to ask and take his concentration from whatever it was that grabbed his attention.

Flicking a glance in her side mirror, she noticed the black car approaching at a high rate of speed. Instant terror blindsided her. "Ethan?"

"Just hold tight." She caught the words even though they were muttered between clenched teeth.

Ethan kept his eyes fixed on the road before him as well as the car behind him. Marianna did the same. Closer, closer. Bracing herself for either the impact or Ethan to swerve suddenly, she was almost floored by surprise when the car flew past in the left lane. Then relief left her shaking.

A breath blew out of Ethan, and she watched the tension ease from him, his fingers relaxing their white-knuckle intensity on the steering wheel.

"Wow." Marianna couldn't keep the word from slipping out.

"Yeah."

Josh continued to play his game in the back, oblivious to the tension oozing from the front seats.

"That was a government car. I glimpsed the license plate as he went by. Stupid. Driving like that. Guy must have been going ninety-five, a hundred miles an hour." Disgust emanated from him.

"Maybe there was an emergency somewhere."

"Humph. In the form of being late for some bureaucratic meeting or something."

Marianna gave him a grin, glad she could find it now that the false alarm had passed. "Don't have a very high opinion of our government officials, do you?"

He slanted her a glance and offered a wry smile. "Only a select few."

Absentmindedly she wondered out loud, "I wonder how the campaign will handle Mr. Luck's death. I guess Steven Marshbanks will have his work cut out for him, although maybe moving from assistant to the campaign manager position into the primary campaign manager position won't be a big deal for him. Who knows?"

"Clayton Robertson will bounce back. Nothing negative ever seems to touch that guy. He oozes charm."

"Hmm…which is why he's so popular with the people, I guess." She lay her head back on the headrest. "I think all my adrenaline just seeped out. Do you mind if I close my eyes for a few minutes?"

"Go right ahead. We'll be there in about an hour."

The rest of the drive passed in peaceful silence, broken only by the sound of the video game coming from the backseat. Finally, Ethan pulled into the entrance to a small, well-kept farm. The long driveway wound around and up to the side of a large white house with black shutters.

Even in January, the grass was green, showing loving

care and skill in the maintenance of the property. Two horses grazed behind the house out in the large pasture. A brown barn nestled underneath a grove of trees gleamed in the bright sun; bales of hay stacked neatly to the side brought to Ethan's mind the one summer he'd gone to a wilderness camp. He'd been about nine years old, and he and his cabin buddies had sneaked down to the barn and scattered and piled the hay about five feet deep under the loft.

They'd had themselves a blast jumping into the mess. He'd been sent home early, and his parents had never let him forget it. But he wouldn't have given up those rare carefree moments for anything...not even his parents' short-in-supply approval.

Marianna's eyes flickered open when he put the car into Park. "We're here?"

"Yep. Safe and sound." Thank You, God.

She gave him a small sleepy smile and his heart lurched. Uh-uh. She was part of a case. Don't get your emotions involved with a case.

Then he wondered what their first date would be like.

Get out of the car, O'Hara.

He climbed out and Marianna followed, opening the back door for Josh. Josh put his game away and let out a squeal when he realized he was home.

As he ran for the fence that held the horses in the pasture, the door to the house opened, revealing a heavyset, gray-haired woman in her late sixties.

Grief showed on her plain face, but her joy at seeing Josh shone through. "Joshie!"

The woman smiled at him hanging over the rail petting the nose of his favorite horse. The change in the boy was remarkable as he leaned over to go nose to nose with his four-legged friend.

Then with sadness replacing her momentary joy, she

headed over to him and Marianna. "Thank you so much for bringing him home. My husband fell last week and injured his ankle, so us driving over to get Josh would have been a hardship."

Marianna reached out to hug the woman saying, "It's no problem, Mrs. Luck. I wanted to be here for Josh and you, too."

Tears welled but didn't fall. "It's hard to believe this has happened; at the height of Roland's career, too." She sighed, shaking her short gray curls. "But I guess it's not always for us to understand."

Marianna kept her own tears at bay through fierce determination. Then Josh's grandmother waved a hand in front of her face as though swatting away a fly and said, "Come in, come in. I have a fresh pot of coffee on. Let's sit down a few minutes."

Everyone trudged into the kitchen, leaving Josh with his horses. He would be fine, Marianna knew. She took note of the house as she followed Mrs. Luck. Pride showed in every part Marianna could lay eyes on. From the scented plug-ins to the plethora of pictures on every available surface. Pictures on the wall, pictures on the end tables, knick-knacks, family mementos. It reminded Marianna a little of her own childhood home. Maybe that's why she liked Mrs. Luck so much. The woman resembled Marianna's mother in a lot of ways. Marianna picked up a picture of Josh when he was about six years old and dressed in army fatigues.

Mrs. Luck saw her interest and stopped to say, "That's Joshie, taking after his daddy. Roland served twelve years in the army along with some buddies of his that he went to school with. Most of them are in politics now." A myriad of pictures cluttered the table, and she wished she had the time to study each one.

"I remember seeing photos Josh brought to school for Veterans Day."

A sad smile curved the woman's lips.

"And that one is my daughter, Lisa, and her family." Marianna studied the picture framed in a simple black rectangle. Ethan stepped up behind her to look. His nearness sent a sudden shiver of awareness zipping along her nerves. When his hand rested on her shoulder, she noticed it felt...right. As if it belonged there.

Briefly, she met his gaze and noticed he'd felt it, too... and wasn't quite sure what to think about it either. He let his eyes linger on hers, his fingers gave a gentle squeeze and pressure danced along her nerve endings.

Mrs. Luck intruded on the moment as she motioned them on.

Ethan let his hand drop to hers, entwining their fingers as he led her to the kitchen.

Sitting at the round table, sipping coffee, Marianna, Mrs. Luck and Ethan chatted for a few moments. Then Marianna ventured, "Well, I guess we need to see about getting a couple of hotel rooms for the night. I know the funeral is tomorrow. Can you suggest a place for us to stay?"

"Why don't you stay here with us? We have plenty of room. All my kids are grown and...gone." Looking away, she got a hold of her emotions once more, then offered a weak smile. "Don't reckon I'll ever get used to thinking of Roland as gone permanently."

"I know it's hard," Ethan murmured, "losing someone you love. I lost my sister three years ago."

"Oh, you do understand then, don't you?" Mrs. Luck nodded. "It's really strange, too, because he had just come home for a short visit."

Mariana perked up at that. "Really? Josh didn't say anything about seeing his father on the weekend." Usually, if

Josh had seen his dad over the weekend, he would come in Monday morning signing, "See Daddy. See Daddy. See Daddy." Sometimes it was all Marianna could do to get him focused back on his work.

"No—" Mrs. Luck shook her head for emphasis "—no, it wasn't on the weekend. It was last week. In fact it was Monday afternoon. It was so odd for him to just show up out of the blue like that. I wondered what was going on, but he claimed he was just here to visit, although it did seem something was bothering him." The woman sniffed and wiped her nose with what was left of the frayed tissue she held. "Well, now I wonder if he had some kind of... idea...inkling that something was going to happen to him."

Again, Marianna felt compassion sweep her. "Who knows what was going on with him? It could have simply been a bad weekend or week for him. You know how it is in politics."

Mrs. Luck gave a watery chuckle. "Well, you're certainly right there. I don't guess I'll ever know what was going through his head." She slapped the table and stood. "Let me check on my husband and see about getting you a couple of rooms fixed up."

Marianna hurried to her feet. "Oh, no. Listen, we really don't want you to go to any trouble. I'm sure you're going to have family and friends descending upon you shortly. Please, we'll just go back into town and stay there."

Mrs. Luck reluctantly agreed, and soon Marianna and Ethan were on their way to the hotel.

After securing two rooms for the night, Ethan asked, "Dinner?"

"Sure. Do you have someplace in mind?"

"Actually, I do know of a little place not too far from here."

They climbed back into the car and, fifteen minutes

later, Ethan pulled into the parking lot of Lakeside Steak-house. He cut the engine. "Uh, guess I should have asked. You do like steak, don't you?"

She grinned at him, loving the way his eyes crinkled at the corners when he was excited about something, yet a bit unsure of how she was going to react. "I love steak. As long as it has broccoli and mashed potatoes to go with it."

"I think that can be arranged. Come on." He got out and rounded the car to open her door. When he placed his hand on the small of her back, sparks shot along her spine. Wow. She was very attracted to this man. Biting her lip, she pondered that as they walked into the restaurant. Ethan was everything Curt wasn't. Self-assured without being cocky; tough as nails without being cruel. Could he also be a man with the sincere desire to take care of her without being overprotective and smothering?

Possibly. Time would tell.

Seated across from him, she asked, "What's your favorite food?"

"Definitely steak." A self-deprecating smile crossed his lips. "I wasn't entirely selfless in bringing you here."

Marianna let out a laugh. "That's all right. You deserve a good steak." She paused, reached over to lay her hand on his. He flipped his over so their palms touched. "Thank you for coming with me."

A corner of his mouth lifted. "I have a confession."

Uh-oh. "What?"

"My boss ordered me to come and I wasn't crazy about the idea. Not," he hastened to assure her, "that I didn't want to be with you, but…"

"But what?"

He waved a hand. "It doesn't matter now. Today has been a—a blessing. And it's thanks to you. I know we didn't end up meeting each other under the ideal circumstances, but I'm not one to turn my nose up at a good thing." He offered another smile. "I'm glad we had this time together and hope we have more in the near future."

Marianna didn't quite know what to say. He was being so open, so...vulnerable. She gulped. "I...I feel the same way, Ethan. I'd like to see where all this is going, too."

"But first we have a killer to catch and you've got to stay out of his way, deal?"

"I'm not going to argue with that one."

By the time they returned, it was pushing eight o'clock and Marianna was exhausted.

Ethan asked her, "Why don't I drop you at the door and you go on in and lie down. I'll park the car and see you in the morning."

She'd agreed. Now, back in front of the door to her room, she slipped the key in the slot. Then stopped. Dread crept up her spine to settle at the bottom of her neck. She shuddered at the feeling of being watched...again.

Unease gripped her as she glanced over her shoulder, down the carpeted hall.

Nobody.

Nothing.

Continuing her perusal, she caught sight of the camera in the upper corner at the far end of the hall. The black eye seemed to be trained on her, zooming in, capturing her fright.

Wrenching the room door open, she stumbled inside and slammed it, leaned back against it and put a hand over her racing heart.

A quick glance around the room showed no disturbance, everything just as she'd left it an hour and a half ago. The room was simple, containing one queen bed and a small sitting area. The bathroom sat to the left of the main entrance.

Convincing herself she was just having some post-traumatic stress after the events of the last week and a half, Marianna did some deep breathing exercises while whispering prayers and managed to get herself calmed down.

Her BlackBerry buzzed, startling her. She read, "Meet me downstairs in the lobby. Catelyn called with some news."

Sweat broke out across her forehead at the thought of opening the door and going back into the hall.

Get a grip, girl. You've fought long and hard for your independence; don't start being a wimp now.

She typed, "Be there in a minute."

Tucking her BlackBerry back into the little clip on her pants, she gripped the doorknob. Then checked the little peephole.

Nothing. Again.

Sighing in exasperation with her paranoia, she opened the door and stepped into the empty hallway. Where was everyone? She felt like the only occupant of the fourth floor.

Scurrying to the elevator, she pressed the down button and stood tapping her toe, willing the doors to open. In the gold-framed mirror to her left, she caught a glimpse of movement. Someone had come up the stairwell and stepped into the hall.

Probably someone staying on the floor, Marianna, don't panic.

The pep talk did nothing to banish the memories of last night's—had it just been last night?—terrifying ordeal in the gymnasium.

Her blood thrummed, adrenaline picked up and heart thudded madly against her chest. Fight or flight? There was another stairway to her right about ten feet away. Paranoia or legitimate danger? Her thoughts scattered like scurrying ants as the remembered feel of her cheek crashing into the bleacher shuddered through her.

The elevator doors slid open. She bolted inside.

Would they close in time?

Ethan leaned back into the leather chair facing the elevators and sighed. A cup of complimentary hotel brew teased his nose, and he took a sip, surprised that it tasted as good as it smelled. Rich, creamy and dark. No sugar.

He glanced at his watch. Eight fifteen. He'd talked to his boss, Victor Shields, briefly and the man had once again imparted orders to keep Marianna safe. Ethan wondered about the pressure. Victor didn't usually take such a personal interest in cases such as this.

The elevator finally dinged and the doors slid open. Ethan stood and smiled as Marianna stepped out. Then he frowned as he noticed she didn't look quite...right. Because she was endowed with naturally dark skin, it took him a moment to notice the stress on her features, that she looked a little pale.

"What's wrong?"

"Nothing." She chewed her bottom lip. "I don't think."

"Then why do you have a permanent crease between your brows and you're about to use your lip as an appetizer?"

Raising a hand to her head, she closed her eyes for a moment, dropped her hand and said, "I'm not sure, but I think someone's followed us here."

Instinct had him glancing around the lobby. A man at the check-in desk, a woman and child playing checkers, two lovebirds on the love seat ensconced in front of the gas logs. An overweight security officer leaned against the wall, reading the paper.

"What makes you think that?"

"I…I'm not sure. It's just…you're going to think I'm losing it."

Ethan took her hand and pulled her over to the leather chairs. "Sit." She sat. "Now tell me."

"I was in the hallway getting ready to enter my room and felt someone watching me. Then when I got your text, I came out of my room, walked to the elevator and *still* felt someone watching me. But no one was there. As I was waiting for the elevator, someone came up through the stairwell and started down the hall toward me. The elevator arrived, I stepped on and…here I am. See? It's nothing. I'm overreacting, right?"

She left out the details of what she must have felt, such as fear, terrifying memories and so forth. Ethan felt a surge of protectiveness hit him. If he hadn't been sitting, it would have brought him to his knees.

God, I don't think I can handle this.

But he would. For Marianna's sake.

"I don't know that you're overreacting. It's certainly understandable that you would be a bit leery, though. However, I don't think there's any reason to call in the police at this time. If someone was watching you, he's probably long gone by now." Jaw tight, he mentally slapped himself. He should have walked her to her room. And for this little meeting, he should have gone up and gotten her, escorted her down to the lobby. "From now on, until we get home, I'm your shadow, okay?"

Protests hovered on her lips. He could see them as clearly as the painting on the wall above her head. She swallowed them and nodded. "You know, I come from a wonderful, loving family, but sometimes I felt…smothered by them. It's as if I had to fight so hard for my independence that accepting help from someone now seems like a weakness."

"Not a weakness. It's the smart thing to do when you're in over your head. So, do we have a deal?" He stuck his hand out for her to shake.

Big sigh, then she said, "Deal." Her small hand slipped into his, and he felt as if she'd just grabbed hold of his heart with a handful of superglue. He was in big trouble.

He then decided to ask a question that had been preying on him since his boss's call yesterday. "Where's your brother Joseph?"

"Huh?" His abrupt topic shift threw her.

"Joseph. Where is he?"

"Mom texted me and said he had to leave to go back to New York this morning. Some big missing person case came up and they called him back early. Why?"

"Just wondering." No doubt Joseph had some connections with the local police department and probably called in a few favors concerning protection for his sister, since he couldn't be in town to personally oversee her safety.

At least that was one mystery solved.

Now, he had to figure out how he was going to keep this woman safe and his heart out of the equation. At least for now. He'd already lost one person he'd failed to protect. He wouldn't survive losing a second. He continued, "What I wanted to tell you was that Catelyn called and said they'd traced the TTY call. It came from the downtown hospital."

"Of course. They have several TTYs throughout the hospital. No one would think twice about someone using one. That's what they're there for."

"Catelyn questioned the afternoon personnel in all locations of the phones. One worker did say she remembers seeing a man using it around four o'clock yesterday afternoon but couldn't describe him."

"What about the hospital cameras?"

He smiled. She was quick. "Catelyn checked those, too.

The only person she could come up with on the camera that might be a likely suspect had on leather jacket and a baseball cap pulled low. There's no way to identify the guy."

Dejected, her shoulders slumped. "So, what now?"

"We go to the funeral, then go home and try to figure out what's going on and what it is someone wants you keep quiet about."

TEN

In line to pay their respects, Ethan took note of the somber crowd. Friends, family and campaign supporters all turned out to say goodbye to a good man and friend. The governor hopeful, Clayton Robertson, had sent his sympathies to the family with regrets he couldn't be there owing to a bad case of the flu.

At the funeral the newly appointed campaign manager, Steven Marshbanks, a handsome man in his mid-fifties with a head full of gray hair that made him look older, gave a short eulogy. "Roland will be sorely missed. He was a good man, a good father and great at his job. His senseless death saddens and angers those of us left behind. Our prayers are with Roland's parents and young Joshua. May God grant you peace in the days ahead."

Then it was time to say their goodbyes and head home. Thankfully, the return trip was uneventful. Marianna and Ethan dropped Joshua back at the dormitory, since his grandparents felt he would do better getting back into his usual routine. He didn't fully understand that his dad was gone for good. Only time would help with that.

They returned the state vehicle, retrieved Ethan's car from the lot and headed to Marianna's parents' house.

Ethan broke the comfortable silence by tapping Marianna on the shoulder. She looked at him, a question in her eye.

"What are you thinking?" he asked.

A hand reached up to rub her forehead. "Just how weird it is that in less than two weeks, two people that I knew have died."

"A bit strange, I have to admit, but I guess we just kind of have to roll with the punches life throws at us…with God's help, of course." Something he was still working on. His phone rang and he grabbed it, sending Marianna an apologetic look. "Hello?"

"Hey, Ethan, it's Catelyn."

"What's up?"

As Catelyn spoke, Ethan put the phone on speaker and set it in his lap. Left hand on the wheel, he signed the conversation for Marianna with his right.

"We got a fingerprint off the car that's not Marianna's or Suzanne's. We're running it through the system as we speak."

"Great. I guess the next step is to question everyone on staff—and the students, too—who was around that night."

"We're already on that. So far no one remembers seeing anything or anyone suspicious. But you might be interested to know that several of the lights around that parking lot had been vandalized. Marianna's car was sitting in virtual darkness."

Ethan remembered he'd had to move away from the car to the light in order to read the note the perp had shoved in Marianna's hand. He'd not thought much about it except that the school needed to put in more lights. Now he found out the lights had been purposely broken.

Someone had put some thought into this—and that chilled him. The question that now occurred to him was: How many people were involved in this attack? Was her car trashed before or after she was attacked in the gym? It really could have happened either way.

"Do they have any security cameras on campus?"

"Nope."

"Figures. All right, keep digging. Marianna and I are almost home. I'll catch up with you in the morning."

"Good deal. See you later."

Ethan hung up, his thoughts racing. Marianna's brow furrowed in thought. She'd followed the conversation well with Ethan signing it.

However, confusion flickered in her tired eyes, and Ethan knew exactly how she felt. It *was* strange that two people she knew had been killed so close together in time. But Roland's death was an accident, having nothing to do with Marianna. Suzanne's death, however, seemed to be another story.

One to which he'd like to know the ending.

By Thursday afternoon Marianna didn't know whether to feel relieved or worried. Relieved because things had been so quiet or worried—for the same reason. Ethan couldn't stay with her twenty-four/seven, so she'd sent him on his way promising she'd be careful and not go anywhere by herself except straight to her students' basketball game. He'd reluctantly agreed but promised to be back and meet her at the game.

Twenty minutes ago she'd entered the gym and that had been hard, memories of her attack pulsing full force. Now the well-lit place buzzed with more activity than a beehive, causing her fears to slowly slide away.

Breathing in the scent of gym socks, tennis shoes, sweat, hot dogs, hamburgers and soft pretzels calmed her and brought her senses into focus. She was here for the students. She could do this. *You're my strength, Lord.*

Soon her girls arrived, and she lost herself in a part of the job she loved. Becoming engrossed in the game allowed her to forget her anxiety. "Let's play, girls!" Even though most couldn't hear her, she still yelled while signing so they could see her encouraging them. A couple of the players had enough hearing that they could hear her cheering for them even if they couldn't understand what she was saying.

Trina dribbled down the court and passed the ball off to Bailey, who went straight to the middle for a beautiful layup. Marianna clapped her hands, cheered and whistled, then motioned for defense to set up.

Then Ethan walked in the door. For five solid seconds she froze, drinking in the sight of him; then warmth filled her and she realized how much she was starting to care for this guy. The whistle blaring caused her to whip her head around, to seeing Paulette signing furiously, her teeth bared in a snarl. "I didn't foul her, Ms. S. That ref can't see. He's blind. Needs to see an eye doctor!"

Forcing herself to concentrate on the action in front of her, not the man behind her, she signed back, "Don't be disrespectful. If the referee says you earned a foul, you earned it." Then she winked and said, "And if you didn't, we'll fuss about it later, okay?"

Paulette rolled her eyes but nodded, accepting Marianna's direction.

When the buzzer signaled the end of the game, Marianna's team had won and she felt so proud of the hard-playing girls.

"Whoo-hoo! This calls for a celebration."

"Pizza!" The team yelled and signed simultaneously.

She'd promised them pizza if they'd won. She would have taken them even if they'd lost.

A hand landed gently on her shoulder, and she turned.

"Ethan." Her heart beat double time at the feel of his touch, and she ordered it to quit. It disobeyed.

Admiration glinted in his eyes. He smiled. "Way to go, Coach."

Heat crept up from her shoulders. Hoping her dark skin would hide the flush she knew would stain her cheeks in mere seconds, she pretended nonchalance. "Thanks."

His wicked grin said she didn't fool him. "So, you're going to get pizza?"

"Yep."

"You have room for one more?"

An eyebrow shot up before she could stop it. "You want to come eat pizza with us?"

He shrugged and seemed a little embarrassed now. "If you don't mind."

Suspicious, she narrowed her gaze. "You found out something?"

That attractive little quirky thing he did with his mouth flashed at her, and her stomach flipped. "Can't hide anything from you, can I?"

"No, so don't try."

"But I'd want to go anyway, lead or no lead."

She gave him a smile that felt a little wobbly. "Come on, you can follow me to the restaurant. The girls will be focused on their pizza, and you can fill me in on what you've found out."

Seated in the booth at the pizza restaurant located about a mile from the school, Ethan waited while Marianna loaded up her plate with the little triangular slices.

He wondered if she'd really eat all that.

She slid in the booth opposite him and grinned. "Yes."

"Huh?"

"Yes, I will eat all this."

He felt his face flush. "Caught me."

"It's okay. On game days, I'm starving by the time everything's over, simply because I'm too worked up to eat beforehand." She turned serious and asked, "So, what did you find out?"

He swallowed his bite of pepperoni pizza and wiped his mouth with a napkin. A swig of tea chased the food. Her gaze stayed steady, waiting. He didn't fool her. A clunk sounded as he set down the glass. Tea sloshed over the edge. "Okay, I'm stalling."

"Just tell me."

"Forensics turned up some DNA at your house. A hair with the root still connected."

"And?" Anticipation mingled with fear danced across her beautiful features.

He hated to disappoint her. "Nothing back from the lab, yet. Sorry."

"Oh."

"But, your car is a different story. The guy was obviously mad at not finding what he wanted. When he busted out all your windows, a fragment of cloth was left on one of the edges."

"What kind of cloth?"

"A very small piece of leather."

"Oh, well that could belong to anyone."

"And the fingerprint we found matched up with your brother, Alonso's, so I guess we're at a dead end there."

A frown marred her forehead. "Alonso's print was on my car?"

"Yeah." He took a few more bites of pizza and looked over at the team of girls, who were laughing and chatting, signing exuberantly, oozing life. Two of the girls were busy texting on their Sidekicks. Ashley would have loved…

Don't. Go. There.

Ethan grabbed the check from the table. Marianna's hand covered his. When he looked up, the sympathy in her eyes told him that, once again, she'd read him as easily as a First Steps reader.

His phone buzzed, sweeping relief through him. "Hello?"

"Hey, it's Catelyn. The boss has called a meeting and wants you here."

"I'm off the clock," he groused.

"Not anymore. We've got a hostage situation and he wants you to take care of it."

All the way home, driving the nice little rental her insurance company had provided, Marianna couldn't get Ethan's words out of her head. Alonso's fingerprint had been found on her car. Usually, that wouldn't be something she'd worry about. But she'd just had the car detailed that very day, and Alonso hadn't been anywhere around it since then. Or so she'd thought.

Aside from her spiritual well-being, there were several things in life she considered important enough to take care of. Her dog, her house and her car. Once a month, someone from Darren's Detailing came and picked up the car while she was at work, and by the time she was ready to go home, she walked out to the parking lot and climbed into a spotless vehicle.

With everything going crazy, she'd kept the appointment as a way of keeping *something* in her life consistent. It would sound dumb to anyone else, but for her it had been important. Something normal in a world gone nuts.

Anxiety dogged her steps as she headed to her parents' home. Fingers gripped her steering wheel with extra force as she wondered whether she should confront Alonso and ask him why his print had been found on her car. Or if she should just forget it.

Okay, that wasn't an option. Maybe she should tell Ethan and see what he came up with, what advice he could offer.

But if Alonso found out, that would put him on the defensive.

Maybe he had a reason to be, she argued with herself. Marianna worried Alonso hadn't quite given up the wild friends he'd used to hang with. But even if he'd started hanging around those guys again, why would he vandalize her car? His sister's car?

She parked on the street so her father could leave in the morning to meet up with his breakfast buddies. Every Friday, barring illness or family chaos, he was up and out the door by six o'clock to head down to The Skillet.

Motion to her left caught her attention. Something on the edge of the driveway, then a shadow darting around the side of the house. Had her mother let Twister out to do his nightly business?

A glance at her watch said eight thirty. No, that was too early for it to be Twister. Besides, he would have run up to greet her.

Unease settled between her shoulders; her gut churned with anxiety. Chewing her lip, she pondered her options. Get out and investigate?

Dumb idea.

Make a run for the front door?

Maybe.

But what if someone lurked ready to pounce? And what if running for the door just led the danger inside? The darkness closed in, suffocating, igniting all kinds of images of danger, the memory of the attack in the gym.

She double-checked the locks on her rental.

Get out? Stay in? Call the police? Call Ethan? She gripped her phone.

Oh Lord, what do I do?

Then the shadow appeared at her window and a scream ripped from her throat.

ELEVEN

Ethan punched his pillow and flipped the lamp on. By the time he'd gotten to the hostage scene, the situation had been resolved. All that adrenaline for nothing. Ethan couldn't decide how he'd felt driving over to the place where a young father had taken his wife hostage until she promised to let him see their children. Ethan had been anxious, nervous, with scenes from his last hostage incident movie running through his mind.

It had only been two weeks since Ashley's funeral, and he'd been going mad sitting around staring at the wall, reliving her death. Insisting he was fine, he'd gone back to work just the day before the incident. He hadn't been on call that night, but, owing to various reasons, he'd been the only one available with crisis negotiation training. Knowing he should refuse, he'd agreed to go.

The images still haunted him.

The gun at her head, Ethan on the phone, the man yelling his demands, the woman turning, fighting, refusing Ethan's orders to be still.

The gun going off…the young woman bleeding to death on her kitchen floor.

And later, his desperate desire to know if he'd done something wrong even though everyone assured him he hadn't. But he knew what they didn't. He'd been drinking. So the thoughts haunted him. If he'd stayed away from the alcohol, would he have said something different, something that would have given everyone a different ending? He didn't know, couldn't know. But he'd made a vow never to place himself in that kind of situation again.

So Ethan had put in for a request his boss had honored. No more hostage stuff.

Until tonight.

But this time, only minutes before Ethan had arrived, the woman had managed to say all the right things and the incident ended peacefully. He breathed a prayer of thanks.

Unfortunately, he was still keyed up and couldn't sleep.

The Bible on the nightstand patiently waited for him. Instead of picking it up, he bowed his head and prayed out loud. "God, You died so I don't have to. You took on the sins of the world so I could be spared punishment. Mentally, I know this, so why do I keep beating myself up? How do I stop punishing myself, and forgive myself?"

Not getting an answer, he dressed and went for a cold midnight jog.

Marianna knew if her heart beat any harder, it would explode. The figure at her window stumbled backward at her hysterical scream. And she recognized him. Fumbling with the car door, she ruptured from the vehicle signing and yelling, "Alonso! Are you crazy? What do you think you're doing scaring me like that?"

Shock twisted to guilt, and his eyes slid away from her. Fury pulsed through her. "Oh, I get it. You're sneaking out."

The guilt left his face so fast she wondered if she'd imagined it. His lip curled into that sneer only a rebellious teenage male can manage. He signed, "You're not my keeper. Stay out of my business."

Immediately Marianna forced herself to calm down, to push aside her initial fear and subsequent reaction to it. She rubbed a weary hand over her eyes. "I'm sorry, Alonso. You're right. I'm not your mother or your keeper. I'm your sister and I love you. I really don't want to see you get in trouble, okay?"

Remorse flickered at her words. Hope ignited inside her that he'd just go inside the house. Because if he didn't, she'd have to be a tattletale. Not her favorite role.

"You'll get me in trouble if I leave, won't you?"

When would this kid start taking responsibility for his actions? "No, Alonso, you'll get in trouble all by yourself. It's *your* choice. You're the one breaking the rules."

The word made her wince, but she didn't berate him, just walked away, praying he'd make the right decision—for once. Questioning him about the fingerprint would have to wait until she had a handle on her nerves—and her temper. If she started in on him now, the neighbors would probably end up calling the cops for domestic disturbance.

And speaking of cops…

Ethan's face leaped immediately to mind. And her heart warmed. She liked him—a lot. Slipping into the house, she greeted her folks. Her mother stepped back into the kitchen, and her dad lay stretched out in his recliner, Twister at his side and a basketball game playing on the television. When she sat on the couch near his chair, he pressed the mute button and asked, "Got a winning team this year, huh?"

"Seems that way." Twister ambled over to her and sat at her feet. She leaned over to scratch his head, avoiding the white bandage that decorated him as a hero. His eyes closed in bliss. "The girls did a great job tonight."

"Did your young man show up?"

An immediate flush made its way up and into her cheeks; she could feel the heat climbing, so she lowered her head and kept her gaze on Twister, then forced herself to look her dad in the eye. "He's not my young man. He's a cop."

That made her father frown. "I know. Have they made any progress on finding Suzanne's killer or who attacked you?"

"I think so. A little, maybe." She didn't think it necessary to go into detail. Her parents were already nervous enough about her safety. Downplaying everything seemed to be the best route to go, although with all of their experience dealing with Joseph's job, she didn't think she was pulling anything over on them. "Where's Gina?"

"Out with her friends. She's leaving tomorrow to go back to North Carolina. Her vacation time is up."

"You hear from Joseph?"

Her father snorted. "Every other hour or so, checking on you." He nodded to the BlackBerry he kept by his side.

"Keep telling him I'm fine, okay?"

Anxiety flashed and he reached over to grip her hand in a tight squeeze, signing with the other, "*Are* you fine?"

She sighed. "Yes, I think so. Alonso scared me to death earlier, but…" Marianna paused, debating whether to say anything about her younger brother's nocturnal activities. No, she'd talk to him herself, first. "G'night, Dad." She leaned over and placed a kiss on his balding head. "I love you."

"Love you, too, sweetie."

She made her way upstairs to her bedroom, thinking about Ethan. She noticed she spent a lot of time doing that lately…thinking about Ethan.

The haunting she saw in his eyes when he didn't realize she was looking made her wonder if it was a result of Ashley's death or something else. The man sure had his secrets. As if he had things he needed to deal with. His sister's death had certainly been hard, but she had a feeling his angst went deeper than that. Twister jumped up on her bed to settle at the foot of it, snout resting between his mammoth paws, but he perked his ears and watched her movements.

Stepping over to her closet, she pulled out clothes to wear to work tomorrow and hung them on the hook on the door. Turning back, she noticed Twister had shifted his attention, his head cocked, his brown eyes trained on the window. She reached to close the miniblinds and stopped. Leaned closer. Twister leaped to the floor and moved under the window. Marianna laid a hand on his head, feeling the rumble of his growl.

A shadowy figure darted behind the bushes to her left. Anger and frustration warred within her. Alonso. She'd hoped her brother would have chosen to do the right thing. Obviously, he'd decided to go his own way, regardless of what his big sister thought.

Immediately, her teeth clamped down on her lower lip, chewing. Resolve stiffened her spine. Turning her lip to mush by pondering her next move would accomplish nothing except for a sore lip. Spinning from the window, she shot from the room, pulling the door shut behind her. No sense in letting Twister out when he was still recovering. She bolted down the steps, bypassing the den where her father now dozed, the kitchen where her mother still puttered, and out the door.

Not bothering to yell because Alonso was totally deaf, she sprinted to the bushes where she'd seen him disappear. A small skipping stone walkway led from the bushes next to the house, to the back part of the yard. Two oak trees towered over her, casting her into the shadows now that she was away from the outside lights of the house.

The walkway connected to the neighbor's backyard.

Once in their yard, it was an easy jaunt around to the front of the house, where he could hop in a waiting car.

Only she was too late. The front yard lay empty, the silence surrounding her; the darkness pressing in. Clenching her fists in frustration, she retraced her steps back to the house, walked in the door and stopped.

Alonso's favorite jacket hung on the coat rack. Trepidation bloomed. Her brother wouldn't leave the house without that coat. But just to make sure…

Marianna took the steps two at a time, made a right at the top of the stairs and stopped at the first door on her right. It was cracked open, a sliver of light snaking its way out into the hallway.

She peeked in and gasped.

Alonso lay on his bed, texting on his Sidekick. No doubt complaining to one of his friends about Marianna's interference in his after-dark plans.

When the fear leaped up to grab her, she had no defense, no excuses, no arguments with which to chase it away. Because if Alonso wasn't the person in her parents' backyard, who had she just sought out in the dark?

Friday morning finally brought some news for Ethan. Catelyn had spent time with the crime lab, pushing, begging, being obnoxious—and getting results. The DNA found at Marianna's house had come back, and the man was in the system because he'd been arrested for DUI. A Gerald Chambers.

The name meant nothing to him, but it might to Marianna. Which was why he was on his way to the school to see her. He didn't want to text her and break the news to her without being there to be a sounding board for her questions. None of which he probably had the answers for.

He was hoping *she* might provide *him* a few. Like who this guy was.

Texting her, he said, "On my way. I have something I need to discuss with you about the case. Can you meet with me when I get there?"

A few seconds later he read, "Sure. It's a teacher work-day. No problem meeting. I'll see you when you get here."

Five minutes later he pulled up to the side of Marianna's building. She waved to him from the window and motioned for him to come up. At the sight of her, his heart did things it shouldn't be doing.

Getting emotionally involved with someone who needed protection—from him. Not a good idea. He'd learned his lesson the hard way. If you cared about someone, you wanted to protect them. And if you failed, sometimes that person died. He couldn't take that chance with Marianna. There was no way he'd live through something like that a second time.

Things had gone well on the trip to Beaufort for the fu-neral, thank goodness, but he'd been tense the entire time. When his boss had informed him that he was going to be responsible in making sure nothing happened to Marianna on that trip, he'd told his boss he wasn't a bodyguard. His boss countered, "No, you're a homicide detective. Make sure we don't wind up with another homicide to our case-load."

The thought of Marianna ending up like Suzanne had sent him racing to her side—even if he didn't want the load on his shoulders. And in spite of the reason he'd been there, he'd enjoyed the time with her. And he had to admit, in different circumstances, he would have already asked her out and been anxious to get to know her.

Like you're not now?

Refusing to answer himself, he finally arrived at her

door, his hand raised to knock, when he heard, "And that's the way we're doing it. If you don't like it, there are several other schools here. Go work in one of them."

He barely had time to move out of the way before a short slender figure barreled from the room. She saw Ethan standing there, gasped and flushed a bright red. "Excuse me," she muttered, then disappeared into the next room down the hall.

Ethan made his way into the classroom where Marianna stood, hands on hips, lips pressed tightly, flames spitting from her dark eyes. Oh, man, she was beautiful.

When she turned that gaze on him, he wondered if he should take cover or run. Thankfully, her eyes softened, sparking something he couldn't identify but definitely wanted to explore. "Problem?"

Marianna mumbled something under her breath. It sounded…Italian.

"Come again? English or sign language, please. I don't do Italian."

A smile peeked at him from the corners of her lips. Then she sighed. "I just don't know why that woman has a problem with me."

"What do you mean?"

"She was fine when we first started working here, but obviously I've done something to warrant her wrath. Now she's blatantly hostile. I may have to report her to my supervisor if this continues."

Warning signs flashed in his brain. "Did she know Suzanne? Would she have any reason to want you out of the picture?"

Marianna blanched. "No, in fact I never once considered it."

"I'll do a little background checking."

She came around the desk to shut the door. "You had something to tell me?"

"Where's your assistant?"

"She called in sick today."

"So, no interruptions, good. Okay, here's the deal. The DNA from your house matched up with someone in the system."

With eyes wide, her jaw dropped, then snapped shut. "Who?"

"Gerald Chambers."

"Who's that?" She cocked her head to the side as though the action would help her to think.

"I was hoping you could tell me."

A hand slapped to her forehead as she walked in a little circle, processing the information. "Gerald Chambers. Gerald Chambers." Dropping her hand, she shook her head. "I've got nothing."

Frustration ate at his gut from the inside. "I thought for sure you'd recognize his name."

"No. I sure wish I did, though." She tapped her chin. "I also probably need to mention that I think someone was hanging around my house last night."

"What? Why didn't you tell me sooner?"

"Because I couldn't decide if it was really someone wanting to cause more problems, or if it was one of Alonso's friends trying to get him in more trouble."

"It doesn't matter, Marianna. I need to know these things. Now it's too late for me to do anything about it."

She dropped her eyes. "I'm sorry."

He reached out a finger and lifted her chin. "It's all right. But next time…"

Julie popped her head around the door, catching Marianna's attention. Guilt pierced her. She'd been so wrapped up in trying to figure out who had killed Suzanne and who was after her, that she'd been neglecting her good friend. Pulling away from Ethan's sweet touch, she said, "Hi, Julie. Come on in."

"I can come back later if you're busy." Julie's eyes said that "later" would include a grilling. Marianna waved toward Ethan. "This is the detective investigating Suzanne's murder. Ethan O'Hara, this is Julie, my friend and fellow teacher."

Ethan held out a hand and Julie shook it. "So, you're the reason I haven't seen much of Marianna, huh?"

Flushing, Marianna met Ethan's amused gaze and shook her head. He grinned, shallow dimples peering out from the beginnings of his semipermanent five-o'clock shadow. "I'll never tell."

"Come on, Julie, you know how the gossip vine gets going around here. Don't add to it, okay?"

Julie turned serious. "You know me better than that."

Relieved, Marianna gave her friend a gentle smile. "I know. Sorry, I just…"

A grin cut a path on Julie's expressive, almost pretty face. "No explanation necessary. Not to change the subject, but I just stopped by to see if you were interested in going to lunch."

"Not today, thanks." Marianna wanted to spend as much time as possible working on figuring everything out. She refused to admit that she hoped Ethan would suggest eating somewhere.

Julie gave a small salute, then signed behind Ethan's back, off to the side where Marianna could see, "He's cute! Definitely a keeper, but if you don't want him, throw him my way."

Trying to act as if she hadn't caught every word, Marianna turned an innocent gaze on Ethan—who had a smirk on his face and was trying not to blush. "What?" she asked. If she didn't know better, she'd swear he knew what Julie had said.

"Guess she forgot about the mirror on that wall over there."

Marianna whirled to look and realized he *had* seen everything Julie had said. She slapped a hand to her head again and groaned. Oh, brother.

Ethan let out a laugh loud enough for her hearing aids to pick up, and she rolled her eyes.

Still chuckling, he reached out to grip her hand. "Don't worry about it. Let's go eat."

Ethan drove them to a nearby restaurant, still chuckling. He had enjoyed the lighthearted moment, glad to have seen Marianna flustered, embarrassed and able to laugh at herself—and him. It was a side of her he found extremely attractive and wanted to see more of.

While they ate, they bounced ideas off each other. Marianna insisted she had no idea who Gerald Chambers was or why he would be in her house. Ethan knew Catelyn was busy scouring every resource she had in order to find out everything there was to know about the man. Hopefully, she would call soon with some news. In the meantime, he would enjoy a few stolen moments with this intriguing woman he was coming to care for a lot.

"Cigarettes," Marianna murmured.

"Huh?"

Staring down at her plate, fork held midair, she didn't hear his confused response. He reached out and tapped the hand with the fork.

She jerked, looking up, eyes unfocused. He tapped again, absentmindedly noticing the fragility of her slender hand and the silky softness of her skin. He cleared his throat. "What about cigarettes?"

Marianna blinked, focused in on him, eyebrows shooting up. "He smelled like cigarettes."

Senses sharpening like a dog on the trail, Ethan leaned closer. "The man who attacked you?"

"Yes, cigarettes and—" she closed her eyes, forehead creasing in concentration "—something else."

"What? Think." With eyes still closed, of course she didn't hear his insistence.

Then she opened them and sighed. "I just can't think of what it was."

"Was it body odor? Some kind of food?"

She gave a negative shake of her head with each question. "No, it almost smelled like cologne, but I don't think it was. It was…it was…something I recognized but can't put a name to." She gave a frustrated sigh. "I don't know. It'll come to me. And probably when I least expect it." A quick glance at her watch had her sighing. "I guess I'd better get going. I have to be back for an afternoon in-service training session."

Ethan stood, regret filling him. Each time they were together, he noticed he wanted more moments. The time always flew when they were together and it constantly surprised him when it was time to part ways. "Come on, I'll take you back. Keep thinking about that smell, okay? And if you can put a name on it, text me."

She nodded. "Sure, no problem."

Marianna stood, stretching the kinks from her frame. The in-service training had been informative, and any other time she'd have been interested, but today she couldn't focus. No matter, it was finally over. Now she'd have to deal with the issue that had been on her mind since last

night before she could look forward to the thought of seeing her younger sister, Catherina, who was flying in from
New York tonight.

Alonso refused to leave her thoughts all day.

She had to know why his fingerprint had been found on
her newly detailed car when there shouldn't have been any
fingerprints at all, not even from the guys who'd cleaned it;
she knew they wore gloves to protect their hands from the
constant exposure to the harsh chemicals. Her prints were
probably on the driver's door, handle and the back door
since she'd gone out to her car after the guys had finished
working on it only because she'd needed to change out of
her teaching clothes into the clothes she wore for coaching.

Unfortunately, she couldn't come up with a good explanation for Alonso's print to be there.

And that worried her.

Pulling the BlackBerry from her clip, she texted Alonso.
"Hey, I need to talk to you. Do you mind meeting me at
home?"

While she waited for his response, she climbed into
the compact rental. The insurance company would have
an estimate on the cost of repairs for her damaged car at
the beginning of next week. Until then, she had to make
do with the rental.

Settling in, she buckled up and reached for the buzzing
BlackBerry attached to her belt. Alonso responded, "Busy
right now. C U later."

The brush-off. Lips tight, aggravation with her brother
gripping her, she muttered, "Oh, you'll see me later, all
right. You'll be lucky if you don't see me with my hands
around your neck."

Instead of typing that message and having him refuse to
even answer her, she punched in, "I need to see you now,

please. If you'll meet me up the street at McDonald's, I'll buy. And give you an extra twenty for your trouble."

"See you in ten."

Bull's-eye. She'd targeted his weakness—money—scoring a direct hit…another reason for more worry. She just prayed he didn't let that influence him into making some stupid, possibly life-threatening decisions.

Although if what she needed to talk to him about was any indication, her worries had already come to fruition.

Pulling into the restaurant parking lot, she dodged mothers and toddlers, teens and ball teams, to make her way inside.

Alonso stood in line waiting to hand the cashier the order he'd already written down. The restaurant was located near the deaf school, and the McDonald's staff were accustomed to deaf customers, which made the process of ordering and collecting food easy.

She joined him in line, noticing once again how tall he'd gotten. Her baby brother had grown into a man. He even needed a shave. Alonso shared her dark eyes, but instead of the straight, heavy hair she'd inherited from their mother, he had the thick curls of their father.

He saw her and signed, "Can we make this fast?"

"What do you need to do that's so important?" she signed back.

"Nothing." He rolled his eyes, then turned to gather his food. Marianna bit her lip. His attitude continued to worsen each time she saw him. She wished she could pinpoint the reason why.

But first she needed to know why his fingerprint had been on her car.

Sliding into the booth opposite Alonso, who'd already dug into his fries, she rested her head on her hands and said a short, silent blessing.

When she looked up, Alonso was staring at her, a faint flush on his cheeks. "Sorry."

Marianna shrugged, knowing it would do no good to lecture him. That would only drive the wedge deeper. "That's between you and God."

"So, what do you need to talk to me about?"

Changing the subject. An avoidance tactic she recognized, but an effective one. "Why was your fingerprint on my car the day it was vandalized?"

"What?" he demanded. "What are you talking about?"

Marianna's heart sank.

Because for a brief moment she'd seen a mixture of surprise and guilt flash in his dark eyes before he slid his gaze down to his remaining food.

Under the table, she gave his foot a light kick. He looked up at her—reluctantly. His defiance speared her. Slowly, she signed. "What did you do, Alonso?"

Jumping to his feet, he knocked the empty tray from the table, drawing startled stares from the other diners.

"Nothing. I didn't do anything, so stop accusing me!"

Shouting in sign language was just as effective as screaming at the top of one's lungs using vocal cords. Large, exaggerated signs, hands slapping together furiously to emphasize words, his facial expression, body language—all of it hollered his involvement in the vandalism of her car.

He stomped from the restaurant, leaving his uneaten food on the table and forgetting to remind her that she still owed him twenty dollars.

Sickness filled her because she knew one thing for certain: Alonso had trashed her car. Now, she had to find out why.

And she needed Ethan's help to figure it all out because she no longer felt safe being alone with her brother.

Shudders racked her as one last horrible question filled her mind: Had Alonso known she would be attacked in the gym that day and allowed it to happen?

TWELVE

Ethan paced his office, staring at the phone on his desk. Another Friday night working had produced no results. Marianna lingered in his thoughts, and several times he'd had to force himself not to text her and ask her to meet him.

She was probably busy with her family. Her younger sister, Catherina, had no doubt already landed and been gathered from the airport. She'd graduate this year from the Rochester Institute for the Deaf with a degree in interpreting and deaf studies. Marianna had practically glowed when she shared that information with him. They were all proud of the young woman.

He'd spent only that one morning with Marianna's family, but they amazed him with their boundless energy and obvious love for one another. He wished...

No, he didn't want to think about his own estranged family. Parents too busy with their country club meetings and tee-off times to pay attention to their special-needs daughter wouldn't be interested in hearing what their son wanted now. They hadn't been interested when he was growing up; they sure wouldn't care at this point in time.

Oh, Ashley's death had hit them hard—he'd give them that—but they'd also almost seemed relieved that the "burden" of their imperfect child had been lifted. After all, it hadn't stopped them from their jaunt through Europe shortly after her funeral. Then his conscience reminded him: They've called you several times, and you've not called them back.

Ethan shook his head, pulled his phone out of the clip once more and clicked his way through the steps until he reached the screen where all he had to do was type the letters and he could send a message to Marianna. Would she want to meet him? He really did need to talk to her because he had found some interesting news about her ex-boyfriend, Curt Wentworth, but giving her that information wasn't a top priority. Just…interesting. Possibly enlightening.

And, yeah, he wanted to see her again.

Then before his eyes, a message light blinked on, indicating he had a new text. Frowning, he pressed the button to pull the words up, and his heart expanded with anticipation.

Marianna.

Eagerly he read her message. "Hi Ethan, I know you're probably busy, but if you haven't eaten and you'd like to join us, we're all going to Wade's Restaurant on Pine Street in about thirty minutes."

He blinked. She'd just asked him to join her family for dinner. He'd rather see her alone, have her to himself, but no way was he passing up this opportunity.

"Sure," he typed. "I'll meet you there."

"Good," she responded, "I need your help with something."

His heart drooped. Oh. She wanted to see him professionally. "No problem. I'm glad to help." And he was, he just wished…

No, not yet. They needed this case behind them before he could think about a future relationship with Marianna.

If he could even consider a relationship. Right now, he had to focus on dealing with the responsibility of keeping her safe. Nope, anything more would be a mistake.

He just hoped he could convince his heart of that before he reached the restaurant.

Marianna slipped into a seat at the large round table. Sure did seem as if she was visiting a lot of restaurants lately. But when her father had declared that her mother was to take the night off, everyone had agreed and decided on this place for supper. On an impulse, Marianna had sent an invitation to Ethan asking him to join them. Hopefully, she'd get the opportunity to ask him for his help with Alonso.

Maybe after supper she could suggest he give her a ride home and they'd get to talk. Alonso hadn't shown up at home in time to ride with the family to eat, but her father had sent the young man a text telling him he'd better get over to the restaurant if he knew what was good for him. Marianna's mother sat to her left, her baby sister, Catherina next to her mother. Her father and Alonso would sit almost across from her.

Alonso still hadn't arrived...but Ethan had. He stepped into the dining area, eyes searching for her. She lifted a hand in greeting even as she drank in his appearance. Yes, she could definitely fall for this guy.

Not a good idea.

Her BlackBerry buzzed, providing a distraction and she pulled it up to see a message from Curt staring back at her. Sighing in exasperation, she deleted the message without reading it and stuck it back in the clip.

A hand on her shoulder brought her head around to see Ethan seating himself in the chair next to her. He smiled and signed, "Hi, everyone. It's good to see you all again."

After the greetings, Marianna said, "Dad's outside waiting on Alonso. They should be here shortly."

"I saw your father on my way in." Ethan linked his fingers and rested his hands on the table in front of him. Marianna felt his gaze land on her, and when he didn't look away, she knew the red creeping up her neck would soon be in her cheeks. What was he staring at?

Absentmindedly, she reached up and smoothed her hair down around her ears, realized what she was doing and slapped her hands to the table. Why did he have such an effect on her? Why did he make her nervous?

Before she could try to figure out the answers, the waitress arrived, took their orders and disappeared again. Marianna's father came in, followed by Alonso. The curl of the younger man's upper lip didn't bode well for the evening. When he noticed Ethan, his entire posture stiffened, his lip unfurled and he sat without meeting Marianna's eyes.

Conversation flowed, except from Alonso, and Marianna enjoyed the evening. No creepy sensations, no feelings of being watched, just a nice time with her family and Ethan. The only distraction was her mental rehearsing of what she'd say to Ethan when she could get him alone for a private conversation.

Then Ethan covered her hand to get her attention. When she looked at him, down next to his leg, he signed subtly, "I need to talk to you about something. Can you get away for about an hour?"

"Yes, I have something I need to discuss with you, too."

Soon the family departed, some leveling, knowing, calculating looks at Marianna and Ethan as they walked out to their cars. Embarrassed, she wished they'd just go on and leave her in peace.

Finally, she and Ethan stood alone in the parking lot. With his hand on her back, he led her to his car. The weather for this time of year fluctuated. Tonight was mild, so she hadn't bothered with a coat. The warmth of his hand seared through the heavy sweatshirt, causing shivers to run up her spine.

A gentleman, he opened her door and waited for her to get settled before he shut it.

When he slid in beside her, he asked, "Starbucks across the street?"

"Sure. I love their mocha lattes."

Ten minutes later, seated on a bar stool at a high round table, Marianna sipped her drink and pondered how to approach Ethan with the subject of Alonso. She'd let him go first.

"What is it you wanted to talk to me about?" she asked.

Ethan studied her pretty features, noticing the strain she couldn't quite hide. "Your ex-boyfriend."

Grimacing, she put her mug on the table between them. "Why would you want to talk about him?"

"I did a little background check on him, and Catelyn did some old-fashioned legwork to see if we could come up with anything."

"And?"

"He's got a pretty airtight alibi for the day of the murder. Some audiology convention in New York. He was the keynote speaker, so I seriously doubt he could have come home, killed Suzanne and gotten back to his convention without someone wondering where he was for that length of time. Add to the fact that there's no airline record of him flying, and it's been noted that he was speaking to a group of about two hundred people the same time Suzanne was murdered…." He gave a shrug. "Not him, if you ask me."

"I didn't really think it was anyway. As unpleasant and

autocratic as the man can be, I can't picture him a murderer."

Ethan toyed with his mug, took a sip, then looked back at Marianna. "And before he dated you, he also dated that teacher you said was so ugly to you."

Shock twisted her features. "Misty?"

"Yep. Catelyn got that information from someone at the audiology office. She started asking questions of the staff and uncovered that nice little tidbit."

"So you think Misty's hostilities stem from her being jealous of the fact that I dated Curt?"

"Absolutely."

"You don't think she could be behind the attempts on my life, do you?"

"I don't know. We know it was Gerald Chambers who was in your house that night. What we don't know is if he has some kind of connection to Misty. Catelyn's working on that one, too."

She blew out a sigh and shook her head. The urge to gather her close and hug her pulled at him. He fought off the feeling and focused on her fidgeting fingers.

Wrapping a hand around them, he looked her in the eye. "Now, what is it you've been wanting to talk to me about all night?"

Marianna locked onto his blue-gray eyes and wondered how this man that she'd known for the grand total of two weeks could read her so easily. The feel of his warm hand around her ice-cold fingers did strange things to her insides. Turned them to mush, caused butterflies to swarm, her blood to hum. Those kinds of things. Things that made her want to snuggle down in his arms and let him take on the burden of all that was wrong with her world.

Reluctantly, she pulled away, straightened her spine. No,

she didn't need a man to take care of her. She could take care of herself. Hadn't she fought long and hard for her independence? Hadn't she proved she was a very capable person who could face a challenge and come out the winner?

Yes, but that didn't mean she didn't need some help. Especially with Alonso.

"I think…my brother, Alonso, can tell you who trashed my car that night in the parking lot."

Surprise lit his eyes. "Why do you say that?"

"I confronted him yesterday. I'm very worried that he's involved with some people he shouldn't be involved with. Doing things he shouldn't do."

"But what made you even ask him anything?"

Marianna sighed, scrubbed her eyes with the heels of her hands, then said, "Because I had my car detailed that day." She told him of her routine. "No one's prints should have been there."

"Well, that explains a lot. The lab guys wondered why it was so clean."

"I'd been out there earlier that day to get some clothes out of my trunk, so finding my fingerprints wouldn't surprise me, but Alonso's…"

"Maybe it was missed in the detailing."

"It was on the hood, Ethan. Not exactly a place that's going to be missed."

He rubbed his chin. "So, what did Alonso have to say about it when you confronted him?"

"He was furious. He stormed out of the restaurant. Now he avoids me, won't look me in the eye."

"Then I guess it's my turn to do a little questioning—and now isn't a moment too soon." The grim expression on Ethan's face told her Alonso was going to wish he'd stayed put at McDonald's and spilled his guts rather than face the man before her.

With mixed feelings, they headed to her parents' house, where she hoped Alonso had the good sense to be.

As they walked in the front door, Marianna noticed Alonso's favorite jacket hung from the peg. She looked at Ethan. "He's home."

"Good, let's do this out on the porch. There's plenty of light, and we won't need to get your parents involved, yet. This isn't a formal interrogation, just a friend doing a little digging."

Relief at the way he was going to handle this flowed freely, yet she still worried Alonso might think that she had betrayed him somehow by bringing Ethan into this.

Shoving aside her feelings of wanting to protect Alonso, she forced tough thoughts: Too bad, kiddo. You did this— now you're going to see some consequences of your actions.

Now, if only she would follow through.

Ethan stepped back out onto the porch to sit in one of the rockers.

Marianna went upstairs to get Alonso, asking him to talk with her. It took threatening him with telling their parents about his recent nocturnal activities to get him to come down the stairs with her, but finally his reluctant clomping steps could be felt.

However, when he opened the door to step outside and saw Ethan sitting on the porch, fear lit up his face like a Christmas tree and he whirled to go back into the house. Only the fact that Marianna stood in the door blocking the entrance and he'd have to mow her down to get back inside kept him on the porch. She signed, "Sit down, please."

"You ratted on me, didn't you?" Fury bristled from him.

"Yes, I did. But only because you wouldn't talk to me."

"So, you called in a cop?" His large signing indicated his extreme agitation.

"Yes, I called in a cop. I'm doing this for you, Alonso."

"Well, forget it. I don't have to stand here and listen to you accuse me of…"

Then Ethan was between the siblings, his fierce expression threatening barely suppressed violence. Alonso took one look and stumbled back.

Marianna bit her lip and refused to allow herself to intervene. She'd fought hard for her own independence, struggling to prove herself trustworthy and capable, pushing her parents away when they hovered. Perhaps she'd done too good of a job and as a result, Alonso had been given *too much* freedom.

Ethan signed, "We can do this here, or I can take you downtown."

Trying to put on a brave front, Alonso bucked up to Ethan, "I didn't do nothing, and you can't take me downtown if you don't have any charges."

With one swift move, Ethan pulled the cuffs from his pocket and had Alonso's wrists shackled together—in front of him. Marianna breathed a sigh of relief. Her brother could manage to sign with his hands cuffed in front. Ethan may have looked like he was on the edge of strangling Alonso, but he was thinking clearly.

"Now," Ethan signed, "one more chance. We can talk here, or I can put you in the car. Your choice."

Alonso dropped his head, scuffed his toe against the porch floor, huffed and signed, "Here."

Ethan uncuffed him and pointed to the rocker on the porch. Alonso dropped into it.

Marianna watched Ethan step in front of the boy and ask, "What do you know about Marianna's car being trashed?"

Alonso deflated; he sagged against the back of the

rocker and closed his eyes for a brief moment. Then he started signing.

"I was supposed to meet my girlfriend, Kelly, outside her dorm. But then she texted me and told me to meet her down by the little pond at the president's house." The president of the school lived on campus in a nice Victorian two-story home. Recently, maintenance had built a small man-made pond that included some beautiful goldfish.

"So, I started walking toward the pond and see this guy writing notes to a couple of my buddies. I go up to see what's going on, and the guy starts freaking out, slapping his head and walking in circles."

Alonso swallowed, looked down. "I pulled out my notebook and started writing notes to him." Most deaf people carried a pad and pen to assist in communicating with the hearing population. "He offered us a hundred dollars each to trash a car." At this point, Alonso's Adam's apple bobbed several times. "I said, sure, to count me in. Then I found out which car…and I tried to back out. I wasn't going to rat on my friends, but I didn't want to be one of the guys who…" All of his defiance had leaked out of him during the telling of this story. Both Marianna and Ethan sat, not wanting to say anything for fear the boy would clam up once again.

"But this guy shoved me up against the car and told me if I didn't cooperate, he'd…he'd…"

"What, Alonso?" Marianna asked gently.

"He'd slit my throat." The signs were slow, as though he didn't want to relive the moment—or tell the two adults about it.

Marianna blanched, sat back and put a hand to her throat as though she could feel the blade pressed against it.

"So, I did it."

"And while you guys were vandalizing Marianna's car,

this guy was staked out in the gym waiting for Marianna to show up so he could scare her to death."

Thoughts swirling, she fought to process everything, line it all up in some kind of order. "But why involve the boys?"

Ethan pulled at his lower lip. "My guess is he got caught."

"What?"

"One, or both, of those guys came up on this dude messing with your car, searching it or whatever. He had to come up with a plan that wouldn't expose him and the only way to do that was to involve the kids. If they had a hand in helping him, there's no way they would go to the cops or volunteer information. Then Alonso walked up, so *he* had to be part of it."

"He warned us about leaving prints."

"What?"

Alonso nodded. "He made us take off our socks to cover our hands so we wouldn't leave fingerprints."

Ethan explained. "If prints were found on the car and traced back to the boys, most likely they would tell what they knew about the man who hired them."

"But he pushed Alonso into the hood of the car before he made them do that."

"Which is why his fingerprint was there. And if you hadn't had the car detailed that day, you never would have thought anything about it." Scary.

Ethan drilled Alonso with his gaze. "Do you remember anything at all about this man? Anything?"

"No, just that he had on a warm-looking leather jacket and a baseball cap pulled down real low. I don't think I ever saw his face, now that I think about it. And he probably didn't belong on campus because he didn't know sign language at all."

Marianna jerked as an idea hit her. "Alonso, do you still have that money the guy gave you?"

Guilt mixed with remorse…and possibly a little relief flashed in his expression. "Yes, I felt so bad I couldn't spend it."

There was hope for the boy, yet, Marianna thought with gratitude.

Ethan caught her eye and nodded his approval, her heart warmed. He said to Alonso, "Show me where it is. Marianna, get me a little plastic bag, will you?"

Three minutes later, five crisp twenties sat in the see-through bag, ready to be processed at the lab to see what evidence remained.

THIRTEEN

Saturday morning found Marianna and Catherina heading for the downtown shops while Alonso confessed his actions to his parents. The police had pulled the other two boys in for questioning and Ethan promised to let her know if anything new came up.

In the meantime, Marianna determined to enjoy herself and see if she could find Joseph a birthday present. Unfortunately, she found it hard to focus, to concentrate on having a good time, when all she could think about were the events of the last two weeks.

And the fact that her fellow teacher and her ex-boyfriend, Misty and Curt, had once been an item—now that was just plain puzzling. Yet, she felt relieved at the same time, too. At least now she had an explanation for the woman's nastiness.

As she and Catherina exited the small antique store to head down the sidewalk, the hairs on her neck stood up and a shiver danced down her spine. Shifting the strap of her purse a little higher on her shoulder, she glanced back, to the side and up ahead.

Normal Saturday shoppers milled, spending money, strolling with children. Everything looked fine. So why did she feel…nervous? Anticipating danger around every corner? Maybe she should have stayed home.

Setting her jaw, she refused to cave in to the fear that could take over her life if she allowed it. No, whoever was causing her all these problems would not win, would not take away the independence she'd fought so hard for. Somehow, someway, she'd figure out who was doing this to her and why. *Lord, keep your hand on this, please. Put all the pieces together for us. Show us the next step to take in figuring all this out.*

In the next shop, Marianna tested the scented candles, picking them up and sniffing them, one at a time. Catherina had wandered off to check the birthday cards. When Marianna turned to put the cinnamon-bun scented jar back on the shelf, she caught movement in the mirror above the display.

She blinked. A man, head bent, studied a rack of antique fishing lures. And he had a ball cap pulled snuggly against his forehead; he also wore a leather jacket. Like the one Alonso had described the night he'd vandalized her car? Coincidence, or was he following her? Did she take a chance on ignoring the guy? Should she just see if he stayed with her or go ahead and put Ethan on the alert?

Subtly, she pulled out her BlackBerry and sent a text to Ethan. "Am shopping downtown shops with sister. Man in leather jacket and ball cap following me. I think. Can you meet me?"

Gripping the device, she waited for a response. And waited. While she stood there, pretending to peruse the inventory, the man turned and went out the door. Relaxing a fraction, Marianna decided that maybe she'd overreacted. After all, there was probably more than one person in town who owned a leather jacket and a baseball cap.

Right?

Still…she glanced at her screen. Nothing yet from Ethan.

Catherina walked up holding a T-shirt that said "Kiss the Cook!" and signed, "I'm going to get this for Joseph for his birthday."

"Joseph doesn't cook. What are you thinking?"

"That he needs to find a woman who does."

Chuckling, Marianna turned back to scan the mirror. Still no sight of the man she thought might be following her. And still no response from Ethan. She realized she missed his presence. When he'd been her "copilot" for the trip to Beaufort, she'd thoroughly enjoyed his company. Shivering, she wished he were here now.

But he wasn't.

Ethan tossed down the paper that held Gerald Chambers's information. Why was this guy so hard to find? Probably because he'd been in the military once upon a time. Not special forces, but still military. Which meant he knew how to take care of himself and stay out of sight unless he wanted to be found.

Obviously, he didn't want to be found. The lab had run tests on the money Alonso had given Ethan and come up with nothing but a bunch of prints that would take forever to identify and would probably mean nothing. The police had an APB out on Gerald and had flashed his military ID on the news asking for information, asking him to "stop by" the station. They'd stressed he wasn't a suspect, just a person of interest they'd like to talk to. Ethan wanted to show the picture to Marianna, but she hadn't returned his text yet.

As far as viable information on Gerald, there'd been nothing that had panned out. Of course they had the usual crackpot phone callers who think they see a bad guy on every corner, but none of those had been the real deal.

And they followed up on each and every lead. His boss, Victor, had been adamant about that. He wanted to catch this guy every bit as much as Ethan did. Ethan gave a wry grin. No doubt Joseph was checking in on his baby sister's case on a regular basis.

Which was fine with Ethan; he'd have done the same thing if it had been Ashley....

He also suspected that Marianna's case was the main reason Ethan's boss was in his office this Saturday morning. He'd just come from the man's office after hashing out the information they had. And it all kept coming back to one man.

Gerald Chambers. Gerald Chambers. For some reason that name was ringing a bell in his mind. Ethan picked up Gerald's file and read some more.

High society, dated a movie star once upon a time. Entered the military against family wishes. Family. That was it. Who was the man's family?

A few quick taps on his computer brought up the Internet, and he typed in a search for Gerald Chambers. He'd already done this once, but this time he was looking for something more specific.

Quite a few pages of information were listed below his search. He clicked and read, clicked and read. Time passed before he found what he was looking for.

A newspaper article. "Gerald Chambers, son of House of Representatives member Chase Chambers, has been arrested for DUI. This comes as a shock to his family, and the senior Mr. Chambers had expressed his disappointment in his son's activities. A bright political future looks to be in question as talks of rehab centers and AA meetings abound."

The article went on to cover Chambers's military career, where he'd had a few scrapes with the law but nothing major. Then the little note at the bottom caught his attention. "It might be of interest to some that Chase Chambers did a little string pulling to get his son honorably discharged from the army and placed on the campaign committee for Clayton Robertson. It seems Gerald is headed for a career in politics whether he wants one or not."

Ethan grunted. No wonder the guy drank. He could almost feel sorry for the man except for the fact that he broke into Marianna's home. And the fact that Roland Luck, also part of Clayton Robertson's political campaign, was dead. Now how did those two facts add up, and what did they have to do with Marianna?

Because there was no way this was all just a coincidence. He reached for his phone to call Catelyn and slapped empty air.

What?

He frowned, glanced around his desk. Nothing.

Then he remembered he'd gone into Victor's office to talk for a brief moment. He'd set it on the side table, then walked off without it. He got up to get it when his boss appeared in the doorway holding the device. "Hey, O'Hara, this thing's been going off for the last ten minutes. You want to get it? I was on the phone or I would have brought it out sooner."

"Yeah, thanks. No problem." Ethan took the phone and looked at the screen. Marianna had sent him a text. Clicking on the button, he pulled up her message and read, "Am shopping downtown shops with my sister. Man in leather jacket and ball cap following me. I think. Can you meet me?"

Cold dread settled in the pit of his belly. "Hey, Chief!"

* * *

Marianna continued to shop, keeping an eye out for the man in the baseball cap. So far, so good. Nothing for the last fifteen minutes or so even though she couldn't shake the feeling she needed to stay on guard. Watch her back.

And while she enjoyed the time with Catherina, she couldn't shut off the part of her brain that insisted on going over every detail she could remember about the case. Not to mention the worry about Alonso. True, he seemed genuinely remorseful over his part in the vandalism, yet…

She sighed, and looked up into the window of the next shop. Catherina touched her arm and signed, "I want to go in there. I've got an apartment to furnish in a couple of months."

"I can't believe you're graduating from college already." She smiled. "Mom and Dad are so proud of you. We all are."

Catherina blushed, but the pleased look on her face told Marianna that her words meant a lot. She nodded toward the store. "Go for it. I'm going to grab an ice-cream cone." If she was being followed, she wanted her sister somewhere else. She wouldn't bring this danger into her life.

Oblivious to Marianna's tension, her sister laughed. "Get me one, too."

"Absolutely."

Catherina disappeared into the store and Marianna turned to walk over to the portable Bruster's Ice Cream stand. As she ordered the treat, she glanced over her shoulder. Maybe she should have stayed with her sister. The man behind the counter held the cones out and Marianna took them.

Then something crashed into her back, her feet went out from under her and she let out a scream as the cones went flying to splat on the ground next to her. Pain shot up from her hip to her spine. Her left elbow hit the concrete and agony seared her arm. She felt her purse ripped from her shoulder, saw running feet pounding past her.

Groaning, she scrambled to her feet, ignoring the aches and pains—and terror—to stumble after the fleeing thief. Then a police car pulled up beside the escaping man and slammed on brakes. The officer—Ethan?—jumped from the vehicle to give chase.

Marianna hobbled along as fast as her throbbing hip would allow. The two men disappeared into a little alley set between two stores. Hurrying, she rounded the corner and stopped. Ethan and the thief were locked in combat, each struggling to get the upper hand.

Marianna had a hard time keeping up with who was who and which fist landed where. Ethan pushed the guy off him, and the man landed on several metal trash cans. Even Marianna's hearing aids picked up the screeching clanging.

A man in an apron stepped out the back door of his restaurant kitchen, frying pan in hand, held as a weapon, to investigate the ruckus. Catching sight of the action before him, with eyes wide, the heavyset chef turned to scuttle back in, but before he disappeared, Marianna grabbed the frying pan from his hand. He offered no protests as he slammed the door.

She turned back to the battling duo and stepped forward, terror racing through her veins, making her shake. She held the cast-iron handle with a death grip and prayed out loud, "Lord, help me, please."

When she focused on the man trying to beat Ethan to a pulp, she had a flash of recognition. She'd seen him somewhere before.

Then the knife caught her full attention.

Ethan reached for his gun but didn't have time to grab it because he had to defend himself against the attacker's rush, knife held out in front of him. Ethan stepped away. The man jabbed again, slicing through shirt and forearm. She saw Ethan grimace, the blood rushing down his arm. He ignored it and set his feet to brace himself for the next attack.

Both men seemed to have forgotten her presence.

As the attacker rushed past her, she brought the frying pan up as hard as she could, aiming for his face, but her blow was off, instead catching the outstretched hand carrying the knife.

Where was his backup? Adrenaline flowed as Ethan scrambled after the perp. His arm throbbed mercilessly. Then a solid thud echoed in his ears, followed by a crunching sound, a scream of pain and the knife spinning through the air to land some thirty feet behind him.

He scrambled for his gun, then realized he didn't have to. Six officers had their weapons trained on the perp, who lay on the ground, grasping his broken wrist, screeching in agony. The ball cap had flown off in the attack, revealing a face Ethan recognized in an instant.

Panting, Ethan made his way over to the man and pulled both arms, wounded or not, behind his back. The groaning and screaming increased, but Ethan was more worried about the damage the man might still be able to inflict than a broken wrist. Especially if he was high on some drug, although the fact that the guy was feeling pain indicated there were no mind-altering substances flowing through his veins.

Except maybe alcohol. He only now just got a whiff. The man reeked of the stuff. Ethan motioned for his backup to haul Gerald off to the squad car, where they'd wait for an ambulance to come. Even bad guys got medical attention before they had to go to jail. Through gritted teeth, Ethan read him his Miranda rights: "You have the right to remain silent. If you choose to give up that right…"

One of the officers took over, pulling the guy to the waiting paramedics. As for himself, he'd get his arm taken care of, then head down the station to question Gerald. He had so many questions burning through his brain that he needed the space to organize them.

"Ethan, are you all right?" Marianna's worried voice cut through the haze of pain coming from his arm.

He grimaced. "Yeah." He gestured toward the man. "That's Gerald Chambers."

A puzzled frown crossed her face as she studied the man, then she shook her head, turning her focus back on Ethan. "You need to get that patched up. Come on, I'll drive you to the hospital."

One of the other officers walked up, and the annoyed expression on the man's face put Ethan on guard. When the cop turned to Marianna, Ethan paid attention. "Nice job with the frying pan, ma'am, but we were right there with our guns drawn. Should have let us do our job."

Marianna bit her lower lip and swallowed hard. "I didn't know you were there."

Disbelief cut across the policeman's face. "I hollered at you to move. You were in the line of fire."

Ethan stepped up. "She's deaf, Joel. Lay off."

Marianna felt slightly sick. Wanting nothing more than to go home and pull the covers up over head and hibernate for the next twenty-four hours, she gathered her courage, her nerves…and her independence.

Coolly, she glared at the two men standing before her. To the cop she said, "Don't worry about it. You couldn't have known." To Ethan she said, "And you didn't need to pipe in and tell the man I'm deaf. I'm perfectly capable of explaining that myself."

When Ethan's jaw dropped at her dressing-down, it didn't make her feel better necessarily, but she had to make him understand she didn't need a keeper. Sure, she knew she needed help in this whole mess, but some things she could—and would—handle herself. "Now, would you like a ride to the emergency room?"

His jaw snapped shut. "Yeah."

As they walked out of the alley and onto the sidewalk, they passed the ambulance where Gerald sat receiving medical treatment for his wrist. She stopped, stared at him, read his lips almost absentmindedly as he whined his innocence, complaining he'd been attacked and wanted to file a police report.

Marianna bit her lip and chewed for a moment until a warm, if dusty, finger pulled it from between her teeth. Startled, she looked at Ethan, who stared at her with a warm look in his eyes. "Thanks for coming to my rescue."

Previous irritation melted, as did her heart. "If I'd known those policemen were behind me, I'd have moved out of the way and cowered in the corner instead."

He laughed. "I doubt you would have cowered, but the fact that you were willing to jump in and help…well, that says a lot. Thanks."

"Sure." The pitter-patter of her heart and the mushy sensation settling in the pit of her stomach goaded her to action. With both hands, she reached up and cupped Ethan's face. His eyes flared in surprise then turned smoky as he realized what she was going to do. He met her halfway and his lips landed on hers with sweet intent. Marianna reveled in the sensations sweeping through her. Then she pulled back and smiled. "Now we can go to the hospital."

She turned back to the man who'd tried to do her bodily harm—again. And she studied him.

Ethan nudged her. "Hey, I'm ready for that ride and I might need another kiss."

She grinned at him and blushed, then narrowed her eyes and said, "I know him."

"What?"

"I think I know that man. Or at least I've seen him somewhere before."

"Where?"

"At Mr. and Mrs. Luck's house. He was in one of her pictures sitting on the sofa table. I remember picking it up to admire it." Confusion tagged her. "So what's the connection between Roland Luck, a dead man, and Gerald Chambers, a man who tried to kill me?"

FOURTEEN

Ethan thought about Marianna's question the entire time he was being stitched up. She'd insisted on waiting for him to be discharged, quietly staying out of the way, but her ever-moving eyes told him she didn't miss a thing going on.

Such as the fact that he refused a painkiller. She frowned as if she wanted to say something, but resisted. He appreciated her restraint. There was no way he was going to cloud his thinking when he still had to interrogate a suspect.

Leaving the hospital, he asked, "Do you feel like going to the station with me? Or do you want me to take you home?"

"Is he there already?"

"Yeah, released from the hospital and transported ten minutes ago. He's on his way to being booked, but I asked the arresting officers if they'd put him in an interrogation room so I could have a go at him."

"I'll go with you. I want to know what he says."

"If you stand behind the two-way mirror, you should be able to see enough of the conversation as it happens."

Her eyes lit up. "You'd let me do that?"

"Sure, you're the one he's after. Seems only right to me."

Ethan let her drive and breathed a sigh of relief when they arrived. Every bump jarred his wound, causing it to be one throbbing mass of pain by the time the station came into sight. It wasn't Marianna's fault; she'd tried to drive smoothly. Pulling himself from the car, he placed his good hand on her back and led her into his second home. Her warmth radiated up his arm and he remembered the feel of her sweet lips on his. He swallowed hard at the intense emotions she roused in him. Wishing he had time to examine them, he instead put them aside for later retrieval and study.

Shrugging off well-wishing and congratulations on his collar, Ethan stayed the course and honed in on the last interrogation room on the left. Spotting a female officer, he asked, "Sarah, would you take Marianna up to the viewing room?"

"Sure."

He turned to Marianna. "Just follow her. Stay there until I come get you, okay?"

Marianna nodded and Ethan watched them disappear down the hall then around the corner. Placing his hand on the knob, he drew in a deep breath, steeled himself against the pain in his arm and opened the door.

Marianna followed the officer to a small room not too far from the door Ethan had stopped in front of. When she entered, two other officers stood there. She recognized them as the arresting officers.

Ethan had taken a seat at the lone table across from the man she now knew as Gerald Chambers.

"Anything you want to say before your lawyer gets here?"

The man's eyes flicked contempt at Ethan before he looked back at the table in front of him. His arm in the cast lay across his belly; his good arm relaxed in his lap.

Marianna could read body language as well as the next

person. Probably better. This guy was not going to talk to anyone. He didn't seem the least bit worried he'd just been charged with attempted murder of a police officer, resisting arrest and assault.

Ethan tried again. "Why are you after Marianna?"

The man sighed, shifted, and shut his eyes as though Ethan annoyed him.

Marianna winced. If Ethan clenched his jaw any tighter, he'd need dental work. While the man's eyes were closed, she watched Ethan struggle to let go of his anger, his tension, to let his muscles relax. He didn't drop his guard, but he did gain better control.

His next question was a common interrogation tactic, ask questions you already knew the answer to, to get the perp's reaction. "What's your connection with Roland Luck?"

That got Gerald's attention. His head snapped up, eyes locked on Ethan. Then he smirked. "Who?"

"Roland Luck." Ethan said the name slowly as though speaking to someone who didn't quite have all his marbles.

"Never heard of him."

Ethan slapped the table in front of him, causing the prisoner to jump. He wasn't quite as relaxed as he wanted Ethan to believe. Good.

"Everybody who's interested in politics has heard of him. Don't give me that."

At this point, Gerald's attorney bustled in, a short older woman named Helen Zanislowski, with eyes like steel. Sharp, intelligent. And highly paid. "Okay, zip it up, Gerald." She zeroed in on Ethan. "You have no right to question my client without me here."

"I was just—talking out loud to myself, so to speak."

She snorted.

Ethan filled her in on the things he'd talked about thus far. "I was just asking him about his connection to Roland Luck—who he claims not to know."

Gerald widened his eyes as though recognition had just hit him, and he spoke before his attorney could say anything. "Oh, yeah, that guy who died in the car accident. Had something to do with the governor's campaign. Right." He spread his hands, or at least tried to, hampered only a bit by the cast, innocence personified. "What's that got to do with me?"

"That's what I want to know."

"Gerald, be quiet, don't say another word."

Chambers ignored his attorney. "And why would you think I even know this dude?"

Ethan leaned forward. Should he play this card now or keep it close to his chest? That was the thing about interrogations. Sometimes you just had to go with your gut. So he did.

"Because Roland Luck's mother had a picture of you, your father and Roland, all dressed in your army fatigues, sitting on an end table in her living room. Not to mention the fact that your DNA was found in Marianna's house. *And,* you're working with the same campaign. Come on, man. Get real." He leaned forward. "You're not doing this alone. Who's pulling your strings?"

Gerald's jaw nearly hit the table; he was clearly shocked that Ethan had so much on him. This time his glance to his attorney was pleading, bravado draining away in the face of Ethan's statement.

She held up a hand. "Oh please, Ethan. There are so many people involved in the campaign that it wouldn't surprise me that Gerald doesn't know everyone. We'll discuss the photo later. I need to talk to my client. If you have any more questions, we'll have to set up a time."

Ethan gave a snort of disgust. "You do that. In the meantime, I'll be gathering the rest of the evidence against your client."

Marianna let out the breath she didn't realize she'd been holding. She'd gotten most of the conversation. Speech reading definitely wasn't a perfected art, and she was better at it than most, but she still missed a word here and there, depending on the shape of the mouth, whether the person talked through gritted teeth or rubbed a hand across his mouth; or maybe as a stranger, she just wasn't used to the way he or she talked. Things like that could mess her up, but for the most part, she'd understood Gerald amazingly well.

And she'd understood that Gerald wasn't talking. What could his connection be with Josh's family? The picture in Mrs. Luck's house gave a good indication that the relationship was more than merely one among acquaintances. It suggested friendship.

Marianna decided that a phone call to Mrs. Luck was in order just as soon as Ethan could make it for her. Oh, she could always use the TTY, but Ethan would speed the process along, get the information faster.

She watched the lawyer leave. The police used special cuffs on Gerald in order to accommodate his cast as they returned him to his holding cell. The charges against him were strong; she just hoped his family's influence wasn't stronger.

Ethan exited soon after, and Marianna turned toward the door so she would be able to see him as soon as he opened it.

Within a minute, the door swung inward. He filled out the entry, broad shoulders nearly reaching from one side to the other. Would he be different? Would he be able to accept her as she was? Hearing deficiency and all? Would he be able to handle her crazy family, including her juvenile delinquent of a brother?

And why was she even going down this road of thought? He was a cop. A professional. Yeah, and one who spoke her language.

Curt spoke it, too, and she remembered how well that turned out. She trusted too easily, too fast. She fell for his charming ways and smooth talk.

All of these thoughts tumbled through her mind with lightning speed. Then Ethan was smiling, satisfaction gleaming. "I think we've got our guy."

"But we still don't know what he was looking for."

"True, but I think in time he'll spill it."

"What about his family? They're pretty powerful here in the state. Won't they have some influence?"

He took her hand to pull her from the room. She followed, letting him lead her as she watched his face. "They'll try. In fact, Gerald's father already has a call in, but with the evidence against him, plus our eyewitness accounts," he said, flexing his arm, "not to mention the fact the man sliced me, I'd say we're pretty good. The father can argue all he wants, but the fact remains, his son's guilty."

Relief slowly eased its way through her. She was starting to believe it might finally be over. Life could return to normal. She gazed at the tall man beside her. But would life ever truly be normal? "Was he the man who made the call from the hospital?"

"Looks like it. Same jacket, even with a piece of leather missing from the sleeve. Plus it was the same hat."

"And the one who attacked me in the gym?"

"Probably." A frown caught at his forehead. "Did you smell alcohol on the man from the gym?"

She closed her eyes, not wanting to remember the incident but forcing herself to relive it. Walking into the gym, knowing someone was there, feeling his presence behind her, the breath-snatching fear, the agonizing moment when she thought she was dead. Her heart rate accelerated just thinking about it. She gripped the door handle, tuned all her senses into that moment. The smell of cigarettes, a sweet sickly, smell of…alcohol?

Instead of pondering that thought, she asked, "No, I don't think it was alcohol. It was more like cologne, a woodsy, yet sweet kind of smell. One I've smelled before and didn't like." She snapped her fingers. "Chewing tobacco! That's what it was, I guarantee it."

"Tobacco?"

"Yes. I'm sure of it. Alonso tried it once upon a time, and it stunk up the place." She shrugged. "What do you think about calling Mrs. Luck and asking her about the relationship between her family and the Chambers family? I'm guessing Roland and Gerald's father were involved in politics together and became friends. And they both had on military uniforms. Maybe they met in the army."

"And Gerald followed in his father's footsteps."

"Yes, all three were in uniform."

"Makes sense. Do you have the number?"

She grimaced. "Yes, but it's in my classroom."

"Want to ride over there and get it?"

"Sure, why not?"

Ethan walked her out to her car and opened the door for her. She climbed in and Ethan walked around to climb in the passenger side. He made only one painful face as he reached up to grab the seat belt.

"Does it hurt that bad?"

He shot her a rueful look. "Kind of like being dipped into a vat of boiling tar."

"Ack. Sorry." Definitely painful.

"It's all right. It'll pass."

The flash of Gerald with the knife, charging at Ethan, and the remembered terror. It was all still too fresh. She swallowed hard. The graze of his knuckles sliding down her cheek caught her, and she flicked him a glance. He said, "Don't think about it."

She started the car. "It's hard not to." The path his knuckles traveled tingled. Her insides shuddered, and she realized she was very attracted to this man. What would happen when this was all over? And it *was* getting close to being finished…she hoped. She fingered her hearing aid and studied him. Could it be possible he was different? Could he truly accept her as she was? Hearing loss and all. Could it be possible she'd finally met a man who wouldn't try to "fix" her?

"Ashley would have liked you."

His out-of-the-blue comment startled her. She wondered if she'd caught exactly what he'd said. "Excuse me?"

"Ashley." He gave her a wistful smile. "She would have liked you. A lot."

"Well…thanks."

"You're a lot like her, different in many ways but alike, too."

"How?" He was letting her in. Opening himself up and allowing her to see the hurting, vulnerable side of him. She remembered their dinner the night before Roland's funeral, remembered his kindness, his willingness to be honest with her about his feelings. It made her want to reciprocate.

For a moment he didn't answer, and she wondered if he was having second thoughts about keeping the conversation on this particular topic. Then he took a deep breath, "She was an incredible girl. Had a deep faith in God you wouldn't expect someone of her age to have."

"I think I remember her going on a mission trip when she was a student here."

A faint smile curved his lips. "Yes, her last one. To a deaf school in Jamaica. She loved it. And came back even more determined to make her mark on her world." Then he frowned. "That's why it's so hard to understand how God…"

"…could let her die?"

His throat bobbed. "Yeah."

"I don't know, Ethan. But I think He understands why you would ask that."

Reaching over, he grasped her hand. "Thanks. I think so, too. I finally had to come to the conclusion that if God is who He says He is, then I have to choose whether I believe it or not. It was a long road, and I can't fathom the purpose of her death, but…"

"God is faithful and just."

He squeezed her hand, then pulled away. "Yeah."

And then there was no more time to delve deeper. And Marianna wasn't sure what to think.

Arriving at the school, she waved to the weekend security guard and drove through the gate, winding around the campus to reach her building.

Two other cars sat parked on the side of the road, and Marianna's heart sank when she recognized Misty's. Great. Often teachers worked on the weekends, but Marianna hadn't even thought she'd run into the woman who continued to aggravate her. She glanced at Ethan, his strong presence a comfort.

But *not* a necessity, she assured herself. She wasn't compromising her independence by being glad he was with her. Was she? She'd come to rely on him…a lot. A niggling sense of discomfort pierced her. She'd fought long and hard to convince her family she could take care of herself. Even having a deaf mother hadn't made a difference. The woman had married Marianna's father right out of high school.

Because Marianna was the first deaf child born, they'd been so protective. Overprotective. Smothering her. Especially Joseph. He'd driven her nuts before she'd finally gotten old enough to stand up for herself. Fortunately, she'd been blessed with a healthy dose of stubbornness that had done her well when it came to dealing with Joseph.

But she didn't need to be so antsy when it came to Ethan. He was here because she was truly in danger, needed someone to watch out for her. Keep her from harm. He didn't smother her or make her feel as if she were incompetent. He didn't try to change her, force her to be someone she wasn't. He just…watched out for her.

She could live with that.

Using her key, she opened the door and stepped into the building. It smelled like…school. Crayons, markers, paper, copies, glue, sometimes popcorn and cookies. She smiled. No matter what school she entered, they all had that same educational fragrance, one that Marianna loved.

Ethan once again placed a hand at her back, and once again she shivered at the contact. Would his touch ever grow old? Would she ever not want to be with him? Breathe in his unique scent? Would the anticipation of waiting for him, watching him walk into the room, dwindle over time?

All of these questions flittered through her mind as she walked to the door of her classroom—and found it already open.

She paused. Ethan moved his hand from her waist to her shoulder, turning her to look at him. "Should that door be open?"

Marianna shook her head. "I always lock up when I leave on Friday. Maintenance people come in to clean, but they always leave the door locked when they finish. I don't know why it would be open. No one knew we were coming up here, so…"

He pulled her back a little, then stepped in front of her. "Let me just take a look."

"I'm sure it's nothing," she protested, but not too forcefully.

"One way to find out." He stepped into the room.

Marianna followed in spite of his order to stay put.

And found Misty going through her desk.

Anger flowed and Marianna clenched a fist to keep it in check. The woman looked up with a deer-in-the-headlights expression on her face. Marianna watched her swallow, clearly incapable of speech, her eyes flitting back and forth between the two who'd just walked in on her.

Ethan said nothing and simply looked at Marianna as he stepped to the side.

And she realized what he was doing.

Since there was nothing life-threatening about the situation, he was deferring the handling of it to her. Something flowed through her at that realization. In the blink of an eye she realized she could love this man.

Unfortunately, she didn't have time to dwell on that. Instead, she focused on the woman still standing behind the desk. *Help me say the right thing, Lord. Show me how to handle this.*

Keep your cool, Marianna. Deep breath. "Is there something I can help you with?"

Misty straightened, and an expression appeared that Marianna had never seen cross the woman's face.

Shame.

Misty dropped her eyes and moved away from the desk. A tear leaked out to trail down her cheek. Then she moved from behind Marianna's desk and dropped into Josh's seat. It swallowed her small frame.

Marianna glanced at Ethan. He motioned he was going to step out of the room to give them some privacy. She shook her head. If the woman said something to incriminate herself in any of the problems Marianna had been facing lately, she wanted a witness.

She moved over and placed a hand on the woman's shoulder. "What can I do?"

The teacher looked up, all traces of animosity gone. "I'm so sorry for everything." She gave a little self-mocking laugh. "I guess the old adage about a woman scorned is true."

Marianna pulled up a chair and faced Misty. Ethan stepped back, but remained in hearing distance. He'd understood why she wanted him to stay.

"You're talking about Curt, aren't you?"

Shock filtered through the shame. "How did you find out?"

"I sort of came by the information accidentally. A friend was…researching something for me and asked me if I'd known you two had dated."

"Yes, we did. For about three years."

"Oh, I didn't realize it had been that long."

"He just wouldn't commit to marriage, and I'm not getting any younger. So—" she shrugged "—I broke up with him, thinking it would send him running back to me. Be a wake-up call, so to speak. Instead, he found someone else." Tears hovered once again as she looked Marianna in the eye. "You."

Marianna ran a hand through her hair, pushing it back behind her ears. "And you want him back."

A hiccupping sob escaped the woman. "Yeah. How dumb is that?"

Real dumb, but Marianna decided to keep that to herself. "Well, we're not dating anymore."

"I know, but he refuses to get back together with me, and I just…" Another sigh. "I just took my frustration out on you. I'm really sorry. Can you ever forgive me?"

"Of course. But why were you going through my desk?"

A flush crept up into Misty's face. "Curt changed his numbers, and I thought you might have them written down somewhere."

"Ah." Marianna reached over and covered the woman's hand. "Don't waste your time on him. You deserve better. Believe me, I know."

More tears threatened, but Misty managed to hold them back. She said, "So I keep telling myself."

"Would you like to come to church with me sometime?"

Once again Marianna had managed to shock the poor woman. "What?"

"Sure. What better way to start over. Trust me, you don't need Curt. He'll just try to change you into what he thinks you should be instead of…" Marianna snapped her lips shut and glanced at Ethan to see a gleam in his eyes. She'd revealed something very personal, and he hadn't missed it.

Marianna stood. "I'm glad this happened."

"You are?"

"Yes. I'm glad I got to see the real you."

Misty shook her head. "So, you're not going to report this?"

"No. I believe you when you say you're sorry. And I hope we can be friends in spite of everything."

"Oh, thank you!" Misty looked as if she might hug her but withdrew at the last moment and left the classroom.

Marianna looked back at Ethan, who had a strange look on his face. She asked, "What?"

"That was a really nice thing you just did."

Embarrassed, Marianna shrugged. He asked, "Is that what's called living your faith?"

She paused and thought a moment, then smiled. "Yeah, I guess it is."

"Well, I think we can safely assume that Misty is not involved with all your latest problems."

"I would agree with that." She went to her desk, pulled open a drawer and found Josh's file. She rattled off the number to Ethan, who dialed it on his cell phone.

Ethan listened to the ringing, impatient for one of the Lucks to answer. When the voice mail picked up, he winced but left a message, asking Mrs. Luck to call back because he had a question for her.

"No answer." He clicked the phone shut.

Marianna grimaced. "Well, we can try again later."

"I'll keep the number on my phone." He looked around. "You ready to go?"

"I guess. I need to check in on Alonso and see how he's doing anyway."

"Let's take Gerald's picture by and see if he can ID the guy as the man who paid him to trash your car."

FIFTEEN

Arriving at Marianna's family home, Ethan ignored the throbbing of his injured arm and the fatigue that dragged at him and found himself once again overwhelmed by the boundless energy of her family. All but her elder brother, Joseph, were gathered in the backyard, playing a game of flag football. Even her mother had on a yellow-and-green jersey with the number zero proudly displayed. Each jersey had the name Santino on the back.

Twister, who'd been lounging on the porch, bounded out to greet Marianna, whining, his hind end giving credence to his name. Marianna laughed and scratched his ears.

Gina had the ball. Catherina ducked around Alonso, and another sister who looked exactly like Marianna shoved her younger brother out of the way—a definite flag-on-the-play kind of shove—and raced for Gina.

"I forgot." Marianna had a confused expression Ethan had never seen on her face before.

"Forgot what?"

"That this afternoon was our annual Santino football game. Even Gina came back. And I forgot."

Marianna's father, ensconced comfortably in a rocker with a footrest, waved to them from the porch and signed, "Did you get my text?"

Marianna fumbled with her BlackBerry and groaned. "I felt it go off when I was talking with Misty, then forgot to check it when we left." She read it aloud, "You ok? We're all here. Ready for some football?"

"Sorry, Dad," she called. "Alissa!"

The twin turned, screeched and flew across the yard to envelop her sister in a hug. Again, envy twinged Ethan's emotions at the tight family bond these people shared, but he refused to let it take hold. But he wished. How he wished...

Ethan's father had called and left him a message the night before last, asking for a return phone call. Ethan had honestly meant to do the courteous thing and call back, but in all the craziness, he'd put if off. He fingered his phone and looked for a secluded area. Maybe he could just slip away.

But the moment was lost when the sisters separated and two little girls burst from the house, followed by a blond-headed giant. When the girls saw Marianna, more screeching ensued, and Ethan had a hard time containing his laughter. Their joy was infectious. With the two bundles claiming ownership to her legs, Marianna turned to introduce everyone. She signed as she spoke. "Ready? This is my sister Alissa, her husband, Matthew, and their two precious leeches, Addy and Amy. Addy is six and Amy is three."

Handshakes all around had Ethan's arm hurting more and his head pounding to remember all the names.

"I'll get Alonso," she said.

Before Ethan could suggest she let him finish the game, she untangled herself from her nieces and made her way over to her brother, signing something he couldn't see.

Alonso nodded and followed his sister from the game, promising to be right back. Ethan let Marianna guide the three of them over to the side of the yard and under one of the oak trees that offered a bit of privacy. But before she could sign anything, Ethan said, "Let's move into the garage." It wasn't the most protected environment, but it was certainly better than the tree she'd picked. She frowned at him and he explained, "Until I'm sure this is over, I think it's best that you stay within walls and away from windows."

Understanding dawned, and she moved into the spacious garage attached to the house. She then signed to Alonso, "Ethan has some pictures he wants you to look at. Will you see if you can pick out the man who paid you to vandalize my car?"

Her brother winced at the memory, but said, "Sure."

Ethan produced the images and Alonso studied them, his brow furrowed, left hand rubbing the stubble on his young chin. Just as Ethan was ready to jump out of his skin with impatience, Alonso pointed to the picture of Gerald Chambers. "That could be him. But it was so dark, barely any light to even read the notes we were writing back and forth. He had a flashlight on him but kept shining it in our eyes. I just can't be sure." He shrugged, anxiety in his features. "I'm sorry, I really do want to help."

Marianna gave him a one-armed hug. "It's all right. And I believe you."

Relief flooded him, and in a sudden move that took them by surprise, he grabbed Marianna up in a bear hug, let her go and then trotted back to the game.

Ethan saw the tears on her lashes before she blinked them away. All she said was, "Well."

Monday morning brought cold wind and freezing rain. Marianna shivered as she got ready for school, shaking her head and grumbling about the wishy-washy weather.

Beautiful day yesterday, yucky stuff today. But that was February in the southeast. Pulling a heavy coat from the hanger, she looked at it and wondered which sister had left it behind. Then she glanced around the room. In spite of the circumstances, she had to admit it had been nice staying here again, allowing her to reminisce about her childhood and teen years.

Blessed didn't begin to describe it. She knew she could never thank God enough for the richness of her life. But it looked as though it would be time to move back into the house she'd shared with Suzanne. Just the thought sent shivers dancing along her nerves.

And she knew she'd never move back there.

Just like that, the decision was made. She'd give her landlord the required thirty days notice and begin house hunting. Until then...

Marianna grabbed a bagel on the way out, opened the door and pulled up short. "Ethan, what are you doing here?"

He sat on the front porch, occupying the rocker her father had only yesterday watched the football game from. Ethan rose and held out a hand. "I'm your escort to and from work until I'm comfortable that this case is closed. Gerald Chambers still isn't talking, and I really think he was working with someone, someone who was pulling his strings. There's just no motive for anything he's done. His actions don't add up."

Warmth tickled her insides as she let him hold the passenger door open for her. He cared. The door shut, she buckled up. Ethan slid in beside her and cranked the car. Marianna said, "Do you think he was the one who attacked me in the gym?"

"I don't know. I'm guessing no."

"Why do you say that?"

"I never smelled cigarettes on him and he never once asked for a smoke during the time we spent together."

Marianna raised a brow. "So, he might have been there to be the decoy?"

"Or simply the lookout. If he saw anyone around, he would cause a distraction."

"Like the vandalism of my car," she muttered.

"He probably had it all planned out if he ran into anyone who questioned him being there. I do think Alonso showing up there was pure coincidence."

Ethan turned left onto Route 56 and headed for the school. "I've got a question for you."

Tilting her head, she shot him a smile. "Sure, what is it?"

"I've been thinking about something. Yesterday, in that alley, that cop yelled at you and you couldn't hear him."

Marianna frowned. "Yes." Where was he going with this?

"Do you ever worry about…"

"What are trying to say, Ethan?" She ignored the familiar scenery zipping by.

"Well, what I mean is, have you ever thought about getting one of those cochlear implant things?"

The crushing devastation that she felt nearly sent her to the floorboard. She stared at him, unable to think, the question echoing through her mind. And then she could only remember Curt's pushing and pushing and then his hand gripping her forearms, fingers squeezing, leaving her with bruises that eventually faded but the final words that never had— "Get a cochlear implant. It's the solution to your problem. Why won't you listen to me? Do as I ask? If you loved me, you'd do it." Then he'd shoved her. Hard.

She'd walked out and never once looked back. And when he'd apologized for his rash behavior, she'd accepted his apology—but moved on without him, recognizing his potential for violence. If he'd kept his hands off her, they might have been able to work through the suddenly obvious issues he had with her hearing impairment, but the combination of the physical abuse and the veiled ultimatum had sent her running. Fast.

Now, as she looked at Ethan, whom she realized had just parked in front of her building, she found she couldn't form an answer to his out-of-the-blue question.

He reached over, took her hand and continued to look at her. Waiting.

Drawing in a deep breath, she shook her head and blew it out, pulling her hand away. "I can't believe you want to change me, too. I thought you were different. I thought I could trust you. I…" She broke off before the tears could fall, stumbling from the car and up the steps to the door.

He probably called her name, but she didn't bother looking back, feeling as though she'd been blindsided, her trust and belief in a future with Ethan shattered into a million little pieces. Marianna stopped at the door, and paused to collect herself. Don't think, don't feel. Get through the day, then get home.

With heart still pounding, her emotions still haywire on the inside, she prayed that at least on the outside she looked normal. A shaking hand opened the door, and she walked slowly toward her classroom. Students began to enter, filtering around her as they went to their lockers. She turned into her room, still feeling zombielike and trying desperately to paste a smile on a face that felt frozen.

Dawn sat at her desk, talking to Victoria, one of the students who'd arrived early to help tutor. The television showed the latest in political news. Slowly, her brain climbed out of the shocked fog, and she began to assimilate the activity around her. Dawn stood and waved, saying, "Since you're here, I'll go run these copies." She grabbed several papers, popped out the door and headed down the hall.

Marianna blinked again, giving an absentminded, belated nod to her disappearing assistant. It was Monday and was supposed to be a day off, a built-in snow day, but since it had snowed right after Christmas break, they'd missed two days. Today was a make-up day. She'd have the older students in her class this morning to help tutor. On Monday, as part of a work program, she had two students, who were interested in the teaching profession, come to her class to help with the kids. Relief made its way through her, and she realized today could be an easy day—if she allowed it. She could sit back and process what had just happened with Ethan.

Then the lights started flashing, the alarm sounded and Marianna groaned in frustration. Why of all days did the administration pick today to run an intruder alert drill? They weren't even supposed to *be* here, for goodness' sake.

A few more students filtered in, and Marianna rushed to the door to begin the lockdown procedures she and the students had practiced only a month ago.

But when she reached the door, terror hit her as she caught a glimpse of a man in a mask headed straight for her.

This was no drill.

It was the real thing.

She grabbed the doorknob to pull it shut, but horror flooded her as she realized she wouldn't have time to twist the lock.

His hand landed on the knob opposite hers…and pulled.

Ethan drove blindly through the campus, absentmindedly noting the students walking and talking as they made their way to class, bundled up against the unexpected chill the morning had brought. At least the rain had stopped about the time he'd pulled up to Marianna's building.

Marianna.

He blew out a breath. Boy, had he ever said the wrong thing. Why had his question sparked such a reaction? A cochlear implant could help her hear, know when danger was behind her, hear music, laughter. Why wouldn't she want to do that? But he already knew the answer to those questions, should have thought it through before sticking his foot in his mouth.

She was immersed in the deaf culture. Those things didn't bother her; she didn't feel the lack. Or what he and other hearing people would consider lacking. To her, her life was normal. And he just realized why she'd reacted the way she had. Flashes of her smoothing her hair down over her hearing aids taunted him; her statement to Misty about Curt wanting to change her sounded in his memory.

He'd insulted her, had made her feel as if there was something wrong with her. Just like Curt.

Ethan groaned and slapped his head. *Idiot.*

Ashley would have raked him over the coals for that one. And rightly so. But he hadn't asked as in making the suggestion that she should *get* one. He just wanted to know if she'd ever *thought* about it.

Turning off campus, he headed for his office. He had until about three o'clock to find out if he could get anything else from Gerald Chambers and to see if he could get hold of Mrs. Luck. She still hadn't returned his calls. Then he'd head back this way to see if Marianna would accept his apology and let him drive her home.

His cell phone rang, jarring him. Pulling it from the clip, he checked the caller ID: the Luck residence. He turned his scanner down and flipped his phone up to his ear. "Hello?"

"Mr. O'Hara? This is Joshua's grandfather, Ed Luck.

We took Joshua out of town over the weekend and just got your message. What can I do for you?"

"Mr. Luck, thanks so much for calling me back. I just had a question for you. Do you know a man by the name of Gerald Chambers?"

"Well, sure, his daddy and Roland were big buddies. Served in the army together and even served on some political committees together."

Nothing he didn't already know. "Is there anything else you can tell me about why Roland came home just before he died? Your wife said his visit was unusual because it was during the week."

"I can't recall anything else. Something seemed to be bothering him, and he spent an awful lot of time in Josh's room. I guess he was missing the boy, or maybe he was feeling guilty sending him to the deaf school so far away. He often said that he should have sent him to some private facility, but what a lot of people don't know is that Roland was a gambler. And while he may have a pretty well-paying job, he had a hard time keeping money in the bank. He couldn't afford a private facility."

That was news. A gambler. Now he might be on to something.

Mr. Luck continued. "I had the impression that he was looking for something and couldn't find it. I'm sorry I can't be of more help."

"No, no, I appreciate your time." The approaching flashing lights caught Ethan's attention. Several police cars whipped by. Then an ambulance. His pager went off. "Listen, Mr. Luck, if you think of anything else, will you give me a call back?"

"Sure thing, son."

Ethan disconnected the call, then looked at the number on his pager. His boss. He pushed the speed dial button and waited.

Without preamble, the man demanded, "That you, Ethan?"

"Yep. What you got?"

"Another hostage situation, and I need you to make sure things turn out right. I'm sending Dallas as your secondary. I'm coming in, too, as commander."

Dread crawled up him. "Can't Mike Umburger handle it?"

"Nope, he's on medical leave as of yesterday."

Great. "Yes, sir, I'll meet you there. Where?"

"The Palmetto Deaf School. Some lunatic's taken a teacher and some students hostage."

He did a one-eighty, praying he'd be there in time. Dread left him. Sheer nauseating terror took its place.

Marianna hovered near her desk, signing for the students to stay calm, watching the intruder's every move, desperately fighting her own escalating horror. Effortlessly, he'd yanked the door from her hand, stormed in and shoved her back against the whiteboard, bruising her shoulder in the process. He had pulled the door shut behind him.

Then locked it.

The ski mask covered his face. Intense blue eyes peered at her from the slits, his nose covered, his mouth a mere outline under the cloth. She watched the outline move. Shaking, she backed up. Knowing her voice wobbled, she told him, "I know you're saying something, but if I can't see your mouth, I can't read your lips."

He made a motion with a gloved hand—the universal sign for scissors. Marianna swung around and got a pair from her desk. What did he want to use them for? A weapon?

But he already had a gun.

Motioning for her to back up, he grabbed the mask, stuck the scissors in the material where his mouth was and started cutting, making an opening and snipping out a large portion that revealed the lower part of his face, which consisted of firm lips and a strong, freshly shaven jaw.

"Wh-what do you want?"

Still not speaking, he tucked the cutaway cloth into his back pocket and jammed the scissors into the potted plant soil behind him.

Oh, dear Lord, please help us.

Thus far, the man hadn't said a word, at least not one that she'd heard or been able to read; he had merely gestured with the gun. Absentmindedly, her senses took in the details. He was tall, at least a little over six feet. Broad shoulders indicated strength she wouldn't want to test. And his scent tickled her nose. Chewing tobacco. It was the same smell she'd noticed the night she'd been attacked in the gym. Along with the odor of cigarettes.

Cold certainty hit her. This was her attacker, the one who'd left the note in her hand telling her he'd be back. He'd picked her. Her classroom. Her school. He'd come here and put all these people in danger. *She'd* put them in danger. Feeling ill, she turned and looked at her beloved students. Fortunately, two of her students were absent today, so she had three regulars and two deaf student tutors.

Josh stared at the man, his features twisted in confusion. Victoria, one of the deaf students who'd come to help tutor, had fear and revulsion emanating from her as she cowered against the bookshelf behind her. But anger, too, glittered in her eyes. Marianna shot her a look that said, "Don't do anything stupid."

Peter had his forehead touching his desk, his hands wrapped around his head, rocking slowly back and forth.

Marianna moved toward him, wanting to offer comfort. The man swung the gun on her. She gasped, backed up, holding her hands up in the universal gesture for surrender.

"What do you want?" she asked him.

Ignoring her, yet keeping the weapon trained on her and the class, he moved to the front of the room. Stepped behind her desk. In a smooth move, he swept the top clean. Marianna flinched. Her purse went sliding, items clattering across the floor.

Next, he pulled the drawers from her desk, rummaging through them then tossing them haphazardly. Still not saying a word.

Glancing around at her terrified students, she signed, "It'll be okay. Just stay calm."

The gun touched her cheek. She froze. Smelled the stale cigarettes again. Turned slowly to see his dark glare. Then he spoke the first words since he'd burst into her classroom. "Don't sign. Understand?"

Marianna nodded, her eyes never leaving his. The eyes of a killer—with a hint of desperation lurking in their depths. She whispered, "Please tell me what you want and I'll give it to you. Anything."

"Sit over there." He gave her a rough shove toward one of the empty student desks. She stepped on an item from her purse, stumbled, grabbed the edge of the chair and sat. He held a hand to his head, looked back at Marianna. "Why is everyone here? No one was supposed to be here."

"Make-up day. It snowed after Christmas so we had to come today."

He kicked a desk and cursed. Then pulled something out of his pocket.

A small plastic bottle full of liquid with wires attaching it to a...cell phone?

Marianna flinched. A bomb of some sort. She'd never

seen one before, but she had watched the news, read books, watched crime shows. She looked around, seeing the students' fear, their horror at the turn their lives had just taken.

Victoria had her arms around Christopher, comforting, patting, her angry gaze never leaving the gunman. Marianna vowed to keep an eye on the hotheaded teen. She tried to communicate with her eyes for Victoria to be still, stay calm. The girl shifted, stuck a hand into her coat pocket. Met Marianna's gaze.

Marianna lifted a brow in a silent question. Victoria pulled her hand back out of her pocket and put her arms back around Christopher, her hands strategically placed, with her right hand covering her left. Marianna caught the sign Victoria subtly sent her. If the man had been watching, he'd have thought Victoria was just shifting her hands, but Marianna knew better.

One word. *Sidekick.*

Oh help. The girl had her Sidekick and could use it practically blindfolded.

Did she dare give Victoria the go-ahead to text a message? But Marianna would have to sign the number to her and pray the girl could enter it in without looking at the screen. Or she could call 911. But she couldn't text 911. Could she?

No, she'd call Ethan to be safe. She gave a small negative shake of her head. Victoria's lips thinned. Under the desk, out of sight of the gunman, who was opening every drawer he could find and dumping the contents onto the floor, she signed, "Wait."

The girl nodded, clearly unhappy at the delay, but at least she obeyed.

Marianna's attention was drawn back to the man who suddenly turned and kicked another unoccupied desk, sending it crashing into the wall. She flinched; Victoria jerked and let out a squeal Marianna couldn't hear but could see escape the girl's lips.

The masked intruder turned back to Marianna, gun waving wildly. "Where is it?" He put the gun to poor Josh's head. "Tell me where it is or I'll blow his brains out."

SIXTEEN

Ethan couldn't get to the school fast enough, his brain snapping with the facts. He had to shove aside the terror he felt because in his gut he knew it was Marianna in danger. She and her students.

Someone had had the gall to enter a building on a busy Monday morning and take a class hostage. Chilled, he tried to analyze what that person must be thinking and feeling.

Someone with nothing to lose. And everything to gain by such a rash act. Desperation shouted. And desperation could lead to deadly action.

Which meant he might never get to tell Marianna he was sorry for asking that stupid question about a cochlear implant; he might not get to hold her in his arms. Never kiss her again. *Please, God...*

Unable to form even the simplest prayer, he just let the Holy Spirit intercede on his behalf. God knew. And God was listening. Shocked, Ethan realized he'd wondered ever since Ashley's death if God really did listen. He'd never had the conscious thought that God was ignoring him, but a smack in the face of self-realization had him newly aware that he'd subconsciously stopped thinking of God as One who hears.

Now, he wanted to know God was listening, that God

heard his frantic prayers for Marianna and the other innocents who were being threatened by this madman.

Please, God...

But better than anyone, Ethan knew that sometimes bad things happened. God allowed innocent people to be hurt. *Please, let this outcome be different.*

Then he was turning back into the school parking lot, his alarm blaring, the lights swirling on the dash. The campus was on lockdown, the entrances barricaded. The main security guard had been replaced by a local police officer, who let Ethan in the minute she saw him heading toward her.

Ethan whipped past the small building; the vast emptiness of the campus and the unnatural stillness during a normally active school day hit him hard. *Lord, it's not right. There should be kids running around here. Please, please protect them.*

Pulling around to Marianna's building, he swung in behind the authorities already there. Along with campus security. He looked around for the person in charge, the one who would be acting as field commander. The police chief had also just arrived and was barking orders into his phone. When he saw Ethan, he motioned him over.

"What do we got?" He tried to stay professional, refusing to let his fear for Marianna and the kids show through.

"The school's on lockdown. Everyone's got their classrooms shut up. He's confined to one room, so unless the guy starts blazing bullets down the hall and into doors, all but the ones in the room with him should be all right for now. We've got guys working their way into the building. They'll try to set up a surveillance system. I want to keep this contained. We've got the outer perimeter established. Now I want the inside done."

"What room is he in?" He already knew the answer,

but couldn't quite help the wave of nausea that swept him when the man pointed to Marianna's window. "That one. We've got a sniper on the roof of the building over there." He gestured behind him. "Guy can see right in, but the teacher's in the way. He's got her sitting in a seat in front of the window. Unfortunately, he's smart."

"Let's pray we're smarter. Has contact been established?"

"Nope. There's no phone in the room. We've got a throw phone but nowhere to throw it." Often when a phone wasn't available in a situation like this, one of the SWAT members would toss a phone to the hostage taker. "I got the teacher's cell number, but she's deaf and hasn't answered it. No answer to my texts either."

But she was alive. He could see her sitting there in plain view, her back to him. Next to her was a male student, probably one of her tutors who came in to help first thing in the morning. The guy may be smart, but he wasn't thinking. He hadn't pulled the blinds yet. "How many in the classroom?"

This wasn't a planned situation. Which meant the guy was trying to think as he went.

"She's got two absent. There are four males and one female student. And the teacher. Marianna Santino."

"All right. We need contact. Also get me the blueprints for this building. I want a microphone and camera in there somehow."

"The boys are working on it. Here's your mic—it's rigged and ready. You say the word and the boys will storm the door. You're the boss here, Ethan. This is what you've been trained for." The man clapped him on the back. "You'll be fine."

So, he hadn't done a very good job of hiding his nerves. Now wasn't the time to think about failure. Failure meant someone would die. And if that happened, they might as well go ahead and dig his grave as well.

Marianna had thrown herself at Josh, wrapping her arms around the boy, who didn't really have a clue he was in danger, and defiantly stared down the man with the gun. She could only pray he couldn't see the sick fear that had her trembling.

His anger was escalating. Not finding what he wanted, he was losing control. But he wouldn't tell her what he was looking for. Every drawer had been pulled out and overturned. Finally, he'd snorted in disgust and moved the gun from Josh.

He was now working on the shelves, pulling stuff off, opening every container, every educational game; he missed nothing. And each time he didn't find what he wanted, he destroyed something else.

And the TV played on above Marianna, creating normalcy where none existed. She wondered if the authorities would soon cut the power. Until then, a commercial depicting Pampers ended and a shot of the two political candidates debating issues flashed. Campaign headquarters celebrated victories. Normal life.

God, please get us back to normal. Safe and normal. But Marianna knew she'd never be the same again.

She shot a glance at Victoria. The girl had sneaked her hand back in her pocket, just waiting for the signal. Marianna gave it to her. While the gunman's back faced her, she quickly signed the first three digits of Ethan's phone number. Victoria moved only a fraction. Marianna blinked—no wonder she'd never caught the girl texting in class. Watching the man move to the next shelf, she waited as he whirled, looked at her, the other students acting like statues, then he went back to his search.

The next four numbers flew from her fingers and Victoria nodded. The number was in. Now for the message:

ONE MAN. MASK. ONE GUN. 9 MM. ONE BOMB. VERY MAD. LOOKING FOR SOMETHING. HE CAN'T FIND IT. HELP PLEASE.

Again, Victoria moved almost imperceptibly, her features paling at the word *bomb,* but didn't stop typing with one hand.

All of a sudden, the man turned toward the window. Victoria froze. He stomped to the window and shoved it open a fraction and listened; then Marianna saw him swear. He turned to her and held out his hand. "Cell phone."

She watched his lips move, but it took a moment for the two words to process. Grabbing her by the arm, he yanked her up, shoving his face closer to hers. "Give. Me. Your. Cell. Phone."

She pulled away. "It…fell on the floor, under my desk when you…" She made the sweeping motion he'd done earlier.

"Get it."

Bending down, she spotted the device—and her can of Mace sitting right beside it.

Ethan held the department cell phone and let Marianna's phone ring, not letting himself think about what he would do if the man refused to talk. Each incident had a personality all its own. There were no absolutes in crisis negotiation. *Help me, God.*

He felt a hand on his shoulder and turned to find Dallas Montgomery standing there. Relief shuddered through him. Backup. Another trained hostage negotiator who could be his secondary, help him out if he needed it.

The phone still rang. Soon it would trip to voice mail.

Then he saw Marianna pulled away from the window. His heart nearly stopped when she disappeared from view. Part of him waited for the sound of the gunshot. He was almost surprised when a voice barked in his ear. "What?"

Ethan's personal cell buzzed on his hip. He ignored it. "Hey, man. My name's Ethan and I'm with the police force here. I've been called in to help with this situation, to see that we can resolve it without anyone getting hurt. Can you help me out?"

Establish contact, offer assistance. The basics of crisis negotiation training.

The phone clicked off.

Ethan growled in frustration. If the man wouldn't talk, Ethan couldn't do his job. And the tactical team made up of SWAT members would have to move in. Which meant Marianna and everyone in the building would be in extreme danger.

One thing Ethan knew he had on his side was time. As long as no one was getting hurt, things could end peacefully.

"Call him back." Dallas started setting up behind him. He'd keep track of the conversation—assuming one happened—and any details he could pick up, offering advice to Ethan as he handled the man.

Dialing the number, Ethan prayed for the man to pick up again. It kept ringing. Then Marianna appeared back in the window, seated once again.

The phone finally clicked. "I'm not talking. Don't call back."

"Wait!"

A sigh. "I'm rather busy. Not in the mood for a chat. *Ciao*."

Click.

Restraining the desire to hurl the phone to the asphalt below, Ethan gripped it until his knuckles turned white.

Dallas shook his head. The big Texan had worry stamped all over his features. "Nothing you can do if he won't talk, Ethan."

Think, think, Ethan.

"He's educated. Cultured."

Dallas nodded. *"Ciao?"*

Ethan's personal phone vibrated that he had a message. Rubbing his forehead, he paced. At the next vibration he snapped the phone out of its case and almost tossed it. Instead, something made him click to see who the message was from.

He didn't recognize the number, but he pressed the button to read it anyway, his mind not on the device in his hands but on how to get the man on the phone and keep him there.

Then the message caught his full attention. And sent fear shuddering through him.

A message from Marianna. Somehow, she'd managed to text him. Probably from a student's phone. He didn't bother questioning how—he was just grateful. But if he responded, would the thing make a noise? He couldn't take a chance, could only hope for periodic updates.

He turned back to Dallas and waved his phone. "I've got contact. One of the students managed a text."

Alarm made Dallas's eyes go wide. "Oh, man, I hope he doesn't catch on to that."

"Yeah. He's got a bomb. We need a bomb squad ASAP."

Dallas immediately got on the radio, calling for the evacuation of the team that had entered the building. They would let the SWAT team go in and remove as many of the hostages that they could reach without the gunman knowing they were in there.

What was this guy thinking? What was he doing? What did he want?

And why wouldn't he talk?

Josh had pushed Marianna away, so she slipped back into her seat, thinking, taking in every detail she could process. She stared at the television. Desperately thinking, praying.

Her cell phone must have rung again, because the gunman pulled it up and pushed a button. Refusing to talk again, Marianna feared. Then he was in her face once again. "Where's that box you keep for that kid Josh?"

"What?"

He gave her a shake and her neck whiplashed back, then forward. She winced. Wanting to shut her eyes and turn from the foul breath on her face, she instead forced herself to watch his lips carefully. "Pay close attention, teacher. Where's the box?"

"That box? This is about that *box?* I don't have it." There was no way she was going to tell him that box was just down the hall in another teacher's classroom. Where another teacher had a roomful of students.

A scream of frustration erupted from him, and Marianna cringed, this time unable to keep her eyes trained on him. He shoved her aside once more, and she fell on the heating/air-conditioning unit under the window. When she looked out, she had the view she'd seen thousands of times over the last few years. Only this time, the entire front part of the building was cordoned off, emergency vehicles surrounding it.

She thought she saw a news camera, various staff members being held back.

And Ethan standing behind a police car was looking up with an expression she'd never seen on his face before.

Sheer terror.

Ethan pushed the raging fear down. Shoved aside the visions of the gun going off and Marianna…

No, he had to focus, to do his job. Pray as if he'd never prayed before. She'd appeared for an instant. He'd seen her come flying against the window. She must have made the guy mad, and if he refused to answer the cell one more time, things were going to have to change. His commander would pull rank and force an entrance.

Ethan didn't want to see that. There had to be a better way. Dallas clapped his shoulder, pulled the blueprints over and pointed out entry points. Kevin, head of campus security, came over. "Can I help in any way?"

Dallas showed him the blueprints. "We've got guys stationed here and here with rifles ready to take him out as soon as we get the word, but he's staying out of the line of fire. As long as everyone else stays in their classrooms, they should be fine. There's no way for him to enter the way they're set up. Our problem is getting into the room this guy's in. Only one entryway. A very small window opening. Not advantageous for us, for sure."

"You'll have to wait him out." Kevin shook his head.

"And we can't get the camera in because of the bomb threat." Ethan said.

"Bomb squad's on the way. SWAT team just arrived."

Ethan rubbed a hand over his jaw and glanced back up at the window, pulled out the official cell and dialed Marianna's number again.

Marianna watched the intruder alternate between swearing and pacing. Then he pulled her phone from his pocket and slapped it to his ear. "Not talking." He hung up and looked at Marianna. "You're lying."

She swallowed hard. *Lord, Jesus, what do I do?*

Slowly, with even, measured steps, he walked over to stand in front of her. "You're lying, and if you don't start talking, I'm going to start shooting." He moved the gun around, "Now, who do you want to be first?"

Victoria cringed. Marianna wanted to scream. Josh just watched with a confused expression on his face. Peter still had his head down, and Christopher kept his face buried in Victoria's arms.

Marianna lifted her chin. "I might have an idea where it could possibly be. If you'll let them go, I'll tell you."

He laughed. "You're not in a bargaining position."

"But we have to move. If you would just let them go and keep me, it'll be a lot simpler."

He studied her, then cursed when the phone rang again. But he picked it up, and listened and then said, "Yeah, I want something. I want a million bucks and to live in the Hamptons, but it's not happening right now."

A pause.

"I tell you what—I'll let all the kids go. Every last one of them. Get everyone out of the building. Except this room."

Another pause.

"I don't care about those kids. I don't want to hurt them. I just need—" he snapped his mouth shut, then continued "—get 'em out, but if I see one uniform in here, I'll start sending out bodies—or just blow the place up."

Hope blossomed in her chest. Why the sudden turnabout? Had she managed to convince him? She looked over at Victoria to see if the girl had caught any of the conversation. She had her eyes on Marianna. Marianna gave her a slight shrug and shook her head. No more texting. Not yet.

What did he need with Josh's box? And how did he even

know about it? What had Josh put in there that would cause someone to take an entire building hostage?

Ten minutes later, to her relief, through the slim side window next to her door, Marianna could see the students and teachers filing past. The gunman simply watched the commotion from his perch on her stool, his little bomb sitting on the smaller desk situated in front of the whiteboard.

Victoria shifted restlessly. Peter still had his head down, refusing to look up. Marianna worried about the long-term effects this would have on him. He was such a sensitive boy. But she couldn't think about that now. She had to stay calm and cool, think about what she could do to help the authorities get them out of this.

The gunman stood. She tensed. He moved the pistol her way. She flinched. "Now it's our turn. Get those kids out of here."

Ethan watched the steady stream of students and staff flow from the building and be pulled behind the police line into the safe zone. The SWAT team kept it efficient as several others entered the building and swept the rooms they could get to without being seen from the gunman's room. As the newly released hostages entered the zone, officers patted down each person and checked IDs. Couldn't be too careful. The principal had been called up to identify each and every person exiting the building as an added precaution.

Two students followed who made Ethan's breath hitch in his throat. He recognized them as students from Marianna's classroom. He spoke into his radio. "Hey, what's the classroom looking like?"

"He had the teacher pull the blinds."

Ethan sent up a swift prayer. Every hostage situation had its own dynamics, but this…this one was driving him nuts; it was so totally off the charts in the crisis negotiation arena. The process wasn't working; following procedure was netting him zilch. He was going to have to go with his gut.

"Chief, I suggest sending the bomb squad in there. I only received one text message, and the guy won't stay on the phone. This feels…weird. This isn't a normal hostage situation. Something tells me this guy hadn't planned on a bunch of people being here today." He shook his head, praying he was making the right decision. He looked his chief in the eye. "Send the team in. Now."

The man stared at Ethan for a brief moment, searching for something and seeming to find it. He nodded and trotted off. Ethan spun on his heel and approached the student he thought was named Peter and signed, "Can you tell me anything about Marianna?"

The boy covered his head and shook. Ethan backed away, sorrow filling him. How had these kids lives been changed? How much damage would this do to them? Fury filled him and he vowed to get this guy.

A hand touched his arm. A dark-headed girl signed, "I'm Victoria. I was in the classroom with Ms. Santino. She told the man she'd show him where something he was looking for was. And she'd show him how to get out of the building if he'd let us go. He did, and I saw him pull her out of the classroom."

Ethan's earpiece crackled; then a voice said, "Classroom is empty. Bomb squad's working on the bomb. Guy's got the teacher and is on the run!"

Ethan swung back toward the girl. "Do you know where she would take him?"

Victoria shrugged, worry pulling her brows toward the bridge of her nose. "No. There's no way out except this door and the one on the other end. Oh, and the one door upstairs."

Ethan envisioned where he had men stationed. All those doors were covered. If the guy so much as stuck his head out, a sniper would put a bullet in it.

He looked around, then back at the building. All students and staff were accounted for—except Marianna and the gunman.

Marianna stumbled along after her captor. She debated taking him down to Cleo's classroom but knew as soon as she gave him what he wanted, she was dead.

Quickly, she'd said, "I don't have what you're looking for. But I might be able to help you find it. There are a couple of places it could be."

"Shut up," he'd snarled. But Marianna persisted.

"I'll help you search the entire building, plus I know another way out, a way past the police. I promise." Another question struck her. Why did he have a bomb with him if he'd thought the building would be empty?

Cold chills broke out over her flesh as she answered her own question. Because if he didn't find what he was looking for, he would blow the place up and leave absolutely no trace of it, just in case it *was* here and he didn't find it. Which meant he couldn't take a chance on someone seeing it.

"I don't have time to search this building. As soon as they realize we're not in that classroom, they're going to swarm this place." His gaze narrowed, "Now find it so I can get out of here."

Her heart fluttered in fear. She started to speak when he flinched. She wondered what he had heard. He grabbed her arm. "Someone's coming." He pulled her around, his blue eyes glittering down into hers, his mouth tight as he demanded, "Get me out of here or I'll blow you away right now...and anyone else I come across, got it?"

"Yes." She shook. He was serious. He wouldn't have any reservations about shooting her. But he needed her right now. She took a deep breath. "Follow me."

"What a waste of..." he muttered. "I can't believe this has...all this trouble for a stupid box that's possibly not even here."

Marianna watched his face, his lips move, the shape of his jaw, the outline of his lips, the slight tilt to his head. And blinked. Could it be? No, no way.

But she knew it was. A deaf person was very aware of body language, and his just shouted his identity.

Shock and disbelief racked her.

She knew him. Knew who this man holding the gun was.

Her mind sputtered, stalled. How? Why?

Her danger meter just rang off the charts. If caught, this man had a lot to lose. And Marianna knew he had no intention of being caught.

And if he realized she knew his identity, she was as good as dead.

Against his boss's wishes, Ethan ran into the building, ordering, "Don't come after me until I call for help. If we all descend on him, he'll kill her."

"Ethan, you're going to get yourself killed." Victor's voice came through loud and clear, but Ethan's focus was on Marianna's safety, not his own. He darted down to the classroom and screeched to a halt. Empty. Just as he'd been told. Where would they go? The roof?

No. As clear as if Marianna had whispered it in his ear, he knew.

The basement.

But no exit door had been shown on the blueprints. He'd specifically looked to see if he needed coverage on one. Why would she go down there? She'd have no way of getting out. Cold terror swept his insides. Marianna was sacrificing herself for her students.

Probably trying to buy some time. Did she have a plan? Did she think she could get away from the guy while down in the basement? Or did she know something he didn't?

Spinning from the door, Ethan headed for the steps that would lead him down. With fingers wrapped around his gun, he kept his focus, his senses tuned to the atmosphere around him.

I'm coming, Marianna, I'm coming.

Marianna felt her ankle twist in the dimly lit area as she maneuvered over and around the accumulation of *stuff.* The basement held tons of storage from years past. File cabinets littered the area along with boxes of long forgotten books, paper, files. A path had been cut through the mess, and she knew this was because maintenance workers had to get down here occasionally to work. Or flip a switch in the breaker box. Her left hand caught on a stack of files, sending them to the floor.

Her captor didn't stop, just tugged her along. She had to figure out a way to get away from the man, who kept a tight grip on her upper right arm. If she could get free and could get to the Mace she had in her front right pocket...

But he hadn't let go of her arm.

Please, Jesus, help me. Let me have a clear mind, be smart.

Think, Marianna. Look around you. Get away from him.

But there was no way. He yanked her around to face

him. "Show me. I need out of here, now. There's no way I'm getting caught, you understand?"

She nodded, her brain humming. He just needed to let go of her. And if she couldn't get to the little canister in her pocket, she needed some other kind of weapon. Meeting his eyes, she shivered at the coldness there. Death stared back at her.

Swallowing hard, she pointed to the back. He pushed her on, over to the window with the broken latch. She had discovered it just a couple of weeks ago when she'd followed a stray cat who'd recently given birth. The cat had slipped inside, and Marianna knew she had kittens she was taking care of.

She'd planned to report it to the maintenance department but had wanted to give the kittens time to grow a bit before they were forced from their home. Now, perhaps her compassionate nature might be the deciding factor in whether this man let her go or shot her.

Depending on if he thought he could fit through the window.

Marianna doubted he could fit but hoped he would try. Maybe it would give her a chance to run, since she feared he would not let her go once he had his escape down. She shuddered. As soon as he was distracted, she needed to be able to act immediately, needed to be quick and smart.

Please give me an opening, just a chance to get away.

She was going to use the fact that she knew the layout of the basement much better than he. If she could just get out of his sight, she might have a chance. But as long as he kept a hand clamped on her arm, she wasn't going anywhere.

Her eyes darted. The lighting was poor, but maybe that could work to her advantage also.

If she could get away, she could hide somewhere—behind the massive number of bookshelves, a filing cabinet; anything would do.

When he shoved her in front of him, she stumbled, her knee banging the side of a file cabinet. Pain shot up her leg, but she ignored it. That was minor when compared with the bullet she felt quite sure was waiting for her as soon as he decided he didn't need her anymore.

"Here." She pointed to the window that sat at face level. He pulled her back, moved her to his right side and gripped her upper left arm with his right hand this time. With the gun, he reached up and shoved the window open. It slapped back down, and he turned back to Marianna.

The voice growled, "Sit there." His lips curved into a cruel smile as he shoved her onto a sturdy wooden crate.

She sat.

Breathing a prayer of thanks, she shoved her right hand into her front pocket. Fingers curled around the can of Mace just as he swung the gun around to aim it point-blank at her heart.

Ethan stepped lightly down the steps, his gun gripped tight in his right hand, his eyes finally adjusting to the darker environment. He heard scrapes, a thud, come from up ahead. The radio crackled in his ear, but he didn't dare answer. Right now, he figured the guy probably thought no one knew where he was. And he sure didn't want to tip off the attacker to the contrary. He kept his breathing shallow, ignored the adrenaline infusing him.

Move slow; move smart. Don't dwell on the fear that if you fail, she'll die.

He couldn't stop the mental picture of him screaming, of Ashley never knowing he called her name, of Ashley being hit by the car, flying through the air. His feelings of helplessness, horror, the crippling guilt that he couldn't protect her.

But now Marianna needed him. He breathed deeply. He ordered himself, to focus, keep it together. *Lord, I need You.*

Three more steps brought him to the bottom of the staircase. Breathing through his nose, he held himself still, tuned his ears to the slightest sound.

Nothing. He kept moving, heard a whisper, felt the chill of musty air brush by like a swish of evil against his face. He shivered, not from the cold but from the oppressiveness he felt. In his mind he quoted every verse he could think of. *I will never leave you nor forsake you. Lo, I am with you always, even unto the end of the earth. Trust in Me. I am the way, the truth and the light.*

Moving forward, he kicked up some papers in the middle of the path. He stepped over them, wishing he could see who he was tracking.

Another slight sound from his left reached his ears, then a single word. "Here." Slowly, he crept forward. One foot after the other until his foot came down on something soft. The yowling screech nearly took his head off, and the bite of sharp claws sank into his left calf.

Marianna knew if she moved a scant millimeter, the man would pull the trigger. Hardly daring to breathe, she watched his eyes. Knew when he'd made the decision. Knew she was on her way to meet face-to-face the God she loved. His finger curled around the trigger.

Lord, I can't give up without a fight. Please let me live to love Ethan.

Her hand gripped the canister. She refused to sit obediently while he blew her away.

A fleeing ball of fur caught her eye just as his focus

swung from her to behind him, his attention diverted, his eyes off her. Marianna dove to the left, pulled the Mace from her pocket and aimed it at his eyes, which were now back on her.

She held her breath and squeezed. Liquid squirted, covering his eyes and his nose, soaking the cloth still covering his face. As though she were in slow motion, she could see his mouth working, could see him stumble away, clawing his face with his free hand. The hand that held the gun jerked toward the ceiling, and she saw the flash of the bullet exiting the barrel.

Then she was back in real time, scrambling from her position on the floor, hurrying away from the man who wanted her dead, her mind looping a prayer: *Please, Jesus, please!*

With her heart thudding painfully in her chest, she moved fast, her elbow catching the edge of something hard, which sent shooting pains into her shoulder. Panting, she followed the trail she'd just walked with the man behind her. Any minute now, she expected to feel a bullet blast into her back. Still, she skirted the debris, maneuvered through file cabinets, boxes. The floor thumped behind her. A bullet pinged from the pole beside her.

She screamed and jerked sideways, tripped and fell.

SEVENTEEN

An agonized cry sounded and chilled Ethan's soul. It echoed madness, fury, murder. Marianna had done something to make the man *very* mad. That was definitely not a good thing. Ethan's heart nearly stopped when he heard the whine and clang of the bullet. Marianna's responding scream froze him for a brief second; then he picked up the pace and headed toward her. He wanted to hurry, to burst on the scene and grab her away.

Still, caution reigned. If he went and got himself shot, he wasn't going to be much help for her. He had to get to her, had to save her. The responsibility weighed heavily on his shoulders as his prayers to God continued.

As he swept the basement with his eyes, his senses, the acid in his stomach churned, ate at him. What if he couldn't save her? What if he failed again? The what-ifs could haunt him.

But God was still in control.

If someone had landed a punch on his jaw, he wouldn't have been more stunned.

It wasn't up to Ethan.

It was up to God.

He swung the gun to the right. Someone still thrashed

ahead. Another gunshot, the bullet grazing the ceiling above him. He ducked.

God was in control.

Ethan was only a tool.

Marianna's life was in God's hands. Not Ethan's.

The realization scared him to death…and freed him all at the same time. What if God chose to let Marianna die at the hands of the man who had her, the man who still screamed obscenities and threats?

Please, Lord, use me. I believe prayer changes things. I know You don't need me, but use me to save her.

Closer, closer to the noise. Where are you, Marianna?

A shuffle to his left. He whirled and stared into Marianna's shocked, fear-filled eyes; then something hit him in the left shoulder, spinning him around to crash against a file cabinet. Again, Marianna's scream echoed around him.

He looked down to see a small stain growing larger. Then searing pain hit him. Marianna grabbed his hand and pulled him behind the makeshift wall of shelves where she'd been hiding. Then the shelves parted, crashing to the ground, and the masked gunman stood, his weapon trained on them. Marianna squealed and Ethan thought she sounded more angry than scared.

The man's blue eyes, rimmed in red, ran with tears—and glittered with rage. Ethan held his gun on him. "Drop it," he ordered.

A guttural laugh scraped Ethan's ears. Then to his horror and fury, the man turned his gun on Marianna and said, "*You* drop it."

Cold fear settled in the pit of Ethan's stomach. If he dropped the gun, they were dead. If he took a chance and shot the man, the guy might get a shot off and Marianna would be dead regardless.

Please, Lord, a little help.

* * *

Marianna knew Ethan would drop his weapon to save her. She couldn't let that happen. He already looked pale, his breathing coming in shallow spurts, the stain on his shoulder growing by the minute. The gunman stared at her, and she swallowed at the evil emanating from him. She'd really made him angry with the Mace stunt. Terror washed over her, and she considered her options.

"Don't drop that gun, Ethan." She knew her voice shook but didn't care. The look on his face said he felt he had to protect her, that if something happened to her, he'd never live through it. Not after what had happened to Ashley.

"Why?" Ethan's simple question caught the man's attention.

He blinked. "What?"

"Why? What do you want?"

A delaying tactic.

"I don't have time to explain my reasons to you. Now either drop the gun or she dies."

She blurted, "He wants Josh's box."

The man gritted his teeth. "Shut up." His finger tightened on the trigger, then Marianna felt herself flying through the air, heard the crack of a gun. Fear cramped her as she heard another loud pop, then gave a grunt as she landed with a thump in a pile of files.

"Ethan!"

No sooner had his name left her lips than SWAT members and local police flooded the place. The gunman lay face-down, screaming his anger, with cuffs encircling each wrist, a steady flow of blood pumping from his right hand. Ethan sagged against a pole, pale, shaken, with a hand pressed against his left side. Blood seeped between his fingers. Marianna scrambled out of the files, ignoring the cloud of dust that hovered around her and scooted over to Ethan. "Ethan, oh, no. You've been shot again."

He grimaced, reached for her and pulled her down to lay a kiss on her lips. When he moved back, he groaned. "I promised myself I was going to do that if you were all right. Are you all right?"

She nodded, tears clogging her throat.

"Then that's all that matters. I can die a happy man now." He gave her a weak grin and she shuddered.

"What on earth are you talking about?"

"I kissed you again. I can die happy now."

Paramedics began easing him into a horizontal position. Marianna wanted to slug him…and kiss him again. "You'd better not die on me. You've got a lot to live for."

He looked into her eyes, and she could see the emotion behind them. "I'm sorry for what I said in the car…about the cochlear…"

This time it was Marianna who leaned down and kissed him. "Don't worry about it. I was just a little sensitive about the issue."

Her heart hurt at the relief she saw flood his face. Then his eyes turned to the still masked gunman. "Who is he?"

She gave a shudder. "Steven Marshbanks, campaign manager for the man who'll probably be the next governor of South Carolina."

Ethan's eyes went wide; then he passed out.

When Ethan wakened, the first thing he noticed was the ache in his shoulder and the fire in his side. The second thing was the beautiful woman sleeping on the couch beside him. Shifting, he grunted at the shaft of pain, but Marianna didn't stir. The door swooshed open and a woman in a white lab coat entered. "Hello, Mr. O'Hara, and welcome back to consciousness."

The stirring of the air must have swept over Marianna, because her eyes popped open and she sat up. Immediately her gaze darted to Ethan and a warmth he'd never felt before coursed through him as he saw the relief in her eyes that he was safe.

And would live.

She gave him a tentative smile. "I'll wait outside if you like."

The doctor glanced at the chart, then looked at Marianna. "That's all right. Mr. O'Hara will be staying with us one more night. If all goes well, he'll be released to head home tomorrow. The bullet in his shoulder passed clean through, causing only some minor damage. The bullet in his side just creased it." She gave him a pointed look. "You are one very lucky man."

He looked at Marianna. "The luckiest."

Then the doctor said to Marianna, "He's healing nicely, and as long as he doesn't overdo it, he will be good as new in a couple of months."

The doctor left and Marianna turned to say something to him, but before she had a chance, the door opened and Victor, Ethan's boss, entered. "Ethan, glad to see you awake. I do appreciate you not dying on me as I need some details filled in on this blank report."

A grin stretched across Ethan's lips. "Good to see, you too, Chief. Try to go easy on the sympathy, will you?"

Victor's expression softened for a fraction of a second. "Glad you're all right, man. We let your parents know what happened. They said they'd stop by shortly."

"Thanks." He wondered if they would, though. Not wanting to dwell on that topic, he said, "So, fill us in. What was so important that Steven Marshbanks risked his career, his life and everything he holds dear to get his hands on?"

Victor nodded toward Marianna. "She gave us the box

that he seemed to be after. Apparently, Josh snatched a flash drive with a lot of incriminating evidence."

"Really? What was on it?"

"An entire list of campaign contributors, the amounts they gave…and where the funds went, a lot of personal spending, bank account numbers, investments—all kinds of stuff."

"Whoa. Where did the funds go?"

Victor grunted. "A lot of places they shouldn't have. And we played a little game with Gerald Chambers. When we told Gerald we had Steven Marshbanks in custody and the man was casting all the blame on him, the boy sang like Tweety."

"What did Chambers have to do with Marshbanks?"

Victor leaned against the edge of the bed, and Marianna spoke for him. "The three of them were all connected, weren't they? Roland Luck, Gerald Chambers and Steven Marshbanks."

"Yep." Victor nodded and Ethan tried to put it all together, but his brain felt a big foggy. He blamed it on the pain meds, not the woman who'd walked up and taken hold of his hand.

"So?"

"So," Marianna said, thoughtfully, "Roland Luck came across the evidence. As the campaign manager, he would have to keep an accounting of the money, know where it was spent, and so forth."

Victor nodded. "Right. Apparently, he noticed something amiss and did a little digging, trying to figure out what was going on. He copied the stuff to a flash drive and took it home with him on a weekend visit to his parents."

Ethan chimed in. "That must have been what he was looking for when he went by his parents' house in the middle of the week. And when he didn't find it, he realized Josh must have snatched it and taken it to school."

"He actually searched your classroom, Marianna," Victor said, "but you never realized it."

"I knew someone had messed with my desk that morning! It was the week after Suzanne's funeral. I went back to work and my desk had been rearranged...everything was...off."

Ethan's lips tightened at the thought of the invasion of her privacy...her classroom, her home...her life. "When he didn't find it there, he went to your house."

"Suzanne," Marianna said, breathing.

Victor nodded. "That was pure accident, we believe. Roland figured the house would be empty for a while, but Suzanne walked in on him. It scared him. She started screaming at him, she grabbed for the phone to call the police and he shoved her. She fell, hit her head and bled to death."

Tears leaked down Marianna's cheeks. "It's all so needless. If she'd stayed at work, she'd still be alive."

Ethan shook his head and squeezed Marianna's hand. He looked at Victor. "So, I'm guessing it's not a coincidence that Roland Luck died in that car accident."

"Nope. We're pretty sure that was a setup. Failed brakes on a steep, winding mountainous road." He shook his head. "Steven Marshbanks arranged the meeting for the campaign coordinators and volunteers. At the top of the mountain. He cut the brake line. Luck got in the car, started down and ended up over the side. Poor guy never had a chance. He was just trying to figure out where the money was going and who was behind the theft of it. So he broke into Marianna's house to find the drive, caused Suzanne's death—and ended up dead himself for his efforts."

"And Marshbanks is spilling all this?"

Victor shrugged. "Hey, we got him for kidnapping, attempted murder, and every other charge you can possibly think of. I think we can even get him for a terrorist act because of the bomb he brought into the school. Against his lawyer's advice, this guy is talking faster than we can listen, trying to cut a deal."

"Okay, Roland killed Suzanne by accident." Ethan mused. "Then Gerald was the one in Marianna's house that night she called me."

"Yeah, the DNA evidence showed us that, plus, he finally confessed. It seems that Roland was so riddled with guilt about what he'd done to Suzanne that he went back and told Marshbanks all about it, including the fact that Roland suspected Clayton Robertson was helping himself to campaign funds."

Marianna took over, thinking out loud. "But it wasn't Clayton. It was Marshbanks—the very man Roland took into his confidence."

"Which is why Roland ended up dead. Marshbanks realized Roland had the evidence but had lost it, couldn't find it at your house.... So, Marshbanks had to get his hands on that flash drive—and fast."

"Which is why he came after me—or rather, Josh's box. He figured I'd put it where I always did. When I didn't send it home as usual, he came after it. And he probably didn't want to call asking for it because he didn't want to draw attention to it. What if I'd been the kind of person who'd look at it? No, he couldn't risk that." Marianna's shoulders drooped. "But how did Marshbanks and Gerald Chambers get together?"

Victor held up a finger. "That one took a bit of work. Roland Luck, Steven Marshbanks and Chase Chambers, Gerald's father, were all in the army together and big buddies for years. Marshbanks knew he couldn't have too many unexplained absences with all the campaigning going on, so he hired Gerald to do some of his dirty work for him. That kid's been in trouble since he got caught with a knife in elementary school. Marshbanks knew this and was able to talk him into breaking into Marianna's house by promising him big bucks and a huge political future. Gerald was dumb enough to fall for it. If he hadn't been caught, I can guarantee you, Gerald would be dead right now."

"At Steven Marshbanks's hand."

Ethan watched Marianna's brain clicking, absorbing the information. He said, "So when Gerald was arrested and the flash drive was still missing, Steven couldn't take a chance on hiring someone else and had to come and do the dirty work himself."

Marianna shook her head. "Only he never expected to run into a campus full of people. But why not wait? Why take a building full of hostages?"

"Greed," Victor said. "On that flash drive was vital information with a deadline. He had to have it for some investment deal or he would have been out millions of dollars."

"It wasn't on the computer Roland Luck copied it from?"

"Apparently not. I think Roland realized to some extent what was going on and in a fit of pique erased a lot of the information, and Marshbanks didn't know how to get it back. A computer forensics person probably would know, but he couldn't exactly ask for help on that. So his only hope was that flash drive."

Ethan leaned his head back and closed his eyes. Exhaustion swamped him. He looked back up at his boss. "Thanks, Victor."

Victor clapped him on the shoulder. "You did a good job, Ethan. You called everything just right at the school hostage scene. You should feel proud of yourself."

Emotion clogged his throat. "I'm just glad no one else got hurt."

Victor turned toward the door, saying, "I'll see you when the doctor releases you back to work."

"I'll be back sooner than you think."

"Ha!" Marianna snorted. "I'll add that to my list of things to discuss with you."

Ethan raised a brow, loving the fire that lit her eyes from the inside. "My pleasure, ma'am, my pleasure."

Marianna couldn't believe everything that had happened in the last twenty-four hours. Incredibly, she felt at peace. About everything. Naturally, she felt sorrow at the death of her friend, the trauma her students had suffered and the destructive greed leading people to make decisions that would negatively impact so many lives.

But for her, peace reigned. God was in control. He'd protected her and her students—and used this wonderful man to do so.

"Mom wants you to come to the house when you're released from the hospital."

Ethan kept a grip on her hand, his thumb rubbing back and forth across her knuckles, causing shivers to dance along her nerves. The light in his eyes spoke about feelings he hadn't allowed to cross his lips yet. She kicked herself. Why had she ever compared this man to Curt Wentworth? The two were as different as night and day.

But she'd been so hurt by Curt that she'd allowed it to blind her to Ethan's true motives. Good motives. She'd been looking at him suspiciously because of one warped experience, and she'd been wrong.

He said, "I appreciate that, but I don't want to put her out."

"She'll be put out if you turn her down." She frowned

at him. "And then I'll get grilled about why I couldn't talk you into coming. So, plan on it, okay?" He pulled her down to sit on the bed beside him, wincing only a little as the bed shifted. She hurt for him. Marianna bit her lip, fought more tears and said, "You saved my life."

The simple words provoked tears. She watched him look to the ceiling, blink them back. "No, I finally came to the realization that I am powerless…except for the power of God."

"You pushed me out of the path of the gun and got shot. You saved me."

He nodded. "I can't explain to you what I was going through in that basement. The whole time I was looking for you, I felt helpless, yet I was praying."

"And God was listening."

"Yes. He used me to help you, and I feel—" he took a deep breath and let it out "—free, I guess, is the word."

"Ashley's death was a horrible, horrible thing, but it wasn't your fault."

His grip tightened for a brief moment. "You can read me like a book, can't you?"

She looked him in the eye. "I love you, Ethan."

Shock flashed back at her—and something else. Pleasure? She couldn't be sure, but she didn't regret saying the words. He opened his mouth, but she placed a finger over his lips. "Shush. You don't have to say the words back to me. They don't come with a required response. They come from my heart, and I wanted you to know."

Funny, she didn't feel embarrassed that she'd told him, nor self-conscious. Once again, Ethan started to say something, then snapped his mouth shut and turned his attention to the door. She understood. Someone had knocked.

The door opened and a nice-looking couple in their early sixties entered.

Ethan's parents.

Marianna stood. "I'll give you some privacy."

He grabbed her hand. "Stay."

Curious looks from both newcomers sent her blushing, but she did her best to ignore it and smiled, holding out a hand. "Hello, I'm Marianna Santino."

"Liam and Margaret O'Hara." The big man who looked like an older version of Ethan gripped her hand in his. "Nice to meet you."

Ethan's mother nodded to Marianna, but her focus was clearly on the man in the bed.

Ethan blinked at the concern in his mother's eyes. He hadn't seen her in almost three months, since right around Thanksgiving when they'd informed him they'd be taking a monthlong cruise for the holidays.

Her fingers curled around his, and she said, "Oh Ethan, we were so worried. Are you all right?"

"Worried?"

Hurt flickered. "Of course. When a mother gets news that her son's been shot, she tends to worry a little."

"Like you worried about Ashley?"

The woman closed her eyes, took a deep breath. "We were wrong in the way we dealt with Ashley, Ethan. I'm so sorry. If we had it to do over again, we'd do it differently, oh, so differently."

He nearly fell out of the hospital bed. She was apologizing? Never before could he remember his mother saying she was sorry. He looked up at his father, stunned to see the man nodding. His dad swallowed hard and said, "After Ashley died, you kept yourself so aloof, so distant from us that we just figured you needed your space and time to deal with your grief the way you needed to. Unfortunately, that distance kept growing, and we've only just now come to understand that we should have done more, been there for you."

Shocked, Ethan's gaze darted between these strangers who were his blood relatives. "What made you come to that realization?"

"Your mom found Ashley's diary while cleaning up after Ashley...died. She wrote over and over about how she wanted us to come to know the Lord the way she did. She even wrote, 'Whatever it takes, Lord, whatever it takes.'"

Tears flowed freely. "How could we ignore what we decided was her dying wish? So, we started investigating the church and everything she held dear...and came to realize that God is who He says He is and we wanted to follow Him."

Marianna subtly placed a tissue box where Ethan's mother could reach it. The woman took a tissue, dabbed her eyes and gave an elegant sniff. Ethan sat stunned. Ashley's death had brought his parents to the saving love of Christ.

He wished it could have happened differently but knew Ashley wouldn't have had it any other way. She'd been on fire for her God, and it had brought about the results she wanted most. She'd made her mark on her world.

God had taken something horrible and used it for something wonderful. He closed his eyes and let the peace flow through him. *Thank you for the gift of forgiveness. I think I can finally forgive myself.*

Ethan opened his eyes and looked at Marianna noticing her tears. And felt love, peace and acceptance finally flow through him. God was good—always had been, always would be. Even in the midst of pain and heartache. Especially then.

His mother patted his hand and stood. "We'll go now. I hope you'll come home to our house to recuperate."

Ethan's eyes sought Marianna's, and she offered him

a small smile and a nod. Her mother would understand. "Sure, Mom, thanks." He cleared his throat but couldn't seem to get rid of the knot there. Then his parents were gone, and he held his hand out to Marianna.

"So, do you think you might want to go out with me?"

She met his eyes and grinned.

Simultaneously, they burst into laughter, Ethan wincing at the sting the motion produced, but ignoring it, willing to suffer anything in order to see her face creased with joy. Then she leaned down and planted her lips against his, and all was right with his world.

EPILOGUE

Four months later, Marianna packed the final box and stored it on the shelf. The last day of school had come and gone for the students, and today meant one more year of teaching under her belt. But that wasn't what had the excitement dancing within her. Ethan had promised her a drive up to the mountains of North Carolina.

Suddenly, warm hands covered hers and she jumped, startled but not scared. "I didn't hear you come in." A familiar wet nose nudged the bare calf not covered by the denim knee-length shorts she'd donned this morning. "You brought Twister!"

The hands fell away and he pulled her around to face him, once more allowing her the privilege of looking into his flashing blue eyes. She smiled, leaning forward to place a light kiss on his lips. He pulled her close for a squeeze then set her back. "Yep. I figured he might as well join us. He's a service dog and has the privilege of going anywhere we go. Now, you're the last one here except maintenance and security personnel. Are you ready to get going?"

"Definitely."

They'd planned to drive up tonight, tour Biltmore House, then have dinner in the main dining room. Ethan was going all out. Biltmore wasn't inexpensive. A new joy emanated from him, and Marianna reveled in it. Not that he would miss Ashley in the years to come, but at least he'd finally made his peace with his sister's death. He was also well on his way to building a lasting, loving bond with his parents and Marianna thrilled at the fact that her own parents had grown to love this man as one of their own.

And he loved her.

She knew he did—his every action shouted it; he just hadn't said the words. But it would come. She just wished he would hurry up with it.

They left the building and climbed into his car, Twister settling himself into the backseat, tongue lolling from the side of his mouth. He'd recovered well.

Marianna silently said her goodbyes to the campus she wouldn't see until fall. Which was fine with her. As much as she loved her job, summer was the best perk the educational business offered.

Conversation flowed, yet underneath the easy words Marianna sensed an anticipation, an edginess about Ethan, and she wondered at it. They'd been on several day trips since he'd gotten out of the hospital and recovered, but this felt different. More exciting.

She shrugged. He'd tell her what was going on when he was ready.

The time flew and it seemed as if hardly any time had passed and they were already pulling into the gated grounds after a short stop to let Twister take care of his business. As they drove along the marked drive, they finally came to the spot to park. When Marianna opened the door, Twister bounded out and she snapped the leash on him and placed the badge on him that identified him as a service dog. Immediately, he settled into work mode and heeled by her left leg.

Ethan came around to take her right hand, and together the trio made their way to the large mansion just ahead.

After a whirlwind tour of the gorgeous interior, Ethan pulled Marianna into the gardens, which contained flowers in full bloom in every color imaginable. "What are you doing?" She laughed at the sneaky look on his face. "Ethan, what are you up to?"

Finger held to his lips, he said, "Shush, follow me."

"But the tour's going that way."

"We're going to have our own tour—now are you with me?" Mischief glinted; his lips twitched to hold in a smile.

"You have a secret." Relenting, her heart racing at what she thought he might be up to, she gave in and followed him through the beautiful Azalea Garden, past the Walled Garden, and into the All-American Rose Garden. The flowers sprang forth, their rich colors surpassing anything she'd ever seen before, every hue, shape and shade. "Oh, Ethan, this is spectacular."

He took Twister's leash from her and dropped it. Twister would stay in that spot until someone picked up the leash handle and led him from it. Then Ethan pulled her close, looked into her eyes and there—with the sun shining down, the scent of roses in the air—said, "Marianna Santino, we've been through an awful lot. God has been so good to see that we've made it to this point. You are the most amazing woman I've ever met. You're loyal, kind, compassionate…."

The flush started up from her neck, and she knew her face would soon rival the red rose she could see over Ethan's shoulder. But there was no way she was going to stop him now. He pushed her hair back around her ear, his fingers grazing the hearing aid. She didn't even flinch. His right hand grasped her left. "Marianna, I know I don't deserve you, but I love you and want to know if you would do me the honor of being my wife?"

A circus of butterflies performed in her stomach, joy nearly caused her heart to explode, tears threatened to fall. She touched a finger to her hearing aid. "I'm bumping up the volume. I don't want to miss a word."

Amusement turned to outright humor, and he threw back his head to laugh. Twister cocked his head and perked his ears. Marianna grinned up at Ethan. "Why don't you repeat that last part to make sure I got it right?"

Laughter still rumbling, he pulled her in close and clamped his lips over hers for a kiss she'd never experienced before, one that left her breathless and yearning for a lifetime of his kisses. When he pulled back, the laughter still lingered, but love, passion and joy simmered in his eyes as well. "I said, you crazy woman, that I absolutely adore you. Will you marry me?"

This time she didn't bother to hold back the tears as she nodded and whispered, "Yes."

Ethan whooped and picked her up to swing in a circle, and Marianna clutched his shoulders, sheer joy running rampant through her. Finally, Ethan settled her back on her feet, kissed her one more time and said, "God is good, isn't He?"

"The best."

Then Ethan reached into his pocket and pulled out a small, square box. Her breath clogged her throat as he opened it and pulled out an exquisite pear-shaped diamond ring. With reverent gentleness, he slid it on the fourth finger of her left hand. A perfect fit.

"How did you know?"

He grinned. "Your mom helped me out."

"My mother knew about this?"

"Yep, your dad, too. I asked him before I asked you."

Another grin slid across his lips. This time it had a bit of smugness to it.

Love filled her. She slid her arms around his neck. "You're incredible. I love you so much, Ethan O'Hara, and I thank God every day that you were there with me during that awful time a few months ago."

His eyes closed. "I never would have wished that time on you, but God brought us through it, taught me lessons I might never have otherwise learned…and bonded us together."

"For always."

"Till death do us part." He leaned down and claimed her lips one more time, sealing the promise to share in the loving, honoring and cherishing.

* * * * *

Dear Reader,

Thank you so much for joining me on Marianna and Ethan's journey. I used to work at our state school for the deaf located here in Spartanburg, South Carolina. Of course I drew upon my experiences there, but I promise, all the characters are completely products of my imagination, as are the activities that take place on the fictional campus.

I know so many wonderful deaf people and love deaf culture and the deaf world so much that I wanted to write about it. Marianna came from a large, protective family that would have allowed her to stay within their loving boundaries, but she was blessed with a streak of independence that enabled her to venture into the world without fear. However, she knew she had the comfort zone of her family to fall back on should she need it. And she did. She also knew God was the one who was going to have to rescue her and keep her safe. Fortunately, He chose to use Ethan to do it. I just love how God allows us to be a part of His master plan, don't you?

I think about this often. I want to make sure that I'm open to what the Lord wants to do with my life, and I pray you do, too!

Thank you again for reading *A Silent Terror*. I would love for you to email me and let me know what you thought about it. You can reach me at lynetteeason.com. I always answer my email personally and find great joy in meeting new people.

I look forward to hearing from you!

God bless,

Lynette Eason

A SILENT FURY

Refrain from anger and turn from wrath; do not fret—
it leads only to evil. For evil men will be cut off, but
those who hope in the Lord will inherit the land.
—*Psalms* 37:8–9

As always, to Jesus Christ.
You are as good as Your Word.

Thanks go out to:

My agent! Tamela, you rock. Thank you for your
unwavering support and belief in my writing.
God bless you!

Thanks to Officer Jim Hall with the ACFW
Carolina Christian Writers group for getting all
my cop stuff right. And if something's not right,
it's my fault!

And once again, I thank my family and friends
for their encouragement and love as I write for
the One who gives me the stories.

ONE

Pack it up, Santino, you've got a murderer and a missing girl to find. His boss's words echoed in his mind as Joseph Santino, Special Agent for the FBI, watched the Greenville-Spartanburg International Airport spread out in tiny detail below him. He'd been fine with the assignment until the man had added, "Oh, and you'll be partnering up with a homicide detective there." He looked down at his papers. "Catelyn Clark."

At that point, Joseph wasn't fine anymore. In fact, he'd done everything to get out of going, short of quitting his job. None of his arguments worked. So, here he was mentally preparing himself to face the one woman he'd never gotten over. The one woman he'd vowed to banish from his thoughts—and failed.

The plane landed, and Joseph grabbed his carry-on, anxious to get this case started so he could get it finished and get back to New York.

An hour and a half later he found himself staring down at the face of a sixteen-year-old girl laid out on the slab in the morgue.

Victim: Tracy Merritt.
Cause of death: blunt-force trauma to the back of the head.

The murder weapon: unknown and still missing.
The suspect: Dylan Carlisle.

Best friend to Joseph's seventeen-year-old brother,
Alonso.

Only the police hadn't arrested Dylan because they
didn't have enough evidence. Yet. Joseph's job was to find
Kelly Franklin, the dead girl's best friend who'd been reported missing the day Tracy's body had been found. It
was suspected that they'd been together and Kelly had been
forcibly removed from the scene. Most likely, by the killer.

What a mess. Joseph sighed and turned away shaking
his head.

His buddy, Victor Shields, captain of criminal investiga-
tions within the local police department, willingly offered
Joseph his services and resources. Joseph had been a uniformed cop under Victor's leadership before moving to the
FBI. About a year after working in New York, Victor had
called him for help. Joseph had responded and found the
man's runaway teenage daughter, bringing her home safely.

Now, business brought Joseph home once again. Only
this time, the missing person hit close to home. A student
at the Palmetto Deaf School, Kelly was not only Dylan's
girlfriend, but she was also a friend of Alonso, Joseph's
deaf brother.

Joseph's heart tightened as he thought about his family.
Having a deaf brother, mother and sister, Joseph, the eldest
of six siblings, had grown up as the protector of the clan.
Active in the deaf community, knowledgeable about the
tight, small world within their own culture, Joseph knew
he was the perfect person for this job. Because he was accepted as part of the deaf world, he could ask questions and
get answers where other hearing cops couldn't. At least not

in a timely manner. And with one girl dead and another missing, time was of the essence.

He looked up at Kip Kennedy, the medical examiner, a balding man in his late fifties Joseph had known from his beat cop days. "I'm going to find out who did this to her."

Kip sighed, shook his head. "I don't know what this world is coming to. Kids dying, teenagers being snatched. It ain't right. Unfortunately, the killer didn't leave his calling card."

"I want to know everything you find on this girl. I don't care if you think it's not important. Okay?"

"Sure. I'll give you everything. I promise." He looked down at the girl who'd never smile, never grow up, never have her own family. "It's the least she deserves, and I'll do my best to give you the tools to find the one who did this to her."

Dead kids tied him in knots. Joseph did his best to shut down emotion and focus on the facts. "Thanks, Kip. I appreciate it."

A young woman in her mid-twenties popped her head in the door. "The Merritt family is here."

Kip nodded, looked up at Joseph and grimaced, his bald head shining in the overhead fluorescent light. "This is the part I really hate."

"Yeah."

Grabbing a lightweight jacket, Detective Catelyn Clark headed back to the Palmetto Deaf School. Tracy Merritt's body had already been removed from the campus and taken to the morgue. As a homicide detective with the Spartanburg police force, Catelyn had been one of the first on the scene. She'd watched the crime-scene investigators do their job and had pitched in where she could. They'd found a baseball jacket and a flip-flop among other things that may or may not be related to the case. The flip-flop had been identified as belonging to Kelly Franklin, the missing girl.

But still, she wanted to go over the scene one more time. Before the yellow tape was removed and the school went back to normal. Her partner, Ethan O'Hara, was away on vacation with his bride of one year. He'd return home tomorrow, but would still have a couple of days off before returning to work. He'd spend them with his wife, Marianna. The man was so happy, it was disgusting. And incredibly sweet. Longing rose up in her, and she immediately vanquished it.

Only one man had ever tempted her to think about the possibility of matrimony, and she'd gotten burned as a result. Two years ago Joseph Santino had been on the verge of asking her to marry him—and she'd been so close to throwing caution to the wind and saying yes. Then she'd found out his true expectations of what he felt a wife should be and she'd shoved him away with both hands—and he'd left, moved to another state. Which was just as well, she reminded herself. Joseph's actions had simply reinforced a decision she'd made long ago. She would never marry another officer—tempted though she might have been once upon a time.

Because if there was one thing she was sure about in this life, it was the fact that two cops married to each other simply created a war zone.

Her parents had certainly taught her that.

And why she was even thinking along those lines puzzled her. It must be because her boss had told her who she'd be working this case with: Joseph Santino. Groaning in frustration at her inability to shove her resurrected thoughts about that man from her mind, she desperately focused on the task before her. Find who killed Tracy Merritt and arrest the creep.

Period.

Pulling into the gate, she flashed her badge at security. This school had seen a lot of police action lately. Just a little over a year ago, teacher Marianna O'Hara, Joseph's deaf sister, had been held hostage in her classroom by a power hungry politician. Thankfully, that situation had ended peacefully.

And now this.

Briefly, Catelyn wondered if she should remove herself from the case. Being the ex-girlfriend of the main FBI agent called in to assist with the case might cause a few raised eyebrows—if they knew.

But that was the past.

She'd worry about him later.

Now, she turned her thoughts to the young man who was the main suspect in the case: Dylan Carlisle. A hotheaded teen who convincingly protested his innocence.

Yeah, right. She'd been up that road before, had the scar to prove it and wasn't buying it this time around.

Dylan hadn't been arrested yet, but if the evidence continued to build, she'd have him in jail so fast his head would spin, convincing protests notwithstanding.

At the crime scene, she pulled to a stop and stepped out of the car. The scene had been cleared by the authorities, but not yet cleaned up. Good. She'd have a chance to go over it one more time.

The lone figure standing inside the yellow tape made her pull up and stare. He couldn't be here already. Surely not. The figure turned and met her gaze.

Yep, it was him.

Sucking in a deep breath, she blew it out slowly, telling herself to calm down. Praying her voice didn't shake at the sudden shock of seeing him, she said, "Hello, Joseph."

* * *

Joseph stared. He couldn't help it. It had been two years since he'd seen Catelyn. Even though he'd returned home to visit family during that time, he'd never run into her. She'd made herself scarce during his visits in spite of the fact that she'd stayed friends with his sister Alissa.

But he'd thought about her. Thought about calling, finding her, asking her to clarify what went wrong with their relationship. And each time he thought about it, he pushed the feelings aside, not wanting to put himself back in a place where he could be hurt again. And she *had* hurt him because she'd seemed to walk away from him without ever making her reasons clear. At the time, he'd been furious with her, confused and pained by her actions—and, he admitted to himself, prideful. So he'd let her have her space and time passed.

But he'd missed her. She'd practically grown up in his house and Joseph had loved her since she'd been a teenager with a chip on her shoulder. She'd fit right in with his family, six brothers and sisters, his mom and dad and a grandmother.

Catelyn had adopted them all and learned the language they'd used most around the house: ASL, American Sign Language.

And now she was even prettier than he remembered. With a glint in her eye that said she wasn't happy to see him.

Well, too bad. He was here to stay until the end. No matter what it took to find Kelly and put Tracy's killer behind bars. Even if it meant dealing with Catelyn and old feelings that had never truly died.

"Hello, Catie."

"Don't call me that. My name's Catelyn."

Nope, she hadn't changed a bit. Just as contrary as she

ever was. "Fine," he clipped. "*Catelyn,* what do you think about this case so far? Any new leads on Kelly or Tracy?"

Compassion softened her gaze for a moment. "No, nothing yet. Kelly's poor family, they're beside themselves. And her brother, Billy..." She shook her head. "He's having a hard time. They go to my church and I've known them awhile. You never had a chance to meet them as they came after you left."

He ignored her dig. She'd been the one to send him on his way. His gaze swept the scene again as he wondered how to respond. Then decided not to.

In spite of the fact that the scene had been cleared, he'd slipped blue crime-scene booties over his shoes so as not to disturb anything in the area. He couldn't help it. He simply couldn't walk a crime scene without them. He watched as Catelyn went ahead and slipped a pair over her shoes. Apparently she felt the same way.

Attention to detail.

Notice everything; mentally record the scene to pull up later. And write everything down. Good notes were essential. He had no doubt Catelyn's would be unquestionably precise and detailed.

"Dylan's jacket was found there," she offered.

"Where?" Joseph's head snapped up. Victor hadn't mentioned anything about a jacket.

She scraped a hand through that silky blond mane that never seemed to stay where she wanted it. He remembered smoothing it down, around her cheeks, his fingers grazing skin so soft, he...

Clearing his throat, he asked, "What was his jacket doing at the crime scene? He doesn't even go to this school anymore now that he's playing baseball with Esterman High."

"I know. We pulled him in for questioning and he claims

he met Kelly here, they were walking, she was cold and he gave her his jacket."

"So how did it wind up on the ground?" He pointed to the marker indicating where the jacket had been found.

"He says he has no idea. That he left his jacket with her and he was going to come back to get it the next day, which would be today. Tracy was found last night. We still haven't heard anything from Kelly."

"You don't believe him." Joseph stated it as fact, his eyes never leaving her face. If he hadn't been studying her so intently, he would have missed the brief flicker of regret.

She shrugged, turning back to assess the scene. He wondered if she was just avoiding looking at him. She said, "I don't know, Joseph. And that's the truth. I don't want to think Dylan capable of something like this. Dylan's aunt is a dispatcher with the department. His mom is a single mother and while his dad's in the picture, he's not around much. Dylan's track record isn't great, and kids do stupid stuff all the time that turns deadly." Another shrug. "Who knows? I'm reserving judgment until all the evidence is in."

"Alonso sent me a text message. Dylan's a good friend of his, of our family. Alonso firmly believes in his buddy's innocence and is begging me to prove it." He blew out a sigh and looked at her. "You've already got him tried and found guilty, haven't you?"

"No." Her eyes got that glint again, the one that said he was walking a fine line, and she was having trouble holding on to her temper. Not for the first time he thought she should have been a redhead. "I didn't say that. I said I'm following the evidence."

"And what if that evidence is all circumstantial and yet still leads back to Dylan?"

"Then I'll arrest him."

* * *

Catelyn hated the tension between the two of them. Once upon a time, Joseph had been her best friend, her confidante, the only man who'd ever made her seriously think about tossing away her personal rule about never marrying a cop. She turned away from him, walked to the edge of the tape.

His voice came from her right. "What else did they find?"

"A ring with some blood on it." She kept her words clipped, professional.

"The girl's or someone else's?"

"Don't know yet. It just went into the lab. You know how fast the turnaround time is." Sarcasm dripped off the words.

Joseph snorted. "Yeah."

Catelyn came closer, asking the question she'd wondered for the last couple of years—ever since he'd left. "So, how have you been?"

"Good. Just working a lot. New York's a fascinating city."

"I'm sure." Now she was stuck. Backed into that awkward conversational corner, silence stretching, making her itch to escape.

Joseph walked the perimeter, just inside the tape. Bending down, he touched the grass. "There was some kind of scuffle here. The grass is really torn up in this spot. I mean, I know it's a school with kids everywhere, but this area's kind of off the beaten path."

Relieved to be back on a safe topic, she said, "Yes, the crime-scene guys looked it over, got the pictures. No prints, though. The ground's too hard."

Glancing at the sky, Joseph lamented, "Could have used the rain that's coming this afternoon a couple of days ago."

She walked a few feet outside the tape. Several strategically placed large boulders lined the curving entrance to the school. More were placed under the shade trees near the pasture where students like to gather in the afternoon. Catelyn scanned them and something caught her attention. She leaned down, pulling the small high-powered digital camera from her pocket. She snapped two pictures of the item, then pulled out a glove. Just because something turned up outside the tape, didn't mean it wasn't evidence. With a steady hand, she picked it up.

Wood. About two inches wide by six inches long.

Looking around, she spied the trees, a wooden play set off to the left, wooden cedar chips had been spread near the horse pasture. The wooden fence. Wood everywhere. Carefully, she studied the piece. Scanned the wood surrounding her once more. It didn't really match anything nearby. Possibly the light, wooden play set.

So what was it?

"What have you got?"

"I was just trying to figure that out. It's a piece of wood, but I don't know what kind or where it came from. There's nothing else around here like it. See, it's smooth on this side, but rough around the edges and underneath."

He came closer, stood next to her to inspect the piece. She shivered at the proximity and had to concentrate on his words so she wouldn't think how wonderful it felt to have him near again. He was saying, "Could be part of that play set. They just built it."

"It's probably nothing, but…" Catelyn snagged a plastic bag from her pocket, one she'd stuck in there just in case. She dropped the piece into it and moved a couple of inches away. She couldn't breathe with him that close. It galled her he could still stir her up when she just wanted to forget the anger and hurt he'd left her with two years ago. "I'll just get this over to the lab. They'll be able to tell us what kind of wood it is."

"Sometime in this century, I hope." He sounded jaded, resigned.

"Ah!"

The guttural cry brought them both around. Alonso, Joseph's brother stood there with Dylan Carlisle. Joseph took note of Dylan's clenched fists, ragged breathing and air of desperation. Seeing he had their attention, he signed, "I didn't do it. I didn't kill Tracy!"

TWO

Joseph strode to his brother and the distraught young man. He gripped Dylan's shoulders and squeezed, hoping to transmit understanding and comfort. Dropping his hands, he signed, "We're going to find out who did."

Alonso shifted, anxiety oozing from him. Joseph had sent a text message to his brother to let him know that he had arrived in town and would see him soon, but after his visit to the morgue, Joseph had come straight to the crime scene.

Alonso and Dylan had come to find him. He studied the lanky young suspect in front of him. Frantic blue eyes, blond hair, a smattering of freckles across a sharp nose and pale cheeks. Then Alonso, who was Dylan's physical opposite. A little shorter with brown eyes and dark skin, he was a younger version of Joseph, their Italian heritage prominently displayed.

A small cut on Dylan's chin looked angry, red. Alonso had a bit of stubble that had already grown out since this morning. His little brother and his friends were already shaving, growing up. *Were* grown up, he realized. Dylan was considered a man and old enough to be tried as an adult if convicted of murder. What would that do to Alonso who fervently believed in his friend's innocence?

Joseph signed, "I believe you. Unless I find solid evidence to the contrary, I believe you. Okay?"

Chest still heaving, Dylan glared back at Joseph, and Joseph flinched at the agony in the boy's eyes. Either the kid was an excellent actor or he was telling the truth.

Catelyn came up to sign, "You two shouldn't be here."

Joseph wanted to tell her to stay away, but she was right, neither of the teens should be here. Wrapping one arm around his brother's shoulder, and the other around Dylan, he steered them back to the idling vehicle Alonso had left in the middle of the road. With his free hand, Joseph signed, "Let's go home. Catelyn will take care of this."

Dylan shot Catelyn one last glare that gradually turned pleading. "Please believe me."

Compassion flickered briefly before her expression solidified into granite. "I'll believe the evidence."

This time Joseph shot her a hard look as he turned the boys toward the car once more. Joseph signed and spoke to his brother, "You two go to the house. I'll follow you there and we'll talk, all right?"

"Wait a minute," Catelyn protested, "this is my case, too. If you're going to question him, I need to be there."

Joseph turned back to look at her, his breath hissing from his lungs. Even driving him crazy, even in the midst of a murder investigation and, yes, even exhibiting her bulldog tenacity, she still had the power to stop him in his tracks with her beauty. He really had to get over that. She'd made it clear she didn't want anything to do—romantically—with him.

Hands on her hips, feet planted wide, she thrust her jaw forward and narrowed her eyes. Arguing with her would be fruitless.

Besides, she was right. They were there to work together. They both had a common goal. Find the bad guy. He had to put aside his personal feelings and keep his heart under control. "I'm not questioning them in any official capacity right now. I'm just talking to my brother and his friend." He paused. "But, all right, come on. I'm staying with my parents right now, so why don't you meet us there?"

Shock at easy acquiescence flashed across her features before she could cover it up. But she didn't hesitate. "Right, see you there."

During the ten-minute drive, Alonso practically superglued himself to Joseph's bumper. Catelyn kept a safer distance back probably trying to figure out his motive for agreeing to her presence.

The truth was, Joseph's gut was telling him that Dylan had nothing to do with the disappearance of Kelly or the death of Tracy. What he wasn't completely sure of was whether Dylan had been entirely truthful about his reason for being on the campus. It made sense, and yet...

Hopefully, they would get to the bottom of this and find Kelly before she turned up dead, too.

Catelyn called in her destination and let her captain know Joseph was in town and they'd met up at the crime scene. Dylan was still a suspect, but the evidence thus far was flimsy. He still had his freedom until something else turned up. Whereas Catelyn thought he was guilty, she could tell Joseph believed the boy.

Great.

They were immediately working the case from opposite sides. *God, I know when I became a Christian all those years ago, You never promised me an easy life, but things are getting too complicated too fast. First my mother, now Joseph?*

Catelyn didn't have any doubts about Joseph's investigative skills. That didn't concern her. Working in close proximity with a man she had once had feelings for, did. Of course those feelings were gone now.

Yeah. Right.

No, if she were honest, she'd admit seeing Joseph had unsettled her. In a big way.

She pulled into the driveway of the home that had become her refuge. Thank goodness for Joseph's sister Gina, who'd befriended Catelyn in high school, or she may never have seen a family as God intended one to be. She'd grown up with the perfect example of what a family *wasn't*. Because of the Santino family, Catelyn grew to love the Lord and came to understand what a personal relationship with Him meant.

Thank you, Lord. Now, about Joseph... She sighed. *I don't even know what to pray, God. Just...be there, please?*

Caught by a long red light, she was the last to arrive. Joseph had parked on the curb, Alonso in the drive off to the side. Joseph, Dylan and Alonso were deep into a signed conversation when Catelyn pulled in behind Joseph. Just as she set the car in Park, a black Jeep swerved around her screeching to a halt, blocking the drive.

She jumped at the sudden intrusion.

What?

A teenager about Alonso's age threw himself from the Jeep and raced toward the boys. The furious expression on his face had Catelyn calling out, "Hey!"

Joseph turned at her yell, concern and shock twisting his features as the boy didn't stop, but tackled Dylan to the ground and began pummeling him with both fists, his shrieks of outrage piercing her ears. Alonso threw himself into the fight, trying to protect his friend.

"Whoa!" Joseph tried to grab a punching fist and caught one on the chin for his effort. His head jerked back and he winced, then waded back in to the fray. This time, he grabbed the boy by his belt and yanked, tossing him to the side. The young guy landed with a grunt, scrambled to his feet and started to lunge back at Dylan. Alonso lurched to take a swing at the teen and Joseph stiff-armed him back.

Catelyn stepped in front of the attacker. The surprise of seeing her had him stumbling to a sudden halt, arms pin-wheeling, feet dancing backward.

Adrenaline rushing at the surprise attack, she placed a hand against his chest and shoved, mimicking Joseph's method to keep his brother out of the action. Knocked off balance, the boy went down on his rear. Noticing his hearing aids, she signed to him, "Stop, now."

Joseph had Dylan's arms pinned down, but the boy wasn't struggling, although it looked like he wanted to. Joseph let him go, and Dylan shook his arms then reached up to dab at a cut above his right eye. Alonso hauled himself to his feet. "Chad? What do you think you're doing?" he signed furiously.

"He killed Tracy!"

"He did not!" Alonso protested. "How could you even think that?" Four hands flew through the conversation. Joseph eyed Catelyn with a warning to stay out of it for now. She backed off and watched the boys yell at each other.

Dylan defended himself, saying, "I was there with Kelly, but I left. Tracy was fine when I left. I don't know what happened later."

"You knew Tracy wanted Kelly to break up with you and you told her to stay out of it 'or else.' I saw you."

Dylan looked shocked, then nodded. "Yeah, I did, but I didn't mean I'd kill her. Get real, man. I just meant I wouldn't have anything else to do with her. I'd get her blackballed from the group." He threw his hands up in the air as though in disbelief.

Catelyn almost believed Dylan. He looked so convincing. She fingered the scar on her left arm. Yeah, so had the kid who knifed her in thanks for giving him the benefit of the doubt. She wasn't falling for that one again.

"We need to either go down to the department where we can hash this all out or find a spot around here to get to the bottom of this." She pulled out her notebook and pen.

Joseph motioned to the porch. Chad's hands shook, his fury still palpable, but Catelyn detected grief beneath the anger. Tracy must have meant a lot to him. And what was that about Tracy wanting Kelly to break up with Dylan?

"Joseph, can you give Dylan's and Chad's parents a call and let them know what's going on? I want to do this by the book. I'm not making an arrest—yet—so we can do this here, but I definitely want these parents aware of what's going on. Plus, Chad's in no shape to drive home. Someone needs to get his car."

He pulled his BlackBerry out. "Sure." He got the numbers from a reluctant Chad and a still-fuming Dylan. Soon he had Chad's parents on the way and had left a message for Dylan's mother and one for the kid's father. They were divorced, but shared custody.

"If this turns into an official investigation interrogation, we'll have to move it downtown," Joseph warned.

"Of course. Right now, I just want to talk to Dylan. Informally. He's over fourteen, I don't need his parents' permission for that."

Nodding, Joseph took a seat on the swing. The still-glowering, yet subdued boys sat in opposite corners of the porch. Catelyn planted herself in a rocker between them. She kept silent hoping one of them would be ready to burst forth with information by the time she got around to asking some questions.

The door to the house swung open and Alonso's father, Geovani Santino, stepped out.

* * *

"I heard a bunch of commotion out here." Spying Dylan, he signed, "What happened to your eye?"

"My friend went nutso on me." Dylan's fingers flew, hands shaped the words and his glare notched up a bit in intensity. Chad Markham, a student at the deaf school and a member of the high school baseball team, fumed, fists clenched at his side.

Joseph raised a calming hand, then watched as a compact car pulled in behind Chad's Jeep. Chad noticed it, too, and snapped his lips together in a mutinous expression of defiance.

Chad's parents bolted from the car and raced up the porch. "Chad? What's going on?" His mother stopped on the top step taking everything in.

Joseph intervened, introduced everyone and explained the situation. Catelyn let him take over. He looked at her face. Take over for now, anyway.

He made sure the parents knew that this wasn't a formal interrogation. Rather just a "getting together" to see what they could come up with and see if any new information came to light.

Once everyone was settled, Catelyn asked, "Chad, tell us why you think Dylan had something to do with Tracy's death and Kelly's disappearance."

"Because he was there. He said he left, but he didn't, at least I don't believe him. He and Kelly and Tracy all had a huge argument earlier that day. He was really mad at Tracy and told her she'd better watch her mouth, or else. I'm Kelly's friend, her best friend. She was tired of Dylan always telling her who she could hang out with and who she couldn't. She told me so."

Catelyn cocked a brow Dylan. The boy leaned over and

grasped his head with his hands. She tapped him on the shoulder and signed, "That true?"

A huge sigh rippled through him. "Yes."

"Anything else you want to add? Because while you keep insisting on your innocence, you're sure leaving out some chunks of need-to-know information."

Dylan shook his head. "We argued. So what? We argued all the time. Tracy didn't like me and didn't try to hide it. I didn't like her, either. She was bossy and pushy and..."

"And what?" Joseph practically growled.

"And Kelly's best friend." He shot a glance at Chad. "Not him. Tracy wanted Kelly to break up with me and date her brother, Zachary. I was afraid..." He trailed off again, rubbing his eyes as though trying to erase a headache. Everyone sat silent. "I was afraid she was going to convince Kelly I wasn't good enough for her so I told her to mind her own business and keep her mouth shut."

"Why didn't you tell us this when we had you in for questioning?" Catelyn demanded.

Tears filled the boy's eyes. "Because it makes it look like I had a reason to...do...something to Tracy." He stood and paced from one end of the porch to the other. Then turned to say, "But I didn't! I swear! I mean, I sure didn't like her, but I would never *hurt* her."

Joseph frowned at the constant protestations of innocence. He watched Catelyn's expressions, her eyes. The more the boy talked, the more she became convinced he did do something. And Joseph had a moment of wondering himself. Could it be that Dylan *had* killed Tracy? Possibly in a fit of anger? An accident?

Blunt-force trauma was the cause of death. Had he picked up a rock and hit her? Pushed her down so she cracked her head against something? But there'd been no sign of that kind of thing at the crime scene. No, the murder weapon was portable.

And the killer either ditched it far enough from the crime scene that the crime-scene unit didn't come across it—or he still had it.

More questioning led nowhere. Dylan said he wouldn't press charges as long as Chad left him alone. The boys were told to stay away from each other, and Chad's parents took him home. Alonso went to his room and shut the door. Dylan's mother, who finally arrived, was filled in on the incident. She expressed her concern, asking to be kept in the loop if anything new happened in the investigation. His father never showed up.

After the mass departure, Catelyn studied the floor of the porch, thinking. She felt in her gut the kid knew way more than he was telling, she just couldn't prove it.

But she would.

Alonso would be upset, and Joseph would hurt for his brother, but...

She stood, straightened her spine as she walked toward her car. He was a cop. A good one. He wouldn't argue the arrest if she had enough evidence, knew he would be right there with her reading the kid his rights if it came down to it. Granted, Dylan's jacket turning up at the scene didn't look good, but his explanation was reasonable. Girls wore their boyfriends' jackets all the time.

So far, nothing had come back from the lab, but she didn't really expect anything this early even with the rush she knew would be on the evidence. With a missing teen, time was of the essence. She'd call Sandy Newman, a tech in the crime lab and a woman Catelyn called friend, to see if Sandy could rush it even faster.

"Hey."

She stopped, turned to find Joseph leaning against a porch pillar, watching her. This time her shiver had nothing to do with anger. She remembered how it felt to slip into his arms and rest her head against his broad shoulder, remembered what it felt like to feel secure, safe. As if the rest of the world didn't matter and everything would be all right.

His sudden change of expectations about certain things in their relationship had crushed her. She'd grown up promising herself she'd be different than her parents, have a different life, a solid marriage.

At first, she'd never thought about dating Joseph simply because he was already rising through the ranks of the local police department.

Then one night, they'd been sitting outside talking after a huge family meal and he'd asked her if she'd like to go on a date with him. She'd hesitated because of his profession, then assured herself that this was Joseph. He knew her dreams, her hopes—her career. During the time she'd been at the academy, all through school, he'd supported her, encouraged her. And so it had begun. She'd fallen head over heels in love with him and he with her.

Until he'd suddenly started talking about "after we're married." About how he was excited because he would make enough money to allow her to stay home. And how God had blessed him in allowing him to find a woman who held the same values as his mother.

And her world had come crashing down. She couldn't believe what she was hearing. He wanted her to shelve her career and become the kind of wife she'd vowed never to be.

At least it had seemed sudden, she thought. Had the signs been there the entire time and she'd just chosen to ignore them?

She'd been devastated that he would ask her to give up

her career to make *him* happy. No way. She knew where that argument would lead.

And yet she couldn't deny the attraction between them had sizzled, both physically and emotionally. She'd been drawn to his softer side, the one he refused to allow anyone to really see. That, and the fact that, deep down, he had a heart for comforting hurting people.

And it was definitely still there—the attraction, all of it. She held her tongue and just looked at him, hoping her face didn't reveal her inner turmoil.

Finally, he started toward her, hands jammed into his pockets. "Can we talk?"

"About what?"

"Us."

"That's not even a topic, Joseph. There is no 'us,' hasn't been for a while now."

"There could be. What we had, Catie…"

She ignored the shortened version of her name. He only called her that when they were alone.

"*Had.* As in the past. You never once said anything about me quitting my job until I was halfway in love with you and thinking marriage. And then you come out with these expectations and blindsided me."

"I didn't realize…and you shut me out."

"Yes, I did."

"Without even giving us a chance to work through it."

"It wouldn't have mattered. You simply reinforced what I already knew. Why it wouldn't be a good idea to marry a cop." She threw her hands up. "And why are we even having this conversation anyway? Look. Your brother's friend is in trouble. Let's just see where all this ends up before we do anything stupid like talk about…us."

His jaw clenched; his fingers curled into a fist. "If you— we—have to arrest Dylan, I'll have to figure out how to help Alonso deal with it. But for now, we have to work together. Without letting our past interfere. Can we do that?"

"We can try."

"Deal."

He reached out to grasp her hand in a handshake and the tingles that danced up her arm told her she might talk a good game about ignoring their feelings for each other, but actually putting her words into actions was going to take a lot more work than she'd bargained for.

THREE

Joseph stared over Catelyn's shoulder at the autopsy report. Nothing new there. And nothing new about his inability to keep himself from noticing how good she smelled. Just like he remembered. A combination of vanilla shampoo and strong coffee.

"Hey, look at this," she said, just as he inched back a tad to put a little distance between his nose and her hair. She pointed to the list of items found with Tracy. "An iPod. An expensive one."

"Did they run the serial number on it?"

"Yes, and would you look at that?"

"Stolen."

"That kind of makes you sit up and go, 'hmm,' doesn't it?"

"So what does a deaf kid do with an iPod. She must not have been totally deaf. Who reported it stolen?"

She shuffled to the next page. "Here. The Whites. Abe and Eva White on the west side of town."

"A breaking and entering. There's been a rash of those lately, hasn't there?"

"Yep. The guys working it think it's gang related, but haven't been able to connect any specific members to the break-ins yet."

"This might be your connection right here. Go back to the autopsy report."

She did and he pointed out the tattoo. "She had a tattoo of a skull around her belly button."

"The symbol of the new and up-and-coming local gang, The Skulls. We just had a whole session on gang training a month ago."

Joseph sighed. "So now they've infiltrated the deaf school."

"But Tracy spent the majority of her school day at the regular high school. It could be that the gang's not originating on the deaf campus, but the local high school campus."

"Or neither."

"Right. So Tracy was a gang member, we know that much. She's also in possession of stolen merchandise. Which brings me to the questions: Does Dylan know about this? Does he know anything about the breaking and entering and thefts going on? Is he a member of the gang?"

"A lot of good questions." He closed his eyes, picturing Alonso's thin, but well-muscled frame. He shook his head. "I can't remember my brother having a tattoo, but I haven't seen him without his shirt, either. I can't imagine him getting involved in that, but I'll ask Alonso later."

Catelyn shot him a look that said she thought he had his rose-tinted glasses back on. Thankfully, she kept her opinion to herself. He'd have to prove Dylan's innocence one way or another. And if the kid was guilty...

"Did Dylan ever say why Tracy was so adamant about Kelly breaking up with him?"

Joseph shook his head. "Nothing specific. Just that her brother wanted to go out with Kelly and she kept turning him down because she was Dylan's girlfriend."

"What's Tracy's brother's name again?"

"Zachary."

"So, we need to talk to Zachary about this gang that his sister was a part of."

"Looks like. And my bet is that if she was a part of it, so is he."

"He's not deaf. He's hearing and goes to Esterman High." She pushed back from her desk and wisps of blond hair tickled his chin sending shards of longing to clench his gut. Somehow, some way, they were going to have to work things out because she had already burrowed her way under his skin in less than twenty-four hours. Just the thought of telling her goodbye again was painful enough to know that having to go through the real thing again would probably rip his heart to shreds.

Pushing aside his personal agenda, he said, "I suppose we should give the family a call and let them know we want to talk to Zachary. I'm guessing he's probably not back at school yet so soon after Tracy's death."

Catelyn got on the phone and made the call. Joseph got up to stretch a minute and say something to one of the other detectives he'd worked with a few years back.

When she hung up, Catelyn turned to him and frowned. "He's not there."

"So, where is he?"

"His mother didn't know. She said he got a text after lunch and said he was going to meet up with a friend. She hasn't heard from him since."

"When's Tracy's funeral?"

"Tomorrow. Visitation is this afternoon."

"I've got a feeling we need to see if he shows up to the visitation."

"And who he shows up with."

Catelyn scanned the sea of faces heading in to pay respects to the family. Mostly teenagers, teachers, probably some church members. The line to greet the family and offer sympathy extended well down the hall to snake around to the entrance to the funeral home. The front door stood open and Joseph waited off to the side, dressed in a suit and tie.

She nearly stumbled in her uncomfortable medium-height heels. She'd never had a problem walking in them before so she couldn't blame her sudden clumsiness on the shoes.

No, it was Joseph. What was she going to do about him? He exuded strength, authority, and was completely at ease in his six-foot-two-inch frame. At five feet eight she didn't consider herself a short woman, but next to him, she always felt petite, feminine. Something that didn't happen very often around other men. And Joseph was definitely the only man who'd ever made her palms sweat. She rubbed them on her black skirt and tried to paste a serene expression on her face.

His smile greeted her with a warmth that nearly caused the upward tilt of her lips to take a downward turn. So much for serenity.

Have a little backbone, Catelyn. And, Lord, if You'd help me control my wayward emotions here, I'd really appreciate it.

He held the door open and she slipped in, nearly jumping out of her skin when his hand dropped to the small of her back. He's only being a gentleman, she told herself. Relax.

Easier said than done. From the back of the line, they waited, watching.

A few more people trickled in, and the line in front of them moved slowly, but consistently. Catelyn kept her eyes peeled. "See him?"

"No, but he's probably with the family in the receiving

room. I can't get a good view yet. A few more inches and I'll be able to see if he's in there."

Catelyn lost her balance and stumbled into the person in front of her. Joseph caught her arm before she could do much damage. The woman turned to see who'd knocked against her and Catelyn felt her face flush. "I'm so sorry. I don't wear heels often and…" She trailed off when the woman laughed and waved a hand as though brushing the incident aside.

"Don't worry about it. Happens to the best of us." A frown pinched her brows. "It's a shame, isn't it?"

"I'm sorry?"

The young woman who looked to be in her early forties stood there holding the hand of a child about six years old. She had a brace on her other hand. "Just a shame. Tracy used to babysit for us on a regular basis."

"Oh, so you knew her well?"

"Absolutely. A great kid. Well, a great kid with a lot of faults, but I liked her. Oh, I'm sorry." She held out a hand that Joseph and Catelyn took turns shaking. "I'm Stacy Dillard. My husband, Alan Dillard, is the baseball coach at Esterman High School." She placed a loving hand on the child's head.

"This is Alan Jr."

"I'm six," the little guy piped in. "My mom hurt her hand."

Catelyn smiled at him and shook his hand. "Nice to meet you Alan Jr."

Stacy gave a self-conscious laugh and held up her hand. "Carpal tunnel. Anyway, I wasn't sure if I should bring him or not, but my mother couldn't babysit today and I didn't want to miss…" Tears welled in her eyes and she blinked them back. Taking a deep breath, she blew it out. "Tracy's brother, Zachary, is our catcher."

Joseph spoke up. "Then you know Dylan Carlisle."

The woman's green eyes brightened, the tears fading. "Oh, sure, he used to hang around Zachary quite a lot. We have the team over for cookouts and such about once a month." Her brows drew together in a slight frown. "I haven't seen much of Dylan lately, though. How's he doing? Is he here?"

"He's upset about Tracy, of course, but other than that, he seems to be doing all right. And no, he's not here."

"I know you consider him a suspect, don't you?" When neither Catelyn nor Joseph responded, she frowned. "Alan said you did. Dylan told him about being questioned by the police." She let out a sigh. "I can't see Dylan as having anything to do with Tracy's death. If the police need a suspect, they need to be looking at Zachary, if you ask me." She herded the child in front of her toward the door. "Well, I was waiting for Alan. He told me he'd meet me in the line, but he's probably talking to someone and got held up. I guess I'd better see if I can find him. It's good to meet you."

She started to hurry off, but stopped when Catelyn laid a restraining hand on her arm. "Wait a minute. Why do you say that? About Zachary, I mean."

The woman shrugged. "He and Tracy fought constantly. I even saw him shove her into the fence one day after a game. I don't know what she said to him, but he didn't like it. Tracy and Dylan argued some, too, but Dylan never put his hands on her like Zachary did. I don't have anything other than just my feelings when I say Zachary should be a suspect." She sighed. "And I probably shouldn't have even said anything. Excuse me." This time Catelyn didn't stop her as she hurried off.

Catelyn looked at Joseph. "So Zachary plays on the

baseball team and has a temper. And Dylan is known to hang out with him. Teammates and friends?"

"No crime in that. She also said she hadn't seen Dylan in a while." He thought for a moment. "Maybe the boys are former friends. I'll have to ask Alonso and see what he says. Maybe it's as simple as Dylan and Zachary had a falling-out and he was avoiding being around him. That would explain why she hadn't seen Dylan around—because he was doing his best to stay out of trouble."

"Maybe."

"I still want to know if Zachary's a part of this gang. And who he was with earlier while his family was at home grieving."

"As soon as we can get to him, we'll find out."

She spotted Stacy Dillard coming back her way. The poor thing looked harried. "I guess I'll just wait here. I can't find Alan anywhere." Still clutching Alan Jr.'s hand, she slipped back into the line in front of Catelyn and Joseph. "Do you mind if I take my spot back?"

"Of course not. Go ahead."

Stacy did and started talking to the person in front of her.

Catelyn stepped to the side to peer around the shifting line of bodies and into the visitation room. "I think I see him," she told Joseph. "Standing next to his mother and younger brother."

"Yep, that's him."

"Just a little closer. Oh, look, everyone's standing."

Zachary shook the next person's hand, looking uncomfortable in his black suit and red tie. Tall, with the build of a natural athlete, he shifted, his eyes moving to and fro. He didn't even bother to try and smile to the people offering condolences; in fact, he looked ready to bolt.

Catelyn leaned in a little closer to Joseph. "You got your running shoes on?"

"I was just thinking the same thing. Why would he run, though? We just want to talk to him?"

"Maybe he thinks that *we* think he knows something."

"Yeah, and he's scared he'll tell us if we catch him."

"Then let's catch him."

Two more steps forward. Zachary's eyes raised, caught on Catelyn's, flitted to the man beside her and widened. The fear in his face couldn't be missed, not even with the distance still between them.

Sweat turned his face shiny and he shifted, glanced at his mother's back, his sister in the now-closed coffin—and the door on the other side of the room.

"He's gonna make a run for it," Joseph predicted.

"I'm going to cover the other door. You get him from this side."

"Right."

Catelyn slipped out of line and headed down the short hall to the door that opened to the hallway around the corner. The open balcony above her now stood empty, occupied only moments before by friends and family who were now greeting the bereaved. If Zachary made it outside to his car, she'd lose him. Or he would have plenty of hiding places in the cemetery with the huge markers.

Rounding the corner, she was just in time to see a figure dart from the visitation room and head in the opposite direction.

"Zachary, stop! We just want to talk!"

The teen looked back once and kept going, picking up the pace to a fast jog.

Joseph came out of the room. He must have cut through in pursuit. No one else followed, so it must have been done discreetly.

"That way," she pointed.

Together, they took off after the teen, then heard a door slam.

At the sound of a loud crack, Catelyn stopped, turned shocked eyes to Joseph who looked back at her with the same expression she knew her face wore.

"Gunshot?"

Catelyn pulled her weapon, shouting into her radio, "Shots fired," as she raced to the door, yelling at everyone to get down. Joseph was two steps behind her, his gun drawn and ready. Shoving it open, she pulled to a stop, the sight before her sending horror up her spine.

Zachary lay in the middle of the parking lot, unmoving, blood pooling under his head.

FOUR

Five minutes later, the ambulance screamed into the parking lot across the street. In spite of the seriousness of the situation, they'd wait for the all-clear from the officers before they'd approach the scene. No matter who was hurt or how bad it was, for their own safety, medical personal could not enter the scene until it was deemed safe by officers.

Was the boy dead? Where were his parents? Were they still shaking hands with visitors, unaware their oldest son possibly lay dying—or was already dead?

Joseph gripped the tie he'd yanked from his neck, wishing he had the shooter by the throat instead. After the gunshot, Catelyn had secured the area, then bolted toward the fallen boy, placing her own life in danger, doing what she could for him while keeping an eye on the area around her.

Joseph had raced to the balcony after the shooter, knowing he was probably too late.

He found nothing but a spent cartridge. The shooter had disappeared as quickly as he'd appeared. Joseph radioed to let EMS know they could approach.

He looked around again. The person had left in a hurry and hadn't bothered to clean up. Joseph turned back inside, studying the room. The shooter had either come up the stairs or the elevator. Joseph would bet the stairs in case there was a camera in the elevator.

But they'd check it anyway.

He walked over to a door just off the room. Twisted the knob. Locked. The sign said Employees Only.

"Excuse me, sir?"

Joseph turned to see a dark-suited man with a name tag that read Butler Dietz. Joseph asked, "What are you doing up here? Can you open this room?"

The man's brow furrowed. "I work here." He pulled a set of keys from his pocket, located the right one and unlocked the door. Joseph glanced in.

A room full of coffins. And everything looked relatively undisturbed. He spoke into his radio, "Set up a perimeter, question everyone, don't let anyone leave the scene." An affirmative answer squawked back at him.

He turned the worker, saying, "Okay, thanks. I need you out of here, too. This is a crime scene and I need to keep it preserved."

Flustered, the man nodded and headed for the stairs, meeting a swarm of cops coming up. Joseph motioned for one of the officers to escort the man down, then filled the rest of them in on the situation. "Crime-scene unit's on the way."

"We've got this covered," a tall officer assured Joseph.

Joseph loped back down the steps to find Catelyn watching a man work on Zachary, the EMTs offering their assistance as it was requested.

She looked up at his approach, question in her eyes.

Joseph pursed his lips and shook his head. "No, he got away."

"He?"

A shrug. "He, she. Whoever. The shooter's gone. Crime scene unit's on the way. Uniforms are preserving the scene." He pointed to the man on his knees beside Zachary. "Who's this guy?"

"A doctor. He insisted on trying to help."

The man looked up. "I was late coming from the hospital for the funeral. I'm a friend of the Merritts. When I saw all the commotion, I thought I'd see if I could help." He looked back down at Zachary who lay still and pale. "The bullet grazed his head. It didn't enter the skull, which is a good thing, but it might have fractured it. I've called a neurologist. He'll be waiting at the hospital when we get there."

"Thanks."

A man rushed up and said, "Oh my…can I do anything?"

"Who are you?" Joseph queried.

"I'm Alan Dillard, the baseball coach at Esterman High. Zachary was…is one of my players. What's going on? Who would do such a…"

"Zachary! Oh, no, oh, my…" Joseph turned to see Zachary's mother rushing from the mortuary. The boy's father was right behind with the younger brother bringing up the rear.

"What happened? What's going on? Why is this happening?" The distraught woman wailed her grief, echoing the coach's questions. Two of her three children: one dead and one severely wounded. His heart went out to her.

Alan Dillard grabbed the woman's shoulder, keeping her from throwing herself across her son and impeding the work being done on him. "He's getting the help he needs, ma'am."

The EMTs let the doctor take the lead, securing Zachary's neck in a brace, then they gently loaded the boy onto the gurney. The doctor helped, supervising the transfer, then washing his hands with the special alcohol-based soap the EMTs left for him. The ambulance pulled out, siren wailing, on the way to the hospital.

Joseph clapped the man on the shoulder. "Thanks. He might have a chance because you were here."

"Quinn Carson." The doctor introduced himself, holding out a hand for Joseph to shake.

"Joseph Santino. That's my partner, Catelyn Clark."

Catelyn nodded and gave a half smile. The ambulance disappeared around a curve.

"I need to get to the hospital. I need to be with my boy." Zachary and Tracy's mother wailed.

Dr. Carson turned to take the woman in his arms. "Sarah, I'm so sorry. Go and I'll be there to check on him shortly."

"Come on, Mrs. Merritt, Mr. Merritt. I'll do anything I can to help. I'll stay here and make sure everything's finished up. Go be with Zachary," Alan offered, his face creased in sympathy and concern.

Tears flowing, cheeks ashen, the woman nodded and took her friend's advice. She, her husband and young son hurried to their car and took off for the hospital. Friends and family dispersed to their own vehicles in near silence, shock rendering them speechless.

Friday morning, Catelyn dragged into work feeling the weight of the world on her shoulders. After Tracy's murder, she'd talked to her parents extensively, but they'd been basically clueless about their daughter's activities. She sighed.

Unfortunately, parents had to work and couldn't watch their teens twenty-four/seven, but still, she would've thought they would have been able to provide more information than they had.

First thing this morning, she'd called to check on Zachary and learned he still hadn't awakened. She did learn that his abdomen sported the same tattoo his sister had. They posted a guard on his door who would also call immediately if Zachary woke up.

A quick call to a buddy who worked in the gang unit confirmed that Zachary was definitely part of the gang and had a record for some petty theft, shoplifting and one incident involving a stolen car. Although, it seemed that since baseball season had started, he'd kept his nose clean.

Deep in thought, Catelyn set her cup of coffee on her desk and tossed her purse in the bottom drawer.

"Good morning to you, too."

She whirled to find Joseph cranked back in an old squeaky chair someone had scavenged from the storage room. A desk had been set up and he looked quite at home. Lovely.

"Hi, didn't see you there. Looks like you're all set up." She hoped her aggravation wasn't too obvious.

"Bugs you, huh?"

Clamping her teeth on her lower lip to control her tongue, she took a deep breath. It was all about self-control. Before allowing herself to respond, she picked up three phone messages and read them.

Set them back down.

Picked up her coffee and took a swig.

Then she turned to face him. And ignored his taunt. "What time did you get here?"

"About an hour ago."

Was he trying to show her up? He'd soon learn she didn't play that game. No, she'd grown up watching her parents trying to outdo each other, show the other who was the better cop. Catelyn had decided she'd avoid that immature behavior.

Actually, if she was honest, she didn't remember that particular trait about Joseph. Was she just being...defensive? She did remember that he could be a big tease, so maybe…he was teasing her?

Withholding judgment, she kept her cool.

He said, "I couldn't sleep so figured I'd just come on in." No sarcasm, no in-your-face attitude. Just fact.

That was a trait she was more comfortable with.

Relaxing, she settled in her chair. "I guess we need to plan out our day."

"I've got some ideas. Do you mind if I run them by you?"

Asking her permission? This she didn't remember. Suspicious, she eyed him. Then offered a shrug. "Sure. Fire away."

A warm smile creased his cheeks and crinkled his eyes. Familiar attraction zinged, and Catelyn deliberately stomped on it.

"First of all, I want to get a record of Zachary's text messages. Then, I thought we might make our way over to the crime lab and see if we can light a fire under someone. I want those DNA results back."

"I checked on Zachary this morning and he's still unconscious. He's got some pretty serious neurological stuff going on. Swelling on his brain and fluid. They've even put him on a ventilator." She shook her head. "They're not sure if he'll ever wake up. The principal of the school and Coach Dillard are letting the students organize a fundraiser for medical expenses for Zachary. The deaf school offered its services, too. Apparently, Alan is well liked in the deaf community, thanks to his having deaf parents."

Joseph nodded. "That's a great thing to do and it'll give the students something constructive to focus on. They've got to be traumatized by all that's happened over the last few days."

"To say the least. The school counselors are working

overtime right now, talking in the classrooms, counseling friends of Tracy, Kelly and Zachary. They're doing all they can do. They've even called in some outside help, so that's good."

"I'm glad to hear that. I just hope someone is helping the Merritt family. To have something so awful happen to two of your children…it's beyond my imagination."

Sympathy clouded her gaze for a brief moment. She nodded and said, "I want to know what it is those two kids knew that someone was willing to commit murder in order to keep it secret."

"And I want to talk to Kelly Franklin's brother today, too. His name is Billy. Let's see if he can shed some light on his sister's disappearance."

"Sound like we've got our game plan."

"Oh, and Alonso's got a baseball game tonight. I'm planning on catching it if you want to join me."

Speechless for a moment, Catelyn processed his statement. Gathering her wits, she shrugged. "We'll see."

He raised an eyebrow, but didn't comment on her evasiveness.

As they headed out, Catelyn ignored the excitement building within her at the thought of spending so much time in Joseph's company. Excitement or no, she reminded herself that this was the man who'd broken her heart two years ago and there was no way she was trusting him with the pieces ever again.

Pulling into the parking lot of the building that housed the local crime lab, Joseph pondered the situation silently while Catelyn called Billy Franklin's mother to ask for permission to visit him at the school, assuring the woman that Billy was in no way considered a suspect, but they just wanted to see if he had anything else to add that might help them find his sister. Sometimes people remembered things later. After the dust settled, and the adrenaline wore off.

Tracy had been killed, and Kelly had disappeared. Why? What did Tracy know that was worth killing for? Had Kelly been at the scene? Had she witnessed the murder and fled? Was she hiding out? Or had she witnessed it and been taken against her will? And why hadn't the killer just killed her, too? Or had he and they just hadn't found her body yet?

Sighing, Joseph waited until Catelyn hung up from a second call before swinging his long frame from the car. "Who was that? It sounded official."

"Victor."

"What did he want?"

"An arrest."

"Don't we all? I vote for arresting the right person, though."

"I know." She pulled at her lower lip with her two top teeth as she thought. Joseph cut his eyes and swallowed hard. He clearly remembered kissing those lips and wanted to do it again. He blinked and focused back in on what she was saying. "I still think Dylan's up to his eyeballs in this thing and knows a lot more than he's telling."

"Possibly. It's just that when he protested his innocence so profusely, I believed him. I didn't see anything that made me think he was covering up a murder."

Catelyn rolled her eyes at him. "Trust me. Kids like that learn how to lie so convincingly *they* probably even believe what they're saying. But they're liars all the same."

"Kids like that?" Joseph raised a brow. Why was she so cynical? He didn't remember seeing this side of her before. Wary about a romantic relationship? Yes. A tough street cop? Yes. But where had her compassion gone? What had happened to change that part of her?

She must have read something in his face because she asked, "I sound harsh, don't I?"

"Yeah, you do."

She chewed her lip again. Then pulled her jacket off and rolled up her sleeve. He sucked in a deep breath. A thin five-inch jagged scar made its way from the inside of her elbow to the center of her arm just falling short of her wrist.

He reached out and pulled it toward him for a closer look. Angry, puckered and red, yet healing. "Compliments of one of *those* kids?"

"Yeah."

"So, you learned your lesson, is that what you're saying? And every kid is guilty until proven innocent?"

She flushed and yanked out of his light grasp. "Something like that."

He let her go. "When did that happen?"

"About six months ago."

He winced. "Ouch."

Shutters came down over her eyes. "Yep."

"You want to tell me about it?" She used to tell him everything. His heart hurt at the memories. He'd missed her. Her laugh, her beauty, her spunk, the way she made him feel when she let him see the pride she felt for him when he collared a criminal. The way she melted into his arms for a snuggle on the couch. Her kisses…

"Nothing much to tell. I had the kid cornered, he acted like he wasn't going to give me any trouble, just blubbering about how he'd been set up. I believed him, let my guard down and he pulled a knife from somewhere. And before you ask, yes, I'd already patted him down. I made a stupid mistake and missed it. It was a little thing, but it hurt. So, no more trusting crying teens protesting their innocence." Subject closed. "Let's go see what we can find out about the DNA. I hope this isn't a wasted trip."

He smiled and let it drop even though he wanted to pursue the fact that just because she had one bad experience with one kid didn't mean they were all the same. But he knew when she got that look on her face, attempting to push the subject more wouldn't get him anywhere. So he said, "The personal touch is never wasted. A phone call might have sufficed, but when you're face-to-face, it's harder for them to put you off...or hang up on you."

She gave a rare grin, one he remembered, but hadn't seen since he'd been back. "Very true."

Why had she bothered to explain about that scar? Catelyn decided having Joseph around could be addictive. Somehow, she was going to have to figure out how to keep her mouth shut around him. Spilling her guts about everything that bothered her was no longer an option. She'd moved on, and he'd just plain *moved*...

"Sandy, how are you?" Catelyn spotted the criminalist and waved her down. A pretty, petite woman in her late thirties, she was part of a team that did their job well. She'd also been one of the people covering Tracy's murder.

The woman's brows arched under her shaggy bangs. "Catelyn? What are you doing here?"

"Trying to solve a murder and find a missing girl. This is my partner, Joseph Santino. He's working on the case with me." Joseph and Sandy shook hands, then Catelyn said, "We need to know if anything's come back on the blood found on the ring."

"Hmm. I'm not sure. We had that murder-suicide on the other side of town and things have been a little crazier than usual around here."

Great. "I hate to be pushy, but do you mind putting a rush on it? There's a killer out there and a missing girl."

Concern flickered across the woman's face. "I heard. I

know Greg was working with the ring. Come on and let's see if he's in the lab."

The three marched down the hall and Catelyn couldn't help feeling the thrill, the excitement that came with her job. Sure, she hated the deaths, the psychos out there who caused such pain and misery to others, but she knew she was right where she was supposed to be.

She was born to be a cop. A detective. Her mission in life was to put the bad guys away. She didn't have time for romance or a family—or Joseph.

Right, God? God had been strangely quiet with the answer to that question lately and she wondered if the pang she felt in the vicinity of her heart meant she wasn't exactly on the right track. *Lord?*

She looked at Joseph, his rugged profile so familiar; one she'd never tired of looking at during the time they'd dated. Pain seared her. The loss of his presence in her life left a gaping hole she realized she'd never completely filled.

It was too bad he'd never understood that part of her personality, the cop part; it grieved her that he couldn't accept she'd never be the traditional happy homemaker he envisioned when he pictured his wife.

Unfortunately, she knew this all too well. After all, it's what had broken them up two years ago. Joseph Santino had wanted her to stop being a cop, stay home and be his wife. A mother to his children. Part of her regretted that it wasn't enough; she grieved the loss of his companionship, her best friend.

But there was no way she'd ever give up her career. Not even for the man she loved.

Just wasn't going to happen.

Joseph watched Catelyn in action. She loved her job, that was obvious. He saw her disappointment when Sandy returned with no news. "But I promise to let you know as soon as it's processed. I've got your cell number, and I'll call you myself."

Catelyn agreed and then she and Joseph were headed back out. He asked, "Where to now? Billy Franklin?"

"Yes. Esterman High School."

He climbed behind the wheel again without asking. He knew she preferred to ride rather drive. He was falling comfortably into old routines.

As they drove through the streets, Catelyn looked out the window. He decided to touch on the past a little. "How's your mom?"

If he'd zapped her with a Taser, he wouldn't have gotten more response. Her head whipped around and she seared him with her gaze. "What?"

"Your mother. How is she?"

"In a nursing home. Dying."

Oops. He hadn't expected that one. He should have done his homework before venturing into uncharted territory. "Aw, Catie, I'm sorry."

She looked back out the window. "You didn't know. Did you let the school know we were coming?"

Her way of saying "Back off." Another topic not up for discussion. But he remembered her mother and genuinely wanted to know about her. Give it time, he told himself.

"Yes, I did." He let the subject drop.

He turned into the parking lot of the high school and she gave him a half grin. "At least you haven't lost your sense of direction."

For a moment he blanked, then the memory rushed forward. The day they'd gone hiking in the North Carolina woods, searching for a specific waterfall.

"This way," he'd insisted, pointing toward a path that branched to the left.

"No Joseph, it's this way. I have it right…"

"Catie, I know exactly where I'm going. Now be quiet so I can concentrate."

They'd wandered around for the next two hours in silence. Finally, he'd stopped and told her he was going to have to call and get directions.

She'd silently handed him her BlackBerry and suggested he follow the map she'd found online two hours ago.

At his stunned expression, she'd laughed herself silly. Humiliated, he'd sat beside her, fuming. But then her infectious giggles eventually got to him, the ability to laugh at himself making its way to the surface, and he'd found himself chuckling along with her.

They'd found the waterfall in a matter of minutes and shared the sweetest kiss he'd ever experienced.

Now, he spotted the glint in her eye. So, she still thought about their times together, too. Interesting. Heartening. Hope rose within him, but instead of making a big deal about it, he gave her a mock glare and said, "Cute."

She laughed and exited the car, leading the way to the front door of the school.

Their mood turned serious as they entered the building. Joseph watched her shutters come back down. All cop now, she was back to business. Flashing her badge at the receptionist, she said, "Did Billy Franklin's mother call to let you know we were coming?"

"Yes, she did."

"Is there a room where we could speak with him privately?"

"Of course."

They walked down a short hall to a conference room. She said, "I'll just page Billy for you."

She left, and Joseph paced.

A few minutes later, the door opened once again and a

young man who Joseph knew to be seventeen years old, entered. He had on baggy jeans and a light sweatshirt with the school logo emblazoned across his chest. He looked scared and tired, like he hadn't had much sleep lately.

Probably hadn't. Not with his kid sister missing.

Following Billy was Coach Dillard. "I'm sorry," Joseph stopped his advancement into the room, "You can't be here."

"Billy asked me to join him. Is it all right?"

Joseph looked at Billy then over at Catelyn. She shrugged. "If he wants him here, I guess."

Alan sat next to Billy at the table. "I assume this is about Kelly."

"You assume right," Catelyn said.

Joseph turned his attention back to the boy. "Do you know if Kelly and Tracy were together at the school Tuesday night?"

Billy licked his lips, his eyes darting around the room stopping when he came to Catelyn. "She already questioned me the day Tracy died. Why do I have to answer more?"

"Because Kelly's still missing, Billy, and we're running out of options to help find her. So, if some of our questions seem repetitive, will you just humor us?" Catelyn frowned at Billy's evasiveness. Joseph didn't blame her. He eyed the kid and started to speak when the door opened.

Another man in his early sixties stepped through the door. "I'm Carlton Bowles, principal here. Do you mind if I sit in on this?"

He held out a hand and Joseph and Catelyn stood once again. Joseph said, "Have a seat."

Catelyn decided it was time for a woman's touch. "Billy, I know we talked right after Tracy was found and I appreciate your cooperation. The only reason Special Agent Santino and I are here is because we're hoping you might have remembered something since I last talked to you. You're not a suspect in any way right now. Do you think you could relax and just try to help us out?"

At her reassurance, his countenance seemed to soften. "Yes. Like I said before, I think she and Tracy were together, but I can't say for sure. She texted me a little after 4:00 that afternoon and said she was meeting some friends." He shrugged. "I don't know if that included Tracy or not. She wanted me to make up an excuse to tell Mom and Dad about why she was going to be late for supper. I did."

"And she never came home, right?"

"Right. I wasn't too worried because she was always late, but then she wasn't home by dark, which still wasn't that unusual. Then around 9:00, I mean, she *still* wasn't home…"

She waited to see if he was going to pick back up with his sentence. He didn't, so she said, "I do have one question that I haven't asked you. Do you know anything about the gang, The Skulls?"

Catelyn knew she'd hit a bull's-eye when Billy's face lost all color. His throat bobbed and shook his head. "No, no. I don't know anything about them. Just what I've heard and it's not good. I don't want to be mixed up in that stuff. Uh-uh."

He placed his hands on the table. They trembled and he shoved them back in his lap. This boy was terrified of something.

Alan lifted a hand. "Um, do you mind if I intervene here?"

Catelyn lifted a brow. "Sure."

"Billy's a good kid trying to stay out of trouble. A fantastic baseball player with a huge future ahead of him. That sister of his…well, no disrespect, but she seemed to be heading toward trouble. I mean, I've heard she was a good kid, so maybe I'm off base, but considering the kids she hung out with…" He shrugged. "From the outside looking in, I would say that if she had her way, she would have had Billy involved in that gang."

"Do you know for sure that Kelly was involved?"

"No, like I said, I only have my suspicions. I do know she was good friends with Tracy, the only other girl from the deaf school who was also part of our mainstream program here. You know, where we bus deaf kids over so they can be around their hearing peers. And I know Tracy was involved in the gang. She made no secret of that fact. We also have a few hearing students who claim they're involved in the gang, but as long as they don't cause trouble here at school, there's not much we can do about it."

"Billy?" Catelyn turned to him. "Was Kelly involved with The Skulls?"

The teen buried his face in his hands for a brief moment before looking back up. "No way!" Then he looked at the two men and muttered, "I don't know. But no, I don't think so, although she never said anything to me about it. And I really don't think she would be involved in that anymore than I would. She wasn't like that even though she was friends with Tracy. Kelly did say something about talking to Tracy about the gang, but I think she was going to try and convince her to quit the gang, not ask to join." He shot a look at his coach, refuting the man's earlier comment. To give the man credit, he just shrugged.

Billy went on, "Tracy and Kelly have been friends since they both started preschool at the deaf school, so if Tracy was involved with The Skulls in any way, and I'm pretty sure she was, she probably did ask Kelly to join, but Kelly would never…" He shrugged and looked away again.

Catelyn glanced at Joseph trying to see what he thought.

An impassive rock stared back her, but she knew he wasn't missing a thing.

She turned back to Billy. Was this kid telling everything he knew? She couldn't tell. He still looked scared. And that made her suspicious that he knew something else.

She leaned forward. "Look Billy, if Kelly's in trouble, withholding information isn't going to help matters. We're going to get to the bottom of this one way or another."

He threw his hands up. "I don't know anything else. I'm sorry, but...I mean I can make something up if you want, but I don't know what else to tell you."

Alan placed a hand on the teen's shoulder. "Calm down, Billy. They're just trying to do their jobs."

"No, of course I don't want you to make something up," Catelyn assured him. "We just don't have much to go on and are doing everything we can to find out what happened to your sister and Tracy. One last question."

"What?"

"Do you think Dylan would hurt Tracy? Did he have any reason to kill her?"

Billy winced then mumbled, "I don't know. I didn't really hang around with Dylan that much even though he was dating Kelly. As for him hurting Tracy, I wouldn't think so, but they had a fight the other day. Kelly told me about it. Zachary, Tracy's brother, wanted Kelly to be his girl."

"And Kelly didn't want that."

"No way. She was all into Dylan."

"All right." Catelyn pressed her palms to the table and stood. "If you think of anything else, you'll call, right?"

"Sure." He licked his lips. "I will. Can I go now?"

"Yeah, go on."

Joseph looked at him. "You have a game tonight, right?"

"Yes, sir."

"Good luck, then. I look forward to watching you play."

Confusion flickered briefly, then he shrugged and said, "Oh, right. You're Alonso's brother. He's told me a lot about you and I've seen your picture. Thanks."

The boy and his coach left. The principal stood and shoved his hands in his pockets. "We want to do everything we can to help Billy. I don't think he would have anything to do with Tracy's death or Kelly's disappearance. He's our star baseball player. Our pitcher. He spends his time on the field. He doesn't hang out with the wrong kind of kids."

"Star pitcher, huh? Scholarship material?"

Pride puffed out Carlton's chest. "National Baseball League material for high school kids, then on to the majors. He's going to put this school on the map. You just wait and see. A couple of years ago, the district was going to cut the team, the whole program, due to a lack of funds. Thanks to an anonymous donor, we got the money. We already had the best coach in the country. Put those two together…" He rubbed his hands together in what Joseph would call glee. "Now, Billy and Coach Dillard are the ones taking the team all the way this year. It's going to be big. So, whatever I can do to help you with this case to make sure Billy stays in the clear, you just let me know."

Joseph frowned. "We're not investigating this to keep Billy in the clear. If Billy's guilty of something, Billy'll take the fall for it."

"I know, I just meant…"

Catelyn jumped in, saying, "Coach Dillard seems very involved with his students."

"Definitely." The man looked relieved at Catelyn's intervention. "All of our coaches are. He even takes a couple of them to church every week. Just the ones who want to go and don't have a ride. We certainly don't force anything on anyone. Alan's also an avid hunter and takes a group up into North Carolina every year. He says it teaches his students patience."

"Sounds like the school is lucky to have him," Joseph said.

"Definitely." They shook hands again.

The secretary popped her head in. "You're needed in the cafeteria, sir."

"Thanks, Alice." He turned back. "Can you two see yourselves out?"

"Absolutely. Thanks again for your cooperation."

"Anytime."

He left and Joseph looked at Catelyn. "Billy knows something, and he'd scared stiff to tell us what it is."

"I got that feeling, too."

"What do you think about the coach?"

Shrugging, she moved toward the door. "He seems nice enough, I guess. Supports his students, a concerned teacher."

"He's also in the running for the Amateur Baseball Association's coach of the year. His team is going to the High School Baseball World Series in July and he's got colleges and the National Baseball League looking at him. Like Mr. Bowles said, Billy's his star pitcher. Colleges all over are looking to snatch him up as soon as he graduates. And the man doesn't want anything to happen to shake that up. I think he'd protect Billy with his life if it came down to it." Joseph shook his head. "And although he comes across concerned and solicitous, I bet he wouldn't feel the same way if it was just his average student in trouble."

"Possibly. Then again, you never know. And how do you know all that about him anyway?"

He grinned. "I read the newspaper."

"Huh. Sounds like Coach has a lot going on."

Catelyn's phone rang, cutting her off. "Hello?"

"Hey, it's Sandy, in the crime lab."

"Sandy." Anticipation jumpstarted her heart rate. "What did you find?"

"The DNA came back with a match for the blood on the ring. You'll *never* guess who."

Catelyn took the information and looked at Joseph smugly as she hung up.

FIVE

"The DNA matched up with Dylan's. I'm shocked."

"Do I detect a tad of sarcasm in that statement?"

They rushed to the car, Catelyn heading for the passenger seat. "Maybe a tad."

"So it was Dylan's?"

"Yup."

Joseph heaved a sigh and climbed in. "I suppose you want to arrest him?"

Looking him in the eye, she said, "No, I don't *want* to, I have to. I'm sorry for Alonso, but I'm not surprised at this development. Dylan claimed he was never there. And now his DNA shows up on her ring?"

"Could have happened before that night."

"The blood was fresh. She hadn't been there long before the security guard found her."

Joseph fell silent for a couple of minutes. "The cut on his chin," he said, almost to himself.

"What?"

"The day he came to the crime scene at the school. I was thinking how Alonso and his buddies were growing up, then realized they were past growing, they were pretty much grown. Dylan had a cut on his chin and I thought he'd probably gotten it shaving. If that's Dylan's DNA on the ring, then Tracy must have slapped him, hit him or some-thing…maybe backhanded him, depending on which way her ring was turned."

"Let's go pick him up. He's at the deaf school. He's a part of the mainstream program even though he does most of his classes here at the high school. Alonso loves the program because he has the opportunity to be around his hearing friends and be at the deaf school, too."

She got on the phone with the deaf school and confirmed Dylan was on campus and informed them they were on the way with a warrant for his arrest. An officer would meet them there with the warrant. The school would call Dylan's mother and let her know what was going on. Joseph drove through town going slower than she would have liked. "You still don't think he's guilty, do you?"

"No, I don't. I think evidence can be misleading. I like to have all the facts before making a decision."

Was he implying that she didn't? Catelyn thought they had more than enough facts. "What about his jacket being at the scene? The ring with his DNA? The fact that he ob-viously lied about being there?"

"I agree. No doubt, evidence is there, but is it the right evidence or simply circumstantial? Sorry, I just…it's a gut thing."

She couldn't discount that. Not when her gut had saved her life more than once. Instead, she turned her thoughts toward arresting the kid, telling herself she was doing the right thing. Doing what she had to do.

Like her job.

No matter what anyone else said or argued. She was a good cop. She'd do a good job. Period.

If the kid was innocent, his lawyer would prove it.

Joseph got into contact with the school resource offi-

cer and put the man on notice that they were on the way
to arrest one of his students.

They arrived at the school and Joseph noticed the activity on the campus. Hands gestured, fingers flew in conversation. Students walking to and from class. A lot of laughter
going on. Unfortunately, one student wasn't going to be
laughing when he was arrested.

The deaf school principal knew they were coming and
stood outside the building to greet them. In his early thirties, he stood around six feet tall, had a dash of gray at his
temples and a commanding presence. He welcomed them
with a pained smile and a handshake. "I'm Cole Pierson.
Are you sure you've got the right person?"

Catelyn sighed. "The evidence says we do."

Shaking his head, he led the way back inside, saying,
"I'm having a hard time with this one. I know I've only
been here a short time, a couple of months since the last
principal retired, but I've gotten to know these kids pretty
well. Dylan comes from a tough background, but I can't
see him doing this. Especially not to poor Tracy. He worshipped that girl."

Catelyn cocked a brow. "In certain circumstances, wor-
ship can turn to hatred real quick."

"That's true, I suppose. I just…" Cole shook his head
again. "Well, let's get to it. We didn't put the school on
lockdown, but our school resource officer has gone to get
him. He'll bring him to the conference room."

As they headed in that direction, a young woman came
hurrying down the hall, speaking and signing at the same
time, "Dylan's gone. Kevin came by to get him, but he
wasn't in my classroom. I think he figured something out
and has run."

Catelyn demanded, "Which way did he go?"

"He came in my classroom for a brief minute, then left. When he went out, he turned left, so he either went to the restroom…or out the end door."

Joseph ran for the exit, Catelyn bolted for the one on the opposite end of the hall, thinking they could close in on him and catch in the middle.

Twenty minutes later, they gave up the search on the campus.

"If he's still on school grounds, we'll never find him," Joseph declared with disgust. "We'd have to get the K-9 unit out here to track him down."

"Yeah, I bet he knows this place like the back of his hand, including all nooks and crannies to hide in." Catelyn stood for a moment, thinking. "And if he's not on campus…where would you go if you were a scared deaf kid?"

Joseph watched her, seeing the wheels clicking in her mind. He answered, "Someplace I'd feel safe, to someone I could count on to help me out and not turn me in."

They looked at each other and said, simultaneously, "Alonso."

Realizing it was probably a waste of time, but having to check in spite of his gut feeling, Joseph raced back into the school building asked the secretary to call Alonso to the office. In the meantime, Joseph tried to text message his brother, however, he got no response even after several attempts. But then, Joseph reasoned, if Alonso was in class, he wouldn't have his phone on.

And if he was trying to help Dylan, he wouldn't bother answering Joseph's text messages. Joseph had a feeling it was the latter.

The secretary looked up from the black notebook. "He didn't sign out, but I called the security guard who said he drove off campus about ten minutes ago."

Joseph hit the glass door at a run and slammed himself

into the car. Catelyn gave him a questioning look and Joseph answered it, "He left campus."

"This isn't good."

Grimly, he told, "I'm aware of that. Let's catch up to them before anyone else spots them." Thinking fast, he told her, "Seems to me, every deaf kid I know has a phone simply for text messaging purposes, a Sidekick, a BlackBerry, whatever. Can we track his phone?"

"Do you have his number?"

"No." Joseph shook his head, then smiled and said, "No, but I've got Alonso's. If we're right and they're together, we can find them that way."

Pulling out her cell, she said, "Give me the number."

He did and she put the request in to the person on the other end. "Call me when you've got it. Thanks." Hanging up she looked at him. "I also put out a Be on the Lookout, a BOLO, for Dylan's car and Alonso's. Both cars are missing from the student lot. If they're in either one, they won't get far. The security guard said both boys left at approximately the same time. I have a feeling Dylan's going to ditch his car and hook up with Alonso."

Joseph said, "I would say that's pretty good reasoning. I can head back to my parents' house, but I'm thinking they probably wouldn't go there."

"Does Alonso have a favorite hangout? Is there a place the deaf kids just go to hang out?"

"The local pizza place over on Union Street or the arcade down on Church. Let's check the pizza place first."

"We also need to get in touch with Dylan's parents and let them know they need to contact us if he shows up at home."

Joseph wheeled the car toward the pizza place. Within minutes, they were driving through the parking lot. "I don't see Alonso's or Dylan's car."

Catelyn sighed in disgust and shook her phone. "How long does it take to track a cell number?"

"If they're having to go through the cell carrier, it'll take a little bit. They're not at the arcade. I'm going to head toward the house."

"That seems like the last place they'd go."

"Do you have any better ideas?"

She heaved a sigh. "He's your brother."

"Right."

Catelyn leaned back and shut her eyes against the headache that was starting. Her phone buzzed, intruding on her brief moment of peace.

"Hello?"

"Catelyn, your target is somewhere on Sugarleaf Street. Um…704, to be specific."

"Thank, Bri."

She hung up. "They're at your parents' house. Or at least that's where Alonso's phone tracked to."

Joseph let a smug look briefly cross his face. She resisted the urge to punch him, decided to let him revel in his cleverness and sat back to finish the short ride while her adrenaline pumped at the thought of arresting Dylan.

Five minutes later, Joseph pulled into the driveway of his childhood home. They hopped out and made their way up the front porch and into the house. His mother greeted them, signing her welcome. "Joseph, what brings you here in the middle of the day? And Catelyn…" Surprise lifted her brows. "Hello, darling."

"Hi, Mrs. Santino."

Concerned flickered across her smooth, chubby face as she looked at Joseph. "What is it, son?"

"Is Alonso here, Mama?"

She twisted her ever present apron between her hands,

then dropped it to sign, "No, he didn't come in the house. At least I didn't feel his usual thumping vibrations. He could have snuck in, I suppose. Is something wrong?"

Joseph told Catelyn, "I'll check his room. You explain to Mom what's going on."

"Okay."

He bounded up the stairs two at a time. Following the well-worn carpet to Alonso's room, he found the door open—and the room empty.

Just as he'd suspected.

Treading back down the steps, he found Catelyn and his mother deep in conversation. Ever since practically being adopted into his family, Catelyn had learned to sign on an expert level. As a CODA, Child of a Deaf Adult, Joseph had learned American Sign Language before he could speak.

He broke into the conversation. "He's not up there."

Confusion stamped plainly on her face, Catelyn turned to go back to the car. Joseph followed. She got in and got on the radio. Within seconds, she had Bri on the line. "Check the signal again, will you?"

A short wait. The radio squawked and Bri said, "Still the same location, Catelyn."

She turned to Joseph and said, "The phone's still here somewhere. The boys at least stopped by here. Do you think they could have left again with Alonso forgetting his phone—or leaving it behind on purpose?"

"Alonso wouldn't leave his phone. It's like an extension of his body."

"Unless he thought we might track him with it."

"I don't think he'd think about that, to be honest. He'd just be doing his best to get away to a place where he and Dylan could talk—or hide out."

"Then they're here. Somewhere." She rubbed her forehead. "I'd call the phone and see if it would ring, but no doubt it's on vibrate. I'm trying to think of some good hiding places from when we played hide-and-seek all those years ago."

"He's not in the house, I…" Joseph broke off and looked her in the eye. "Granny's suite."

"Excuse me?"

"The basement. I almost forgot all about it. Come on."

She scrambled from the car as he led the way to the side of the house. "It has a separate entrance and everything. We never use it, haven't used it in forever. It's been closed off since our grandmother died. With Alonso being the only kid left at home, Mom didn't need the space and didn't want to have to worry about cleaning it, so she just closed it down."

They reached the door. Catelyn looked down. "Footprints."

"Recent ones. Just the right size for a couple of teenage boys, too. See those prints there? They're different from the ones on this side."

"No use knocking, they're both deaf."

He twisted the knob and the door swung inward. "They didn't bother to lock the door." He stepped inside taking in the large area jam packed with antiques, family mementos and other unused, probably forgotten items.

A light snuffed out and darkness shrouded them. Joseph stated, "Yep, they're here."

"But they don't want us to know that they are."

"Back up."

"What?"

"Just do it, will you?"

Huffing a sigh, she did it. Joseph pulled the door shut as he exited.

"What are you doing now?" she demanded.

"Waiting. Now, you head around to the side and cover

the window." Thunder rumbled and he looked at the sky. Gray clouds billowed overhead.

"Fine, what are we waiting on though?"

"One of them to check and see if the coast is clear. It'll save us hunting through that dusty mess and trying to chase down a scared kid. Let's just let them come to us."

Realization crossed her face.

"You're still a rat, Joseph."

"But a clever one, you must admit." Oh, how he loved it when the red flush took over and she looked at him in annoyance. But she couldn't help the small smile that tried to curve her lush lips.

"All right," she admitted, "a clever one." She left him and he watched her round the corner.

"Joseph?" she called. "They've already managed to get out. I can see them running. I'm going after them!"

"What? How?" He made his way around to find Catelyn racing off in the direction of the road.

Five minutes later, Catelyn leaned her palms against her knees and puffed, "Nice work, Colombo. Very clever."

"Hey, how was I supposed to know they'd move so fast? They ran up the stairs and out the back door. Mom's still shaking her fist at them."

"If we'd just gone in and…never mind. How far away could they be?"

"Far enough. There's tons of places to hide around here, and it's not a far hike into town to some of the stores."

"Then let's get officers here to set up a perimeter and a K-9 unit."

"We need a chopper, too."

Joseph was already talking into his radio. When he finished, he looked at her grim-faced and furious as he pulled out his BlackBerry.

"What are you doing?" she asked, annoyance still evident.

"Telling Alonso to haul himself back here and that he'd better hurry up and talk his friend into turning himself in."

"You think he'll listen?"

"There's always hope. He's been making some good decisions lately. Let's hope he adds this one to the list."

Catelyn sighed. "Running from the cops doesn't seem like a very good decision to me."

"You're right, it doesn't." He ran a hand through his hair. "I really think Alonso will come through. He's got a baseball game tonight. That is if it's not cancelled." He looked at the clouds that were threatening to release a downpour. "There's no way he'd jeopardize the team's status by not showing up. When he shows, I'll grab him and grill him, okay? And if it's cancelled, I'll figure something else out."

Indecision marred her features and he wanted to reach out and smooth her wrinkled forehead. Instead, he clenched his fingers into a fist. "Let's get in the car and see if we can track them down."

"Fine."

They hurried to his vehicle and he pulled the door open. A raindrop smacked his nose before he had a chance to duck inside.

Catelyn's door slammed and she pointed. "That way.

"Do you see them anywhere?" she asked as he circled the block.

Her question distracted him for a moment. "No, I'll try this other side street."

Catelyn watched him drive, competent, strong…intense. Swallowing hard, she refocused her attention on the search. She picked up the radio and called for backup in the neighborhood. Joseph sighed, but didn't protest. He wanted to find these kids as soon as possible, too.

The drizzle turned into a steady downpour.

"We're never going to be able to spot them in this mess. They've most likely holed up somewhere." He slapped the steering wheel, frustration stamped on his forehead.

"Let's get the dogs out. They can track anything, even in the rain."

"I'll call it in."

While he did that, she answered her ringing phone. Slapping it to her ear, she stared out her window at the rain. "Hello? What? When?" She whirled back around to look at him.

His gaze sharpened, and she knew he could see the worry on her face. "What is it?"

"I'll be right there." She hung up and bit her lip.

"What?" he insisted.

"My mother." Her voice shook. She cleared her throat. "She's taken a turn for the worse. They can't wake her up. She's…"

He stopped the car, then did a three-point turn. "I'll take you back to the station to get your car. You go see about your mother and I'll take care of the case—and Alonso. Call me as soon as you know something."

She hesitated, stared up at him like she wanted to say something.

"What is it?"

"Thank you, Joseph."

"For what?"

"Just…" She shrugged. "Thanks."

Five minutes later, he pulled up beside her car and placed a hand on her arm. "I know you need to go, but…be thinking about what you want, Catelyn, okay? When all this is over, could we please sit down and have a major talk?" Intense brown eyes held her captive.

What she *wanted?* Have a major talk?

"What do you mean, Joseph? I want to solve this case. I want to find Kelly Franklin, I want…"

His finger covered her lips and she froze. "I mean—" his throat bobbed, betraying his cool, seemingly unaffected attitude "—is there a possibility for there to be an 'us' again? Could you possibly want to explore these feelings that are still there between us?"

Catelyn shut her mind against the instant rush of wonderful memories with this man, and instead, focused on the reason they'd split up.

"You're a cop."

His brown eyes glinted. She hadn't denied she still had feelings for him and he'd picked up on that. "I'll agree with that."

"Well, so am I. And I'm not giving that up."

"Did I ask you to?" Confusion flickered as he sat back to stare at her.

"Yes, Joseph, you did."

The stunned look on his face floored her. Did he not realize? "I told you about my father and you started acting just like him."

Stunned, he countered, "How did you come up with that? You said he wanted your mother to stay home and be mom and a wife. What's wrong with that?"

"Everything!"

How could anyone so smart be so dense?

She hopped out of his car and into hers, cranked the engine and sped off.

Women.

Joseph drove back to his parents' home with the vain hope that Alonso had come to his senses and returned there. The dogs would be here shortly to pick up the scent. Joseph would let them do their job while he did his.

Parking in the drive, he shook his head, opened the door and dashed through the rain into the house. *Having grown up in a household full of women, you'd think I would understand them by now, but I don't, God, especially not Catelyn. What did I say that was so wrong? So I would prefer that she think about staying home instead of working. Is that so wrong?*

Guilt gnawed at him as he thought about the conversations that seemed to come in spurts. He'd never asked her to quit being cop.

Not in so many words.

But what did his actions say? Was he *not* saying something that he should put into words?

But what? How could he reassure her that they could work everything out? What did she need to hear to put her fears to rest?

Lost in thought, he intended to make his way to the back bedroom, the one across from his parents' master bedroom, but his mother stepped out of the kitchen cutting off his path. "Is everything all right?" she signed.

Not wanting to worry her, he signed back, "I think it will be. Nothing for you to be anxious about, okay?"

She waved aside his words then planted her hands on ample hips before lifting them one more time to sign. "I may not be a big bad FBI agent, but I'm still a mother and I know when something's wrong." Narrowing her eyes, she signed, "If you don't want to tell me, fine, but don't try to tell me everything's all right when your face, the tension in your shoulders and your heavy footsteps tell me another story."

"Mom, I'm sorry." He tamped down his impatience to get moving. "No, everything's not all right, but I don't want to say anything right now. There, is that better?"

"Much." She stood on tiptoes while he bent at the waist.

She pressed a kiss to his cheek then she reached up to pat it with a soft hand. "You need to shave. Your father and I are going out to eat with friends. Alonso's game has been canceled due to the rain. You're welcome to join us or eat the casserole in the fridge."

"I'll take the casserole, thanks." He backed toward his room, needing to get going.

"I think we're going to go see one of the late movies after we eat, so don't worry about us if we're not home until midnight or so, okay?"

She headed back into the kitchen to grab her purse, and Joseph bolted for his room.

Even as he kept an eye out for the K-9 unit, love for his mother filled him. He heard his dad's footsteps heading in the direction of Joseph's mom. All his life, his mother had been a living example of the kind of woman Joseph wanted to marry.

Without warning, Catelyn's pretty features flashed into his mind. Ruthlessly, he shoved them away. Catelyn had made it clear she wasn't interested in marrying a cop. And, too late, he'd discovered she wasn't interested in being a stay-at-home wife and mother, which is the kind of woman he'd always pictured himself settling down with. The thought of marrying a career woman had never held any appeal for him. Call him old-fashioned, but that was just the way he was. And the thought of Catelyn being hurt or killed was just more than he could bear. His heart cramped at the thought. But he'd figured they'd work through it. Find a solution, a compromise that would make them both happy. However, before he could even present the idea to her, she'd refused to see him, have anything to do with him. So when he got the call from New York saying the FBI job was his if he wanted it, he'd taken it.

Maybe he should have pushed harder to get her to talk to him, but…he'd been hurt, too. So, he'd left.

Only now he had regrets. Lots of them. And he'd come to realize a future with Catelyn would be completely different than what he'd always pictured. She didn't meet any of the expectations he'd mentally placed on his future spouse; add in Catelyn's reserve about marrying another officer and he had hurdles in his path that he didn't know if he could successfully leap over.

And he wasn't interested in a job change. Although, if it meant doing it for her…

Was he willing to revamp everything he'd ever thought about when it came to marriage and family?

He sighed and focused his attention back to the case. He simply had to put Catelyn and their relationship out of his mind until this case was over. So he turned his thoughts to his brother.

He heard his parents leave. Two minutes later, the unit arrived. Grabbing Alonso's pillow from his bed, he carried it downstairs to meet the handler, Christine Palmer and her K-9, Zorro.

"Hey, Christine, how are you?"

The petite redhead nodded at him. "Doing well, Joseph. Good to see you again."

"Yeah, you too. I just wish it wasn't for this reason." He held the pillow out to the German shepherd at her side. The dog took a good sniff and Christine put him to work.

"Let me know immediately what you find, will you?" he hollered at her disappearing back. "I'll be right here working on what I can from this end."

"You got it," she yelled.

Worry about Alonso engulfed him. His suspicion that the game would be cancelled had come to fruition. That meant Alonso was out there somewhere. With a BOLO out on both boys, it wouldn't be long before he would be getting a phone call that they'd been picked up. His heart ached at the thought of his brother's involvement. He just hoped it didn't come to the point where he had to excuse himself from the case.

He still had a couple of hours before darkness would fall.

He pulled out his laptop and connected to his parents' wireless server. Then ran a specialized software program that would ensure privacy while he used the Internet.

For an hour or so, he worked, running another background check on all the individuals involved in the case. There was nothing on any of the teenagers except Dylan Carlisle. The boy had been arrested as a juvenile for shoplifting, minor vandalism, joyriding without a license—and assault and battery.

Old news.

His phone rang. He grabbed it before the sound faded. "Hello?"

"Joseph? This is Christine. The dog tracked the scent down the road a bit, then I think the boys got into a car because Zorro completely lost them."

Great. He sighed. "Thanks. Give Zorro an extra treat from me."

"Sure thing."

So now he would wait and see if an officer picked them up. Who would have given them a ride? A question Alonso would answer just as soon as Joseph caught up with him.

A little more research into Dylan's background showed the assault and battery was a school fight. The charges on that had later been dropped. He'd had a shoplifting charge and served some community service for the shoplifting charge. Other than that, the kid really didn't have a record.

Still, it didn't look good for the boy.

And yet, Alonso obviously believed in his friend enough to help him at the risk of some major trouble for himself.

Another hour flew by before his stomach growled, reminding him he needed to eat something. Time had passed quickly with Joseph so engrossed in what he was doing, he hadn't noticed the sun going down.

His phone rang.

Catelyn.

He picked it up on the second ring. "Hello?"

"Have you found the boys yet?" She didn't waste any time getting to the point, did she?

"Not yet. The K-9 unit came out, but the boys must have gotten into a car because the dog lost them. I'm trying to decide the next step in this case. I traced Alonso's cell phone again and got nothing. I think he's pulled the battery out. Same with Dylan's. I finally got ahold of Dylan's mother and she gave me the number."

"Great. Well, look, I'm almost home. I need to pick up something to take back to my mother, then I can meet you somewhere. Back at the office or wherever, or we can try to find Alonso and Dylan again."

"Fine, give me a call when you're ready. I'll keep working it from this angle. How's your mom?"

"She had an allergic reaction to something she ate, but she's doing better, thanks. I'll call you shortly, okay?"

"Sounds good."

She hung up, and Joseph just sat there for a moment trying to figure the woman out. He looked back at the computer and then realized how dark the room had become.

Squinting through the blackness, he reached for the switch on the bedside table when the floor creaked under the weight of a footstep.

He froze. Listened.

Another creak. Like a person shifting his weight.

Alonso? No, that kid would burst into Joseph's room unannounced with no hesitation—at least he would've before today.

Whoever it was, he—or she—was standing just outside the bedroom door, making no attempt to knock or announce himself. Could it be his dad?

Probably not. Engrossed in his work, Joseph's mind had absently registered the sound of the door closing behind his parents when they'd left the house hours ago.

Not wanting to call out and let the person know Joseph knew someone was outside his door, he eased his way over to the drawer of his nightstand, slid it open and wrapped his fingers around his gun.

Could it be Alonso after all? Trying to work up the courage to face his brother?

Or someone with a more sinister motive in mind?

Catelyn drove toward home, her mind in a jumble. Her mother was fine. A false alarm. The allergic reaction had been resolved with a whopping dose of Benadryl. As a result, the poor woman had just been too tired to bother to respond to those trying to wake her.

Catelyn stayed as long as she felt necessary. When her mother had awakened long enough to look at her with that blank expression on her face, Catelyn's heart nearly broke and she knew it wouldn't matter if she stayed or left. On her way out, a nurse stopped her and asked, "Do you know what your mother may have meant by the words fun album?"

Confused, Catelyn thought. "No, why?"

"She was asking for it earlier. Wanted her fun album."

"Um…no, not really. I can't think of what she might have…" Realization dawned. "Wait a minute. I might know what she's talking about after all. I have a photo album at home. It has pictures in it of the one time we actually took a family vacation."

"Could you bring it next time you come?"

"I'll bring it back tonight."

"Oh, but you don't have to…"

But Catelyn was already out the door. If her mother wanted that album tonight, she'd have it.

Her stomach growled reminding her she hadn't eaten in a while. If she waited too much longer, she'd get the shakes. As she drove past the grocery store nearest her house, she recognized a car in the parking lot.

Sandy.

On impulse, she spun into the lot and parked still thinking about her continued interaction with Joseph.

Why on earth did *that man* still have an effect on her emotions, her heart, her—everything? It made no sense.

Lord, I gave him up two years ago. I told You I would dedicate my life to You and serve You in the capacity of being the best cop I could be. What purpose do You have in bringing Joseph back into my life?

Anger stirred beneath the surface. What right did he have to come back and interfere? Acting like everything should be all right between them? Wanting to talk about "us"?

"Hi. Catelyn."

Startled, she turned at the sound of her name. Just the person she'd been looking for.

"Oh, hi. Sandy. How are you doing?"

"Fine thanks. Just taking a little break from work to grab a few of the necessities. My cupboard is looking a little bare."

Catelyn gave a small laugh. "I know what you mean."

"How's the case progressing?" Sandy tossed a pack of chocolate chip cookies into her cart.

Catelyn grabbed a ready-made roast beef sandwich and a bag of chips. She grimaced and shook her head. "Actually, I saw your car in the parking lot and thought I'd come hunt you down. I was going to ask you the same question. Unfortunately, it seems like we're spinning our wheels on this end. Although, if I could go without sleeping or eating, I might have it solved by now."

"Well, I don't have anything from the lab for you yet, sorry."

Shrugging, Catelyn stepped into the line to pay for her sandwich. "It's all right. I know you'll call when you do, I just decided to stop..." She paused.

The woman offered a commiserating smile. "So...you're working with Joseph Santino?"

Catelyn might have known this subject would come up. Taking a deep breath, she nodded sighed, and handed her sandwich and chips to the cashier as she dug in her front pocket for a ten-dollar bill. "Yes, I am."

"How's that going?"

Sandy knew the history there. She'd been there with a shoulder for Catelyn to cry on two years ago. "It's definitely interesting."

Sympathy flashed on her friend's face. "Well, if you need me, you know where to find me."

"Yeah, the lab. You work too hard."

"Isn't that the pot calling the kettle black?"

Catelyn grimaced. "I suppose it is. And thanks for the offer. Actually, to be honest, I'm not sure what's going on. The feelings are still there—on both sides. I'm just..."

"Scared of getting hurt again?"

"Right. Thanks for beating around the bush."

"Well, it's no wonder. I don't blame you. But I think you're dumb if you let him get away again. He's not like your dad."

Catelyn blinked at the woman's directness. "Maybe not, but I'm afraid I might be too much like my mom."

"There is that. But you need to keep one thing in mind."

"What's that?"

"I don't know Joseph very well. Just what I've heard. But I do know he's highly respected and lives his faith. You do, too."

Confused where she was going with this, Catelyn wrinkled her brow and waited.

Sandy didn't disappoint her. "You and Joseph are both believers. You love God. Your parents didn't have that."

Stunned, Catelyn could only stare at Sandy as she processed that statement. Then looked at the cashier. The woman patiently waited for Catelyn to pay. Catelyn handed over the money with an embarrassed shrug.

Sandy smiled sympathetically. "I'll see you later. Take care and let me know how it works out. I'll be praying for you guys. And I'll also let you know as soon as I have something from the lab."

Pulling into her driveway ten minutes later, Catelyn realized with a start she had no memory of the drive home. Great.

Climbing out of the car, she grabbed her sandwich from the seat beside her. At least it had finally quit raining.

Her empty house loomed in the evening light. Soon it would be completely dark. And she would be alone once more. Normally, she didn't mind the solitude, but now that Joseph had come back, she found herself longing for his company once again.

And that just wouldn't do. She'd fallen for him once, then learned he expected her to quit her job to stay home and be his dutiful little wife.

Catelyn shuddered, grateful she'd found that out before she married him. She would have been her mother all over again, living a life of misery, full of arguments and…

Nausea churned in her as she shut down that line of linking. What a disaster that would have been.

She sat there for a moment, considering whether or not to eat her sandwich right there or take it inside.

Inside might be better. She could grab the album then get back into the car to make the drive back to the nursing home before she hooked back up with Joseph to continue working on the case. If she just sat here, she'd keep thinking about Joseph.

Climbing out of her car, she unwrapped the sandwich and took a bite. She needed to hurry. Kelly was still missing; Alonso and Dylan needed to be found. She had no time to waste and felt a little guilty for stopping to eat when so much needed to be done. And Joseph would be waiting for her call.

Joseph. She stomped up the steps of her front porch. He should have just stayed in New York. But he hadn't. He'd come back. True, it wasn't because he'd opted to do so. It was because of a case, but he was back and she wanted him to stay.

Really, really wanted him to stay.

With her.

Exasperated with herself for her inability to purge him from her thoughts, she grabbed her key, inserted it and turned it to the right.

And stopped.

There had been no familiar click.

Her door hadn't been locked.

Shut, but not locked.

Had she forgotten when she'd left for work this morning? Not likely.

With careful, watchful movements, Catelyn unsnapped

the strap holding her gun in the holster just under her armpit. Pulling the weapon out, she stepped just inside the door.

Did she have an intruder, and was he still here?

The brief thought that she should call for backup flittered through her mind. But if she'd simply forgotten to lock the door, she'd feel pretty silly calling this in. She'd never live it down.

Not that she should let pride get in the way of safety, still...

The small foyer curved around into the den.

Again, she came to an abrupt halt.

It had been trashed. In one sweeping glance, she took in the destruction. Her television sported a gaping a hole, jagged glass grinning at her like an evil jack-o'-lantern. It looked like it had been wantonly smashed with a blunt object. The rest of her electronics were gone, bare spaces on her entertainment center mocking her.

Shock and revulsion filled her. Not that the scene was anything new. She dealt with this kind of thing every day. Only now, it had happened to her.

She found it chilling. Horrific.

Scary.

Backing out of the room, she reached for her cell phone. She needed help.

That's when she heard the running feet coming up behind her.

SIX

Joseph swung the gun up, keeping the nose pointed toward the threat that could possibly be waiting on the other side of the door. Sliding his feet out of his shoes, he crept toward the door.

Positioning himself to the side, he waited.

Listened.

Heard nothing.

Then a scrape, like the shuffle of a foot. And his mom thought his shoulders had been tense before. The muscles across the base of his neck felt ready to snap.

With his left hand, he reached for the knob.

Before he could get a good grip, he felt it turning under his palm.

Pulling his hand away like he'd touched a hot stove, he raised it to join his right hand, wrapping his fingers around the butt of the gun in a two-hand hold.

He stepped back so that he was an arm's length away from the door. Just the right distance between him and the head of the person who entered.

Light filtered from the attached bathroom opposite the wall where he stood. The faint glow enabled him to see the knob turning. Instead of watching it finish its journey around, he raised his eyes and brought his arms down to aim the weapon at head level.

And waited.

Slowly, the door opened. The hinges squeaked and the person on the other side paused.

And waited.

Breathing coming more shallowly, Joseph felt his adrenaline surging, could feel his heart pounding. But his cool professionalism never wavered.

Who was it?

Catelyn whirled to confront her intruder and got a glimpse of a ski mask before the person rammed into her, knocking her back against the foyer wall. Her feet went out from under her and she landed on her backside.

With a whoosh, her breath left her; her gun flew from her fingers and skittered across the hardwood.

Pounding feet moved in the direction of the front door.

Oh, no you don't, you little punk.

From her sprawled position on the floor, lungs still screaming for a deep breath, she threw out a foot and connected with a shin of the escaping thug.

"Ah!" He went down.

But before she could react, he threw a punch in her direction. It caught her on the cheek, snapping her head back against the floor.

Stars danced in front of her eyes.

No time to pass out. Get the gun.

Shaking off the dizziness and a sudden wave of nausea, she scrambled toward the weapon. More pounding feet. The slam of the door and her aching head left her ears ringing.

She reached for her cell phone and punched in the direct work line to her friend, a dispatcher for the 911 service here in Spartanburg.

"911. What's your emergency?"

"Hey, Tara, it's Catelyn," She winced at the breathy sound of her voice and cleared her throat.

"Catelyn? Are you okay?"

"Ah, no, not really. My home was broken into and I surprised the creeps."

"I'm dispatching a unit right now." The familiar, friendly tone in her voice disappeared as she turned into the skilled professional she'd been for seven years. "Do you need an ambulance? Are you hurt?"

"No, not too bad."

"That means you're hurt. You get an ambulance."

"No, no, seriously, I think I'm all right. Just a few knocks and bruises. It could have been a lot worse."

"Just stay on the line with me."

Catelyn did because she knew if she didn't she'd wind up with more than just a police cruiser in her driveway. Vaguely, she registered Tara's dispatch speech, the codes she used and knew the woman was sending an ambulance whether Catelyn wanted one or not.

She just hoped Joseph wasn't in his car listening to the scanner.

Joseph kept the gun steady. The door continued its inward swing to land on the opposite wall from Joseph. As soon as the figure stepped inside, Joseph placed the gun against his head.

The person froze.

And thanks to the moonlight, Joseph got a good look at his intruder.

Dylan.

Joseph quickly pointed the gun elsewhere and flipped on the light switch. The boy's eyes were wide and scared, his hands held out from his body.

Signing with one hand, Joseph demanded, "What do you think you're doing, sneaking into someone's house, Dylan? Not smart."

"I need help."

"You bet you do. Go in the den while I put this away." Joseph made sure the safety was on, but slipped it into the waistband of his pants. He believed Dylan was innocent, and yet...

Exiting the room, he made his way into the den where he found Dylan sitting on the couch chewing a thumbnail to the quick.

Sighing, Joseph signed, "Why'd you run, Dylan? And why are sneaking around this house? That's a pretty good way to get yourself shot."

The boy threw his hands up and signed back, "I was scared. I don't want to go to jail. I didn't kill Tracy, but nobody believes me." He swallowed hard. "Actually, I did knock, but when you didn't answer, I decided to come find you. I didn't want to leave because I was scared someone else might be looking for me and you're the only one who even thinks it's possible that I might be innocent."

Had he been that into what he was doing that he hadn't heard the knock on the door? Must have been. "You should have rung the bell," he grumbled. "Did you know there's a warrant out for your arrest?"

Dylan's throat bobbed again in time with the jerky nod of his head. His right hand curled into a fist that he shook with the sign for "Yes." "I know. I saw the teachers talking about it in the office. They didn't know I'd come down there to turn in some papers. They were saying that you were on the way to arrest me."

"So you ran." A statement.

Dylan nodded.

"And got my brother in the middle of it. What kind of friend does that?"

Tears gathered in Dylan's eyes and Joseph hated to be so harsh, but the kid needed to realize the seriousness of his situation.

Dylan nodded, signing, "I know. That's why when Alonso insisted I come find you, I had to do it."

"He insisted, huh? Where is Alonso anyway?"

"He's waiting on the porch. He said I had to do this. Turn myself in and let you see that I'm not guilty. That I'm willing to let you help prove that I'm not a killer. So, will you help me?"

Joseph stood and strode through the room, into the foyer and opened the door. His brother sat on the two-seater swing, rocking like he hadn't a care in the world. He looked up when Joseph appeared in the doorway to sign. "Get yourself in here, little brother."

A frown marred the teen's forehead, but he didn't argue, just rose and followed Joseph back into the house.

Once in the den, Alonso looked at Dylan and signed, "Well, did you ask him?"

"Yes."

Joseph looked back and forth between the two. He signed to Alonso, "So you convinced him to turn himself in."

"Yeah. Running was stupid and I told him that. I also told him that you would prove he didn't kill Tracy or hurt Kelly but he had to turn himself in."

The weight of his younger brother's unwavering faith fell heavily on Joseph's shoulders. "You told him that, huh?"

Alonso shrugged, signing, "Sure, it's what you do and as you're always saying, it's what you do well, so why wouldn't you be able to help my friend out?"

Joseph paced from one end of the room to the other, then

turned to face his brother and sign, "All right, Mom and Dad went to the late movie after supper. I want to get this taken care of before they get back. So, here's what we're going to do. I'm going to call Detective Clark and let her know that I'm arresting you, all right?"

Dylan's eyes went huge, but he didn't say anything. Joseph continued, keeping his signs fluid, "You may have to spend some time behind bars, but I've got friends in the system and can probably get you in a cell by yourself, all right? So no one would bother you. It'll buy us time to find out who's behind all this, okay?"

Some of the fear left Dylan at Joseph's reassurances. Being deaf, the kid would be terrified to be in a place where communication would be limited. Not that there weren't other deaf inmates, but the majority of them were adults. No way was Joseph letting this kid be subjected to that if he could help it. "Who gave you a ride when you ran from here earlier?"

"Chad drove by and we hopped in."

"Chad, huh? I thought he was mad at Dylan."

"Naw, they made up. After he calmed down and he and Dylan talked about it, he doesn't think Dylan had anything to do with killing Tracy any more than I do."

"Why wasn't he in school?"

Alonso flushed. Joseph answered for him. "Skipping, huh?"

His brother offered a shrug and looked away.

Joseph picked up his BlackBerry and punched the number he had on speed dial for Catelyn.

Officers crowded her small cottage-style house. The two-bedroom, two bath home glowed brighter than a Christmas tree on December 25.

Neighbors peered out windows, some stepped out onto

their porches, and Catelyn knew she'd be the recipient of more casseroles and desserts than she'd be able to eat over the next few days. Not that her neighbors didn't genuinely like her and visit occasionally, but Catelyn had a feeling visits would triple. They were good people, just a nosy bunch.

Paramedics and medical personnel swarmed her and she fought them off claiming she was fine. They insisted on bandaging the cut on her cheek. She let them just to get them off her back. Itching to get back in and help the crime-scene guys process her den, she finally pushed the good-intentioned hands away and hopped off the back of the ambulance. "Thanks, guys."

Before stepping through the door, she scanned the front of her house and driveway. Four police cars sat outside her home. "I only wanted one unit," she muttered under her breath.

And yet, she was secretly touched. They'd heard about one of their own being in trouble and had immediately responded. Couldn't ask for more than that.

Sighing, she braced herself and went inside. Silently, she surveyed the mess. Then heard her phone ringing—somewhere. Where had she left it? Looking around, she spotted her purse on the table just inside the foyer by the door. Oh, right. Grabbing the bag, she fished the phone out and answered it on the last ring.

"Hello."

"Catelyn?"

"Joseph?"

"Yeah. You busy?"

She looked around and gave a small laugh devoid of humor. "Um, a little bit, yes. Can I call you back in a couple of hours? Oh, wait a minute, what time is it?"

"It's around eight-thirty, I think. I just wanted to let you know I've got Dylan Carlisle here my house. I'm placing him under arrest. You want to meet me at the station or come here?"

The floor shifted beneath her feet. "Excuse me? Did you just say you had Dylan Carlisle?"

"Nothing wrong with *your* hearing, is there?"

"Um, okay, right. It's just I'm a little busy. Someone broke into my house and I'm dealing with the aftermath."

"What?!"

She winced and pulled the phone away from her ear. "Nothing wrong with my hearing, remember?"

"Are you okay?" he demanded.

She was so tired of telling people she was fine. "I'm fine. I'll be there in a few minutes."

"You got it. We'll be waiting on you."

Ten minutes later, Catelyn finished giving her statement and once again assuring everyone she suffered no serious side effects of her run-in with the attacker.

Finally, the crime-scene guys packed it in. Sarah Hinson, part of the CSU team, stopped her as she rushed for the door. "We'll check out the prints and stuff, but I'll tell you right now, this is looking similar to the break-ins going on over on the west side of town."

"I've heard about those, heard the chatter in the office, but haven't really kept up with what's happening."

"Whoever's involved is getting bold. They broke into a home with the owners there."

Concern pinched her. "Was anyone hurt?"

"Nope, the old man was asleep on the couch. His wife was downstairs in the basement in their home office. Perps walked in an unlocked door and started hauling stuff away. Started in the bedrooms and worked their way forward. By the time the guy woke up and realized someone was in his house, it was too late. They ran, climbed into a waiting van and took off. The guy just said it was a nondescript blue van. Didn't even get a license plate because he didn't have his glasses on."

"Scary." And it was. "Look, I've got to run. Thanks for all your help."

"Just doing my job. Take care of that head of yours."

Wincing, Catelyn raised a hand to touch the knot at the base of her skull. Her cheek throbbed, too. "I will."

She picked up the album that had fallen to the floor and placed it on the small table to the left of her front door. Her mother would just have to wait. She had a murderer to put behind bars.

Joseph heard her car pull into the driveway and let the boys know Catelyn had arrived. Dylan immediately lost what little relaxation he'd managed to achieve. Alonso blew out a sigh between pursed lips and eyed his friend.

When the knock came at the door, Joseph crossed the room to open it. She entered, her gaze zeroing in on Dylan. Seeing his slumped, dejected form, she stopped. For a brief moment, she looked like she'd rather be anywhere else; doing anything other than what she'd sworn to do.

Uphold the law.

"Catie." Joseph breathed as he took in her bruised cheek and disheveled appearance.

She held up a hand. "I'm fine."

Then she straightened her shoulders and marched into the den, signing, "Get up, Dylan, and let's go. I suppose Joseph's already read you your rights." At his affirming nod, she signed as she talked, explaining that the DNA on the ring had come back matching Dylan's. He raised a hand to his chin. To the cut Joseph had noticed his first day back. The cut he'd just figured had been a result of shaving.

Hesitantly, fear radiating off him in waves, Dylan rose

and held out his hands. Catelyn efficiently snapped them into place and signed, "Let's go."

Joseph frowned at her brusqueness. Normally, in a situation on the street, he wouldn't have thought twice about it, but here in his parents' living room with a scared kid who'd just turned himself in, she seemed so…uncaring.

It hurt to watch. The Catelyn he'd known two years ago would've…no, he couldn't think about that. At least she'd cuffed the kid's hands in front of him so he could still communicate. Joseph turned to Alonso and signed, "I'll be back. Tell Mom and Dad what's going on when they get back, all right?"

He followed her to the squad car. An unmarked, beige Town Car that shouted "Cop." Dylan obediently allowed Catelyn to herd him into the car.

Joseph settled into the passenger seat. He noticed she didn't offer him the keys. "You've changed."

Cranking the car, she ignored his statement. At least that's what it looked like to him. They drove in complete silence to the jail. Things didn't improve as they walked inside to the booking area.

Joseph cleared his throat. "I called his parents while we were waiting for you. They should be here somewhere. At least his mother will. You never know with his dad."

She didn't even blink, just nodded. "An interpreter is on the way."

Even though he and Catelyn were both highly skilled in ASL, it would be a conflict of interest for either of them to act in the capacity of interpreter.

Twenty minutes later, Jonathan Wise arrived and jumped into his job with skilled professionalism. Dylan knew the man from the deaf school and seemed relieved, if a little embarrassed to see him. Dylan's mother arrived shortly after the booking process began.

The interpreter explained to Dylan that he would have a hearing within seventy-two hours. Dylan shrugged. He'd been through this before, but had never been charged with something so serious. Once booked, Joseph led him to an interrogation room, the interpreter dutifully following.

Once in the interrogation room, Catelyn stood against the wall while Joseph sat down opposite of Dylan. The teen's mother waited in another area and his lawyer was on the way.

Staring at Catelyn, he wondered at the expression on her face. Tense, resolute. Poor Dylan.

The door opened and a heavyset woman in her mid fifties entered the room. "I'm Rose Donovan, Dylan's lawyer."

After handshakes all around, the lawyer and her client faced off the Special Agent and the Homicide Detective.

Here goes round one, thought Joseph.

"Now, what's my client being charged with?"

Catelyn sucked in a deep breath and repeated everything she'd told Dylan when he'd been arrested. The interpreter didn't miss a thing.

"Now," Catelyn concluded, "Jocelyn's already read Dylan his rights, the interpreter was there and we've got it on camera. He understands everything." She passed the paper to the lawyer who tapped it and nodded. "The big question tonight is why Dylan's DNA was on Tracy's ring when he claims he never saw her that night."

The boy signed. "All right. Here's the truth. The rest of it anyway."

So, he had been holding back. Joseph felt anger twist his insides. "You should have come clean long before now, Dylan."

Defiance flashed for a brief moment, then he dropped his eyes to the table. When he raised them to Joseph, he asked, "Just wait until I tell you everything before you get all mad." Another deep breath. "I didn't kill Tracy, so I didn't think it would matter."

Catelyn stomped to the table, leaned over and growled as she signed, "Spill. And if you leave out a single, solitary detail, I'll nail your hide to the wall, do you understand me?"

Dylan recoiled, his own anger bubbling just below the surface. Joseph could see it clearly.

"Catelyn, back off a little, huh?"

She whirled. "Don't tell me how to do my job."

Whoa. Her eyes snapped a clear warning. He held up both hands in the universal gesture for surrender. "Fine."

She gritted, "Thanks." Turning back to Dylan, she took a deep breath. "Go ahead."

Catelyn felt the raging anger deep down inside. Anger at Dylan, anger at herself for being a sucker once more, anger at Joseph for butting in and coming home. And anger at God.

Her knees nearly buckled at the realization. Stiffening her spine, she made sure none of her emotions showed on her face. Professionalism in its purest form radiated from her. She'd deal with this newfound self-awareness later.

Dylan started signing. "Yes, I was there with Kelly, just like I told you before. But—" his signs slowed "—Tracy was there, too."

Catelyn blew out an annoyed breath. Dylan didn't notice but Joseph shot her a look. She ignored it. "Go on."

"When I walked up to meet Kelly, she and Tracy were arguing. I only caught part of the conversation, but what I understood was that Tracy wanted Kelly to get involved in something and Kelly didn't want to."

"What was she trying to get Kelly involved in?"

"I'm not sure."

"But you have an idea?" This question came from Jo-

seph. The lawyer's sharp eyes missed nothing and Catelyn knew she'd stop her client if it even looked like he was
going to say something to incriminate himself.

Dylan nodded. "I think Tracy was trying to get Kelly
to join The Skulls. The gang. It's getting really popular,
growing by pretty big numbers."

"But Kelly didn't want to?" Catelyn furrowed a brow,
concentrating hard.

"No. She thinks gangs are stupid. She and Billy both do.
They're more into the church scene, not the criminal stuff."
With a sense of relief, Catelyn took note of Dylan's use of
the present tense when he talked about Kelly. If he did know
where she was, he just told them that she was still alive.

If he knew where she was.

"Anyway, I asked her what they were arguing about and
she refused to tell me. Tracy started yelling at me about
staying out of her business and told me what a loser I was."
He swallowed at the memory and wiped a hand across his
lips, closing his eyes for a brief moment.

Catelyn and Joseph shared a look. And waited.

"Kelly got mad—" Dylan opened his eyes and finally
signed, "At Tracy. She lost her temper and told Tracy she
was done with their friendship, that blackmail was really
low, but if she ever got her life straightened out or if she
ever needed any help, Tracy could count on her to help, but
if she kept doing the stuff she was doing, then they were
done as friends."

"Wow, that's pretty heavy stuff," Joseph empathized.
"Blackmail, huh?"

Dylan nodded, then stared at the table as though gathering his thoughts.

Catelyn leaned in, not bothering to hide the ire she felt.
"Wait a minute, Dylan, you didn't mention the blackmail
issue before. You didn't think that was important?"

He dropped his eyes from hers. "I didn't actually re-member it until just now."

She tapped his hand and his eyes rose to meet hers. "Do you know who she was blackmailing?"

Keeping his gaze locked with hers, he signed, "No, I promise. I don't have a clue who she'd be blackmailing." He ran his fingers over his eyes, rubbed the bridge of his nose and signed, "Kelly was wearing my jacket. I'd given it to her earlier that day at school. When we turned to leave, Tracy grabbed the back of the jacket and jerked. Kelly's arms pulled back and the jacket slipped off. Tracy gave it a toss—" he mimicked the move like he was flinging some-thing aside "—and when Kelly stumbled, Tracy pushed her to the ground."

"And you came to Kelly's defense, didn't you?" Joseph signed and asked the question at the same time, his voice soft, his signs slow. The interpreter mimicked his move-ments for the camera.

Dylan looked miserable. "Yeah, I did. When Kelly fell, Tracy went after her and lifted her foot like she was going to kick her right there on the ground." He looked around the table. "I couldn't just let her do that. I grabbed Tracy to pull her away from Kelly."

"So you pushed her?"

He gave a shake of his head. "No. I just grabbed her arm and pulled. That's when her hand flew back and her ring…" Fingers touched the healing spot on his chin.

Understanding crossed Joseph's face and he gave her another look. She kept her gaze on Dylan. "Then what?"

"I let go and told Kelly to come on. She refused. I begged her and she said she had unfinished business and wanted me to leave. I started to argue with her, but she was get-ting mad, yelled at me to go away, so…I left. I don't know what happened after that."

Startled at the abrupt ending to the story, Catelyn sat back with a thump. "That's it?"

Dylan shrugged. "That's it. That's why I didn't say anything about being there. I don't know what happened after I left," he reiterated. "I didn't think it was important. I didn't think anyone would believe me. I just..."

Catelyn stared at him as he trailed off. He met her gaze, then dropped it to the table. Did she believe him?

Joseph did, she could see it written all over him. And she trusted Joseph's judgment although she gave him a hard time sometimes. Frustration gnawed on her insides. Blackmail. That put a new twist on things.

Who was Tracy blackmailing and what kind of information did she have on that person?

Glancing at her watch, she saw that it was pushing 11:00 p.m. "Joseph, do you have any more questions?"

He looked surprised at her inquiry, like it shocked him that she'd bother to include him. Hurt bit her heart. Did he really think she was that hard-nosed? That she didn't respect him as a professional?

Well, it's not like you've been the most cooperative person in this partnership, her conscience sniped at her. Shame filled her and she avoided his gaze by watching Dylan's lawyer gather her stuff.

Joseph nodded. "I've got two questions. What was the relationship between Tracy and Zachary?"

"They were brother and sister."

"We know that," Joseph said patiently. "But did they get along? Hang out? That kind of stuff."

"No, they didn't like each other much. I mean, they did and they didn't. When Zachary did what Tracy wanted, they got along fine, but Zachary wanted out of the gang. He said something about coming into some cash and didn't need the gang anymore."

"Wait a minute. Do you know what he meant by that?"

"No, I never saw him with any big amount of money. Anyway, Tracy didn't want him to try and leave and was pushing him to stay in, calling him names and stuff, bullying him about being weak." He twisted his fingers. "I think she was scared that if Zachary tried to leave, the gang members would come after her and make an example of her. I don't know if that's what happened or not, but it wouldn't surprise me."

Joseph made a notation in his notebook. Catelyn felt her mind whirl with this new information. Then Joseph signed his last question. "Dylan, where did you go when you left Kelly?"

The boy paused then signed, "I just drove around, went downtown and watched the people coming and going from the bars, wishing I was old enough to go in."

"So there's no one who can vouch for you at the time of the murder?"

Dylan shook his head then dropped it into his hands. His shoulders shook as he sobbed.

Catelyn turned and left the room.

SEVEN

Joseph reassured Dylan once more that he would do everything in his power to prove his innocence and to just hang in there.

Then he went after Catelyn.

Locating her was easy. Out in the parking lot, she stood facing her car. Unmoving, still as stone.

When he placed a hand on her shoulder, she flinched, whirling to face him. "You said I've changed. What made you say that?"

He didn't answer right away. Instead, he suggested, "Why don't you take me home? We'll talk on the way."

She gave a short nod and pressed the keyless remote to unlock the doors. Silence filled the car for the first few minutes of the drive as he pondered how to word what he wanted to say, then he took a deep breath and ventured, "When I said you'd changed, I meant you're different. You were so…emotionless when we brought Dylan in. I don't remember that about you. You seem to have a new…hardness about you. Where's your compassion? The deep caring that you used to express for each and every person you come in contact with? The belief that everyone was innocent until proven guilty?"

Shocked, she stared at him for a full five seconds before swinging her eyes back to the road.

More silence as several miles clipped past.

Uh-oh. Had he done it now? Pushed her completely away?

He saw her shoulders lift as she breathed deep. But she still didn't respond. He gave her a couple of more minutes and right before she pulled into his driveway, he asked, "Catie?"

Staring straight ahead, she told him, "Just get out, Joseph."

"So, you're going to push me away again?"

Whiplike she faced him. That's when he saw the tears trembling on her lashes. "You left me! You left, packed up and moved away before…"

"Before what, Catie?" Her pain seared him, but maybe now they could find the answers they'd left in limbo two years ago. "You told me to leave, if I remember correctly. You said you couldn't ever be what I wanted, and that you needed space and time, that you didn't know if you'd ever be ready for marriage, especially to another cop. Is any of this ringing a bell?"

He should have left that last part off. But she didn't blast him on it. Her shoulders shook, and in the moonlight, he could see the tears fall. "But you weren't supposed to just… go. You lay out these expectations about how you want a wife like your mother—" she paused, thinking "—and I didn't want to quit my job."

She stopped, her frustration evident.

"I never asked you to quit your job!"

Catelyn realized she was losing the battle against the storm of tears threatening to unleash itself. "Yes, you did! I can't talk about this now, Joseph."

He opened his door and Catelyn stared in shock as he slammed it. Then he marched around to the driver's side, unbuckled her seat belt and pulled her out of her seat. "Hey!"

"Come on."

"What are doing?" she protested, but didn't fight him.

"What I should have done two years ago."

He led her through the front yard, around to the back and down to the little pond that sat on the edge of his parents' property.

His touch turned gentle and he rubbed her shoulders before pointing to the bench that faced the water. "Sit down, please, will you?"

She hesitated a fraction, wondering where he was going with this then lowered herself to the bench. The moon offered enough visibility that she was able to see his face. He'd shocked the tears from her throat with his high-handed, albeit gentle, maneuvering. She had to admit, he hadn't physically hurt her once. She could have pulled away and left had she chosen to do so…and she knew he wouldn't have stopped her.

He demanded, "Now, talk to me, please?"

She bit her lip; looked away. The urge to run away threatened to overpower her. The desire to share with Joseph the hurt in her heart took precedence. "You know as well as I do the kind of woman you want to marry. Only you didn't share those expectations with me until we were already…until it was too…"

Oh, Lord, give me the words. "My mother and my father were cops, you know that. I just never told you—in detail—what a lousy marriage they had," she said through gritted teeth. "I made the decision not to get involved with a cop… and then you came along and I thought maybe it would be okay. But—" she blew out a breath "—I now know that I can't live the life of what it would entail."

"I haven't asked you to marry me, Catelyn."

She flinched at the reminder. "True, but you were going to two years ago, weren't you?"

This time he jerked. "Yeah, I was."

She felt the tears trying to surface again and only stopped them through sheer willpower. "You want me to be like your mother, stay home, do nothing but care for a family, have babies, all that. And like you said not too long ago, 'what's wrong with that?' And the answer is—nothing. There's absolutely nothing wrong with that—if that's what a woman wants to do." She lifted her hands, palms up. "I don't."

He rubbed his chin and looked at the ground, a flush covering his cheeks. "And you think I would expect that of you?"

"Yes!" He averted his gaze and she knew she'd hit a bull's-eye. But she wanted him to understand completely why they were wrong for each other. "Oh, maybe not at first, but eventually you would because, in your heart, that's what you want. You would drop little hints in the beginning, then those hints would turn to suggestions, then to outright demands. And when I didn't comply, not only would I feel guilty for not following my husband's requests, you'd resort to begging, guilt trips, whatever."

"You think you have me figured out pretty good, don't you?"

Catelyn could see his face, but couldn't read his expression. She thought she saw some anger, maybe—pity? But he didn't deny her accusations, either. Instead, he squatted in front of her. "Is that what your parents' marriage was like?"

She snapped her mouth shut, but it gave a betraying tremble. Instead of being angry with her, taking offense at her blunt, possibly overreactive words, he was trying to understand, offering her compassion, empathy.

The dam broke and the tears dripped one after the other down her cheeks. His hand lifted to wipe them away, but there was no stopping the flood.

Catelyn blurted, "Yes, and it was awful." Her voice squeaked, but she didn't care. "They loved each other in the beginning, had such high hopes and dreams. They had me." She tapped her chest then let her hand drop. "And they just pushed it all away, like it wasn't important. They shoved me to the wayside. The job became everything and they started competing with each other. Who could earn the most decorations, make the most collars, be the best cop." She whispered, "Hurt the other one the most."

"Aw, Catie. Why didn't you ever tell me all this?"

"I...just couldn't. It makes me so mad, so hurt, I try not to think about it."

"So that's why you needed space and…" His quiet words struck her heart. She'd hurt him, too, two years ago.

"And when you left like you did—" she broke off, bit her lip "—I'm sorry, Joseph. I've got to go." *Before I say anything else.* She stood and he rose from his crouched position, grimacing as his knees popped.

A small watery chuckle escaped her, breaking the tension a bit. "You're getting to be an old man, Santino."

"We don't have to be your parents, Catelyn." He lifted a hand and stroked her cheek, not letting her sidetrack him with a poor attempt at humor. "I care too much about you to let you sweep this under the rug. I think what happened two years ago goes a lot deeper than what you've touched on here."

She drew in another deep breath. "I need to leave, Joseph."

He followed her back to her car without another word.

She could tell he wanted to push it. To get all the answers out of her. But right now, all she wanted was to go home, crawl into bed and pull the covers up over her head for at least a week.

But she couldn't. She still had a missing girl to find— and if Joseph's instincts were on target, there was still a murderer wandering free.

She definitely had her work cut out for her.

Emotions and feelings would have to wait.

Joseph let her go.

She almost wondered if she'd really blown it this time. Had she pushed him away for good?

Sighing, exhaustion cramped her and she pushed the emotion aside. She just couldn't deal with it anymore.

Pulling into her driveway, she noticed things had changed a bit since she'd left a few hours earlier. Crime-scene tape still covered the area, but the house stood in darkness. She'd forgotten to leave a light on.

Memory of the earlier incident spooked her and she shivered as she put the car in park and turned it off. She really wished she'd left some kind of light burning. Or that she'd asked Joseph to follow her home.

Get a grip. You're a cop.

True, but sometimes criminals returned to the scene of the crime, she had no backup with her—and she'd never liked coming home to an empty, dark house. She had enough of that when her parents had worked the same shift late into the night during her early teenage years before her father...

Unclipping the strap from her Glock 23, she decided she'd rather be safe than sorry.

Inserting the key, she unlocked the door.

At least it was locked this time.

Slowly, she inched it open and stepped inside. And just stood there.

Listening.

Two minutes passed. Three.

Nothing moved. Not a whisper of a sound that shouldn't be there.

Breathing a little easier, she flipped on the foyer light, walked into her den and winced. Quickly, she gave her house a walk-through.

All clear.

Back in the den.

What a mess. "Great. Just what I want to deal with tonight. Lord," she said aloud, "I don't know how this case is going to turn out, but help me remember You're still in charge. And I don't know where all this is going with Joseph, why I felt so compelled to spill my guts like that, but…"

Cutting off her prayer, she waded through the mess to pick up a picture knocked facedown on the mantel. She turned it over and felt tears well up again.

Her parents on their wedding day.

Never had two people looked so happy. Her dad in his uniform dress blues and her mother in a gown of white. Big grins and bigger dreams.

Oh, God, why? What happened? Where did it go wrong? Why couldn't they work it out? Compromise? Something? How did they turn into enemies? These two people who were supposed to have each other's back?

She studied her dad's face and a fury like she'd never known herself capable of filled her. She screamed aloud at the photo, "How could you leave me like that? How?"

Frisbee style, she flung the picture across the room where it whacked the wall and fell to the floor, broken glass littering the hardwood.

Just like her heart.

A thousand tiny pieces. Shattered, never to be put back together. *Why didn't You do something, God? Why? With all Your power and all Your love, how could You just let them...*

With shock, she stopped her anguished prayer and dropped to the couch. What was she saying? Was she blaming God for the downward spiral of her parents' marriage and the twists her life had taken as a result?

Breath whooshed from her lungs as she considered that.

Maybe she did blame God.

But she loved God.

And God had failed her. At least that's how she felt.

Tears coursed down her cheeks as she got up, still pondering this self-realization she'd stumbled onto. Mindless, she began to clean the mess left by her intruder. Zombielike, she walked into the kitchen for a trash bag, then back to the den to throw away broken pieces of one lamp and other odds and ends she'd had sitting on her mantel.

Mad at God.

He'd failed her.

He'd left her when she needed Him.

Just like her father.

Just like Joseph.

Which brought her back to why she could never be with Joseph. She couldn't live up to his expectations for one, and she didn't know if she could get past her fear of what marrying another officer would entail.

Numb, she moved to the entertainment center. The large wooden structure had been jerked away from the wall so the thieves could unplug the DVD player and other electronic equipment she'd had.

For a moment, she studied the television. The great gaping hole in the center of the screen stared back her, a one-eyed monster. It definitely looked like it had been smashed on purpose. The TV was an older model. Maybe they were mad that it wouldn't bring much money and had decided to take the anger out on the object.

Whatever. She almost didn't care. She'd been battered one too many times tonight, emotionally and physically.

Grasping the edge of the large piece of furniture she pulled it back. As she stepped for another tug, she felt something soft under her foot. Bending down, she picked it up.

A baseball cap.

With the logo from the deaf school on it.

With two fingers, she carried it into the kitchen. Grabbing a brown paper bag from under her sink, she placed the hat in it and folded the top of the bag closed. A chill slithered down her spine. Was this break-in related to the case? If so did that mean she and Joseph had someone worried? Was someone after her? She set her jaw with determination. Well, no amount of danger would scare her off. A girl was missing and Catelyn was determined to find her. Alive.

Time to see who the hat belonged to. Hopefully, the perp left a few strands of hair with the roots intact. Catelyn gave a tight smile.

DNA was a wonderful thing.

And maybe if she tried real hard, focusing on the case would keep her from focusing on herself—or Joseph's truthful words.

After Catelyn left, Joseph drew in a deep breath and shoved his hands in his pockets. His heart hurt for her, this woman that he still loved. He was surprised the admission came so easy to him.

But he did. Loved her still. Even after she'd broken his heart. The hurt had been so acute, he'd run. To a new job, a new state, a new life.

And still, not for a lack of trying, he'd never forgotten her or successfully moved on. Simply put, he'd missed her.

Turning, he walked up the steps to the front porch and settled himself on the swing. The clear night allowed him a good view of the Big Dipper, the Little Dipper, a glimpse of the Milky Way and the rest of the scattered twinkling stars. God's tapestry.

What do You see, God? Up there from the other side? Where do we go from here? Personally and professionally? Kelly's still out there, Lord and I know there's a team searching even as I sit here. I pray You're keeping her safe. Keep Catie close, let her know You're there for her. So much to pray about, God. I'm glad You know my heart. Show me how to reach her, how to help her face her past and her fears.

Joseph's thoughts and prayers turned to Dylan. During the questioning, Joseph had carefully observed the boy. He'd not shown any signs of lying. Yes, he'd been scared, worried, anxious. But not guilty.

Although he'd been deceitful in not telling the full story the first time he'd been questioned, Joseph could see why he'd felt he could leave out his being at the school. If he was telling the truth, and Tracy was alive at the time he'd left the area, then, in his eyes, he wouldn't have anything of relevance to add. Of course, he should have come clean, but Joseph could understand why he hadn't.

If his story was the real deal.

Tomorrow, he and Catelyn would spend their day investigating the case. Another Saturday spent working. But at least he'd be with Catelyn. Maybe she'd open up more with him tomorrow during the course of the day.

He had a feeling she'd left a lot unsaid tonight.

The door opened and his dad stepped out. "Joseph? Are you all right?"

"Fine, Dad. Just sitting here...contemplating, praying a little. When are Ethan and Marianna coming home?"

"They'll be back tomorrow. Said they had some news for us."

His interest piqued, he quirked a brow at his parent. "Really? What kind of news?"

"Not sure. Ethan's been thinking about transferring into South Carolina Law Enforcement Division, so they may be moving to Columbia."

"Ouch. What does Mom say to that?"

"She's not happy about it, but wants what's best for all."

"Yeah." His thoughts returned to Catelyn.

"Catelyn's gotten ahold of you again, huh?"

Startled at his dad's astute assessment, Joseph let out a low laugh. "Now what would make you say that?"

"We're a visual family, Joey," his dad said, pulling his childhood nickname from the past. "I see a lot. And you didn't take off two years ago for New York because your life was going along smoothly."

"But I never said..."

"You didn't have to, son. Some things a dad just knows."

"Huh."

"So, she's gotten ahold of you again."

"Yeah, she has." Why bother to deny it? "But she's got this...anger deep inside her about something. It's like a silent fury that's bubbling underneath the surface ready to erupt. I think it has something to do with her father's death, but I'm not sure. I just get that idea from reading between the lines. I think she's got a lot of anger towards God, too. And until she gets that resolved, she and I really can't go forward."

"Wow. That's a lot to deal with."

"For her and me. Because I want to be there for her when it happens. I think it's going to have to in order for her to be able to move on with her life. I just wish she'd share it all with me."

"Are you up to it?"

He met his dad's eyes. "I have to be. I think if we can get through whatever's going on inside her right now, we can deal with whatever the future throws at us. I think."

"All right, well I'll be praying, too. She's a lot different from your mom, but she's a good woman. A man could consider himself blessed with a girl like that. Night, son."

Speechless, Joseph watched his father reenter the house. Then he raised his eyes back toward the heavens and in suspicious wonder, said, "Huh."

His phone rang.

Catelyn.

He listened as she kept her tone professional and distant. "I'm on the way to see the graveyard shift at the lab. I found a baseball cap behind my entertainment center. I'm going to see if someone is willing to process it tonight to see if we can get anything useful from it. We've got to find Kelly, Joseph. I really feel like her time is running out."

EIGHT

Sluggishly, Catelyn pulled her weary body from her bed. A late-night run to the third-shift crime lab to drop off the hat had her arriving back home for the third time that day and climbing in bed around two in the morning.

She'd allowed herself five and half hours of sleep before rising and dressing for the day ahead. Anticipation and dread churned within her at the thought of seeing Joseph again. He had told her to call him if she got anything, but the lab had been crazy and she'd finally left without getting the information she wanted to grab a few hours of sleep. Hopefully today she and Joseph would learn something new.

Joseph.

Now that she had time to contemplate her revelations to him last night, she felt almost embarrassed, wondering if he'd think less of her for revealing some of her innermost feelings.

Her mind said he wouldn't, not the Joseph she'd known two years ago, but her heart still wondered. Gulping down a bagel and some coffee, she headed toward the office. She didn't bother to call Joseph, knowing full well he'd probably be there when she arrived.

Sure enough, when she pulled into the parking lot, his

car sat in the spot nearest the door. Butterflies tickled her insides. As much as she wished it wasn't so, she realized she really looked forward to seeing Joseph.

In spite of her embarrassment over last night's outburst.

Entering the building, she strode to the elevator and rode up to the third floor. Stepping out when the double doors opened, she ran smack into a hard chest made harder by a Kevlar vest. "Oomph."

Masculine hands grasped her upper arms and set her back. "In a hurry, Clark? If I'd known you were that anxious to throw yourself into my arms, I would've done something before now."

"Back off, Johnson," anther male voice demanded.

Tim Johnson's brows shot Heavenward and he obeyed Joseph's order, holding his hands in the universal sign for surrender. "I was just kidding. Catelyn and I are old friends."

Catelyn stared in surprise at the danger glinting in Joseph's dark eyes. Catelyn shot lasers at Joseph and he stared for a moment before shrugging. "Right."

He turned and walked back to his desk. Catelyn gave Tim a disgusted look and trotted off after Joseph. He sat at his desk, not bothering to look up when she approached. "You think that was necessary? That I can't take care of myself?"

Finally, his eyes lifted to meet hers. Innocence radiated from him. "What?"

She opened her mouth to reply then snapped it shut. "Forget it. We've got a girl to find."

"I agree."

Her phone buzzed and she grabbed it. "Hello?"

"Hey. This is Sandy."

Crime-lab Sandy. "What's up?"

"I've got that DNA from the hat."

"What? Already? When I left last night, the place was a zoo."

"You're a friend who was victimized. I stayed late."

Touched, Catelyn responded. "Wow. Thanks so much."

"If you can get me a sample from whoever you think it belongs to, I can try to match it up for you."

"That'll be what I'm working on today. What color was the hair?"

"You're looking for a redheaded male. Good luck."

"Yeah, and thanks again," she said.

She hung up.

Great.

"What do you have?" Joseph asked from his spot behind his desk.

Nothing about last night. Good. Breathing a sigh of relief, she said, "Sandy extracted the DNA, but we need something to match it up to."

"You've got a picture of the hat?"

"Yes."

"We can show it around, but it could belong to anyone. However, just giving an educated guess, I'm willing to bet that it belongs to someone between the ages of fourteen and eighteen."

"Redheaded and male, too."

He quirked a brow. "That helps."

"I know. At least it's a start. And if we come across a redheaded teen, we can ask for his DNA."

"Let's start with Billy Franklin again. There was just something about that kid when we talked to him at school. He was nervous, scared. And he has reddish-blonde hair. Let's catch him at home."

"Sounds good to me."

On the way to the Franklin residence, Catelyn called to check on Zachary only to be told there was no change in his condition. She told the nurse, "Please call me as soon as he wakes up."

"If he wakes up, I will," came the sympathetic response.

"Right."

Catelyn relayed her conversation to Joseph, who sighed then said, "I have another question for Billy. Not only do I want to know who the hat belongs to, I want to know if he knows who Zachary hangs out with and who he could have been with the day before his sister's funeral."

Ten minutes later, they pulled into the Franklin's driveway. Catelyn had called and let Mrs. Franklin know they were coming. Fortunately, they'd been home and were free to meet. Billy was on his way home from his coach's house where he'd been hanging out with some friends of his from the baseball team.

Joseph knocked on the door then stepped back, his badge in his hand. Less than a minute later, Mrs. Franklin opened the door. "Hello."

"Thanks for agreeing to meet with us."

"Anything to find Kelly."

The forty-something woman opened the screen door and stood back to allow Catelyn and Joseph to step inside. Then she led the way to a small family room where she gestured for them to have a seat.

Running a hand through her mussed gray hair, she said, "Billy's on his way. I called his cell a few minutes ago and he promised to be here soon."

"That's fine," Joseph said. The woman looked worn out. "I know this is an incredibly difficult time for your family, but I promise we're doing everything possible to track down your daughter."

She gave a small sad smile. "I know. It just seems like

there should be something more that I could be doing. Some way to help find her."

"Unfortunately, there's not. You're staying by the phone, keeping your cell phone charged in case she sends you a text message. That's about all you can do." He didn't bother to tell her they'd already tried to trace Kelly's cell phone and hadn't had any luck.

The door slammed and Billy entered the den. He'd lost weight. His hands shook as he nodded at the two officers sitting in his den. Joseph frowned. The poor kid was falling apart. "Hi, Billy."

"Hi." He slouched onto the couch, shoulders hunched, his head pulled low, like he was trying to impersonate a turtle.

"Sorry to pull you away from your friends."

"It's all right. I wasn't having much fun anyway. Alonso was there, though. You should…" He stopped and looked away.

"I should what?"

"Nothing."

"You've got a big game coming up in a few days, don't you? Play-offs?"

"Right." No enthusiasm whatsoever. Depression? Possibly.

Joseph pulled the picture of the hat out of his pocket. "Do you recognize this hat?"

Billy leaned forward and took the proffered photo. He studied it for all of three seconds before he said, "Sure. Practically every kid at the deaf school has one. Kelly even has one. They give them away the first day of school in a kind of welcome-back-to-school package."

Catelyn pulled in a deep breath. Joseph flicked a glance in her direction. Great. "Do you know anyone it could possibly belong to?" The break-in happened last night. Plus the hat probably belonged to a deaf kid.

"No, I don't know."

"All right, one last question." The real reason for their visit. "Do you know who Zachary was hanging out with the day before his sister's funeral? His mother didn't know and no one can tell us."

Billy's body language went from slouched and lethargic to ramrod straight and tense. His eyes slid to his mother then back to Joseph, before ending their journey on the floor. "I don't know. I saw him right before the visitation, but he never said anything about being with anyone. He just seemed mad."

"Mad? Not sad?"

The boy jerked. "No, he wasn't sad. He didn't like his sister that much."

Well, that sort of went along with what Dylan had told them. Catelyn shifted, but didn't stop writing on the pad in front of her. Joseph probed deeper. "Why do you say that?"

"She was mean. And always causing trouble for Zachary."

"Do you think Zachary killed his sister?"

"No. As much as she got on his nerves, he wouldn't kill her."

"Why not?"

Billy shrugged, glanced at his watch and shifted. "I don't know, I just don't think he would have. I mean he didn't like her, but she was still his sister, you know?"

"The first day we started this investigation, a young boy by the name of Chad thought Dylan killed Tracy. What do you think?"

"Chad was in love with Tracy. He'd never have hurt her. He was obsessed with her or something. But Tracy thought he was a loser and wouldn't have anything to do with him.

Dylan and Tracy used to be friends until he started dating Kelly. For some reason Tracy didn't like that, but I don't know why. She never said anything. I do know Zachary wanted Kelly for himself, but Kelly was a good girl." His throat bobbed again. "She wouldn't have anything to do with Zachary." This time his eyes met Joseph's. "I wouldn't let her."

"Because of his gang affiliations?"

"Yeah, mostly."

"What do you know about the gang, The Skulls?"

Fear bleached his face white. "I already told you. I stay away from them. I don't want to have anything to do with them."

"But they've infiltrated the deaf school. They've got deaf kids joining this gang. Do you think they've done something to Kelly?"

Tears flooded his eyes and he sighed, glanced at his watch one more time. "I don't know." He stood. "Look, I wish I could help, but I can't."

"You keep looking at your watch. Do you have somewhere you need to be?"

"I told Coach I'd be right back. We're discussing baseball strategy for the game on Tuesday night."

Joseph looked at Catelyn. "Do you have any more questions you need to ask?"

"Just one, if I gave you a description of a redheaded deaf teen, who would be the first one to come to mind?"

Confusion flashed across his face along with a smidge of irritation. "I don't know. Um, Lee Myers, maybe."

Joseph stood, facing the teen. "All right, thanks. If you think of anything else, give us a call, will you?"

"Right." Billy looked at his mother. "Gotta go, Ma. Coach is feeding us supper. Cooking out. I'll be home around nine, okay?"

Anxiety written on her features, Mrs. Franklin nodded. "Fine. I'll tell your father."

"Thanks." He leaned over and kissed her cheek. Waving to Joseph and Catelyn, he slipped out the door.

After thanking the woman for her time, they headed at a fast clip for the car.

"What's your hurry?" Catelyn asked.

"That kid is up to something. I want to follow him and find out what."

Catelyn hurried around to her side of the car and hopped in. Joseph climbed behind the wheel and pulled from the curb. Billy's taillights flashed for a brief moment at the stop sign at the end of his street. He turned left and Joseph followed a safe distance behind.

"That kid is royally scared of something," Catelyn muttered as they pulled out of the subdivision onto Pine Street. Cars whizzed by, but Joseph had no trouble keeping Billy's vehicle in sight.

"Yeah, I get the same feeling. I just want to know what it is."

"Or who it is."

"Right."

Catelyn rubbed her eyes, turned to him and said, "He saw us there and didn't ask any questions about Kelly."

"You noticed that, too?"

"Right off. Most people worried about someone see us and immediately ask if there are any new developments."

"True, but he is a seventeen-year-old kid."

"Granted. However, he just sat there. He also shows symptoms of depression. Although, I guess those could be attributed to whatever he's afraid of, too."

He wheeled around the next corner and entered a very

prestigious subdivision. "Hey, isn't this where Coach Dillard lives?"

"Sure is. And there's his house."

"Well, it's exactly where Billy said he was going."

Joseph pulled up to the curb. They had a pretty good view of the huge backyard from their vantage point.

"Look, they're signing."

"And there's your brother."

Joseph frowned. "He didn't say anything about a baseball get-together today."

"I guess he doesn't feel like he has to report in to big brother about his activities." She gave him a smile.

"Guess not."

"Who's that?" Catelyn pointed to another young man. One she recognized as the kid who attacked Dylan at Joseph's house. "That's Chad, right?"

"It sure is."

"And look, there's a redheaded kid signing to Alonso."

They exchanged a look then Joseph shook his head. "Naw, it couldn't be that easy."

"Of course not. And we don't have any reason to ask him for his DNA."

"I see several of those hats on heads over there."

"The deaf school and the high school have really come together to give these kids a great opportunity. A lot of good deaf baseball players at the deaf school, but no team. A high school that needed good players. Couldn't ask for a better combination."

"Not to mention a winning one. That coach, Alan Dillard, sure is committed to his boys, isn't he?"

"It's good to see. Kids need role models like that."

Billy came out of the house and Coach Dillard immediately walked up to the boy and put his arm around his shoulders. Billy kept his eyes on the wooden flooring of the deck.

The coach leaned over and said something in Billy's ear. Billy shook his head, shoving his hands into the pockets of his baggy jeans. Coach Dillard nodded, slapped him on the back and then stepped up onto the large wooden deck. He clapped his hands, waved his arms and motioned for the boys to gather around.

Coach Dillard started to talk and sign at the same time and Joseph turned to Catelyn. "I've seen enough." They started forward and Catelyn grabbed his arm and pointed. Billy had turned from the crowd and isolated himself in a far corner.

"The kid's hurting…or something. Something more than his sister being missing is going on with him," she murmured.

"I agree." Joseph sighed and shoved a hand through his hair. "All right, I'm going to talk to Alonso about that hat. I also want to ask Coach Dillard to let me know if one of his players is missing a hat that he normally wears. Feel free to eavesdrop if you can see what we're saying. You coming?"

"Absolutely." Catelyn followed behind him, approaching the house from the front. Stacy Dillard answered the door and soon she led them through the house, to the sliding-glass doors and out onto the wooden deck. Alonso immediately spotted Joseph, surprise and curiosity drawing him toward his brother.

Joseph waved to the coach, who frowned and walked over. "Something I can help you with?"

"Just need to ask my brother a few questions."

The man's brows rose. "Can't this wait?"

"If it could I wouldn't be here."

Coach Dillard shrugged and backed off. "No problem, then." Joseph pulled Alonso aside and the two talked for a moment. Catelyn decided to take advantage of the time and crossed to catch Coach Dillard before he could get into another conversation. She had a few questions of her own.

Joseph signed, "Sorry to intrude, but I wanted to ask you a couple of questions."

Irritation darkened the young man's eyes, but he didn't protest, just nodded. "What do you want to know?"

Joseph pulled the photo of the hat from his pocket. "I'm seeing these things everywhere. Now, I know where they came from, I just need you to tell me if one of the guys here lost one between last night and today."

Alonso shrugged. "Not that I know of. I can keep my eyes open, though."

"It would be a redheaded kid who wears one all the time. The hat is worn and practically falling apart. My guess is, the kid wears it every day. I wanted to ask you because you're on both campuses."

Blowing out a breath, Alonso thought for a moment. "Either Ron Camp or Tyler Hathaway. They both go to the deaf school."

"Do you know where they live?"

"Ron lives across the street from the school in that neighborhood, but I don't know which house. Tyler lives in Gaffney. He's a day student and buses in every day."

"Does he play baseball?"

"No, neither of them is on the team. And I'm glad because I don't like them much."

"Why not?"

"I think they're involved in that gang. The one Tracy was with. From what I hear, they're always causing problems in school, but haven't done anything to get themselves kicked out, yet."

Interest definitely piqued, Joseph made a note to visit

these two young men as soon as possible. "Thanks, Alonso. You've been a big help."

Alonso left and Joseph turned to find Catelyn heading his way. "Ready?"

"Yep."

"You disappeared on me. Did you learn anything?"

"Not much. Coach Dillard said he'd keep an eye out for one of his guys who lost a hat, but said some of these kids wear a different hat every day."

"He's right about that. All right. I guess that's it for here. I've got two guys we need to track down. Redheaded deaf kids that wear the hat with the school logo on a regular basis."

"Let's go then."

Twenty minutes later they arrived at Ron Camp's house. Joseph climbed from the car and looked around. "Doesn't look like anyone's home."

"Should have gotten the number and called."

"No, I don't want to scare these guys off. If they're somehow involved, they could pull a major disappearing act."

"True."

Joseph walked up the path to the front door and rapped his knuckles on the wood.

No luck.

Catelyn's cell phone rang and she lifted it to her ear. Joseph watched her listen then her eyes shot to his as she said, "Thanks, Sandy."

"What does she have?"

"She said she managed to pull off some writing that had almost completely faded from the edge of the hat."

"What was it?"

"The initials, *T.H.*"

Joseph gave a little smile. "Well, well. Let's head to Gaffney and pay Mr. Tyler Hathaway a little visit."

NINE

Tyler Hathaway proved to be an elusive young man. No one answered the phone at the residence. "That doesn't mean he's not there." But he wasn't. Joseph sent a text message to Alonso. "Quick question. Where does Tyler Hathaway hang out?"

Alonso's response came back immediately. "At the arcade on Stead street. Likes the free meals next door. That church on Stead Street. If he's not at home, you can count on him being there—if he could get a ride in. At least that's where they were hanging two weeks ago."

"Thanks." He looked at Catelyn. "Want to head over there?"

"Absolutely—" she looked at her watch "—but if he's not there, I'm going to have to leave pretty soon."

"Got something to do this afternoon?"

"An appointment. It'll just take me about a couple of hours. Then I can meet back up with you."

"Okay." He was quiet for a moment as they climbed into the car and took off. Catelyn thought he might ask her what she needed to do. He didn't.

She volunteered, "My mother. I need to go see her. I need to take her something she asked for before I walked in on my intruder."

She felt him grasp her hand and looked over at him. Compassion flared brightly in his eyes. "I'm sorry." He squeezed her fingers.

Catelyn shrugged. "I deal with it."

"Will you let me go with you?"

She hadn't expected that one. "Why?"

"Because I want to. I want to be there for you if you need me."

"But…" What did she say to that? "Are you sure?" The thought of having someone to lean on, to care about her, to care about the effect visiting her mother had on her emotionally was almost overpowering. Something she desperately wanted.

But did she dare trust him? With her life, yes. Her heart? Not there yet.

Visions of her childhood brought sheer anxiety shooting through her. "I don't know, Joseph. It's not exactly the most pleasant thing to do."

He tugged her hand and she leaned in closer.

"I want to," he insisted.

What if she let him close again and he decided she wasn't what he needed, what he wanted—again?

But what about what she wanted? Needed?

He let her go, concentrating on the drive. "It's a simple thing, Catelyn. Why are you having such a hard time letting me back into your life when you know it's what we both want?"

Catelyn reeled away from him. "But I don't, Joseph. I don't know that that's what I want." But it was and yet… "And why are you pushing so hard when you've made it clear that I'm not wife material?" His flinch singed her heart, but she had to make him understand. "I just—" She broke off and pointed. "Isn't that Tyler Hathaway?"

Joseph blinked, pressed the brake and followed her pointing finger. "That's him."

"You got the paperwork we need to arrest him?"

"Got it right here on the computer."

"Excellent. Let's go get the twerp and see what he has to say for himself." He gave her a hard look. "But don't think this conversation's over. It's not."

Catelyn ignored him and kept her eyes on the young man standing outside the arcade next door to the church smoking a cigarette.

Joseph pulled up next to the curb and they got out. Their activity caught the young thug's attention and he straightened, eyes narrowing.

"He's going to run."

No sooner had the words left her lips than Tyler threw his cigarette to the pavement and took off, legs churning as fast as he could push them.

Joseph and Catelyn were right behind him.

Down the sidewalk they went, dodging the occasional pedestrian. Catelyn could feel Joseph right on her heels.

The kid was fast.

Fortunately, she ran three miles almost every morning. She knew she had the endurance to outlast him—as long as she didn't lose him.

He darted around the corner of the next building and Catelyn felt a surge of satisfaction. She raced after him with Joseph breathing down her neck.

Around the corner, down the next alleyway, she heard his running steps skid to a stop. The clank of a chain-link fence.

Soon she had him in her sights.

He was clawing his way over the fence.

Without slowing down, Catelyn pounded up to him, grasped the back of his belt with both hands and pulled.

Tyler gave a harsh yell, but didn't let go.

Two seconds later, Joseph added his strength to the situation and within the blink of an eye, had Tyler on the ground, his hands cuffed behind his back.

Catelyn placed her hands on her knees and drew in a deep breath. Joseph was a little winded himself but that didn't stop him from patting the kid down and pulling out a knife and a pair of brass knuckles. "Nice assortment here," he grunted as he hauled the kid to his feet.

Catelyn shook her head to dispel the images of a previous arrest where she'd been stabbed. Nausea churned. She covered it up by signing, "If you'll promise not to fight, Special Agent Santino here will move your cuffs to the front so you can communicate."

Fury emanated from Tyler. He wasn't happy being caught. Too bad. She wasn't too happy with *him*. Catelyn continued. "Looks like you need a little time to calm down. Your interpreter will meet us at the jail."

Joseph jerked him to the car while Catelyn signed his rights to him. They'd have the interpreter do it again, just so no one could come back and say anything about her not being certified in sign language.

Tyler understood her. His glare never lessened. She told Joseph, "Better keep those cuffs in the back."

"I think you're right. We'll get him to the station and in the interrogation room and see how tough he is there."

The teen never once made an attempt to communicate on the way to the jail. Catelyn figured he was doing his best to figure out how to get out of this mess. He also didn't put up a fight once inside and they were able to remove his cuffs so that he would be able to talk should he choose to do so.

The interpreter was waiting when they arrived.

Once in the room, Catelyn sat across from Tyler, the interpreter next to her. Joseph sat at the end of the table. She stared at Tyler, trying to decide the best way to approach questioning him.

She glanced at Joseph. "You want to start?"

"Sure, you got the video set up?"

"Taping as we speak."

Catelyn informed him once more of his rights and he signed the paper saying that he understood them. She told him that he was being taped and then Joseph said, "You want to tell me what you were doing in Detective Clark's house, who was with you and where her stuff is?"

Joseph watched the kid jerk like he'd been punched on the chin. A new emotion crossed his face.

Anxiety.

Good.

"I don't know what you're talking about," Tyler signed.

Joseph leaned in, making sure the kid still had the interpreter in his line of sight. "Sure you do. You broke into Detective Clark's house, trashed it and stole a lot of her electronics. We know you were there. We have a warrant for your DNA and as soon as it comes back, we'll match it to the hat you left behind."

Tyler's eyes rounded slightly.

"Yeah, Tyler," Catelyn pushed, "you know, the one with the deaf school logo on it that has your initials on the inside edge?"

The teen shifted, his left eye began to twitch and he ran a hand through his greasy red hair. "Where's my lawyer?"

Joseph gave a mental groan. Up to this point, the kid hadn't said a word about wanting a lawyer although they'd offered. Catelyn looked at Joseph and sighed. "I'll let them know he wants legal representation."

Another long night loomed ahead. Joseph watched

Catelyn leave, then turned back to the kid. And just stared at him.

Tyler refused to meet his eyes.

So Joseph just waited.

Finally the boy signed, "What?"

Joseph shrugged.

The interpreter glanced between them but kept quiet. She was a veteran interpreter and professional all the way.

Tyler stood abruptly. The officer standing just outside the glass door watched intently. He placed his hand on his gun. Joseph tensed, but signaled the man that he had the situation in hand. The officer relaxed, however he kept his hand near his weapon.

Joseph caught Tyler's eye. "Problem?"

"Do I have to wait for my lawyer?"

"I would if I were you."

Licking his lips, Tyler paced from one end of the room to the other. Joseph let him. He could handle the teen if he decided to turn violent.

The clock ticked. Tyler turned. "Do I get some kind of deal if I help you?"

Excitement leaped within Joseph. Finally, they were getting somewhere. He kept his expression neutral and signed, "Possibly."

Catelyn chose that moment to return, a portly, balding gentleman with a keen glint to his eye, in tow. She gestured to him and said, "Meet Edward Hale. Defense attorney for Mr. Tyler Hathaway."

After handshakes all around, they got right to it. Mr. Hale advised his client not to say a word, but the client had other ideas.

"I changed my mind, I don't want a lawyer. I want a deal."

Joseph rubbed his hands together and leaned closer, pushing a piece of paper in front of the kid. "Sign here and tell us what you know."

TEN

Catelyn decided to leave Joseph to the questioning. As soon as he was finished, she knew he'd call her. She had to get to the nursing home. Her mother expected her to be on time.

Actually, her mother seemed to be slipping more and more into her own little world and Catelyn wondered if she'd even notice her daughter was running about thirty minutes late.

Bounding up the steps and through the automatic sliding doors, she waved to the nurse behind the desk. "Hi, Thea."

"Hi, Catelyn."

"Sorry I'm late. I'm working a case that doesn't seem to have stopping points."

A sympathetic smile flashed across Thea's face. "I understand. She's awake and seems to be having a good day today. Much better than yesterday."

"Great, thanks." She hurried down the hall to the second room on the left and slowly opened the door. "Mom?"

"Catelyn, is that you?"

A good day. Her mother remembered she was coming, was waiting on her. Catelyn slipped into the room and blinked at the sight of her mother. Always she seemed to age a little more between each visit. In no way did she resemble the vibrant young woman pictured in the wedding photo that Catelyn had thrown across her den. White hair had obliterated the shining blond strands that used to hang in carefully groomed waves. Her clear blue eyes had the look of confusion more often than not now.

But not today. Today Marilyn Clark's gaze landed on Catelyn with a shrewdness Catelyn hadn't seen in weeks.

"Sorry I'm late," Catelyn said as she entered the room.

"Big case?" The fact that Catelyn now worked as member of the same force her mother had served on was a huge source of pride for the woman.

"Yes." She changed the subject. "Here. I brought you something."

Her mother took the album from Catelyn and studied it. "I haven't seen this in years."

"Thea said you asked for it."

"I did?"

"Must have."

Her mom opened the book and looked at the first few pictures. Without raising her head, she said, "We had some good times, didn't we?"

Catelyn sighed. "Some." She shifted, uneasiness twisting within her. "You look like you're feeling good today."

Setting the album to the side, her mom said, "I'd feel better if you'd tell me what you're working on."

So Catelyn did, falling into the routine of acting like everything was fine and that the past hadn't happened, that her parents hadn't destroyed each other with Catelyn suffering the effects of their selfishness. Instead, she pretended, played the dutiful daughter, didn't vent, didn't ask why they hadn't loved her more than...

Pulling in a deep breath, she finished her account of the case. By this time, two hours had passed and Catelyn itched to leave.

Then her mother did something she hadn't done since she'd been in the nursing home. She reached over and clasped Catelyn's hand. Startled, Catelyn looked at her mother. The woman had never been big on affection and hadn't reached out for a voluntary touch in years. "Mom?"

"I'm sorry."

Heart thudding, Catelyn started at her mother. "What?"

Tears built in those aging blue eyes, and her mom looked away, giving a small sniff. "I'm sorry."

Perplexed, Catelyn stepped around to gaze at this woman she'd called mother all her life, but didn't really know. "For what?" She figured she was treading on thin ice, but had to know what her mother was sorry for.

"For what we did to you," came the quietest whisper.

Pain shafted through her. Why now? What had incited her to bring this up now?

"It's—" she couldn't say it was all right because it wasn't, but "—it's in the past, Mom. Just…forget it."

"I can't. I know I will soon as a result of this horrid disease, but while I'm thinking clearly…" She pulled Catelyn closer. "I'm sorry. Will you ever find it in your heart to be able to forgive us?"

Lightning zapping her wouldn't have shocked her more. What did she say?

Say, I forgive you, she told herself.

Say it.

Her throat worked, her lips moved, but she couldn't vocalize the words. Too much hurt rested within her. Instead, she pushed the words through her tight throat and whispered, "Did you know what Daddy was going to do that night? Did you know he was going to put that gun in his mouth and pull the trigger?"

Her mother flinched, her chin wobbled. "No. I promise, I didn't know."

A whimper escaped Catelyn, but she leaned down and placed her forehead against her mother's. Anger, hurt and resentment battled within her, but the need to feel her mother's arms around her won out over her need to express her rage at this helpless woman. "I want to forgive you. Hug me," she pleaded. "Just…love me."

Slowly, thin, wiry arms lifted and wound around Catelyn's stronger, youthful form.

And for the first time that she could remember in a very long time, her mother hugged her.

Catelyn sobbed on her shoulder and thought she heard the words "I do love you."

Joseph stepped back from the room. Catelyn wouldn't appreciate it if she knew he'd followed her here.

He'd walked down to the room to find Catelyn in her mother's arms, sobbing out enough tears to fill Lake Bowen. Heart aching for her, wanting to be a part of the solution to her problem, he turned to go back to the waiting area.

"Joseph?"

Uh-oh. Caught.

He did a one-eighty back to face the door. She stood in the doorway wiping her eyes, looking about fourteen years old.

"Hey, sorry. Look, I didn't mean to interrupt…"

"What are you doing here?"

"I decided to come over after we finished up with Mr. Hathaway. Plus, I got the text message information from Zachary's phone for the day of the funeral. Thought you might want to see it. And, we need to track down Billy again."

She sniffed. "You have really rotten timing, you know that?"

"But a great sense of direction."

A chuckle escaped her. She wasn't mad at him. Relaxing a fraction, he opened his arms. "Need a hug?"

More tears flooded her eyes at the question, but she shook her head. "No. I need to get back to work. We need to go over those text messages."

"You can take a few minutes."

She sucked in a deep breath. "What else did you learn after I left?"

"Quite a bit, actually. I called to check on Zachary again, too. He's still in a coma, although the doctors are more enthusiastic about his waking up sometime in the near future. I told them to call us as soon as he starts to stir."

"Excellent."

"I've still got a guard on his door just in case the person who shot him decides to finish the job. He says the kid has some regular visitors like Coach Dillard and some of the other players, but it's been quiet with no problems."

"Good." Another deep breath and she was fairly composed.

He wished she'd taken him up on his offer of a hug. "Hungry?"

She nodded. "Starving. Have we stopped to eat today?"

"I don't remember."

She gave another laugh. "Then I'd say it's time."

"Let's grab something while we wait on a search warrant for the Hathaway residence."

"Tyler gave you enough for that?"

"Yep. Just waiting on the call."

They hurried out to their cars, Catelyn following behind Joseph back into town. They decided on a pizza place that served buffet style.

Joseph settled into the booth opposite her and admired the way she could be tough and delicate all at the same time. Strong on the streets, yet ate her pizza with all the grace of a lady. He smiled. His dad was right. Catelyn was different from his mother, but a man would be blessed to be loved by her. He cleared his throat.

"Did you have a good visit with your mother?"

She paused, pizza hanging in the air in front of her mouth. Then she deliberately took a bite and chewed.

Joseph just waited.

She swallowed and looked him in the eye. "It was interesting."

"Emotional?"

"To say the least."

"Are you going to share it with me?"

His phone rang, interrupting her answer. He winced, but snatched it up. "Hello?"

Catelyn swallowed the last of her water and watched Joseph give her the thumbs-up. He hung up. "We've got our search warrant and a team's on the way to the house. They'll meet us there with a copy of Zachary's text messaging log for the last week. We can see if any number stands out."

She tossed some bills on the table. "Let's go."

Joseph added his money and they took off out the door.

Catelyn watched the scenery whiz by.

Soon, they pulled in behind a black-and-white cruiser. Joseph stepped out. "Anyone home?"

The uniformed officer shook his head. "Not that we can see. No one's answering the door, anyway."

Joseph and Catelyn approached the house. Catelyn said, "Knock it in."

"What's going on?"

They turned at the sound of the voice coming from the street. A gentleman in his early fifties stood at the curb, two officers blocking his approach. Catelyn strode over to him. "Who are you, sir?"

"I'm David Hathaway. This is my house."

"We've been trying to get in touch with you. We have your son in custody and have a search warrant for this property."

Outrage turned the man's face a scary shade of purple. He exploded. "What do you mean you have my son in custody! Why wasn't I contacted? Where is he and no, you can't search this property!"

The two officers placed their hands on their weapons. Catelyn held up a soothing hand. "Sir, if you'll just calm down…"

"I will not calm down. What is the meaning of this?"

Catelyn explained the situation, adding the fact that his son's DNA had been found on the hat left in her house and they had tried to call to inform him but hadn't been able to reach him. Then she asked, "Will you please open the door?"

By the end of her explanation, the man's face had gone through several different shades of red to wind up a pasty white.

Without another word, he approached the house and opened the door. Stepping back, he waved them in.

Joseph asked, "Do you have any idea where Tyler might hide any stolen goods?"

"No, of course not. When can I see my son?"

"You're welcome to go down to the jail anytime."

A shout from the garage pulled Catelyn and Joseph in that direction. An officer led them through the garage into the backyard and over to a shed sitting on the corner of the property.

"Crammed full, Detective."

Catelyn stuck her head in and gasped. "Wow."

Tyler's father had followed. "What in the world? Where did all this come from?"

Joseph looked at him. "I take it you don't ever come out here?"

The man never took his eyes from the goods in the shed. He slowly shook his head. "Never. Once I started working so many hours, I hired a yard service that comes once a week. They have their own supplies. Tyler has some pretty bad allergies so I never asked him to do anything outside." He took in the scene again. "I can't believe this."

Joseph sighed. "What you want to bet this is related to all of the break-ins we've been having over on the west side of town?"

"I do believe you could be right," Catelyn agreed.

"All right, I'll call the guys in charge of that case and we'll let them come take a look."

"Hey, Joseph, look over there. A flip-flop and a backpack. Looks kind of out of place in all of those stolen goods. I sure would like to know who those belong to."

"Definitely."

Two hours later, they had matched up the flip-flop with the one found at the crime scene. It belonged to Kelly Franklin. Surprisingly enough, the backpack was Billy's, Kelly's brother. Once again, they had the third-shift crime-scene guys working overtime.

Joseph turned to Catelyn. "I think we need to find Billy and see what he has to say about his backpack being in that storage shed."

Catelyn stifled a yawn. "Sounds good to me." She glanced at her watch and groaned. 9:00. It was going to be another late night.

Joseph was eyeing her like he wanted to say something else. Not up to a big discussion, she slid around him and out the door, calling over her shoulder. "Come on, let's get going."

"Catelyn…"

"Yeah?"

He shook his head. "Nothing. Let's go find Billy."

Catelyn crawled into the passenger seat of the car and let Joseph drive. She leaned her head against the back of the seat and sighed. *Please, Lord, let us find Kelly before it's too late.*

"Hey, you okay?"

"Yeah, just tired."

"We'll find her."

She gave him a weary smile. "I sure hope so."

He cranked the car and pulled away from the curb to head for the Franklin house. They'd called ahead, but had gotten no answer. Which was really strange considering the family was desperate for news about Kelly.

Joseph let the car idle in front of the dark, empty-looking house. "Huh. Wonder where they could be?"

"Do you have cell numbers for the parents?"

"Yeah." He pulled the mounted laptop around in front of him and typed a few keys. As he rattled off the first number, Catelyn punched it into her phone and waited. She looked at Joseph. "Voice mail."

He frowned and gave her the next cell phone number. "That's the dad's number. Bryan."

"Got it." She waited again. "Voice mail."

"I'm not getting a good feeling about this."

"Do you have any next-of-kin numbers?"

"I can find out. Hold on." He tapped a few more keys on the keyboard and gave her another number. "It's Kelly's aunt, her mom's sister. She lives on the west side of town. Libby Darlington."

Catelyn dialed it and perked up when someone answered. She pressed speaker so Joseph could listen in. "Hello? Mrs. Darlington? This is Detective Catelyn Clark with the Spartanburg Sheriff's Department. I need to…"

The woman interrupted. "Have you found Kelly?"

"No ma'am, we haven't. I'm sorry, but I need to ask you if you know where Mr. and Mrs. Franklin are."

"They're at the hospital. We think Bryan had a heart attack."

Catelyn gasped. "Oh, no. I'm sorry to hear that. I'll call if I have any news on Kelly. Thank you so much."

She hung up.

Joseph raised a brow. "To the hospital?"

"Yeah."

ELEVEN

The first person Joseph spotted when entered the waiting room was Alan Dillard. The man saw him and Catelyn coming toward him and rose from his seat to greet them.

After handshakes all around, Joseph asked, "How's Mr. Franklin doing?"

"We're still waiting to hear."

"Is Billy here? We need to talk to him."

"No, I haven't seen him. He's really the one I came down to support. Mrs. Franklin called me and asked if Billy could stay with me while they were here at the hospital. I came to pick him up, but…" The man shrugged. "I haven't seen him. Which is really strange."

Catelyn and Joseph shared a look. "Well, if you hear from him, will you give us a call?"

"Absolutely."

Joseph handed his card to the man then turned to Catelyn. "Why don't we go check on Zachary while we're here?"

Coach Dillard spoke up. "You can check on him, but I just came from there. There's been no change. Stacy, my wife, is up there, too, with Zachary's family."

Joseph thought for a moment. "I guess we'll see if we can track down Billy."

"I've already been calling all his buddies and no one's seen him. I hope he hasn't snapped."

"What do you mean?" Catelyn asked.

"I've seen some symptoms of depression. I've tried talking his parents into letting him talk to a counselor, but they're not having any part of it. They're consumed with finding Kelly. And now this…" He lifted his hands, palms up then dropped them to his side. "I don't know. I have to say, I'm worried, though."

Joseph shook the man's hand again. "Thanks for your help. If we find him, we'll let you know."

Alan nodded and returned to his seat.

Joseph turned to go and caught sight of two familiar figures walking arm in arm toward the exit located just ahead. They'd come from a different part of the hospital that shared the exit with the heart center. It was his sister and her husband.

"Marianna? Ethan?" he called.

Ethan turned, pulling Joseph's sister to a stop. He spotted Joseph and nudged the woman, signing Joseph's name with a crooked pinky twisted next to his right eye. She whirled, her long black hair fanning out behind her. Excitement lit her face and she ran to throw herself into her brother's arms. Joseph gave her a gentle squeeze. He pulled back to sign, "You've gained some weight, little sister."

Marianna whacked him on the arm. "Thanks a bunch." Then she smiled. "It's so good to see you. What are doing here? Is everything all right?"

Joseph held up a hand. "Whoa, whoa. Yes, everything's fine. Just a case we're working on."

Ethan approached with an outstretched hand. Joseph shook it while Catelyn hugged Marianna. Ethan said, "Good to see you. We just got back from our mini vacation and haven't had a chance to let everyone know."

"What are you doing here?" Catelyn asked, signing so Marianna could easily follow the conversation rather than have to try to read lips.

Marianna and Ethan exchanged a look. Ethan cleared his throat and shrugged. "Just paying someone a visit. Nothing major. Anyway, we're headed over to see your parents. We both head back to work tomorrow." His gaze sharpened as he zeroed in on Catelyn. "Anything I need to know about?"

She snorted. "Captain has work waiting for you, don't worry. And I'll fill you in when I can, but right now, we really need to get going. We've got a missing girl to find."

Marianna frowned. "When can we get together?"

Joseph rubbed her back with one hand, signing with the other. "After this case is finished, I promise, we'll all go out for some fun. Maybe dinner and a movie, okay?"

Marianna, used to Joseph's and Ethan's workaholic ways simply rolled her eyes and linked her arm back through her husband's. With her right hand she signed, "Come on, you're not going back to work until you have to. And that's an order."

Ethan looked torn, but finally succumbed to the soulful, dark brown eyes peering up him. He shrugged. "Catch you later."

Joseph and Catelyn said their goodbyes and left the hospital to climb back into the car. Two hours later, Joseph slapped the wheel.

"It's almost midnight. He's not at any of his friends' houses. Where could he be?"

"I don't know." She rubbed a hand across weary features. "He's got that big game coming up. Surely he wouldn't do anything to jeopardize the team's chances for winning the tournament."

Joseph shrugged, thinking she might be right, then said, "If he is depressed, he might not be thinking clearly."

"True."

"Okay, so I'm going to call in a BOLO for Billy and then I'm going to take you back to your car. There's really nothing more we can do tonight."

"Right, let's grab a few hours of sleep and meet back in the morning."

He drove in the direction of the station. Pulling a water bottle from the cup holder, he uncapped it and asked, "Are we going to finish our conversation?"

"What do you mean?"

"At the restaurant before we were interrupted. You were telling me about your parents."

Catelyn drew in a deep breath and Joseph held his. Had he stepped over the line in asking? He took another swig of the water as he waited to see what she would say.

"My father killed himself when I was seventeen."

Joseph choked, spewing the small sip of water he'd just taken. Catelyn didn't look in his direction, just stared out the window. He said, "I never knew that. I just thought it was an accident with his gun."

"That's what everyone believed. But the official report was he ate his gun. I've hated him ever since. I think I've had a lot of suppressed anger, too." She spoke in a calm, deliberate way, almost as though talking about someone else. "But now that I've figured that out, I'm going to be able to deal with it. I'm going to *have* to deal with it."

"Catie…" he whispered.

"Don't." She held up a hand. "I don't want your sympathy right now. I'll start blubbering."

"You never told me."

"I…couldn't. Until today. Because of my mother." She shook her head. "Amazing."

* * *

The numbness faded leaving a gaping wound in her heart. She felt the tears surface again. "Anyway, after he... died...my mother...she, um, she just...she kind of withered away. Quit the force, quit life, quit...me."

He reached across to take her hand. "I don't know what to say."

Catelyn pulled away. "There's nothing you can say. Your home became my haven. My escape. If your family hadn't treated me as one of your own, I don't know where I'd be today." She gave a short laugh. "The only reason I never tried alcohol or took anyone up on those many offers of drugs was because of your parents. I...didn't want to blow a good thing. I knew if I got caught up in that kind of stuff, your parents wouldn't let me back in their home."

"That's not true. They loved you and would've helped you, would have still treated you like one of their own kids and gotten you any help you might have needed."

She gave a small laugh and brushed at nonexistent lint on her khakis. Then she nodded. "You're probably right." Her eyes finally lifted to his. "I do believe you're right."

"See, God was looking out for you after all...in spite of the parents you were born to."

Tears flooded her eyes again and she sniffed, desperate to turn them off, but not quite succeeding. He changed the subject and she gave a grateful sigh.

"But why become a cop?" He turned into the parking lot and pulled the unmarked cruiser to a stop beside her car. "Why this profession when it seems to be the reason your parents messed up so completely."

This time the laughter that escaped her had a harsh ring to it. "Because I thought it would help me understand. I thought if I *became* them, if I walked in their shoes, I could somehow find some answers."

"And have you?"

She shrugged. Had she? With a start, she realized that those few moments with her mother today had gone a long way toward dispelling the raging fury she'd carried in her heart for so long. More so than working as an officer had. "I don't know. I don't know if I'll ever know."

"I want to be there for you, Catie."

"And I want you to be there, but I don't think I'm capable of having a relationship with another cop." She stared into his eyes and took a deep breath. "No matter how much my heart might want to."

With that, she climbed out of his vehicle and into her own, not bothering to look back. Because if she looked back, she knew he'd be watching her and she'd cave in to the urge to run into his arms, eating her words and throwing caution to the wind.

And with visions of the screaming matches she'd grown up with flashing in her mind, she knew she just couldn't do that.

Arriving home, Catelyn pulled into her garage this time and went in the back door. A quick inspection told her no one had been in the house during her absence except for the professional cleaning service she'd called in to repair what the vandals had destroyed.

Her house looked good, finally back in order—if missing a few electronics. She'd get an insurance check for that soon enough. No time to watch TV anyway.

She kicked off her shoes and looked longingly toward her bedroom. Fatigue gripped her, numbing her mind, pulling on her body. The day had been an eternity what with the visit with her mother, telling Joseph about her father, avoiding her feelings for Joseph and trying to stay on top of this case.

Now, she just wanted to sleep for a few hours before starting all over again.

But first she checked all the doors and windows one more time. Just to be sure.

Not usually nervous about turning the lights out, she realized she didn't want to be in the dark tonight.

Leaving the hall light burning, she crawled into her bed and prayed. *Lord, You've shown me some pretty incredible things about myself lately. I'm not sure what to think about everything, to be honest. Especially this thing that seems to be between Joseph and myself. I guess I'm going to have to leave that for You to figure out. And as for today with my mother—thanks. I needed that. I still don't understand why my father did what he did, I don't know why You couldn't have just...*

She cut off the prayer feeling the anger rise back up in her. It would take time, she figured. Time to process it all again. Maybe she'd never be at peace about it. The thought terrified her because more than anything, she wanted peace.

Peace, Lord. Please give me peace...

She must have drifted off because something awakened her. She lay still, wondering what it could have been. Usually once she fell asleep, she slept until her alarm went off.

Something had disturbed that. The air in her room seemed different. A smell that she didn't recognize. A combination of body odor and cigarettes?

Then she realized...

...someone was in here with her.

Her nerves bunched. Frozen, her eyes probed the shadows. Very little moonlight made its way through her heavy curtains. Usually she liked to sleep in pure darkness. The light from the hallway was out. Now the night seemed to press in on her.

Her heart pounding, her palms slick, she pondered what to do. How to react. Which way to move. Where was he? Not daring to move to alert whoever was in the room that she was awake, she calculated how long it would take to roll to her left, grab open the nightstand and palm her gun.

The shadows shifted.

He was beside her bed.

She tensed her muscles to roll to the right.

Without warning, something soft fell across her face and pressure from above kept it there.

She was too late!

Flinging her arms up, she tried to push the object away. Felt hard fists clenched into the fabric.

She couldn't scream, couldn't breathe!

Someone was trying to kill her by smothering her with her own pillow. She kicked, bucked, turned her head and managed a small gasp of air before the small opening closed.

God, help me!

Churning her arms, she tried to punch. Her feeble blows fell on a bare arm. Panicking, she dug her fingernails in.

The arm flinched away from her and she managed to push the pillow to the side while her attacker fought to maneuver it back into place.

Another gasp of life-giving air. Then the pillow returned heavier than before. Brain racing, she frantically brought both hands up and felt a head, ears. She pushed, but couldn't budge the person above her.

Help! Help me! Her mind screamed; terror nearly scrambled her thinking.

Then an idea filtered through the fog of fear.

Fisting her hands, she laid her arms spread-eagle on the bed then brought them up with all her strength, effectively boxing her attacker's ears.

A howl of rage and pain reached her as he flung himself back. As he jerked away from her, she grasped the mask covering his face. The sliver of moonlight caught on a lantern-shaped chin. Then he was in the dark and disappearing fast.

Kicking at the covers, Catelyn rolled to her right and landed on the opposite side of the bed. Fleeing feet headed for her bedroom door.

"Oh...no...you...don't!" she ground out through gasps for air and gritted teeth.

But she was on the wrong side of the bed. Her gun was in the other nightstand. Flipping herself over the bed, she grabbed the drawer and yanked.

Gun in one hand, cordless phone in the other, she took off after the escaping thug. She could hear him pounding through her kitchen, then the slam of the back door.

She punched in 911 and headed out after her target.

TWELVE

Joseph lifted his head from the kitchen table, rubbed the sleep from his eyes and looked around. He'd fallen asleep over the case files.

What time was it?

The stove clock read 1:38.

Time to get comfortable and get some sleep. He still had his gun strapped to his arm and his phone on his belt. His gaze dropped to the picture of the missing girl. Kelly Franklin. Was she still alive? Was she hurt? Suffering? Or was she already long dead, Tracy's killer striking twice. But she'd been alive after Tracy had died. That much he thought he knew. The flip-flop left at the first scene indicated she was at least still alive when she was taken from the campus.

And the other found in a storage shed full of stolen goods. Was she a part of the ring? Or had she stumbled on all of this accidentally? Digging into her life had shown her to be a "good girl" who hung out with the right crowd with the exception of Tracy Merritt. Kelly went to church every Sunday. Was friends with Alonso, girlfriend to Dylan, who had a bit of a shady past, but seemed to be trying to turn it around. Maybe Kelly was a positive influence on him.

Why was she at the school that night? To meet Dylan

as he'd said? But neither were dorm students. Because she lived in town, normally, Tracy wouldn't stay on campus overnight, but because she played basketball, she was allowed to be a temporary residential student.

So, Kelly and Dylan had planned to meet that night at the school for whatever reason. Kelly arrived early and got into an argument with Tracy. Dylan came upon them fighting, got into the thick of it, then left when Kelly wanted to finish whatever she and Tracy were arguing about.

He pulled out the text message log from the phones. Kelly and Dylan had arranged their rendezvous. Nothing about meeting Tracy. So it hadn't been prearranged. Tracy's cell had no texts that evening.

Zachary's had several to his coach about meeting for practice, confirming game times, baseball chit-chat, and then telling him about Tracy's funeral. Nothing unusual. Nothing revealing. Nothing to indicate who he was meeting with the day of the funeral. He could have received a text anytime during the day and met up with the person several hours later.

However, there was one text that Zachary had received about an hour before he was reported to have left the house. It read "Stay out of stuff that's not your business or you'll be very sorry."

The text came from Stacy Dillard's phone. This was a new twist. What was the woman doing sending that text to Zachary? Definitely something to ask her about tomorrow.

Joseph sighed and put the papers aside then reached up to rub his eyes.

And then there was Catelyn. What was he going to do about the only woman who'd ever driven him to distraction? Made him pace the floor at night thinking about how much he missed her and wished God would intervene to change her heart.

Her parents had done a number on her. Especially her father. Suicide…whoa. No wonder she was so angry.

Joseph sighed—and nearly jumped out of his skin when his phone buzzed.

Dispatch. What?

"Joseph here."

"This is Margo in dispatch. Sorry about the lateness of the call, but I just got a 911 call from your partner's house reporting an intruder. I know Catelyn pretty well and know you guys are working together. Figured you'd want to know."

"You figured right. I'm on my way. Thanks."

Joseph punched in Catelyn's number as his steps ate up the distance between the kitchen and the back door. Her phone rang four times then went to voice mail.

He hung up as he threw himself into his car. He could be at Catelyn's in approximately seven minutes. He planned to make it in five.

Where was he? Fury battled common sense. Her gun gripped in her right hand, she followed the path she thought her intruder had taken. Flashing lights pierced the darkness letting her know help had arrived.

But the guy she was after was getting away.

Had gotten away.

She'd lost him.

Winded, she leaned against the nearest telephone pole, and searched every nook and cranny within seeing distance.

He was around here somewhere, she felt sure, but with so many houses, bushes, trees, open garages, there was no way to figure out where he'd gone.

But they would search.

The squeal of tires caught her attention and she spun to see taillights disappear around the corner.

Picking up her cell, she dialed dispatch again. She needed Margo to patch her through to whoever was going to be in charge.

Eyes still scanning the shadows, she listened to it ring. Margo picked up before the first ring ended. "Catelyn, is that you?"

"It's me. He got away. I think he's heading north down Kendall Street. Get a car after him, will you?"

"You chased him?" She sounded outraged.

"I knew you were sending backup." Catelyn winced at the slight whine in her voice. "Anyway, I need some manpower out here to search the area and make sure he isn't taking refuge in someone's house or garage. I'm pretty sure he was in the car and is long gone by now, but we've got to check."

"It's on the way."

"Catelyn?"

She turned and her heart nosedived to her toes before banging back up. "Joseph? What are you doing here?"

"Margo called me."

"Ah. Well, she needn't have bothered. Sorry to get you out of bed."

"I haven't made it there yet. What happened?"

Remembered terror flooded her and she shivered. "I was asleep, or at least dozing. Something woke me up and I realized I wasn't alone in the room. Then I felt a pillow slam over my face…" She broke off and swallowed.

"Catie," he whispered, and wrapped his arms around her.

It felt like coming home.

The shakes set in and she felt the tremors rock through her. Yes, she was a cop, but she was still human. And she'd been personally attacked twice now. Her house and now

her physical person. It was enough to throw the strongest
person off her game.

She pulled in a deep breath and stepped back. "Thanks,"
she whispered without meeting his eyes.

"You're welcome. Are you okay? Did he hurt you?"

"I'm all right. I'm just wondering how he got in."

"Let's check it out."

Catelyn started back the way she'd come. She hadn't
gone too far from her house when she'd lost the guy. Back
in her driveway, she noticed something for the first time.
"My garage door is open."

"You didn't open it?"

"No. I was stunned and mad when I came out chas-
ing that guy and didn't stop to think about it, but I always
close my garage at night. Maybe that's what woke me and
not the smell."

"Did you lock the door going into the house?"

She sighed and rubbed her eyes. "I think so. I remember checking all the locks before going to bed, so yes, I'm
pretty sure it was locked."

He stepped closer. "Let's see if we can get some prints
off this. I can't tell by just looking at it, but I bet someone
picked your lock. Did you notice if he was wearing gloves?"

She closed her eyes, forcing herself to remember what
she'd felt when she'd reached up and felt his arm, his head,
his fists. His ear.

"No, he wasn't and he was wearing two earrings in his
left ear. Plus, I pulled a ski mask off and caught sight of his
chin. Unfortunately, I couldn't see anything else.'

"So you wouldn't recognize him if you saw him again?"

"No," She sighed. "Probably not."

Two hours later, the crime-scene unit had finished up
and the clock was pushing 3:45. There'd been no sign of

her intruder. Joseph walked into her den and sat on the couch beside her. She had her knees pulled up, her forehead resting on them.

He reached over to rub her shoulder. "Are you going to be all right?"

"I don't know" came her mumbled response.

"It's a good thing you scratched him. The tissue they scraped from under your nails will be helpful—especially if it matches up with a guy who's got two earrings in his left ear."

"I know," she said to her knees.

Tilting her chin, he looked into her eyes. Eyes so blue, they usually reminded him of the ocean on a clear day. Only tonight, they were stormy gray. Vulnerability shone through the clouds and his heart clenched with sympathy.

He leaned closer, placing his lips on hers, feeling their softness, remembering their texture. He waited a moment, giving her the opportunity to pull away if she wanted.

Instead, a soft sigh escaped her and she let him kiss her. Just a soft, comforting kiss that touched his heart with tender fingers, yet left him longing for more.

Then he transferred the kiss to her forehead and she wrapped her arms around him to let him hold her.

Never had a moment been so sweet. He cherished it while he could, figuring when she got her feet back under her, she'd be off and running again.

"You'd better go," she mumbled against his chest.

"I know." He didn't move. She was letting him hold her, letting him see her vulnerable side and he didn't want the moment to end.

"You're not going to get much sleep," she warned him.

"I've gone on less."

With a sigh, she pulled away and his arms ached with

loneliness. The sensation startled him, then he realized she was right. He should go.

He stood, and she gave him a small shove. "Give me a wake-up call, okay?"

"Sure. Try not to worry. Your guy's probably not coming back."

"Probably not, but I'm still getting an alarm system put in."

"I can't believe you don't have one already."

She shrugged. "I've thought about it, of course, even had a company come out and give me an estimate. They're pretty expensive and with Mom in the nursing home…"

"Doesn't her pension pay for that?"

"No. She quit the force, remember?"

"So you…"

"Yeah, me." She waved him to the door. "Go on, get out of here. I'll see you tomorrow…um, today…in a couple of hours."

He lifted a hand and ran a finger down her cheek, started to say something, then closed his mouth and walked out the door.

THIRTEEN

Catelyn couldn't believe it. First, she'd let him kiss her after she'd given him a list of reasons a relationship between them would never work. And second, the big lug had slept in his car for the past—she looked at the clock—three and a half hours. She'd fallen into bed after setting her alarm and only rolled out fifteen minutes ago. She'd slept hard, her body craving the rest, and yet she'd been restless, too, worried her intruder might come back. And feeling guilty for resting when Kelly was still missing.

Joseph hadn't told her that he was planning on standing guard because he knew she wouldn't let him…or would, at the very least, lose sleep over his act of chivalry because she'd feel guilty that she was snug in her bed while he earned a crick in his neck.

The man knew her well for the most part.

Standing in her kitchen sipping a cup of the strongest coffee she could stand, she looked out her window and watched him stir.

He cared about her. She'd have to be comatose not to see it. The thought warmed her and scared her to death.

But she just couldn't get past her parents' lousy marriage—and the fear that she couldn't live up to Joseph's expectations of what being a wife entailed.

Although she realized she desperately wanted to. As long as she could be his wife and do her job. But that wasn't to be. He wanted a wife who'd be happy staying at home and there was no way that was going to be her.

That line of thought startled her. For so long, she'd refused to even consider marriage to another cop simply because of her childhood. But Joseph, ever since their first meeting when she'd been a hurting teen and he'd been the brother of her best friend, they'd had a connection…a…something.

So, did that mean if Joseph suddenly decided he would be happy having a cop for a wife, she'd change her stance on marriage to a police officer?

Groaning, she reached up to massage the back of her neck with her right hand, then finished of her coffee. She set the mug in the sink and looked back at the man in the car.

She did know one thing, though. No matter how conflicting her feelings, she cared for the guy. Maybe even loved him. Probably did. Okay, definitely did. Always had. Always would.

Pouring the rest of the ten-cup pot of caffeine into a thermos, she grabbed her lightweight police jacket and headed out the door and over to the car.

A light tap on the window roused him. He opened one eye and glared at her. She smiled and remembered the times he'd fallen asleep at his parents' home after a large family meal. His mom or dad would try to wake him and Catelyn, Marianna and Gina, two of his sisters, would watch and giggle about how grumpy he would be. Nothing had changed in all those years.

The window slid down. "Go away."

"You're an idiot," she said, hearing the affection in her voice.

"I know, but I couldn't just leave. I was…"

"Worried?"

"Huh. Maybe. I know you can take care of yourself pretty well, but…" He shrugged and opened the other eye. "Is that coffee?"

She laughed at the pleading tone in his voice.

Opening the door, she settled in the passenger seat. "You drive and I'll pour."

"Deal." Cranking the car, he pulled away from the curb and rubbed the stubble on his chin. "Guess I'll clean up when we get to the station."

"What's the plan today?"

"I want to talk to Billy Franklin about his backpack and that flip-flop showing up in the storage shed."

She handed him the brew. "We probably should have pulled him out of bed last night and demanded some answers."

"I think we had enough to deal with last night. So, we grabbed a couple hours of sleep. We have to watch out for ourselves, too."

She rubbed her eyes. "I know you're right, it's just that Kelly's missing and we've still got a killer out there. It feels wrong to sleep even for a minute."

Joseph placed his coffee cup in the holder and reached over to squeeze her hand. "I know. We'll find her, though. Right now, I want to find Billy Franklin. I haven't been able to track him down all day."

She smiled at him, remembering his tender gentleness only a few hours earlier. Her dad never would have…

Her smile slipped and she said, "Have you called Coach Dillard?"

"Yeah. He said he hadn't heard from Billy and didn't have any idea where the kid might have gotten to. He did mention that Billy wouldn't miss the big game."

"How's his dad doing?"

"Better. It wasn't his heart. He had an anxiety attack."

"No wonder. I can't say I'm surprised."

Joseph reached for his coffee once more as he drove and Catelyn considered her feelings for the man. She wanted things to work out between them more than she'd thought possible.

Especially after last night...

But could she lay it all on the line like that? Trust him with her heart? Fully open herself up to someone else. A cop? One who wanted a traditional stay-at-home wife? Could she get past her own fears of what marrying another cop would entail?

She shuddered at the thought, but couldn't help the yearning desire to answer each question with a resounding yes. But the truth was, she just didn't know.

"Give me fifteen minutes, then we'll head over to the Dillard house. I want to talk to Stacy Dillard about that text message she sent Zachary."

She nodded. "She may be at church. Let me call and see if anyone is home."

He disappeared into the building and Catelyn got on the phone.

Mrs. Dillard let them in, albeit reluctantly. Joseph stepped through the door, taking in his surroundings—and the fading bruise on the woman's left cheekbone.

"What's this about, Detective? I have a sick child upstairs."

Joseph raised a brow. Were they going to do this in the foyer?

As if reading his mind, Stacy motioned for them to precede her into the den area. Catelyn sat on the edge of the nearest recliner. Joseph chose the love seat.

Stacy stood in the doorway, arms crossed. Joseph cleared his throat. "Mrs. Dillard, why don't you have a seat?"

She did.

Catelyn intervened. "I'm sorry Alan Jr. is sick. We won't take much of your time, but we need to ask you about Zachary."

"That's what you said on the phone."

"When we saw you at the funeral, you said you didn't understand why we thought Dylan would be a suspect in Kelly's disappearance. You thought we should be looking more at Zachary."

The woman took a deep breath and nodded. "Yes. Yes, I did say that."

"Then Zachary ends up shot and we find a text message on his phone from you."

Stacy paled, her right eye twitched. "I see."

Catelyn looked at Joseph. He nodded. He'd noticed she didn't ask which text message they were asking about.

"You threatened him."

She grimaced. "I wondered when that would come back to haunt me."

Joseph got up and wandered over to the glass gun rack. "That's a nice set of rifles you have there."

"They're my husband's." She twisted her fingers.

"Did you shoot Zachary?"

The woman let out a laugh. "What? You've got to be kidding. I was standing there in line with you when Zachary took off with you guys right behind him. When would I have been able to shoot him?" She waved a hand. "And I didn't want to shoot him anyway, I just wanted him to keep his mouth shut."

The woman had a point. She didn't shoot Zachary and she had two police officers who could give her an alibi. But did she know who shot him or did she hire someone to do it? He made a note to pull her financial records. "What was the text about?"

"Zachary knew Alan and I were having problems. I... met with a...friend. Zachary saw me meeting with...this friend. I was desperate—and stupid. I thought if I took a tough stance, Zachary would back off."

"Did he?"

"No, he wanted money to keep quiet."

"Blackmail?"

"Yes." She swallowed hard. "I asked him for some time to get the money together."

"So you were going to pay him?"

"Yes."

And that was as much as she was going to say, Joseph could tell. He wondered if her reticence to talk had anything to do with the bruise on her cheek. "I'm going to need the name of your...friend."

His phone rang. "Excuse me." He left Catelyn talking to Stacy while he took the call from one of the dispatchers. "Hello?"

"Billy Franklin was spotted at the church where he attends. The one on North Spring Street."

"Thanks."

Joseph hurried back into the den. "Come on, Catelyn. We've got to go pick up Billy." He turned to Stacy. "We're not done yet."

She shrugged. "I'm not going anywhere." Then she bit her lip. "Just don't tell Alan, please."

Joseph didn't make any promises, just followed Catelyn's brisk jog to the car.

FOURTEEN

Catelyn threw herself into the seat and slammed her door. "She didn't shoot Zachary."

"Nope. I think she's got some major marital problems, but I don't think she shot the kid to keep him quiet."

"What do all of these boys have in common?"

"They're all in high school. And they all play baseball."

"Right. That's what I've come up with. But there's something else tying them together, too. I just can't figure out what it is." She gritted her teeth as he took another turn. "Sandy said she'd put a rush on the DNA, to see if the evidence they got out from under my fingernails matches anything in the system."

"Okay, so what else? Somehow these guys with the baseball team are involved."

Joseph rounded a corner then took a sharp left.

Catelyn's breath whistled between her teeth as the scenery zipped past her window. "And Billy knows more than he's telling."

"You think someone's got his sister and is threatening to kill her if he tells what he knows?"

"It's possible, but what does Billy have that's of use to someone else? He's just a kid."

"He saw who did it and they're using Kelly to keep him quiet."

"But why not kill him, too? Kill both of them?"

"I don't know."

Catelyn's phone rang. "Hello?"

"Hey. This is Sandy."

"Sandy, do you ever sleep?"

"Not when I've got a case this big going on. The tests finally came back on that wood chip you found. It's the kind of wood that baseball bats are made of. It's ash wood and yes, ash is used for a lot of other things, but after studying that piece more, my guess is it came from a baseball bat."

"Was any blood or anything on it?"

"I found a piece of hair, no blood. Tracy never bled on the outside of her skull, just the inside. The hair matches up with Tracy's. I believe if you find a baseball bat with a missing chip, you'll find your murder weapon."

"You're worth your weight in gold, my friend. Thank you so much."

"Okay, now I'm going home to sleep for a few hours."

Catelyn saw they were getting close to the church. "You've more than earned it. If you hadn't stayed on top of things in the lab like you've done, we wouldn't be anywhere near solving this thing."

"This one kind of hits close to home. I'm friends with Dylan's mom, too."

"Thanks again, Sandy. Catch you later."

Catelyn hung up and relayed the information to Joseph. She finished up just as they pulled into the church parking lot.

Both hopped out of the car and entered the church. The service was over, people spilling from the auditorium.

Keeping her eyes open, she looked for any familiar faces milling around. Seeing none, she nodded for Joseph to take the opposite end of the lobby to watch those exiting the sanctuary.

She signed to him, "Do you see anyone?"

"No," he signed back.

She pulled back into the lobby and finally spotted a group of deaf kids signing near the exit.

Joseph caught her eye and followed her over to them. "Excuse me," she signed. "Would you guys mind talking to us outside?"

The boys stilled, eyes on the two cops who'd just interrupted their conversation. "This way, please, all of you."

Eyes darting back and forth to one another, they followed her outside where Joseph thanked them for their attention. Catelyn got down to business. "All right guys, have any of you seen Billy?"

"None of your business, Cop."

Catelyn honed in on the smart mouth. "Excuse me?"

"Bobby, shut up."

Joseph turned to the young black boy who'd just spoken. "And you are?"

"R.J., Ricky James, but I go by R.J. Yo, Coach and Billy left a while ago. Billy said he had to make a phone call and went to the lobby. Coach Dillard asked me what was up and I told him. He took after Billy like a streak of lightning."

Catelyn met Joseph's eyes. That didn't sound good. "Do you know where they went?"

"Nope. When Coach Dillard asked me where Billy went I told him and he said for us to catch a ride with one of the youth workers who would help get us home."

"Do you guys come to church every Sunday with Coach Dillard?"

The boy shrugged. "Most Sundays. Coach is real religious and likes us to come with him. He says we're his future and he's watching over his investment. Or something like that. We like Coach and think he's cool. Church is all right, too."

"All right. Thanks, R.J."

"I hope you can help Billy out. He's been real depressed lately what with his sister missing and all."

"You wouldn't happen to have any idea what happened that night she went missing would you?"

"No, man. I wish I did. I like Kelly, she's a good kid."

Joseph turned to the rest of the crew, signing and voicing at the same time. "Do any of you know where Coach Dillard and Billy might have gone?"

Bobby, Mr. Smartmouth, spoke up. "They had business and went to take care of it, obviously."

Catelyn lasered him with her eyes. "What kind of business? Gang business?"

A flush crept up into his cheeks. "Wouldn't you like to know?"

Joseph wanted to pop the kid in the mouth—or at least arrest him for something. Catelyn looked like she felt the same way. He ignored the kid and turned to the one who seemed willing to help. "R.J.?"

"That, I don't know. Coach Dillard just said he had to take care of something and it wouldn't wait."

"Where would they go to take care of this business? Someplace special?"

"Probably at his house. That's where he does everything. But I don't think Billy would go there. He's been mighty weird about Coach Dillard lately. Maybe at the high school? Coach's got an office there and spends a lot of time in it, studying teams, videos of different players and stuff."

Catelyn looked at Joseph. "You think?"

He shrugged. "I think that would be way too easy. But let's give it a shot. We just came from his house so I doubt he'd take his business there with his wife and kid."

"Right. Let's head for the school."

They thanked the boys and headed over to the high school.

The place looked deserted. Knocking on the door brought no response. Joseph peered in another window. "So do you think Tracy's death is related to the gang situation with Zachary wanting out or something else?"

"That's been in the back of my head ever since Dylan told us about it. But I'm thinking it's connected to something different. Tracy's death doesn't seem like a gang killing. She was cracked in the head with a blunt object—probably a baseball bat—and that sounds more like an impulse killing, spur of the moment, she made someone mad kind of thing."

"Yeah, that's what I think, too. The evidence isn't there for a gang killing."

"I sure wish Zachary would wake up so we could talk to him."

"I'm worried about the person who doesn't want him to wake up."

"That's why we've got a guard on him."

Fifteen minutes later, they pulled in the parking lot of Esterman High. Two cars sat in the parking lot. Joseph recognized the red Bronco from their visit to Coach Dillard's house. The blue Toyota looked familiar, too.

Joseph draped his wrists over the steering wheel, his brow creased in thought. "You know how we were brainstorming what all these guys had in common?"

"Yes."

"What about a coach?"

He nodded. "But why kill Tracy?"

"I have no idea. Let's go ask."

He blew out a breath and pulled his phone from the

cup holder. "All right, let me call for backup, then let's see what we've got."

"Go for it."

He had the first six digits punched in when a shot rang out.

FIFTEEN

Weapons in hand, Joseph and Catelyn headed to the gymnasium where the shot had come from. Nerves bouncing with every step, she visualized various scenarios. Had the bullet found its target?

Catelyn got on her radio and called for an ambulance. "Shots fired."

"Backup's on the way," the dispatcher reassured her.

"Tell them to keep their sirens off. I don't want to alert anyone we're here yet."

"Ten-four."

Joseph found a window and looked in. Catelyn approached the door, and standing off to the side, reached over to turn the knob. It twisted easily beneath her palm.

The door swung inward.

She nodded to Joseph and, leading with his gun, stepped through the opening. Catelyn followed then moved ahead of Joseph.

Moving slowly, feeling Joseph at her back, she kept her ears trained for any warning sound. Her eyes took in every detail of the building. They'd come in the side door that opened directly into a hallway lined with closed doors on either side.

Catelyn tried the first one she came to.

Locked.

Joseph tried the next three.

All locked and no sound coming from behind them.

The door she and Joseph had entered just moments before cracked open. Catelyn swung her weapon around to train it on the opening. Joseph did the same.

Heart pounding, she waited. A gun came around the edge.

And Joseph stepped in front of her.

She snapped her gun so the muzzle pointed to the ceiling and stepped to the side so she could watch the door.

What was he doing?

She had to push aside the anger thrumming through her. She'd have to deal with that—and Joseph—later.

A uniformed officer slid inside followed by three more.

Catelyn released a whispered breath of relief. Joseph motioned for the officers to hang back. They nodded.

She shot Joseph a we'll-talk-later look and turned back, trying door knobs as she went.

Then she heard voices.

Catching Joseph's eye, she motioned him over.

Silently, he joined her.

"Where is she?!" Another shot and a bullet pierced the door. They both jumped.

Billy. Catelyn raised a brow and Joseph moved in, twisted the knob and pushed the door open, yelling, "Freeze! Police! Put the weapon down."

They stayed in a safe zone on opposite sides of the open door. Catelyn sneaked a look around the door frame.

Three pair of startled eyes focused in on the sudden intrusion. Billy held a gun in his right hand.

"Hands in the air, now!" Catelyn ordered.

"Billy," Joseph said, "put the gun on the floor."

The boy, tears streaking his face, shook his head. "No

way. He knows where Kelly is but won't tell me. I'm out of time!"

"We're here now, Billy, just put the gun down so we can sit down and figure it all out."

"You'll just let him go, but you don't know what they've done."

"Then tell me. What has he done?"

Coach Dillard interrupted. "Nothing. Billy's distraught. He needs counseling."

"And you're going to need a doctor if you don't tell me where my sister is!" Spittle flew from his mouth as he screamed at his coach.

Joseph intervened. "Billy, come on. We can't settle anything if you have that gun."

"He'll kill me," he practically sobbed. "He killed Tracy and he's got Kelly."

"Who, Billy?"

"Him!" He waved the gun at Coach Dillard.

Catelyn watched a look of frustration pass over Alan's face. He held his hands up as though in surrender. "I don't know where he got this idea or why he's chosen me, but I can assure you, I had nothing to do with anything happening to the girls."

"Liar!" The gun waved wildly and Catelyn's heart clamped at the thought of shooting this kid.

"Billy, Billy," she soothed. "I promise, we'll work it out, just put the gun down."

She wondered if she was going to have to call in the hostage-negotiation team.

Joseph met her eyes. He was thinking the same thing.

"Here, look." Billy's hand reached for his pocket.

"Wait!" Joseph hollered. Billy froze.

"What are you going for?" Joseph asked a little more calmly.

"Pictures."

Catelyn saw Alan Dillard's body tense. She asked, "What kind of pictures, Billy?"

"Pictures of Kelly."

Joseph's mind raced. What if the kid was telling the truth? He'd noticed the subtle change in Dillard's posture. A sudden awareness that this situation might not go in his favor?

The tension, already thick, just tightened a bit more.

"Billy..." Coach Dillard started.

"Be quiet," Joseph ordered the man. He turned back to Billy. "Show me the pictures."

The kid reached into his pocket with his left hand and pulled out several snapshots. "He sent me these. I know he did."

"How do you know? Did you see him?"

Billy's brow creased even further. "No, but it had to be him. No one else knows what I do." He motioned with the gun for the coach to move back away from him. Then he walked forward and threw the pictures on the table just inside the door.

Unfortunately, he stepped right in front of Joseph, turning so the gun was pointed away from Alan for a brief second.

Alan took advantage of that and launched himself at Billy as the kid stepped back. The gun went flying, only to land inches from Billy's fingertips. He screamed and scrabbled for it.

Catelyn and Joseph reacted immediately. She went for the gun while Joseph went for Billy. Catelyn knocked the weapon from his grasping fingers.

Alan Dillard had him pinned on the floor. Several

SWAT members swarmed the large office, guns pointed at everyone not wearing a badge.

Joseph pushed the man off Billy and hauled the youth to his feet. "Please, please, believe me. I promise you'll understand. Just look at the pictures."

Catelyn's skeptical look didn't escape Joseph's notice; however, she seemed to make a conscious decision to deliberately soften her stance and walked over to pick up the photographs.

A gasp escaped her as she studied the first one. He handed Billy over to one of the uniformed officers and crossed the room to look over her shoulder.

"Whoa."

"What's the date on that newspaper?"

"Yesterday."

Hope leaped within him as he studied the face of the terrified young girl glaring at the camera holding a newspaper. "She's still alive."

"Looks like it. But for how much longer?"

Joseph told Coach Dillard. "All right, fellas, let's head down to the station and see if we can hash all this out."

Alan narrowed his eyes. "Is that necessary? You saw who had the gun." He looked at Billy. "What happened, Billy? Why would you do this?"

Not giving Billy a chance to respond, Joseph said, "Yeah, it's necessary. I want to know why he thought he needed a gun to confront you and why he thinks you sent these pictures of his sister."

"Can we do this here? I'd prefer it if we could keep the media from getting ahold of this."

"Sorry, we'll expect you in our station within fifteen minutes." He didn't have any reason to arrest Alan—yet. But he still wanted to talk with him.

"Are you arresting Billy?" Alan demanded.

"Absolutely. You can't just go around waving a gun at people. But I also want to hear his story." He turned to one of the officers. His name tag read Bud Bridges. "Will you see Dillard gets to the station?"

"No problem."

"All right. You ready, Catelyn?"

She nodded, her eyes still on Billy, a frown creasing her forehead. Joseph asked, "What's wrong?"

"Nothing." She shook her head and rubbed her nose. "I... Nothing. Let's go."

They headed for the station, Joseph praying that they could finally resolve this case in the next few hours. His churning gut told him it probably wasn't going to be that easy.

Catelyn stomped into the interrogation room. She was starting to feel like she should move her bed into one of the rooms and change her address.

Billy fidgeted, crossing his arms in front of him then fiddling with the sleeve of his plaid shirt. He plucked a button from one cuff and it rolled to the floor. He didn't even blink.

Catelyn sat across from him and his parents who flanked him on either side. "Mr. Franklin, are you sure you're feeling up to this?"

The man nodded, weariness and despair oozing from him in almost visible waves. Catelyn took a deep breath and laid the pictures of Kelly out so they were visible for all to see. Mrs. Franklin sucked in a deep breath and studied her daughter. Then she said, "But this is good, right? It means she's still alive." Hope gleamed in her eyes.

She turned the tape recorder on, went through the list of introductory questions having him verify his name, birth date, etc. Once done, she said, "Start talking Billy. What happened? Where have you been?"

Tension had his body nearly vibrating. "I need to find Kelly. I've tried and tried, but I can't…I just…can't. I've run out of ideas and…time…"

"Who took her?"

"Coach Dillard did."

"You say that with absolute certainty. How do you know?"

Billy swallowed hard. "Because she called and told me she saw him kill Tracy. She didn't know I was just a minute away from the school. She begged me to help her then her phone got cut off."

"Why call you? Wouldn't she text message you? And don't say she did, we already checked her records."

"Normally she would have text messaged me—if she'd had time, but she sounded desperate and scared. She might be deaf, but she can still talk."

Catelyn murmured, "I did some checking on her. Her hearing loss is a lot like Marianna's." Joseph's sister couldn't hear much, but she had excellent speech.

Joseph nodded. "Okay. So she called you."

"Yeah. When Kelly didn't come home, I went looking for her. I figured she was probably meeting Dylan, so I went to the deaf school. They liked to meet there and hang out with the other kids before curfew."

"Did you see her?"

He sighed and rolled his eyes to the ceiling. "Yeah. When I got there, it was already dark. I saw Tracy lying on the ground—" his Adam's apple bobbed once "—dead, I think. Behind Tracy, I saw a man. He was arguing with Kelly. Kelly was hysterical, screaming that he'd killed Tracy. He was trying to get her shut up. He had her by her left wrist and she was trying to kick and hit…" He swallowed again. "He lifted the bat to hit Kelly and that's when I stepped out of the bushes and told him to put it down."

"Who was it, Billy?" Joseph pressed, leaning in to stare the kid in the eye.

"Coach Dillard. I told you, he killed Tracy and grabbed Kelly."

Catelyn jumped in. "Why haven't you told us this before now?"

He swallowed hard. "Because Coach said if I told anyone he'd kill her! I couldn't let him hurt Kelly." He swallowed again. "While Coach was dragging Kelly away, she signed, 'Coach and Tracy lovers.' And something about a secret room."

"Whoa." Joseph sat back. "Alan and Tracy were having an affair? What about this secret room? Did she say anything more about that? Where it was, who it belonged to? What was in it?"

Billy blinked at all the questions then said, "I guess they were having some kind of affair, I really don't know. And I don't know about a secret room, but that's what she signed. I wanted to go after her, but—" he rubbed his head "—I didn't dare. He was serious about killing Kelly."

"So, you just watched him put her in his car and drive away?"

"Yes." Shame flashed, then impatience stamped his face along with worry. "I thought I could find her! I thought I could...get her away from him and then go straight to the police, but he was too good, too smart for me, too... Look, you've got to find Kelly. He knows that I'm going to tell you all this and he's going to kill her!"

"Relax, Billy," Joseph said. "We've got him in a room down the hall. He can't get to her right now."

The boy sat back in his chair with a huff. He rubbed his arms and his sleeves slid up.

Catelyn reached out and grabbed his wrist. "What's this?"

Billy jerked away from her. "Nothing, I scratched myself."

She sat back with a thump. "Scratched yourself, my eye. That was you in my house! You tried to kill me?"

Billy leaped to his feet, fists clenched at his sides. "You're crazy."

Catelyn eyed Joseph who kept a watchful eye on things.

She planted herself in front of the boy. "You tried to kill me. Don't try to deny it. I pulled the mask off your face, you've got the scratches on your arm that are going to match up to the DNA in the system. Why don't you just come clean and tell us everything?"

Billy buried his face in his hands and let out a sigh. He seemed to wither into himself as he slumped back into his chair. "He told me I had to get rid of you. He said you were getting too close, interfering in everything." He looked up and had tears in his eyes. "I'm sorry, but he said he'd kill her if I didn't do it."

"Why didn't you just tell someone?"

"Because who would believe me?" He exploded. "Coach is like a god. Everyone in this town thinks he's the greatest thing in the world. And me?" He shrugged. "No one would believe me. Coach even laughed at me when I said I would tell. Then he said he'd send Kelly to my parents…bit by bit." His Adam's apple bobbed again. "I believed him. I couldn't take the chance. I…didn't want to hurt you…I didn't want any of this to happen…I just didn't know what else to do!"

Catelyn stood and paced, ignoring the boy's shocked parents. She looked at his ear. He'd removed his earrings. Billy's mother cried quietly. His father stared at the son who'd just confessed to attempted murder.

She whirled back. "Were you in on the break-in at my house that night? Stealing my stuff?"

"Yeah. I was there."

"And your backpack in the shed?"

He swallowed hard again. "I told Coach I'd had enough. I wanted him to let Kelly go and I promised I'd keep quiet, I'd keep Kelly quiet, too, but I couldn't keep doing what he wanted me to do." A tear leaked down his cheek. "He gave me the flip-flop. Said if I didn't obey him, the next thing of Kelly's that he gave me would be a finger. I had the backpack with me when we unloaded the stuff. I guess I left it there in the shed."

"Maybe hoping someone would find it? And force you into a confession?" Joseph questioned softly.

Billy shrugged. "I don't know. Maybe."

"All right." Joseph sat back and crossed his arms. "You'll have a hearing, and your parents can post bail for you—if you make bail. Attempted murder of a police officer is serious stuff."

Billy was already shaking his head before Joseph's last word. "No way. I want to stay here. I'll be safe here. Coach is going to be so mad. He knows I've squealed on him. If you let me go, he'll kill me." His lips tightened. "I just couldn't figure out why he hadn't killed Kelly and me both yet. That's the thing. I kept thinking what's he waiting for? Why does he keep dragging it out? Then it hit me. He's waiting for the big game. He's waiting for me to win it." This was said without any cockiness whatsoever. The kid was a brilliant ball player and he knew it.

And he was probably right. Coach Dillard wanted to move up in his career—and felt he couldn't do it without Billy's help.

Leaving Billy in the hands of jail personnel, they made their way to the room where Dillard was supposed to be waiting. Catelyn looked in. "It's empty."

Joseph frowned. "Try the other one."

She marched to the next room and gave a disgusted grunt. "What is this?"

"What do you mean?"

"It's empty, too."

"Who was the officer we left him with?"

"I think his name is Bridges."

"Great." Joseph headed for the information desk. Catelyn followed.

He asked the officer behind the computer, "Could you page Officer Bridges, please? I need to speak with him."

The man nodded and picked up the phone. A minute later, he hung up. "He's not answering. Let me call him on his phone." He punched in a few more buttons and asked for the man. "No answer there, either. I don't understand. Let me just get into this program…" More typing on the computer. Then his brow shot up. He looked up from the screen. "He called for help about five minutes ago, declaring an officer down."

Catelyn nearly screeched. "What?"

SIXTEEN

Joseph and Catelyn bolted for the door and raced for the car.

He told her, "We need to find Dillard. If everything Billy is saying is true, he's going to go after Kelly. I should have told Bridges to cuff Alan."

"But we had no reason to place him under arrest," Catelyn protested as she yanked her car door open.

"Yeah, I know. Guess we do now." His jaw clenched, he slammed his door and cranked the vehicle.

Catelyn buckled her seat belt. "He knew he was busted as soon as Billy opened his mouth. Attacking and injuring an officer is the least of his problems if he's caught."

"I have a feeling we're seriously running out of time to find this girl alive." Wheeling out of the parking lot, he asked, "So, where to first? The coach's house or back to his office? Where would he go?"

"I'm going to get someone to cover all the bus stations, highway exits and the airport. There's no way he'd go back to his office or his house—would he?"

Joseph hesitated at the stop sign. "You wouldn't think, but if he's got Kelly at one of those locations, he's going to have to go there to get her." He grabbed his phone. "I'm going to get units covering both places immediately."

She nodded. "Sounds good."

He placed the calls then gripped the steering wheel. Finally he turned left.

Catelyn added, "But something else is bothering me."

"What?" He wondered if she was going to confront him about his actions in the gym earlier.

There went her teeth again, digging into her full bottom lip. He looked away. Now wasn't the time to notice how attractive she was. Instead, he focused on her words, which were about the case, not his faux pas—the one where he stepped in front of her. Relief flooded him. Maybe she was going to let it go.

He wasn't going to hold his breath on that one.

She said, "Those pictures of Kelly. They're really nagging at me."

"Okay, let's go over them."

Catelyn pinched the bridge of her nose and closed her eyes. "She's sitting in some, standing in others."

"And she's holding a newspaper in all of them, pointing to the date."

"What kind of room is she in? There's something about the room."

Joseph pictured the frightened teen and his gut clenched. They really needed to find her. "I couldn't really tell anything about it. It was a pretty close-up picture."

"Paneling." She snapped her fingers.

"What?"

"That's it, it's got to be. It's the paneling, the wall behind her."

He was confused. "That stuff is very commonplace. Nothing special about that."

"But it's the same as the paneling that was in Coach Dillard's office." Her eyes had the satisfied look of someone who'd just figured out a difficult puzzle.

"Well, if that's where they took the pictures, she wasn't there earlier when we came in on Billy threatening them with the gun."

"But what if they have her nearby? What if she's being held at the school somewhere?" Catelyn's excitement started to grow. Joseph could see it in her snapping blue eyes.

"How would that be possible?" Joseph played devil's advocate as he took a left turn to head for the school like she'd suggested instead of the coach's house. "There's a cleaning crew and people there practically around the clock. Someone would have seen or heard something."

"Just think about it. Alan Dillard's office is set apart from the main school building. It's on a back hall in the gym. All he has to do is put a sign on the door asking for maintenance not to enter his office. And remember, Billy said something about a secret room."

"Someone would get suspicious."

"Maybe not. Baseball season is intense right now. No one would question him spending a lot of time at the school or in his office after hours. So—" her words slowed "—tomorrow's the big game, right?"

"Right." He wondered where she was going with this line of thought. With Catelyn, he was never sure, but she usually made sense in the end. So he listened.

"Okay, so Coach Dillard is warning him against going to the cops. Why? He has to know inevitably, the kid is going to crack and say something."

"Like today."

"Exactly. So, he was hedging his bets and hoping Billy wouldn't say anything until after the game tomorrow."

The light came on for Joseph. "And that's why Billy was running out of time. As soon as the game is over, he and Kelly lose their value and are dead."

The school came into sight. "Right."

Catelyn blew out a sigh. "Well, his car's still here."

Joseph put the car in park. "Because you were right on it when you said he had unfinished business to take care of. Come on, we can't afford to wait on back up. Kelly's life is on the line."

Catelyn called and got a warrant on the way. She wanted to search that office. Every nook and cranny. And like Joseph said, there would be no waiting for backup. If Alan had Kelly, every second counted.

In what felt like a rerun of their actions just a few hours earlier, Joseph and Catelyn drew their guns and entered the building.

This time, though, they knew which door to aim for.

Once again, they took their positions on either side. "Police! Open up!"

Nothing.

Catelyn shot a look at Joseph who nodded. He stepped back, lifted a foot and kicked the door. It slammed in against the wall and bounced back. Joseph moved in, gun raised, using his body to block the door from banging shut.

The room was empty.

Catelyn walked over to the nearest wall and started tapping. "You got the door covered?"

"Yep."

Tap. Tap.

She worked her way around the room. Up one wall, down the next. Tap. Tap. Thud. Thud.

"Hello, what have we here?" She quirked a brow at Joseph. She was onto something.

Fingers explored the paneling and then her palm brushed up against a slight bulge in the wall.

She pushed it and the paneling separated, revealing a door as tall as she.

Catelyn swung the door open to expose a small living area with a door that must be a closet and a bathroom complete with a sink, shower and toilet.

"Joseph!"

He rushed up to stand beside her. A teenage girl lay on a twin-size bed, hands bound in front of her, but not moving.

"It's Kelly. I'll call an ambulance." He reached for his phone.

"I don't think we'll need that ambulance after all."

Catelyn swung her gaze up to see Alan Dillard, gun in hand, step out of the room she'd figured to be the closet.

SEVENTEEN

A mixture of fear and anger coursed through Joseph. Fear for Catelyn and anger at himself for not covering the closet.

Catelyn's nostrils flared, her gaze flitting between the man with the gun and the girl on the bed. "Well, well, came to finish up your dirty work, huh?" Disdain dripped from her voice.

"Shut up and drop your weapons."

Catelyn slowly lowered her piece to the floor, keeping her eyes trained on the man in front of her. Joseph did the same. "So, you're so hard up for entertainment you have to threaten kids to get your kicks?"

"Not hardly. I should have just killed the two of them, but I needed Billy. Now," Alan said, "move into the room with Kelly and over against that wall."

Catelyn moved first, obviously anxious to check on the unconscious girl. Joseph wracked his brain to try and figure a way out. He moved two steps in that direction.

Stopped.

"Wait a minute. We think we're pretty sure why you kept Billy alive. You needed him for the big game. I want to know about Tracy."

"Unfortunately, we don't always get what we want, now get in there."

Joseph narrowed his eyes. "You had money on this game, didn't you? You rigged it?"

Fury flashed in the man's eyes, and Joseph realized he'd nailed it.

"This girl needs a doctor," Catelyn interrupted. She glanced at her gun then back up at Joseph. He saw the intense worry on her face and knew he needed to move fast.

Alan Dillard refused to budge. Joseph tried again. "You killed Tracy, why?" He knew the answer but wanted to hear the man say it—and stall for backup to arrive. Where were they?

"I'm not playing the stall-for-time game. Now move." He fired the gun and the bullet pinged off the ceiling raining plaster on Kelly and Catelyn. She flinched, but never took her eyes from the man.

Joseph moved slightly, watching, waiting for Dillard to get a little closer—then dove for him, just as the man stepped back and fired again.

Catelyn screamed, "Joseph!"

The bullet kicked up the floor just under his armpit. He rolled again and surged to his feet. Alan leveled the gun at Joseph's head. "Don't move. I won't miss again."

Joseph froze.

He'd failed to take the man down. Where was their backup? He'd called it in about three minutes ago when he realized they might find Kelly stashed somewhere in this office.

The gun moved to center on Catelyn and Joseph felt nausea churn in his gut. "Stop!"

Catelyn eyed the gun from her perch next to Kelly. She turned her gaze on Joseph, her look speaking volumes. He was to do whatever it took to disarm this guy.

"You move again, and the lady cop gets it. You understand?"

Joseph swallowed hard, his heart pounding in his throat. He wanted this guy as bad as she did, but he wouldn't do a thing to place her in any more danger. He needed to stall. Surely, backup would be here soon.

"How did you get mixed up in this?"

"When our baseball program was close to being cut, I came up with the bright idea to form a gang, leaked some stories to the press about them and boom, we had money-hungry kids willing to break into houses and steal. Kids who thought being a part of a gang was cool."

"And of course you picked kids that had a psychological need. The need to be accepted, the need to feel like they're a part of a family, a group."

The man smirked. "Of course. Now into the room. I've got to get out of here."

"One more question." Joseph didn't give the man the option to refuse, he just asked it. "Why shoot Zachary?"

Startled, Alan jerked. Then he smiled and shrugged. "I didn't shoot Zachary."

"Who did?"

"I don't know and I don't care. Now move."

A siren sounded from outside and Alan cursed, his gaze moving toward the window.

And Joseph reacted, taking advantage of the split second distraction. He hit the floor and rolled for the man, hooking a hand around an ankle. The coach gave a startled yell as he went down, crashing into a filing cabinet before smacking the floor.

Joseph's senses took in Catelyn diving for her gun.

He flipped over and grabbed for Alan's wrist but not before the man managed to pull the trigger again. Plaster rained down as the two scrabbled across the floor.

* * *

Catelyn searched the floor for her gun. It had been kicked aside in the scuffle. She found it halfway under the bed. Snatching it up, she turned toward the action.

A bullet splattered the wall above her head and she ducked.

Joseph was having a hard time subduing the angry man.

Finally, Joseph had the man's wrist pointed elsewhere and she was able to point her gun, yelling, "Freeze! Drop the weapon!"

Uniformed cops stormed the room, yelling for Dillard to let go of his gun.

And still the man fought. Catelyn lined up a shot. She didn't want to kill him, but she would if she had to. Then they rolled again. She lowered the gun, heart pounding, adrenaline surging.

She didn't dare pull the trigger when Joseph could make a sudden move; she might hit him. But if she didn't... Alan moved the gun around, leveling it with Joseph's head.

Catelyn pulled the trigger. And got him in the shoulder of his gun hand.

"Ah!" Alan jerked back, screaming, arms flailing, yet he still kept a grip on his weapon. Catelyn stepped forward and soccer-kicked his gun hand. Another pained yell escaped him and Joseph pinned him to the floor.

An officer moved in and helped cuff the enraged man. Bridges. He'd rejoined the action, obviously feeling the need to redeem himself.

Joseph, panting and gasping, rolled away and groaned. "Thank God."

Bridges stated over his radio, "Scene's clear."

The ambulance arrived and paramedics rushed in.

Catelyn pointed them to Kelly. Joseph wiped his eyes

and took a deep breath. Concerned for him, she knelt beside him then offered him a hand up. "Are you all right?"

"I gotta get to the gym more," he grunted, ignoring her hand. "That guy's an ox."

Officers escorted the man to the nearest squad car. Right now he protested it was all a misunderstanding and he needed medical attention.

Catelyn snorted. Right. Watching the paramedics, she said, "I'm going to check on Kelly."

"I'm going to…sit here…one more minute."

Every muscle in his body quivered at the stress he'd just put it through. But satisfaction surged. They'd found Kelly and captured Tracy's killer. But what about Zachary? They still didn't know who'd shot the teen. Unless Alan was lying, which was a distinct possibility.

But for now, Alonso was right. His friend wasn't a murderer. He'd be pleased and Joseph would be his hero. Joseph smiled at the thought. More than likely, Alonso would ask him what took him so long.

Getting to his feet proved to be a painful process, but he did it with only a small grunt escaping his lips.

Now that he'd caught his breath, he had a few questions he wanted answered.

Catelyn moved back to him and he asked, "How's Kelly?"

"Drugged up, malnourished and will probably be in the hospital a while."

The crime-scene unit entered and Catelyn greeted Sandy. "Hey, what are you doing working the field?"

"I decided I wanted a break from the lab. I'm trying my hand out here for a bit."

"Aw, Sandy, don't do that. Who am I going to call when I need a rush on evidence?"

Catelyn turned serious once more. "I'll be real interested in everything you find. We still have questions that need answers."

Joseph spoke up. "Yeah, like who shot Zachary Merritt."

"I want to search Alan Dillard's house."

"Sounds good. I'll request a team to get out there and do that right away."

"And I want to talk to Alan personally. Sounds like he had a little side funny business going on with his female students. I'm willing to bet Tracy's not the first."

"Maybe not, but she's sure going to be the last."

At the hospital, Joseph and Catelyn hurried through the door and approached the front desk. Joseph obtained the information that Kelly was being admitted and that Alan's shoulder would require surgery. The bullet had lodged in his collarbone.

They decided to head for the waiting room. Catelyn nudged him. "Look."

"Stacy Dillard."

"Right. You want to talk to her or should I?"

Catelyn shrugged. "Maybe I should. She might relate better to a woman right now."

"Go ahead, I'll go see if my badge earns me any information."

Catelyn strolled over to the woman who sat staring out the window. "Mrs. Dillard?"

She jumped and turned, placing a hand over her heart. "Oh, you startled me."

"I'm so sorry about your husband."

"I'm not."

Ouch. Catelyn winced, but couldn't say she didn't understand the woman's bitterness—not if the woman was aware of her husband's extracurricular activities.

Stacy continued. "I'm not sorry about that. Sorry about a lot of other things, but not him."

"So you know about him and…"

"Tracy. Yes." She stood and crossed her arms. "I never thought him capable…and yet, I suppose I'm not terribly surprised, either."

"Why is that?"

"He's always had an eye for the young ones. I suppose after a while I just stopped wondering where he was and who he was with. I stopped caring."

"But you're here now waiting for him to get out surgery."

The woman drew in a deep breath. "Yes. Yes, I am. And as much as I might hate…well, let's just say he's still Alan Jr.'s father, right?"

Outwardly Catelyn nodded. On the inside, she was questioning everything. The woman had almost just practically admitted she hated her husband, yet here she sat waiting for the man to come out of surgery. Her son's father or not, that seemed strange to her. To each his own, she supposed.

"Mrs. Dillard?"

The two women turned as one. Stacy said, "Yes, Jill."

A blond nurse approached. "I just thought I'd let you know that Zachary's waking up. It's so sweet of you to be so concerned about him. His parents are with him now, but they gave me permission to pass the word to you."

Stacy Dillard drew in another deep breath. "Really? That's wonderful. When will I be able to see him?"

"Shortly, I suppose. The doctor's in with him now."

"Thank you so much."

Catelyn's brain hummed with this new information. "Great. Finally." She turned to the nurse. "Do you think he'll be able to tell us who shot him?"

"Oh, I think it'll be a while before he can talk. He's still on the ventilator, but I would hazard a guess that sometime tomorrow he'll be able to tell you what he knows about that day."

Another delay. Catelyn smiled her thanks and turned back to Stacy. "I'll be praying for your husband and family."

"Even though he's a terrible person?"

"God still loves him." Catelyn nearly choked on the words, but knew they were true and maybe this woman needed to hear them. She was working on her anger, striving for the compassion she knew Jesus felt toward the man. Maybe if she gave lip service long enough, she'd actually feel it. Praying for the people she arrested was a new thing for her—and a tough one.

"Well, I don't need God right now, I need some news on Alan. I'd really like to know if he's going to live or die."

Catelyn blinked. She wasn't sure if the woman meant that to sound as cold as it did or if she was just still in shock over everything.

Giving her the benefit of the doubt, Catelyn shifted and watched Joseph pace back and forth, phone pressed to his ear.

"How's your son?"

"What?"

"Your son. He was sick when we came by earlier?"

"Oh, yes, he's better. Just a cold, I think." She grimaced. "I'll have to change his name just so he doesn't have to be ashamed of it." A huge sigh blew out of her. "He's with my mother right now. She'll keep him until I pick him up a little later. I don't know what I'd do without him. He's been my whole reason for..." She broke off and Catelyn handed her another tissue from the box on the table beside her.

Small talk over, Catelyn sat with the woman while Joseph pressed for answers from the CSU team. His brows rose at something said by the person on the other end of the line. Then he looked over at Catelyn and Stacy Dillard.

Crossing the room, he stopped in front of the woman. "Did Alan know that you were filing for divorce?"

EIGHTEEN

Joseph watched a number of expressions cross Mrs. Dillard's face. Fear, anger, resignation. She finally sighed and looked at the ceiling. "No, but I suppose you'll be talking to him about that when he comes out of surgery."

"Is there some reason you're waiting to let him in on your plan? The papers the crime-scene unit found were hidden pretty well and are dated three months ago."

"I...wanted to make sure I was making the right decision. Alan had threatened to take my son away if I ever left him. I had to make sure I was up for the fight." She gave an odd little smile. "But I guess today sort of clinched the deal. I can finally be free of his bullying and abuse, can't I? I can toss those divorce papers in his face. I don't have to worry about him anymore, do I?"

Compassion softened Joseph's face. "No, I guess you don't." He changed the subject and asked, "Zachary met with someone the day of his sister's funeral, but we can't figure out who that person was. Do you know if it was Alan and if he had a reason to want Zachary dead?"

Stacy shrugged and shifted her eyes to the door that separated her from her husband. "I don't know if they met or not. As far as if Alan had reason to want Zachary dead, it's possible. If Zachary found out about Alan's propensity for young high school girls, I'd say Alan would have some motive, wouldn't you?"

"Definitely. But did Zachary know?"

She leveled her gaze on him. "He knew. Zachary's been like a son, a troubled son, to me. He was angry with Alan for cheating on me. Zachary's the one who told me about Tracy."

"And you confronted Alan about this?"

"I did."

"What did he say?" Catelyn asked.

"Gave me a black eye and told me I had a good life. He said if I didn't want to lose it, I'd better be real careful about what I said and who I said it to."

"So, what did you do?"

"I kept my mouth shut and made divorce arrangements." Stacy used shaky fingers to pick at nonexistent lint on her faded blue jeans. "And I was working on a way to…get away from him. Forever."

"Then chickened out at the last minute?" Joseph pushed.

"No…" She paused. "Like I said, I just needed time."

"With your…friend?" There was no condemnation in his voice, but the woman still flinched.

"My *friend*—" she stressed the word "—is part of an underground organization that helps women and children get out of abusive situations. That's who Zachary saw me meeting with and interpreted it a different way. I couldn't tell him otherwise."

He stood. She was lying, but he wasn't sure why. It would take some digging to find out. "All right, Mrs. Dillard. Thanks for your cooperation. Let us know if there's anything we can do for you. It's a hard road you have ahead of you."

"Thank you."

* * *

Joseph and Catelyn moved to a separate area of the waiting room to continue to wait to hear about Alan and Kelly. However, it looked like their timing might be just about perfect. According to the nurse, Zachary was showing very real signs of waking, so they decided to hang out and see if he came around enough to be able to tell them who shot him.

Catelyn said, "I guess since they're not taking the ventilator out until tomorrow, we could leave and come back."

"We could, but if he's responsive, we could at least get some yes or no answers to a few questions."

"True. He can also fingerspell anything he has to tell us."

"Right. I'm hoping he gives us a name."

She sat next to him and studied Alan's wife. She looked...hard. And worn down, sad and mad all at the same time. Like life had dealt her one blow too many.

The woman looked over at them and frowned, glanced at her watch, rose and headed for the exit. Probably had to pick up her son or something. Watching her leave, Catelyn asked Joseph, "Do you believe her?"

"What do you mean?"

"I don't know. She seems awfully eager to give up her husband." Catelyn chewed the thought.

Joseph pursed his lips. "He's done some pretty bad stuff to her. What about a woman scorned and all that?"

"Maybe."

"Why, you think she's lying?"

"I don't know. We've been lied to so much lately that I don't know that I'd recognize the truth if it bit me."

"Yeah, I know what you mean."

She looked at him. "Where was Alan during visitation for Tracy? Do you remember?"

"No, I just remember talking to his wife while standing

in line. I never got to see who was sitting where. But I do remember she was looking for him. I wonder where she found him—*if* she found him?"

"We can ask her when she gets back." He moved closer to her and placed a hand over hers.

She jerked and looked at him. What was he doing?

"Catie, we need to talk."

Emotions swept over her at the tone in his voice. "No, we don't." Anger flooded her as she remembered him moving in front of her when they didn't know who was coming through the door of the gym. "You made yourself clear what you thought about me as a cop. Nothing more needs to be said. We're going to finish this case then go our separate ways. There. We talked."

"Okay, maybe I deserve that. But…"

"You say you have no problem with me being a cop yet you think I need protecting out there? Hello? It doesn't work that way. You have to have confidence in me."

"I know and I do."

"Well, you sure have a funny way of showing it! You stepped in front of me, Joseph. What does that say to you? It says tons to me."

Hard hands gripped her shoulders. "It says I care about you. It says I want to protect the woman I love."

Stunned, she couldn't react at first. He moved back a little, giving her some space. She couldn't believe he just said that. She remembered her father's definition of protection. He'd gotten so bad he hadn't wanted her mother to even leave the house. "I don't want that kind of love."

Joseph flinched and she realized she'd spoken her thoughts out loud. But he persisted. "Catie, you've got to understand. It wouldn't matter if you were a schoolteacher, I'd still want to protect you from some things. It's the way I'm wired. It's the way God made me. I won't apologize for it. If you'd been any other female cop in that hall with me, I never would've stepped in front of you. But…it was you."

"Which just clarifies why we aren't right for each other."

"No," he said. "No, it just means we can't *work* together. Sure, I might worry about you out working a case like any husband would, but that's normal. Can't you see that?"

She shook her head. "No, I really can't. All I can see are the fights, hear the yelling, the accusations, the harsh words. I don't know what normal is."

"Yes, you do. You've practically grown up in my parents' house. How can you say you don't know what normal is?"

Her mouth worked and nothing came out. Flashes of his parents, their disagreements handled in a totally different manner, their laughing, teasing one another, the support for each other in everything they did.

So opposite of everything her parents had stood for.

Could she possibly hope to be the kind of wife he wanted? Deserved? "But you want a wife who'll stay home, have dinner on the table every night, etcetera. I just can't promise that I can do that."

Her phone rang and Joseph leaned back with a groan. Snapping her attention to the phone, she answered the call, listened for a moment then hung up. She looked up at Joseph and forced herself to see the man as only her partner right now. Told herself to ignore the longing she still saw in his gaze. Finally he cleared his throat and narrowed his eyes. "What?"

"CSU found the gun they think was used to shoot Zachary."

"Found it in Alan's house is my guess."

"Right."

"Well, I suppose that answers that question. Alan Dillard shot Zachary."

"Excuse me, officers?"

They both looked up at the nurse. She said, "Zachary is awake. His parents said that you could come in and see him if you'd like."

NINETEEN

When they entered the room, Zachary looked rough. Various tubes extended from him and monitors clicked and beeped. But at least his eyes were open. They widened when he spotted them. His heart rate picked up and Joseph said, "We're sure glad you're awake."

The boy lifted a weak hand to sign, "Yes."

"We're also hoping you can tell us who shot you. Do you know who?"

"Maybe."

Catelyn stepped forward, intensity radiating from her. "Can you spell his name."

His fingers moved, slowly, but with clarity. H-E-R.

"Her?" Catelyn glanced at Joseph and frowned. Then went wide with understanding. "It was a woman?"

Another signed yes.

"It wasn't Alan Dillard?"

"No." His fingers moved as in slow motion.

"Who? Do you know who?"

His eyes shut and his mother moved in to touch his hand. "Zachary, please, honey. Try to stay awake. Tell them who did this to you."

Zachary's lids fluttered. Closed, then opened once more.

Joseph pressed, "Who was it, Zachary?"

Fingers slowly formed the individual letters to spell: D-I-L-L-A-R-D.

Joseph blinked. Maybe the kid had been confused when he spelled H-E-R. "Alan Dillard? He's in surgery as we speak."

Zachary's eyes drooped, then closed. Joseph patted the kid's hand, but he was back out cold.

Joseph looked at Catelyn. "Let's see if Mrs. Dillard is back in the waiting room and ask her a few questions."

Catelyn shook her head. "He specifically spelled H-E-R. What if Stacy heard Zachary was waking up? What if she wasn't here to see her husband, what if she was waiting to finish the job?"

"I don't know. What reason would she have to want Zachary dead?" He addressed the question to Zachary's parents.

Both looked shocked at the recent developments and Mrs. Merritt said, "I don't know. I know my children were mixed up in that gang. I…didn't want to admit it at first, but I can't really deny it at this point." She looked down at her son. "I guess my husband and I've been so focused on our careers, we lost sight of what we were working so hard for…our family."

Joseph felt a pang of sympathy for the woman. Her husband ran a hand down the side of his face and grunted. "Well, we've got a second chance with Zachary and Justin. As soon as we can, we're going to have a family meeting and get some things straightened out." He frowned and glanced at the door. "I have a hard time believing Stacy Dillard shot my son. She's been nothing but kind and caring toward him."

"Your son is the one who told her that her husband was having an affair with a fellow student."

"What? Zachary wouldn't do that. He worshipped the

ground Alan Dillard walked on—and he didn't care much for Stacy. He said Alan deserved a better wife than her. If the man was having an affair and Zachary learned of it, there's no way he would have said anything to her, not out of concern for her feelings, but because of Alan."

"You know, I felt Stacy was lying to us at the hospital. She's the one that pulled the trigger."

Calling for a car to go by the Dillard house and see if Mrs. Dillard went home and orders to pick her up if she did, Joseph then asked Catelyn, "Are you ready to track this woman down?"

"Absolutely."

They left with promises to call as soon as they knew anything and Mr. and Mrs. Merritt agreed to get as much information out of Zachary as soon as he woke up again.

Joseph watched Catelyn exit the door ahead of him and knew his time with her was running short. They needed to get this case solved so they could get back to resolving the situation between them once and for all. *Lord, help us please?*

The drive to the Dillard house was silent. The woman hadn't been in the waiting room when they'd returned to the area. A call from the cruiser sent to check her house confirmed the woman wasn't there. either.

"Her son," Catelyn blurted.

"What?"

"If she's going to make a run for it, she'd probably grab her kid first." *At least that's what I'd do.* But what kind of mother was Stacy Dillard? She had a feeling the woman's child was everything to her. "She said her mother had her son. We need to find out who her mother is and where she lives."

Joseph got on the radio and started the process to find

out the information they needed. A call to the child's elementary school principal found him at home on this Sunday afternoon. He instantly provided the woman's name.

Cheryl Frazier.

Within minutes, Joseph had the address and, with siren wailing, headed in the direction that would take them to the west side of town. He also had backup units on the way.

Catelyn watched the scenery whiz by. A middle-class neighborhood came in to view. She shut the siren off and Joseph wheeled in. They found the house without incident. She just prayed Stacy and her son were still here. They pulled up to the curb and quickly assessed the scene before them.

"Looks quiet," Catelyn observed.

"Looks can be deceiving," he answered, scanning the front of the well-maintained home. "Be ready for anything. This woman shot a teenager."

"I wonder what he did that had her pulling that trigger. Somehow I don't buy the story she fed us at the hospital. And yet, she was in front of us in the line at the funeral." Confusion crimped her. "I just don't see how she would have had time to get up to the balcony, get her gun ready and shoot Zachary."

"She left to find her husband."

"Then came back to talk to the people in front of us, remember?"

"Yes, I do. So, maybe Zachary didn't run because of our presence, he saw her and took off."

She shrugged and unclipped her shoulder holster. "It's a theory, but I still don't see how she made it up to the balcony in time to shoot him. And how would she know he was going to run out of the mortuary?"

He pulled out his phone. "I don't know. All good questions. Let's see if anyone answers the number here so we can get those questions answered."

Dialing the number, he waited. Two more cruisers pulled in next to the curb, their sirens silenced, not wanting to further upset an already possibly frantic woman.

Joseph slipped the phone back into his pocket. "No one's answering."

"You want to do the honors?" she asked, motioning to the door. Joseph stepped up on the porch and knocked.

The window next to him exploded in a crash of flying glass. He ducked out of the way, to the side, the glass missing him by millimeters. "Hey! Police! Freeze!"

Another gunshot sounded. Then a small voice, "Mommy! Mommy!"

Catelyn spun herself up against the side of the house away from the broken window, heart pounding. "Joseph, are you okay?"

"Yeah, fine. We've got to get that gun away from whoever's in there."

"I don't want to start shooting back, there's a kid in there."

"Absolutely." Gun held pointing up, he yelled, "Mrs. Dillard, I need you to throw your weapon out."

"No!" A trembling voice came from inside. It sounded close to the window, to Catelyn's left and they could hear her clearly. "Mrs. Dillard, is that you?"

"No, it's Cheryl Frazier, Stacy's mother, and you need to leave now."

Catelyn shot a look at Joseph and mouthed. "The mother?"

He shrugged. "Zachary was pretty out of it. Maybe he was trying to spell Mrs. Dillard's mother. Who knows?"

Right now it didn't matter. At least Mrs. Frazier was

talking. Always a good sign. If she was talking, she wasn't hurting anyone. "Where's your daughter and grandson?"

"In here with me. They're safe. My poor Stacy…she's just not in her right mind right now. She's had too much put on her with everything. We're taking Alan Jr. and we're leaving, do you understand? We've worked so hard…" A muffled sob broke through.

Catelyn spoke up. "Ma'am, you know we can't let you do that."

"Then I'll…I'll…I don't know what I'll do, but…something."

They needed a hostage negotiator. Catelyn shifted and licked her lips. "Your grandson's listening to you, isn't he?"

Shifting, a scrape. Catelyn tensed, felt the butt of her gun against her palm. She really didn't want to shoot anyone, especially not Alan Jr.'s grandmother.

"Yes."

"You don't want to scare him, do you?"

Sniffling, a moment of weeping. "It wasn't supposed to be like this."

Looking around, she spotted the two uniformed officers who'd arrived at the home just minutes after she and Joseph pulled in.

And Ethan O'Hara.

She gave a small wave to the man who was her usual partner and was Joseph's brother-in-law.

Ethan waved back and motioned to Joseph he'd help cover him. Joseph looked surprised to see Ethan, but nodded for her to keep talking. He was going around the back of the house. He held up two fingers.

She nodded, two taps on his radio would mean he was inside. She'd continue talking to Cheryl Frazier and pray she could remember everything she'd ever learned about hostage negotiations until a trained negotiator arrived.

"How was it supposed to be, Cheryl?" She used the woman's first name, hoping it would keep her focused on the conversation and not on whatever Joseph and Ethan were doing around back.

Another sniffle. "I just wanted to get us away."

"Why?"

"Because I'm so ashamed of my son-in-law, so hurt, so *mad* at him for what he's done to Stacy and Alan Jr. How could he do that to them? To his own son?" Cheryl's fury exploded from her as she spat the words.

Catelyn flinched at the venom in the woman's voice. "I understand. It was a terrible thing he did. A total betrayal of their vows, their trust. And an ugly legacy to leave behind for Alan Jr." Mention the kid as often as possible. Keep her mind on her grandson—and the fact that he needs her.

"Yes! Yes it was."

Joseph crept up to the back door and tried the handle. Locked. Of course.

Ethan stayed behind, covering him.

Joseph moved through the shrubbery trying the windows. Finally, the last one on the end lifted. A quick glance inside told him the room was empty. Hoisting himself in, he landed silently on the carpeted floor and looked around. This must be where Alan Jr. slept when he visited. A twin bed with a puppy-dog bedspread sat against one wall with a little white dresser beside it.

"What are Stacy and Alan Jr. going to do if you go to jail, Cheryl? He's already lost his father. What's he going to do if you get arrested or—worse? You said your daughter's not in her right mind. That leaves you to care for the boy. Do you have another family member who can keep Alan Jr.?" he heard Catelyn ask. Her voice carried through the broken window.

Dead silence from the house.

Joseph slid down the hall toward the den where the action was taking place. Where was the kid? The mother?

It was a typical ranch-style house and a quick sweep showed all three bedrooms and hall bathroom to be empty. So that left the kitchen, dining and den areas.

The end of the hall opened up into the den. He could see Stacy sitting on the couch holding a little boy on her lap.

"Mom, put the gun down, please." The woman had her eyes trained on her mother. Tears stood out on her cheeks and she raised a palm to brush them off.

"Stacy, you just hush. I'm taking care of you, just like I always have." Her mother never turned from the window.

Joseph stepped inside the den then to the right into the living room so he couldn't be spotted. He needed to get Stacy's attention so he could get her and the boy out of there. Assuming she wouldn't turn him in.

A chance he'd have to take. He waited until she turned her head slightly, then stepped into her peripheral vision. She started and he raised a finger to his lips. Her eyes narrowed, then shot to her mother, who stood staring out the window. Her mouth opened as though to call out and Joseph raised his gun a tad. If the woman turned from the window to shoot at him, he'd have no choice.

Sorrow crossed Stacy's features but she clamped her lips together and didn't give him away.

Instead, she shifted her son and rose with him on her hip. He wrapped his arms around her neck and leaned his head on her shoulder. He looked scared stiff at the upheaval going on.

Cheryl whirled and Joseph jerked back. "Stacy, what are you doing?"

"Going into the kitchen. I need to give Alan Jr. his medicine."

"Leave Alan Jr. there. On the couch."

Stacy paused, then sighed and set him down. He clung to her and said, "Don't leave me."

Grief spasmed her features. "All right, baby, I'll stay with you."

Joseph sucked in a relieved breath. She hadn't given away his location yet. And they were still in the line of fire. She'd been trying to get the boy away from them, trying to open up the opportunity for Joseph to get Cheryl.

The child hadn't seen him, so hopefully he would stay put on the couch. He reached around his mother to pick up a stuffed turtle, clutching it close while never taking his eyes from his grandmother and the gun.

Joseph stayed put behind the cover of the wall, tapping his radio twice to let Catelyn know he was in. She tapped back once. Good, she got his message.

"Cheryl," he said. The woman whirled to stare at him in shock.

"How did you get in here?" she demanded.

He ignored her. "Why did you shoot Zachary?"

Catelyn figured her negotiating time had run out. Joseph was inside. She raced the few remaining steps to the broken window, doing her best to stay out of the line of fire should someone decide to send another bullet that way.

She knew Ethan had Joseph's back.

Officers swarmed the house, weapons drawn.

Looking through the window, Catelyn saw the woman was distracted, noticed Joseph watching. Slowly, she reached through the broken window and silently unlatched it and raised it in one smooth movement. She slipped in and landed in the den—and came face-to-face with Cheryl Frazier as she whirled toward the noise. "Drop your gun, Cheryl."

Tears of frustration streamed down the woman's cheeks. Alan Jr. sat on his mother's lap, his little hands covering his ears, eyes squeezed shut, as he rocked back and forth. Catelyn softened her voice. "Your family needs you, Cheryl. Don't add anything else to your list of things to fight."

Stacy begged, "Stop, Mama. I need you. Alan Jr. needs you. Look around you. You can't fight them and win."

The hand holding the pistol shook. Cheryl drew in a steadying breath. "Get them out of here." She motioned to Stacy and Alan Jr.

Catelyn gave the order to the officers. Immediately, they ushered the two out of the house. The woman started moving toward the kitchen, the gun held out in front of her not aimed at anyone. Yet.

"Ma'am, I really need you to stop and put the gun down."

"I really didn't want to hurt anyone. I was just taking care of my family, just like I always have."

Ethan appeared in the hallway. He looked at Catelyn and she could almost read his mind. He had a clean shot. She shook her head.

Joseph held his gun steady as he moved with the woman. "I understand that, ma'am. You were just protecting your family. But we can't resolve any of this as long as you hold on to that gun." Cheryl stepped into the kitchen, still facing Joseph and now Ethan.

Catelyn stepped next to Joseph so she could see the woman. "Cheryl, what are doing? You need to put the gun down."

"I didn't want to get blood on the carpet." She spoke casually and it didn't occur to Catelyn what she meant until she swung the gun up to rest the business end against her temple.

"Stop!"

Joseph had gone to his knees the moment the gun started

moving. Ethan had pulled back around the corner against the wall and Catelyn had done the same move with the opposite wall. Now she realized what Cheryl meant when she said she didn't want to get blood on the carpet. Kitchen linoleum was much easier to clean up.

For a brief moment, the woman's face morphed into Catelyn's father's. She blinked. Joseph, still on his knees, kept his gun aimed just in case Mrs. Frazier decided to swing her weapon around and point it at him.

And Catelyn wanted to step in front of him.

The feeling stunned her; shook her to the core and swept her entire being with nausea.

She pushed it away. They had one more thing to deal with. "Mrs. Frazier, why did you shoot Zachary?"

Mrs. Frazier's gun hand shook, tremor after tremor. Catelyn prayed she wouldn't spasm and pull the trigger. "He was going to tell Alan that Stacy was going to divorce him. Alan Dillard was that boy's hero. He never knew…"

"He never knew what Alan was, right? He never knew what was going on between Alan and Tracy? And he never told Stacy that Alan was having an affair, did he? She lied to us in the hospital to protect you, didn't she?"

"Yes, she lied. I think Tracy tried to tell Zachary that Alan wasn't all he was cracked up to be, but the boy just wouldn't listen. And when Stacy came home…the day of the visitation, right before the visitation…she was hysterical."

Joseph asked, "Why?"

"She'd met with Zachary and tried to reason with him. He wouldn't have any part of it. He was going to tell Alan the next time he saw him."

"And Stacy was afraid of Alan's reaction?"

The gun lowered a tad as her elbow drooped. Her arm was getting tired. Keep her talking, Joseph.

"Stacy was afraid of Alan, period."

"He was abusive."

With a tight jaw, the woman nodded. "In every way imaginable. But when Alan went after Alan Jr...."

Catelyn winced—every mother's nightmare. "She'd had enough."

Her arm trembled, the gun shifted. "He threatened to take Alan Jr. from her and never let her see him again." A harsh laugh escaped her. "And I have no doubt he would have followed through with it. Stacy tried to find help, even went to the police to see what she could do."

"Why is there no record of this on file? We did an extensive background check on Alan."

"Did you come across who Alan's favorite poker buddy was?" she snapped.

"No."

"Try Mayor McCloud."

Understanding darkened Catelyn's brain. She made a mental note to do a little research into Mayor McCloud's life. She watched the gun in the woman's hand. It was almost pointing to the ceiling at this stage. She was so busy telling her story, she wasn't paying attention to the weapon. Just a little bit more and she could...

"So, Zachary and Stacy met the afternoon of the visitation. Stacy tried to talk him out of telling Alan about the divorce. But, wait a minute...how did Zachary know about it in the first place?"

"That stupid kid went over to my Stacy's house looking for Alan one afternoon after his sister was killed. Just walked right in. Stacy was in the kitchen going over the papers. Zachary saw them and stormed out with Stacy yelling at him not to tell, that she was just thinking about it and didn't really mean it."

"So she came to you, and you decided to take care of the situation."

She closed her eyes as though pained at the memory.

And Catelyn struck.

She gave a flying tackle and clipped the woman around the knees. Shrieking, Mrs. Frazier went down, Catelyn landing on top of her.

Joseph was beside them in a heartbeat, kicking the weapon aside. Ethan grabbed her arms and pinned them behind her back.

And then all the fight went out of her.

Panting, Catelyn rose to her feet and helped Joseph pull the weeping Mrs. Frazier to hers. Ethan went to tell everyone that it was over.

Catelyn said, "Just one more question, how did you get off the balcony of the funeral home without anyone seeing you?"

Tears dripped off the woman's chin and she sniffed. "It was so easy. I simply crawled into one of the coffins in the room off the balcony. There were plenty to choose from." Hands now cuffed behind her back, she shrugged. "I chose an empty one."

Joseph spoke up. "You used Alan's gun to shoot Zachary. How did you get your hands on it and how did it wind up back at his house? Our CSU guys found it."

"I have a key to the house. I simply went by when no one was home. I was hoping you would find the gun and blame the shooting on Alan."

Catelyn shook her head. Oh, what a tangled web we weave...

Now that the case was officially closed, Catelyn had one last thing to take care of. She had to decide if she was strong enough to love a cop—and if she could be the kind of wife Joseph wanted.

She finally admitted it to herself.

She loved Joseph. Had loved him for a long time.

But did she love him enough?

She wanted to. And that scared her and yet thrilled her all at the same time. And Sandy was right. She and Joseph did have something her parents had neglected from the start of their relationship.

God.

But could she quit her job for him? She just didn't know.

She dreaded the next item on her to-do list for the day, yet was determined to get through it. *Please, Jesus, I need Your strength.*

She thought she heard someone call her name, but not in the mood for conversation, she ignored it and continued on like she hadn't heard. Climbing into her car, she cranked it and took off. In the rearview mirror, she could see Joseph standing in the parking lot, hand raised.

Guilt hammered her. That was really rude. She was going to have to talk to him at some point. But she just wasn't ready for the conversation she knew he wanted to have.

And she wanted to be ready.

I could have just talked to the man. Told him I needed some space. Lord, what do I do? What do You want? I'm so messed up inside over my parents, I just don't know if I can ever have a normal relationship with another cop. Especially an overprotective one. But I do know what I need to do right now. I need to let go of my anger, Lord. I need to let it go and I need Your help to do that.

She picked up her phone and punched in Joseph's number. He answered on the first ring. "Hey."

"I'm sorry."

"For?"

"For ignoring you in the parking lot. I just…I've got something I need to do and I…want to do it alone."

"All you had to do was say something." She winced at the hurt in his voice.

"I know. I had a brief moment of cowardice. That's why I'm calling. I owed you an apology."

"Apology accepted. So when do you think you'll be ready to talk?"

"Soon, okay?"

"Do you want me to come with you wherever you're going?"

She thought about what she was going to do. "Yes. No. I'm not sure."

He gave a small laugh. "Okay, that's clear."

Heaving a sigh, Catelyn turned to make her way through the gates of the cemetery. Winding around the narrow paths, she said, "I guess not. Maybe I need to do this on my own. Face my demon, so to speak."

"Call me when you're done?"

"Yes. Yes, I will."

"All right. See you soon."

She hung up and turned right. She'd only been here one other time, the day of the funeral, but the way to her father's grave was permanently embedded in her mind.

Parking to the side, she slowly climbed from her vehicle. Not really sure why she felt the need to do this to herself, she kept a prayer on her lips as she made her way over to the grave.

Someone had left fresh flowers. Who? A buddy from the force, no doubt.

Catelyn knelt, not caring if the grass left a stain on the knees of her faded jeans. She touched the headstone. Traced the words that had been carved into it.

Harold James Clark. Family man and devoted defender of the peace. Gone too early.

Yeah. Too early. Well, whose fault is that?

Then the grief hit her.

And the memories flooded her. The good ones. Ones she hadn't thought about in over a decade. The ones that had been overshadowed by the anger she felt toward the man who'd given up and killed himself. The ones recorded in the "fun book" she'd taken to her mother the day after they'd arrested Cheryl Frazier.

"Oh, Daddy," she whispered, "I miss you."

She closed her eyes and let the tears fall. She'd been his pride and joy when she'd been small, riding on his shoulders, laughing, giggling and wearing his uniform hat.

Why was she just now remembering this?

She remembered the swing in their big backyard. He'd pushed her to the sky, so high her toes could "touch God."

She remembered his big booming voice every day, the minute he walked in the door. "Gimme a hug, kiddo!" And she'd run to him and he'd swing her up in his big muscular arms and squeeze the breath out of her. She remembered her mother watching the two of them and smiling. Catelyn let out a sob. She remembered her mother *smiling. Oh, thank you, God, for that.*

The rush of memories tripped over themselves in her mind, stealing the hate and anger from her heart.

Not caring if she looked like a fool, not concerned about who might be watching, she leaned forward and wrapped her arms around the cold headstone, wishing it was her daddy's warm hard chest. She lay her head against the smoothly carved words and pretended she could hear his heart beating one last time. Pretended she could feel his arms wrapped around her in one last breath-stealing squeeze.

"I've hated you for so long, been so filled with anger that I'm not sure how to do this, but I hope this is a start." She took a deep breath, smelled the scent of freshly turned dirt, a hint of rain and felt the possibility of the sun as it struggled to peek through the clouds. "I forgive you, Daddy. I have to. It's the only way I'm going to be able to love someone of my own. It's the only way I'll ever have peace."

Tears dripped to the soft green earth. The wind blew, and time passed as she prayed and talked to her dad. Finally, bones creaking and muscles aching, she let go of the headstone—and her anger—to sit back on her heels and caress the letters etched into the head stone. "I love you, Daddy, and I miss you."

She raised her eyes toward heaven and let the tears continue to fall.

Joseph stood against his vehicle, arms folded across his chest as he watched the scene play out before him. Never had he witnessed such an outpouring of grief. He felt like an intruder. And yet he couldn't leave her. She might need him.

Right, he mocked himself, when has she ever needed you?

But she might—this time.

Hopefully.

Anxiety tightened his gut as he watched her weep, her silent tears nearly ripping his heart out. And when she'd wrapped her arms around the headstone, he couldn't stand it and had to turn away from the scene.

Forcing himself not to go to her, he let her have her moments with her father, praying, crying out that somehow God would give her the peace she so desperately needed.

Finally, he turned back to see her sitting on her heels,

mopping up her face, the emotional devastation of the storm passed.

He took several steps in her direction, then stopped, wondering if he should intrude. Wondering if she needed more time.

She pushed herself up to her feet, and he closed the gap placing his hands on her shoulders.

Catelyn didn't even jump as she felt a pair of hands lightly fall on her shoulders. She'd smelled Joseph's cologne, a woodsy, masculine scent that she never tired of, about thirty seconds ago and knew he stood behind her.

Shuddering, broken and yet finally at peace, she felt cleansed. Ready to make a new start in life.

But was Joseph the right person to make that start with?

She hoped so.

As long as he understood some things.

Sucking in a deep breath, she turned, looked into his eyes—and nearly felt her knees buckle at the look of love shining there. Tears of sympathy glistened, and she simply wanted to melt into his arms and let the world fade away.

Oh, Lord, help me.

He smiled. "Hey, can I do anything to help?"

"You followed me—again," she said, referencing the nursing home incident. "And it's the second time you've found me in tears."

"I want to be there for you, Catelyn."

She swallowed hard. "I know you do, Joseph, but I don't know that you can do that without wanting to protect me. I don't want to compare you to my father, but…" She shoved her hands in the back pockets of her jeans and started walking.

Joseph followed her behind her. "Catelyn, I'm not your father."

"You stepped in front of me. A fellow cop. And one with a gun at that. What if I'd chosen to pull the trigger at that moment?" She shuddered at the thought.

"You wouldn't have. You're too good a cop."

"Then why did you feel the need to step in front of me?" she demanded.

"Catelyn, I told you I wasn't protecting the cop. I was protecting the woman I love." He ran a hand through his dark hair, causing a sprig to stand up. "Excuse me for that being a crime."

"Oh, Joseph, it's not a crime. It's…it's…"

"What I'm supposed to do. I'm wired that way, both by God and by my upbringing. I could no more let you stand in the path of a bullet than I could sprout wings and fly. I don't know what else to say to convince you."

And it hit her. She remembered in the house when he was in the line of fire. She remembered the urge she felt to step in front of him, get him out of the path should the woman decide to pull the trigger.

Why? Because she loved him. Would she have felt that way if it had been another cop standing there?

No.

Suddenly, she saw things in a different light, from a whole different perspective. His perspective.

He loved her. Really, truly, loved her.

Loved her enough to step in front of a bullet for her.

Loved her enough to die for her.

Just like she felt for him.

Excitement swirled within her. "How can we make this work?"

"Well, we can't work together, that's for sure."

She choked out a laugh. "Okay."

"You've been under the impression that I don't want you to be a cop. And I'll admit, two years ago you that would have been the case. But recently, I've been thinking, praying, picturing us together…and I realize I tried to make you into someone you're not. And that's okay, but I fell in love with who you are, not who I wanted you to be."

She sucked in a hiccupping sob and tried to speak, but he placed a finger over her lips, so she'd kept quiet. He went on, "I'll worry about you while you're on duty, but I don't think I'll obsess about it. I'd appreciate it if you would check in with me when you can. And I'll be sure to do the same with you."

Surprise lit her eyes. "You'd do that?"

"Well, sure, why wouldn't I?"

"My father told my mother what he was doing was none of her concern and would get furious if she even suggested that he check in with her and…"

He grasped her upper arms and pulled her closer. "Aw, Catie, I'm really not like your father. I love you, I love the Lord. We'll rely on Him to get us through the rough times and rejoice with Him through the good times. It's true that all my life I figured I'd marry a woman like my mother. And then God dropped you into my life. A woman completely opposite from Mom is some ways…and yet very similar in all the ways that matter. Especially when it comes to loving the Lord. I'm fine with you being a cop, I promise."

Tears clogged her throat. "You're a very good man, Joseph."

"And you're an amazing woman who's been harboring a lot of anger for a long time."

"Huh. You noticed that, did you?"

"Yeah, I noticed."

Catelyn took a deep breath. "Well, I…think it's been bubbling beneath the surface for a while. Ever since my father shot himself, I've been…afraid."

"Of?"

"Of being abandoned."

This time it was Joseph's turn to suck in a swift breath. "Aw, Catie…and I…"

"Yes, when you left me two years ago, it just about killed me."

He flinched, her words wounding him with their honesty. She held up a hand and said, "But you were right to do what you did. I was too…insecure. I kept waiting for you to leave me and that's no way to have a relationship. My father said he loved me, then he killed himself. I was begging God to intervene with my mother and He didn't seem to be listening. And then you…you were too good to be true. I couldn't believe someone like you could love someone like me." She gave a small laugh. "I had some real self-esteem issues didn't I?"

"But I never saw those. You always seemed so confident, so in charge, so…"

"Bullheaded?"

"You said it, not me." He quirked a smile and was relieved when he got one in return.

"Right. Bullheaded. Anyway, when you left, it just confirmed what I'd been afraid of all along. I told myself I was better off, that if you hadn't left when you did, you'd leave me eventually."

"But I didn't want to."

"I know. I drove you away. And it was probably for the best at the time. It made me realize that God was still in control. That no matter what was happening with my life, no matter how far away I thought He was, He was still there, just waiting on me to come back to Him. And I had to trust Him with you."

"And He brought me back."

Dear Reader,

This story was such a blessing to write. Thank you for joining me as we met up with the Santino family once again. What a great group of brothers and sisters we have here who all love the Lord—and the special people He picked out just for them.

Catelyn had such a deep anger left over from her childhood, and as a result, while she still prayed to God, she felt distant from Him. Once she got that resolved, she found a new, deeper relationship with Him—and was able to let herself love Joseph the way he deserved to be loved. I pray that you are walking closely with the God who loved you enough to die for you. Let Him wrap His arms around you and bring hope, joy and peace into your life.

I love to hear from my readers. If you get a chance, drop me an email and let me know what you think about Catelyn and Joseph. You can reach me at lynetteeason.com. I always answer my email personally and find great joy in meeting new people.

God bless,

Lynette Eason

"Much to my dismay at the time."

"I was never so happy to accept an assignment as this one. Oh, I fought it at first, especially after I heard who my partner was going to be, but then I saw you standing there by the crime scene…and those two years just kind of faded away and I wanted back what we'd had—and more."

She nodded, the tears now dripping from her chin. "Me, too," she whispered.

"I love you, Catie. Will you marry me this time if I promise to refuse to work with you?"

Laughing, she reached up to encircle his neck with her arms. "I will."

"Good." He leaned down and met her lips with his, relishing the feeling of coming home. There'd never been another woman for him and he'd missed her desperately during his time in New York; now he reveled in the knowledge that she loved him as fully as he loved her.

He lifted his head a bit and looked down at her. "When?"

"When what?"

"When will you marry me?"

"Um…soon?"

"Yeah, soon is what I kind of had in mind." He touched the tip of his nose to hers.

"I want my mom to be there."

"Absolutely."

She pulled his head back down for another tingling kiss.

Yeah, he'd definitely come home.

To stay.

* * * * *